The Faber Guide to Victorian Churches

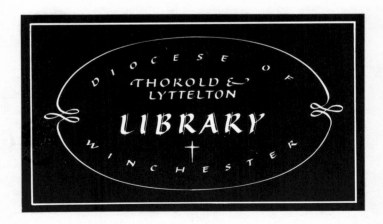

The Faber Guide to

VICTORIAN CHURCHES

edited by

Peter Howell *and* Ian Sutton

in conjunction with

THE VICTORIAN SOCIETY

faber and faber
LONDON · BOSTON

First published in 1989
by Faber and Faber Limited
3 Queen Square London WC1N 3AU

Phototypeset by Input Typesetting Ltd, London
Printed in Great Britain by
Richard Clay Ltd, Bungay, Suffolk

British Library Cataloguing in Publication Data

Howell, Peter
Faber guide to Victorian churches.
1. Church architecture—England—
History—19th century
I. Title   II. Sutton, Ian
726.5'0942   NA5461
ISBN 0–571–15274–0
ISBN 0–571–14733–X Pbk

*Library of Congress Cataloging-in-Publication Data
has been applied for*

Contents

Sources of photographs

Nearly all the photographs in this book were taken by Gordon Barnes and are now held by the National Monuments Record, London. The exceptions are as follows:

National Monuments Record but not taken by Gordon Barnes: Albury, Apostles' Chapel; Bath, Prior Park College Chapel; Ditton, St Michael; East Grinstead, Convent Chapel of St Margaret; Leicester, former Baptist Chapel; Liverpool, Unitarian Chapel; London, Westminster Cathedral; Lowfield Heath, St Michael (photo D. Robert Elleray); Manchester, Holy Name; Manchester, St Francis of Assisi; Newbury, Methodist Chapel; Preston, St Walburge; Preston, St Wilfred; Todmorden, Unitarian Chapel; Truro Cathedral.

Royal Commission on Ancient and Historic Monuments of Scotland: all churches in Scotland except the Barclay Church in Edinburgh and St Mary, St Paul and St Salvador, Dundee (*see below*). The photographs of the Gardner Memorial Church, Brechin, and the Stenhousemuir and Carron Church, Larbert, are by Bedford Lemere.

David McLaughlin: Barbon, St Bartholomew; Finsthwaite, St Peter.

Cadw: Welsh Historic Monuments: Baglan, St Catherine.

Stewart Tod and Partners: Edinburgh, Barclay Church.

Colin F. Wishart: Dundee, St Mary.

Dundee University Library: Dundee, St Paul and St Salvador.

Edwin Smith: Cheadle, St Giles.

Martin Harrison: Brithdir.

A. F. Kersting: Halkyn, St Mary.

The photograph of the Holy Rood, Watford, is taken from C. Nicholson and C. Spooner, *Recent Ecclesiastical Architecture*, London [n.d.]
We are grateful to the Council for the Care of Churches for allowing us to copy some Gordon Barnes prints that were not available at the NMR.

Preface

This book had its origin in a suggestion made by the late Gordon Barnes. He was an enthusiastic admirer of High Victorian church architecture, and used his talents as a skilled and sensitive photographer to build up a fine archive of photographs (which is now available to the public at the National Monuments Record). He proposed that a gazetteer of Victorian churches should be illustrated by his photographs, and that he should take additional photographs where necessary to achieve a balanced coverage. Unfortunately the deterioration of his health made this impossible, and it is a source of deep regret that he died in 1985, while this book was still in preparation. We dedicate it to his memory.

First, a few words to explain the principles on which the book has been compiled. It covers England, Wales and Scotland, and includes not only parish churches, but cathedrals (if wholly Victorian), the chapels of private houses, religious houses, colleges, schools, and hospitals, and Nonconformist places of worship. The initial and terminal dates are those of the reign of Queen Victoria (1837–1901). This is, of course, arbitrary, but all the same these dates are not entirely without significance for church architecture, in that the 1830s mark the turn towards a more seriously archaeological approach to style, and the influence of the Oxford Movement on liturgical ideas, while the turn of the century saw the flourishing of the Arts and Crafts Movement, and a more permissive attitude towards style in general. On the other hand, it follows that some architects are represented only by churches from the end, or beginning, of their careers.

A few churches are included which are pre-Victorian in origin, but only if their character is now predominantly Victorian. Not all the churches described are still in ecclesiastical use: where they have been declared redundant, converted to another use, or simply allowed to fall derelict, the fact has been indicated, but inevitably more will have gone out of ecclesiastical use even by the time the book appears, and some (though we hope not many) may even have been demolished. When a church has been very substantially altered, or when its new use renders it virtually inaccessible, it has been omitted.

The selection of churches to be described has been extremely difficult, and is bound to seem more or less arbitrary. The editors made a preliminary list, but the individual contributors were encouraged to make their own selection. Contributors were chosen for a variety of considerations: some because they were experts on particular architects, some because they were experts on particular geographical areas, some because they were experts on particular denominations. Readers may find interest in the choices made by the various experts, but it is bound to be the case that churches have been omitted which could well be claimed to be of superior quality to others which have been included. A partial justification for this has been our desire to achieve a fair geographical spread, and, in particular, to include plenty of churches by good provincial architects, who have tended not to receive their due. The former consideration may have led us to include fewer churches in the big cities (and especially London) than we might have done.

One inevitable result of the large and varied cast of contributors is that their entries show considerable variations in style and approach, which no amount of editing could have entirely ironed out. We hope that they will not be found too disturbing, and that they may instead add spice to the mixture. The authorship of each entry is indicated by initials (identified on page 2). The book is in one single alphabetical sequence, the name of the town being followed by its modern, post-1974 county. Within a town, churches are arranged alphabetically by their dedication. See also the note on London churches, page 72. It has not been an easy book to edit, and we must express our gratitude to our authors for their patience, their helpfulness, and their forbearance in enduring editorial interference.

Introduction

When Queen Victoria came to the throne in 1837, the great 19th-century boom in church building was already gathering momentum. In 1818 it had been estimated that the population exceeded the available seating in the buildings of the Established Church by no less than two and a half millions, and in that year an Act of Parliament set up a Commission to make grants for building churches. Most of the 'Commissioners' Churches' were cheap and of little architectural pretension. They usually had shallow chancels and galleries on three sides, with the characteristically Protestant emphasis on the pulpit rather than on the altar.

However, in 1833 John Keble preached his famous Assize Sermon at Oxford, which marked the launching of the Oxford Movement. Its aim was to reaffirm the Catholic tradition of the Church of England. Although primarily theological and liturgical, the Movement had in addition a strong archaeological side, and this led to the formation in 1839 of both the Oxford Society for Promoting the Study of Gothic Architecture (later the Oxford Architectural Society) and the Cambridge Camden Society (after 1846 the Ecclesiological Society). The Oxford society devoted itself mainly to the study of old churches, but the Cambridge one exercised enormous influence on both the building of new churches and the restoration of old ones, mainly through its journal the *Ecclesiologist*. Until 1846 this had a strongly polemical tone, but even after that date, until it ceased in 1868, it continued to spread the gospel of 'Middle Pointed' or Decorated Gothic, regarded as the purest style.

The most important single person in the advocacy of Gothic was not, however, a member of the Church of England, for in 1834 Augustus Welby Northmore Pugin had been converted to Rome. This was the only logical conclusion for a man so fanatically devoted to the Middle Ages. He was the son of a French émigré artist, who was himself one of the pioneers of the publication of accurate drawings of medieval buildings and their details, along with other pre-Victorian antiquaries such as John Britton. The Catholic Emancipation Act of 1829 had finally given Catholics full liberty, but their lack of money meant that Pugin rarely had a chance fully to express his ideals in actual buildings, and his influence was chiefly exercised through his brief and trenchant books, with their wiry but telling illustrations. The most remarkable of these is *Contrasts, or a Parallel between the Noble Edifices of the Fourteenth and Fifteenth Centuries, and Similar Buildings of the Present Day, and Showing the Present Decay of Taste*, which came out in 1836.

As far as the Church of England was concerned, the combined influence of the Oxford and Cambridge societies ensured that Gothic was established as the best style for church architecture. Usually this was the canonical Decorated, though sometimes Early English was preferred (for one thing, it was cheaper), and very occasionally Perpendicular (regarded as late and debased) was attempted. In the 1840s there was a brief fashion for the Norman style. Until about 1850 archaeological accuracy was aimed at and praised, rather than originality, but William Butterfield's All Saints, Margaret Street, London (1849–59) marked a turning-point. Built under the patronage of a leading Ecclesiologist, and under the influence of Ruskin's *Seven Lamps of Architecture* (published in 1849), its 'constructional polychromy' and originality, in both massing and detail, had a tremendous impact. It also showed clear influence from North German Gothic, and this again was revolutionary. In the late 1850s the leading architects of the Gothic Revival came to be more and more interested in Continental Gothic architecture, especially French and Italian, though German and Spanish influences were also felt. This trend, coupled with the contemporary interest in geology and in geometrical patterning, led to the 'High Victorian' movement, whose outstanding exponents included, as well as Butterfield, G. E. Street, James Brooks, and William Burges.

In about 1870 another turning-point occurred, when G. F. Bodley, hitherto a notable practitioner in High Victorian Gothic, along with Thomas Garner (who became his partner in 1871), led a return towards the use of English models, usually of the latest period of Decorated Gothic. The crucial churches here are All Saints, Cambridge, and St John, Tue Brook, Liverpool. Some architects towards the end of the century preferred the full-grown Perpendicular style, some chose to blend elements of Decorated and Perpendicular. The last quarter of the century is in fact marked by much greater stylistic laxity: not only were Romanesque and Byzantine churches built, but even classical styles could be used, especially of the Renaissance variety.

Those designing churches not for the Church of England had in any case never had such strong stylistic prejudices. Ultramontane and Counter Reformation sympathies naturally ensured that throughout the whole century Roman Catholic churches were built in classical or Renaissance styles. Nonconformists were, as might be expected, comparatively unprejudiced about style, though tending throughout the century to prefer something vaguely classical, partly for practical reasons, partly for reasons of tradition. (When the prominent spire of Colchester Congregational Church was damaged by an earthquake in 1884, some saw this as a judgement from above.) However, in the second half of the century the Nonconformists emulated the Anglicans by erecting many good Gothic churches, and they too experimented in other styles, sometimes adapting them with great ingenuity to the demands of their own worship.

The demands of worship naturally had as much effect on the appearance of church buildings as did stylistic preferences. For the followers of the Oxford Movement, the medieval type of church seemed the perfect vehicle for the revival of Catholic practices: a long, dignified chancel provided plenty of space for ceremonial, gave dignity to the altar at which the Eucharist was celebrated, and made room for stalls for the surpliced choirs which soon became *de rigueur*. This was the type of church, complete with rood-screen, which Pugin in his later years insisted was the only one allowable, although earlier he had designed churches (especially St Chad,

Birmingham) whose breadth and openness were more in keeping with the Counter Reformation spirit, which laid emphasis on the ability of the whole congregation to see the altar and the ceremonies taking place at it. Pugin's eldest son, Edward Welby, along with other Roman Catholic architects, was to develop a plan which put this scheme into Gothic form. Roman Catholic architects designed ever more elaborate high altars to incorporate not only the tabernacle for reservation of the Sacrament, but also a throne where the Sacrament could be exposed at Benediction. Other Roman Catholic requirements included side-chapels and shrines, and confessionals, often set in a row along an aisle.

The 'higher' the ritual at an Anglican church, the nearer it would tend to approach to the Roman Catholic type. Thus the High Victorian, High Church architects like Butterfield and Street favoured a comparatively short, often apsidal chancel, divided from the nave only by a low screen, but with the altar well raised up on steps so as to form the focus of the whole building. Aisles were sometimes reduced to mere passages for access to the seats. At the opposite extreme, Low Church buildings would tend to be more similar to Nonconformist ones in putting the emphasis on the sermon rather than on the Eucharist. However, Tractarian ideals were so pervasive that not only is it extremely uncommon to find any Victorian Anglican church in which the pulpit actually dominates the altar (as it so often had in the 18th century), but the Nonconformists themselves often built churches virtually indistinguishable from Anglican ones. This was naturally most often the case with the 'higher' denominations, such as the Unitarians and Congregationalists. Many congregations, however, expected their architects to provide seating for enormous numbers, who had to be able to see and hear the preacher, and the challenge produced some extremely striking and original results. One altogether exceptional denomination was the Catholic Apostolic Church, founded in 1832 by an expelled Presbyterian minister, the Revd Edward Irving: it favoured a particularly elaborate ritual, and built many churches, which include some remarkably fine examples.

Towards the end of the century, the preference in High Church Anglican architecture was for a type of church which emphasized the historical continuity of the Church of England with the Middle Ages, and appealed to the antiquarian tastes of architects and patrons: deep chancels, wide aisles, and rood-screens again became fashionable, and the resulting inability of many of the congregation to see the altar was countered by writers such as the architect J. T. Micklethwaite and the influential Revd Percy Dearmer (in his *Parson's Handbook* of 1899) with the argument that a church was not a theatre. The illogicality of this forcibly struck the Prussian critic Hermann Muthesius, who published his fascinating but little-known *Die neuere kirchliche Baukunst in England* in 1901: as a Protestant himself, he was deeply impressed by the bold experiments in church planning of architects like James Cubitt and Alfred Waterhouse, and he denounced Micklethwaite's backward-looking attitude as a blind clinging to an outmoded ideal. He went so far as to claim that the form of Anglican worship had derived from the planning of churches, rather than vice versa.

The best-known architects of the Victorian period are the great men with London offices, numerous assistants, pupils, and clerks of works, and practices often extending over the whole of Britain (or even beyond). Such, for example are Sir Gilbert Scott, William Butterfield, G. E. Street, Alfred Waterhouse, and G. F. Bodley. However, many of the best Victorian churches were built by comparatively obscure architects, sometimes lesser-known London men such as R. J. Withers or G. H. Fellowes Prynne, sometimes local men. Many of the latter built up extensive ecclesiastical practices in their own districts: the bread and butter usually consisted of the restoration and remodelling of old churches, and the erection of new schools and parsonages, but some of them built many new churches as well. Examples of first-rate provincial architects are John Prichard of Cardiff, John Douglas of Chester, R. J. Johnson of Newcastle, and Paley and Austin of Lancaster. Most architects tended to specialize in work for a particular denomination, though later in the century this became less universal. So, for example, both Alfred Waterhouse (a Congregationalist) and J. F. Bentley (a Roman Catholic) built Anglican churches.

The extraordinary quantity, and frequent grandeur and elaboration, of the churches erected during the reign of Queen Victoria are bound to raise the question of who provided the money. The majority were naturally in the towns, where the phenomenal growth of population, combined with the fact that in existing churches comparatively few of the seats were free, and so available to the poorer classes, produced the greatest need. Adequate provision of churches was regarded not only as of spiritual benefit, but also as a means of social control (religion as the opium of the people). The chief source of funding must usually have been the landowner, whether this was a wealthy individual (aristocrat or industrialist), an institution, or an industrial company. When it came to collecting funds, the bulk was provided by the prosperous middle classes. Only very rarely can the 'pennies of the poor' have counted for much: even in the case of Roman Catholic churches in Liverpool, the facts disprove the myths. Many clergymen were wealthy enough to pay for their new churches themselves. As regards country churches, these too were often erected by the landowners, sometimes as memorials to members of their families. When the Tractarian Robert Raikes bought the Treberfydd estate in 1848, he employed J. L. Pearson to build a new church (Llangasty Tal-y-llyn) before building a new house. On the other hand, W. S. Dugdale later came to regret his lapse in duty in having rebuilt Merevale Hall before restoring the parish church.

Sadly, the amazing achievement of the Victorians in erecting so many churches has been followed by shifts in population (especially away from inner cities) and a decline in church-going, which has meant that an especially high proportion of these churches have become superfluous to the needs of their denominations. Even before the Church of England's Pastoral Measure of 1968, many town churches were demolished, though country churches were less at risk. However, the Pastoral Measure not only formalized the concept of 'redundancy', but positively encouraged dioceses to dispose of what up-to-date churchmen like to refer to as their 'surplus plant'. Consequently much pressure has been put on combined parishes to have their less-used churches declared redundant, when encouragement from above might instead have prompted their congregations to continue to make a communal effort to keep them going.

A redundant church faces three possibilities:

(i) It may be vested for preservation in the Redundant Churches Fund. The Fund has, however, sufficient resources to take on only outstanding examples, and so far these have included few Victorian buildings (one example is All Saints, Cambridge). The Church Commissioners are very reluctant to vest inner-city churches in the Fund.

(ii) It may be sold, either to another denomination (like Henry Clutton's church at Tavistock, which became Roman Catholic in 1951), or for a secular use. In the latter case, the ensuing alterations frequently destroy the church's character. Furthermore, it may be rendered virtually inaccessible (which explains the omission from this book of J. Croft's splendid little church at Cold Hanworth, Lincs.).

(iii) It may be demolished. Particularly unfortunate cases of demolition of notable Victorian churches have recently included Holy Trinity, Rugby (G. G. Scott); St Michael, Stourport (G. G. Scott); The Saviour, Bolton (Paley and Austin); All Saints, Cwmafan (Prichard and Seddon); All Hallows, Inchinnan (Sir R. Rowand Anderson); and The Assumption, Rhyl (R. C-J. Hungerford Pollen).

Churches that have remained in use have often suffered grievous alteration in recent years. The liturgical changes brought in by the Second Vatican Council of 1964 have led to widespread reordering, often unnecessarily destructive, and the fashion has spread to the Church of England. Nonconformist congregations, who often see their old buildings as impediments to their work, rather than assets, have for many years resorted to internal subdivision as a way of making more economical use of the space. Once again, the Church of England is following suit, and an ever-increasing number of its churches are being treated in this way. Notable Victorian examples include St Clement, Ordsall and St Matthias, Richmond, Surrey (G. G. Scott).

The maltreatment of churches is facilitated by the existence of the so-called 'Ecclesiastical Exemption'. When the Ancient Monuments Bill was passed in 1913, all buildings in ecclesiastical use were exempted from its provisions. This was on the grounds that the Church of England had its own Faculty System, and wished to remain independent. At that date other denominations were not reckoned to possess buildings of sufficient architectural or historical merit to warrant concern. The exemption remains in force, despite the introduction of state aid for churches in 1976, so that ecclesiastical buildings are still exempt from most of the control to which listed secular buildings are subject. It is greatly to be hoped that this anomalous situation will soon be rectified. The Victorian Society has strongly urged the total abolition of the exemption for all denominations.

SCOTLAND

1 Inverness
2 Ellon
3 Aberdeen
4 Dunecht
5 Braemar
6 Fort William
7 Tarfside
8 Brechin
9 Dundee
10 Perth
11 Larbert
12 Greenock
13 Dumbarton
14 Cumbrae
15 Largs
16 Paisley
17 Glasgow
18 Edinburgh
19 Dalkeith
20 Penicuik
21 Shiskine
22 Irvine
23 Galston
24 Ayr
25 Kelso
26 Moffat
27 Carnsalloch
28 Dumfries
29 Castle Douglas

ENGLAND

30 Alnwick
31 Crosby-on-Eden
32 Bamford
33 Carlisle
34 Warwick Bridge
35 Farlam
36 Whitfield
37 Wreay
38 Alston
39 Hunstanworth
40 Cullercoats
41 Newcastle upon Tyne
42 Sunderland
43 Bournmoor
44 Hetton-le-Hole
45 West Rainton
46 Durham
47 Ushaw
48 West Hartlepool
49 Hartlepool
50 Stockton-on-Tees
51 Darlington
52 Richmond
53 Plumbland
54 Lamplugh
55 Cleator
56 Ambleside
57 Tebay
58 Finsthwaite
59 Millom
60 Heversham
61 Preston Park
62 Dalton-in-Furness
63 Field Broughton

64 Barbon
65 Giggleswick
66 Whitby
67 Goathland
68 Fylingdales
69 Eastmoors
70 Appleton-le-Moors
71 Wykeham
72 Scarborough
73 Healey
74 Studley Royal
75 Ripon
76 Skelton
77 Baldersby St James
78 Bagby
79 Thirkleby
80 Sproxton
81 Whitwell-on-the-Hill
82 Castle Howard
83 East Heslerton
84 Howsham
85 West Lutton
86 Helperthorpe
87 Sledmere
88 Aldwark
89 York
90 Lancaster
91 Middleton
92 Scotforth
93 Fleetwood
94 Winmarleigh
95 Singleton
96 Preston
97 Blackburn
98 Witton Park
99 Crawshawbooth
100 Todmorden
101 Blubberhouses
102 Ilkley
103 Saltaire
104 Bradford
105 Halifax
106 Copley
107 Cleckheaton
108 Heckmondwike
109 Leeds
110 Clifford
111 Everingham
112 South Dalton
113 Scorborough
114 Cowick
115 Ellerker
116 Altcar
117 Kirkby
118 Parbold
119 Daisy Hill
120 Howe Bridge/Atherton
121 Westleigh
122 Lever Bridge
123 Bury
124 Rochdale
125 Worsley
126 Eccles
127 Salford
128 Manchester
129 Ashton-under-Lyne
130 Reddish
131 Dukinfield
132 Stockport

133 Haughton Green
134 Hyde
135 Low Marple
136 Bamford
137 Sheffield
138 Wentworth
139 Doncaster
140 Scunthorpe
141 Burringham
142 Liverpool
143 Rainhill
144 Ditton
145 Warrington
146 Higher Walton
147 High Legh
148 Bowdon
149 Alderley Edge
150 Macclesfield
151 West Kirby
152 Oxton
153 Prenton
154 Thurstaston
155 Bromborough
156 Hooton
157 Chester
158 Eccleston
159 Christleton
160 Pulford
161 Eaton
162 Whitegate
163 Sandbach Heath
164 Crewe Green
165 Odd Rode
166 Edensor
167 Matlock
168 Mansfield
169 Clumber Park
170 Perlethorpe
171 Moorhouse
172 Lincoln
173 Nocton
174 Haugham
175 Little Cawthorpe
176 Leek
177 Stoke-on-Trent
178 Cheadle
179 Alton
180 Denstone
181 Calverhall
182 Welshampton
183 Llanyblodwel
184 Llanymynech
185 Peplow
186 Slindon
187 Hoar Cross
188 Dunstall
189 Stretton
190 Derby
191 Nottingham
192 Shrewsbury
193 Meole Brace
194 Hopwas
195 Leicester
196 Deeping St Nicholas
197 Spalding
198 Fosdyke
199 Birmingham
200 Richard's Castle
201 Tenbury

232 Highnam
233 Daylesford
234 Milton-under-Wychwood
235 Leafield
236 Hailey
237 Freeland
238 Milton
239 Horton-cum-Studley
240 Westcott
241 Woburn Sands
242 Woburn
243 Ridgmont
244 Steppingley
245 Hitchin
246 Tutshill
247 Selsey
248 Woodchester
249 France Lynch
250 Hatherop
251 Filkins
252 Marston Meysey
253 Watchingfield
254 Oxford
255 Cowley
256 Wheatley
257 Dorchester
258 Prestwood
259 Langleybury
260 Ayot St Peter
261 Woolmer Green
262 Waterford
263 Bayford
264 Old Hall Green
265 Stansted Mountfitchet
266 Ford End
267 Twinstead
268 Leiston
269 Coalpit Heath
270 Bristol
271 Bath
272 Leigh Delamere
273 Oare
274 Chute Forest
275 Fawley
276 Brightwalton
277 Leckhampstead
278 Newbury
279 Greenham
280 Midgham
281 Beech Hill
282 Reading
283 Wokingham
284 Marlow
285 Dropmore
286 Boyne Hill
287 Gerrards Cross
288 Farnham Royal
289 Clewer
290 Windsor
291 Datchet
292 Staines
293 Englefield Green
294 Watford
295 Epping
296 Loughton
297 Bentley Common
298 Brentwood
299 Southend-on-Sea
300 West Quantoxhead

301 Wells
302 Downside
303 Chantry
304 Hornblotton
305 Sutton Veney
306 Fonthill Gifford
307 Wilton
308 South Tidworth
309 Andover
310 Ecchinswell
311 Hursley
312 Itchen Stoke
313 Newton
314 Privett
315 Clanfield
316 Hawkley
317 Blackmoor
318 Fleet
319 Shackleford
320 Slinfold
321 Hascombe
322 Grafham
323 Blackheath
324 Albury
325 Ranmore
326 Kingswood
327 Lower Kingswood
328 Dorking
329 Holmbury St Mary
330 Lowfield Heath
331 East Grinstead
332 Titsey
333 Chiddington Causeway
334 Hildenborough
335 Langton Green
336 Tunbridge Wells
337 Kilndown
338 Hawkhurst
339 Sheerness
340 Murston
341 Ramsgate
342 Dover
343 Tuckingmill
344 Truro
345 Little Petherick
346 Biscovey
347 Tavistock
348 Revelstoke
349 Down St Mary
350 Washford Pyne
351 Exwick
352 Exeter
353 Babbacombe
354 Torquay
355 Collaton St Mary
356 Bicton
357 Honiton
358 Buckland St Mary
359 Monkton Wyld
360 Bothenhampton
361 Melplash
362 Cattistock
363 Bryanston
364 Colehill
365 Longham
366 Bournemouth
367 Kingston
368 Lyndhurst
369 Marchwood

370 Whippingham
371 Newport
372 Ryde
373 Gosport
374 Farlington
375 Portsmouth
376 West Lavington
377 Chichester
378 Petworth
379 Arundel
380 Worthing
381 Lancing
382 Hove
383 Brighton
384 Eastbourne
385 Netherfield
386 St Leonards
387 Hastings

WALES

388 Deganwy
389 Colwyn Bay
390 Rhyl
391 Bryn-y-Maen
392 Bodelwyddan
393 Trefnant
394 Halkyn
395 Shotton
396 Buckley
397 Pentrobin
398 Llandwrog
399 Llanberis
400 Betws-y-Coed
401 Llanbedr Dyffryn Clwyd
402 Bersham
403 Bettisfield
404 Llandegwning
405 Maentwrog
406 Barmouth
407 Caerdeon
408 Brithdir
409 Bwlch-y-Cibau
410 Welshpool
411 Leighton
412 Carno
413 Llangorwen
414 Penrhyncoch
415 Elerch
416 Abbeycwmhir
417 Beulah
418 Lampeter
419 Llangasty Tal-Y-Llyn
420 Capel-y-Ffin
421 Abergavenny
422 Nicholaston
423 Morriston
424 Neath
425 Baglan
426 Port Talbot
427 Pentre
428 Merthyr Mawr
429 Pontypool
430 Llandogo
431 Malpas
432 Newport
433 Roath
434 Cardiff
435 Penarth

THE CHURCHES

NA	Nicholas Antram	DM	David McLaughlin
CB	Chris Brooks	MM	Michael Morris
DB	Donald Buttress	JO	Julian Orbach
BC	Bridget Cherry	KP	Ken Powell
RO'D	Roderick O'Donnell	AQ	Anthony Quiney
DRE	D. Robert Elleray	AJS	Andrew Saint
TEF	T. E. Faulkner	MS	Matthew Saunders
DH	Douglas Hickman	GS	Gavin Stamp
REH	Roger Homan	CS	Christopher Stell
PH	Peter Howell	IRS	Ian Sutton
RMH	Rodney Hubbuck	ANS	Anthony Symondson
PJ	Paul Joyce	DW	David Walker
ENK	Edward Kaufman	LW	Lynne Walker
DL	David Lloyd	AW	Alexandra Wedgwood

* denotes that the church is illustrated in the plate section

Abbey Cwmhir, Powys
St Mary

In the 1860s the Phillips family of Manchester built
here a house and church which are the quintessence
of High Victorianism. Their architects were Poundley and Walker. The church, of 1866, has a nave, an
apsed chancel, and a porch beneath a vigorous spirelet
which turns octagonal, all in knobbly brown stone
and Early French Gothic. Inside, there is elaborate
carving, and good glass. The W window is by Clayton
and Bell, but the chancel windows by Heaton, Butler
and Bayne (1866) are even finer, with rich, deep
colours and intense emotion. [PH]

Aberdeen, Grampian
Queen's Cross Church (Church of Scotland)*

A very original French Gothic church in grey granite
by John Bridgeford Pirie, 1880–1. Broad six-bay plan,
two slightly advanced as transepts, W front with
massive gabled doorway on huge cylindrical dwarf
columns, SW tower of extraordinary profile, mullioned treatment composed of immensely tall triple
lancets through several stages, arched and gabled
belfry-stage over cantilevered balcony, octagonal
spire interrupted by open stage of dwarf colonnettes.
[DW]

Aberdeen, Grampian
St Mary (Episcopal)

Financed and designed by the Revd Frederick George
Lee, and said to have been based on a scheme obtained
from G. E. Street; executed by Alexander Ellis,
1862–4. Italian Gothic, very tall, of grey granite
banded with red; plan of so-called Gerona type but
inspired more by Florentine and Sienese prototypes;
short nave with flush transepts entirely lit by circular
mincer-plate windows high up; crow-stepped gables,
chevroned slating and transept pinnacles with elaborate wrought-iron finials; single-bay chancel with
aisles, and aisleless three-sided apse, again with
circular windows; rebuilt without crow-stepped
gables after bomb damage, 1952. Frescoed interior
with open timber roofs. [DW]

Abergavenny, Gwent
Our Lady and St Michael (RC)

This grand and lofty church, in elaborate but pure
Decorated Gothic, was built in 1858–60 by Benjamin
Bucknall. It is beautifully detailed: the arcades and
rose-traceried E window are particularly fine. The
elaborate high altar reredos, with angels in an orgy
of adoration, is by Edmund Kirby of Liverpool (1883).
[PH]

Addiscombe, Greater London
*St Mary Magdalene**

E. B. Lamb's last church, built in 1868–9 for the Revd
Maxwell Machluff Ben Oliel, a Jewish convert who
achieved such popularity as a preacher that a group
of supporters offered to build him his own church,
though without diocesan authority, so that it was
technically a Nonconformist church. It follows the
pattern definitively stated at Gospel Oak but worked
out many years earlier of combining axial with centralized spaces. The wide-span timber roof is Lamb's
most fantastic, mounting up into a trellised pyramid
over the crossing, capped dramatically by a lantern.
The stonework is personal too, with its transitions
from crisply faceted bases to strangely flowing,
biomorphic colonnettes; the great detached columns
standing at the ends of the transepts provide a dramatic accent which would have been easier to under-
stand when they framed passage-aisles along the
perimeter, i.e. before the original seating was removed
and the altar brought down into the crossing. When
Lamb died in 1869, St Mary Magdalene was unfinished, and so it remains. Hugh Mackintosh designed
the tower in 1927, and Lamb's son, Edward Beckitt
Lamb, contributed many of the decorative fittings.
But the projection of the nave beyond the crossing-
area is truncated, finished off with a blank brick wall
instead of a W façade. [ENK]

Albury, Surrey
The Apostles Chapel (Catholic Apostolic
Church)*

The Gothic chapel which Henry Drummond built in
the years 1837–43 as the spiritual centre of the
Catholic Apostolic Church was designed by William
Wilkins and his associate W. McIntosh Brookes,
though some of the fittings in the chancel may be

the work of Pugin. It comprises an aisleless nave, transepts and chancel, a W tower, and vestries, some of later date, at the E end. The most unusual feature is an octagonal chapter house or conference room on the S side. The chapel, although maintained in perfect condition, has not been used since about 1950 and is not open to visitors. [cs]

Alderley Edge, Cheshire
St Philip

Built by Joseph Stretch Crowther in 1851–2. With his partner Henry Bowman he had measured medieval buildings and they adapted features such as the broach-spire (rare in the NW) and the flowing window tracery from the finest Northamptonshire examples. The random wall masonry is carefully textured and looks almost 'real', whereas the polychromatic roof-slate patterns do not. There are three parallel roofs and no clerestory so that the interior, although plastered, is dark. There is one good Morris window of 1873. [DB]

Aldwark, North Yorkshire
*St Stephen**

By E. B. Lamb, 1851–3, and one of his most important works. With its low-browed, high-soaring roofs, St Stephen has an appealingly cottagey flavour which disguises its brash originality. For this is one of the earliest and most striking examples of mid-Victorian constructional polychromy, a technique initiated by William Butterfield in 1849. At Aldwark, Lamb radically reinterprets Butterfield's innovation, replacing his smooth, hard materials with handmade bricks and rounded cobbles straight from the riverbed. The oddly vaned tower, small and upward-straining, is pure Lamb, with all his concentrated expressive force. Inside, the dominant material is wood. The open timber roof is an imaginative variation of medieval traditions, with some surprises: note especially the dramatically sloping valley rafters over the angle-bays and the daringly cantilevered purlins which meet in a pin-joint over the corners of the crossing. The wooden furniture reveals an eye for simple outlines and sheer mass, and the powerfully chamfered altar table bears comparison with the best furniture of Street or Webb a few years later. But none of this explains the mysterious quality of this small but intricate space, part axial and part central-ized, humble and low-roofed, yet full of flickering light and Gothic wonder. [ENK]

Alnwick, Northumberland
St Paul (RC)

This former Anglican church was commissioned by the 3rd Duke of Northumberland to accommodate the growth of Early Victorian Alnwick and to provide a town church for his personàl use. He commissioned Anthony Salvin, a native of County Durham, whose work here was a prelude to his extensive activity at Alnwick Castle. Also available were the duke's estate workers, whose careful craftsmanship imparts real quality to the stone and wood carving of the interior. This monumental church was consecrated in 1846 but the duke only had one year to enjoy his private box over the E door before his death. That was the occasion for a long series of memorials which begin with his own recumbent monument by J. E. Carew, and culminate in the E window, made by Ainmiller of Munich to the designs of William Dyce, and erected in 1851–6. [LW]

Alston, Cumbria
St Augustine

A large church dominating the steep slopes of this Pennine market town with nave, S aisle, and a large tower and spire (completed in 1886) at the SE. The design by J. W. Walton, of 1870, is not typical of any particular Victorian style. The interior reflects the English parish-church tradition but the details show a mixture of Gothic forms, as in the use of Purbeck marble for the columns of the nave arcade, squat and with heavy capitals, richly carved. [TEF]

Altcar, Lancashire
St Michael

Built in 1879, this church is exceptional for John Douglas in being completely timber-framed, with red-tiled roofs. The bell-cote has a pyramidal roof. The inside is spacious, light and cosy, with excellent roofs, and a timber arcade to the passage-aisle on the N. Everywhere are texts carved in the wood. The pulpit and other fittings are in Douglas's vernacular style. There is one window by Edward Frampton (1885). [PH]

Alton, Staffordshire
St John (RC) and *Castle Chapel* (RC)

A. W. N. Pugin's first major project for the Earl of
Shrewsbury, begun in 1840, was the Hospital of St
John, intended as an ideal religious community,
modelled on medieval examples, with chapel, school
and lodgings for the warden, poor brethren and
schoolmaster. Built in the local red sandstone round
three sides of a quadrangle, it has chiefly been used
as a parish church, convent and school. The church
has a nave and chancel with an adjoining priest's
house to the S, which has a S entrance tower. Inside,
there is a fine roof to the chancel and a splendid
alabaster altar and reredos. The E window is by
Willement and there are large brasses by Hardman
to the 16th and 17th earls. After the tranquil Englishness of the church, the chapel to the castle, built
several years later, is a complete contrast. It is
dramatic and Continental in inspiration, with a steep
roof of coloured tiles, Geometrical window tracery,
and a polygonal apse. After an antechapel of two bays
and great height, the chapel proper is tall and narrow.
It is also rib-vaulted in stone with angel corbels to
the vaulting shafts. [AW]

Ambleside, Cumbria
St Mary

An imposing design in late-13th-century style by Sir
George Gilbert Scott, built in 1850–4. Sandstone
dressings contrast with the basic fabric of grey-blue
Lakeland stone, but the dominating feature is the SE
tower, with broach-spire rising to 180 feet. The
spacious interior, with hammer-beam roof to the
nave, is correct and academic; there is a marble
reredos of 1895 and some fine stained glass. [TEF]

Andover, Hampshire
St Mary

Sidney Smirke took over the construction of this large
and impressive church from Augustus Livesay of
Portsmouth when structural difficulties arose in the
course of its construction. Begun in 1840, it was not
finished until 1846. A cruciform composition with a
high pinnacled tower at its W end, it soars above
an elevated site and, lit by lancets throughout, is
recognizably Early English. It has a remarkable
interior with plaster-vaulted ceilings supported on

extremely thin six-shafted columns having crisp stiff-
leaf capitals. The shafts of the triple-arched screen
veiling the apse are extremely attenuated. [MM]

Anerley, Greater London
The New Church (Swedenborgian)

An interesting example of early concrete construction.
The designer in 1883 was W. Henley and the style is
eclectic Gothic. The principal feature is a large rose
window between twin spires over a SW portico. The
church is lit by coupled lancets and small round
windows for a gallery that never appeared, leaving
its intended doors stranded high in the wall. The
interior is spacious and is spanned by a great chancel
arch. In accordance with Swedenborgian principles,
fittings are functional but not ornamental. [REH]

Appleton-le-Moors, North Yorkshire
*Christ Church**

Designed in 1862–3 by John Loughborough Pearson
and built in 1863–5, of local limestone. Externally,
its lines are bold and clearly stated; inside High
Victorian Gothic ornamentation contrasts with plain
walling and unchamfered arches to give it a severely
primitive character. Pearson was inspired by many
divergent medieval sources: as far away as Italy
for the rounded, unbuttressed apse, and tower and
pyramidal spire, placed like a campanile on the S
side; as near as Byland Abbey for the W end with its
rose window over a porch set between buttresses. The
carved capitals of the nave arcade are a notably
vigorous interpretation of Early French Gothic and
the incised pictorial band round the apse boldly
emphasizes the E end. Stained glass is by Clayton
and Bell. [AQ]

Arundel, West Sussex
Cathedral Church of Our Lady and St Philip (RC)

Erected in 1870–3 from designs by J. A. Hansom at
the expense of the 15th Duke of Norfolk to commemorate his majority, this was the most costly Victorian
church in Sussex, and must be considered the triumphant climax of Roman Catholic building in the
county, though it only became a cathedral in 1965.
The style, based on 13th-century French Gothic, is
telling in the manipulation of spatial effect rather
than convincing architectural detail. The plan is

cruciform; there is vaulting throughout, but no triforium; the tall clustered nave columns lead to an impressive apsidal chancel with ambulatory of pointed arches surmounted by five windows. There is good glass by Hardman and Powell. The W front has a large rose window. The massive NW tower remains incomplete. [DRE]

Ashton-under-Lyne, Greater Manchester
St Michael

Medieval in origin although the aisle walls had been raised to accommodate the galleries by the end of the 18th century. The church was extensively reconstructed between 1840 and 1844 by an unknown architect. The timber panels of the ceiling follow the ancient form but are enriched by extra plaster bosses; the walls and arcades are deeply moulded with plasterwork. The dark woodwork of pulpit desks and pews is lavishly enriched by ornament made of fireclay and plaster, adapted from the plates of Halfpenny's *Gothick Ornaments of York*. Pews face the pulpit midway down the nave and not the altar. The tower was rebuilt and grandly enlarged by John Crowther in 1886–8. [DB]

Atherton, Greater Manchester
St John the Baptist

The immense size of this Paley and Austin church of 1879 is all the more amazing as it has no churchyard, but is crammed on to a tight corner site right in the middle of an industrial town. Pinnacled octagonal buttresses clasp each corner of the massive four-stage tower which is just attached to the S aisle. The clerestory windows catalogue what Late Decorated tracery can do within the confines of a square – quatrefoils, swirling Curvilinear, trefoils set in a cusped rose and more. The Curvilinear six-light E window (with stained glass of 1896 by C. E. Kempe) sits on a diapered ground of fleur-de-lys, roses and emblematic shields. [DM]

Avon Dassett, Warwickshire
St John the Baptist*

Finely sited on the steep hillside, this church was entirely rebuilt in 1868–9 by Charles Buckeridge of Oxford. In warm local ironstone, it is his masterpiece – an elegant essay in 13th-century style, with a soaring broach-spire. The aisle arcade is Transitional. The excellent fittings, including the blue-grey reredos and woodwork, are by Buckeridge, who also built a cusped recess N of the chancel for the Forest marble tomb-chest of a deacon (*c.* 1210). The church has been declared redundant. [PH]

Ayot St Peter, Hertfordshire
St Peter*

Built in 1874–5 by J. P. Seddon. Seen from the road to the E it makes an impressive picture: the round-roofed apse, the canted S chapel and the tall flanking tower and complex spire form a fascinating composition of subtle geometry. The material is mainly rich red brick with polychrome patterns using buff and black. Inside it is a complete church of the early period of Arts and Crafts influence, with painted panels on the chancel roof; chancel arch in grey ceramic; green and brown chancel tiles; font with a colourful mosaic representation of a landscape and glass in W windows by Seddon himself. The delicate iron screen dates from 1908. [DL]

Ayr, Strathclyde
Holy Church (Episcopal)

Early English, by J. L. Pearson; chancel, chapel and vestries 1887–8, nave completed 1900 but tower then left unfinished, completed without spire 1952. Nave with aisles of the same height presenting a tower and two unequal gables to the street, vaulted narthex with gallery over in the first bay. Nave arcades have clustered piers with higher wall-shafts carrying chamfered transverse arches and king-post roof; chancel with clerestory opening into N side of chapel; square E end with two tiers of triple lancets. Excellent Late Gothic triptych reredos with coloured and gilded *alto relievo* of Madonna and Child and the Wise Men, wrought-iron choir and chapel screens by F. L. Pearson, 1902–3. [DW]

Babbacombe, Devon
All Saints*

All Saints is one of William Butterfield's most important churches and one of the definitive statements of High Victorian Gothic. The nave was built in 1865–7, the remainder in 1872–4. Straightforward in plan, the exterior – built in blue-grey limestone – is relatively quiet, although characteristically personal qualities are evident in the spiky profile of the tower and spire, the squeezed chancel vesicas and the restlessly varied diaper-work on chancel, porch and steeple. The interior is spectacular. The diaper motif reappears as a stone wall-trellis, superimposed upon polychromatic brick and tile; polychromy, indeed, is employed everywhere, Butterfield exploiting the availability of local marbles. Particularly fine are the font and pulpit, strongly architectural, fascinatingly intricate in construction, and using a whole range of polished marbles with colours from black and pure white to greens, pinks, browns and ochres. The chancel is a fitting climax to the whole, elaborately playing decorative and constructional schemes against one another, and everything to Butterfield's design: the candle standards and all the metalwork; the windows, executed by Gibbs; the reredos mosaic, made by Salviati. For all its visual diversity, All Saints has an intensity of concentration, a consistency of expression, that makes it unforgettable. [CB]

Bagby, North Yorkshire
St Mary*

A small masterpiece of 1862 by E. B. Lamb. Like nearby Aldwark, Bagby explores the interaction between an axial or Latin-cross and a centralized plan, but in contrast Bagby drives towards radical simplification, and to a paradoxical grandeur at miniature scale. The massing is tautly geometrical, an intersection of primary forms. Inside Lamb throws the entire central area of crossing and transepts into a single space which rises grandly into a turret-capped pyramidal roof. The dizzying timber arch-braces suggest parallels both with medieval monastic kitchens and with the Mozarabic star vaults of Spain, but the total effect is Lamb's own, not least because of the paradoxical distortion of scale: one can practically lean on the eaves of this monumental but miniature structure. [ENK]

Baglan, West Glamorgan
St Catherine*

Above the spreading suburbia of Port Talbot rises the pinnacled spire – strong but elegant – of John Prichard's masterpiece and swan-song. Consecrated in 1882, it was paid for by his cousin Griffith Llewellyn of Baglan Hall. In Geometrical Decorated style, the exterior is of red stone, with refined detailing. The interior, which has a passage-aisle on the N, is astonishingly rich and colourful. Pink alabaster (from Penarth) contrasts with different shades of grey stone. All the arches have coloured voussoirs, irregularly arranged. The floors are of mosaic. The striking reredos of incised marble is by H. H. Armstead. N of the chancel is the Cosmateque tomb of the founder (died 1888). All the glass is by the Morris firm, and dates from 1880. The crucifixion in the E window, and the lovely St Cecilia in the S transept, were designed by Burne-Jones: the other windows have pretty flowered quarries. [PH]

Baldersby St James, North Yorkshire
St James*

The church of 1855–7, its spire a landmark in the flat landscape, is the centrepiece of a model village designed by William Butterfield. It is a major work. The severe stone exterior conceals a warm and beautifully controlled interior, rich yet not strident, with walls of mellow brick banded with stone. The chancel is appropriately enriched with alabaster facings and fine tiles. Typically excellent Butterfield roofs crown the whole. Everything in this interior is in keeping: forcefully designed font and cover, pews, chancel fittings, even a splendid Butterfield clock. The glass is by various makers – E window by O'Connor, W by Wailes, aisles and clerestories by Preedy of Worcester. [KP]

Bamford, Derbyshire
St John the Baptist

Erected in 1856–60 by William Butterfield who also designed the adjoining vicarage and the gateway with stepped gable. The exterior is dominated by the slim NW tower with pyramid spire rising in unbroken line straight from it. Entry is by way of the tower and a narthex into the nave with a N arcade which, unlike the rest of the church, is traditional for Derbyshire. The windows have a variety of Decorated-inspired tracery motifs with quite original Geometrical patterns that could only be Victorian. Excellent glass of 1860 by Preedy in the E, W and S windows, with wonderfully bold lines and powerful faces. The fittings are plain and there is a circular, tapering marble font. [NA]

Barbon, Cumbria
*St Bartholomew**

This beautiful fell church by Paley, Austin and Paley with a broad central tower was built in 1891–3. A tiny window nestling down on each side of the S transept roof floods light into the crossing. Internally, the SE tower staircase is expressed as a diagonal buttress merging with the tower pier. The arches of the two-bays nave die gently into the broadened octagonal piers – a beautiful detail. The E respond dies into the flat solidity of the tower pier, from which the S transept arch flows. On its chamfered reveal are carved squared roses (so beloved by Austin). The mullions of the freely styled Perpendicular E window die into curving pierced transoms. Austin's joy in detailing is well expressed in the font, with its tiny diagonal buttresses and its three-stage timber cover. [DM]

Barmouth, Gwynedd
St John

Perched up on the steep hillside above the town, the grey and red stone of this mighty church makes a striking contrast with the black rock and yellow gorse behind it. It was designed by Douglas and Fordham and begun in 1889, but in 1892 the broad central tower collapsed, and it was not completely rebuilt until 1898. The interior is grandly spacious, with a short but lofty chancel with stone reredos. There is excellent woodwork, and Kempe glass. The marble font, an angel holding a shell, is by Davidson of Inverness, after Thorwaldsen. [PH]

Barnet, Greater London
St John

Designed in 1889 by John Loughborough Pearson. The E parts were finished in 1891; the nave was built in 1901 and the W end, to a modified design by Frank Loughborough Pearson, in 1911. Frederick Hall, the patron, had been impressed by the ruins of the Gothic Heisterbach Abbey in the Rhineland and asked Pearson to build him a version of its semicircular apse and flying buttresses. Pearson complied, though the design is characteristically his own with quadripartite rib-vaults for the interior, sparse ornament beyond the Decorated tracery of the clerestory, and a sense of space encompassed within small dimensions. The aisled nave leads to the apsidal chancel and its ambulatory, and there is an apsidal S chapel acting as a foil to the main body of the church. A N tower and spire were never completed. [AQ]

Bath, Avon
Prior Park College Chapel (RC)*

The great Palladian mansion of Ralph Allen would have been the centre of the revived Roman Catholic Church in the West of England if Bishop Baines, who bought it in 1830, had had his way. The chapel, added next to the W wing of the mansion, was begun in 1844 by J. J. Scoles but remained roofless for many years, being finally inaugurated in 1882. The interior is a spectacular Neo-classical basilica of the type evolved in late-18th-century France from Palladio. Giant Corinthian columns of Bath stone divide off the aisles and carry a magnificent continuous cornice above which springs a coffered barrel-vault. The E end is apsed with attached paired columns. Scoles intended it to be filled with mosaic. [JO]

Bath, Avon
St John the Evangelist (RC)

The 220-foot-high steeple is the most conspicuous feature in the S side of the city. It was C. F. Hansom's first important High Victorian church, dating from 1861–3. The exterior is rock-faced with Bath stone and elaborately roofed, with a W narthex, cross-gabled aisles, transepts and five-sided apse. The rich interior is largely intact, with sculptures and altars by Earp, Hardman glass, and contemporary rood-screen. [RO'D]

Bath, Avon
St Michael

One of those churches of the 1830s that wholeheartedly adopt the Gothic without losing the confectionery look of their less correct Georgian predecessors. The local architect G. P. Manners selected almost all his detail – triplets of lancets, gable-capped buttresses, cornices and other patterned mouldings – from Salisbury Cathedral, but the smooth Bath stone, the box-like shape and most of all the tower and spire give away the 1835–7 date. The octagonal spire (182 feet high) with a tall gabled opening on each face letting light right through stands on a solid tower, a conflation of Salisbury bits with added small rose windows. The inside is tall and plaster-vaulted, with slim piers that once held galleries. [JO]

Batsford, Gloucestershire
St Mary

A late example of Neo-Norman, designed by W. F. Poulton of Reading and built in 1861–2. Nave and apsed chancel have round-arched windows; the remarkable spire, somewhat French in outline, has big square pinnacles and is ringed by excessively hefty gabled lights. The interior is plain except for the carved chancel arch and rib-vaulted apse. Lovely white marble tomb-chest of the foundress by William Burges, with interlacing design of foliage and birds of Celtic richness set against gold mosaic, *c.* 1866. [JO]

Bayford, Hertfordshire
St Mary

Built to Henry Woodyer's designs in 1870–1. Though small – it consists of a nave and chancel with a grand flèche over their junction – it has several features characteristic of Woodyer's ingenuity. Most unusual is the splendid way the roof at the junction of nave and chancel sweeps downwards and outward to be broken by a large dormer with a round opening as though to form transepts, but in fact to form vestries. The chancel is entered through a wooden rood-screen with tall, cusped openings, and it terminates in a polygonal apse. The ornate pulpit is carved with diaper, quatrefoils and figures. [AQ]

Beccles, Suffolk
St Benet (RC)

An ambitious French-Romanesque-style cruciform church by the local Roman Catholic architect, F. E. Banham. It was intended to be the centrepiece of a small Benedictine monastery. The nave was ready by 1901 and the building was complete by 1908. It is tunnel-vaulted throughout, with groin vaults to the aisles. The nave has seven-bay arcades, tribune and clerestory, and the S doorway and porch are richly decorated with chevron, billet and dog-tooth mouldings, all in a hard West Country stone. The 1880s is a surprisingly late date for the use of a Neo-Romanesque style, which had been briefly popular forty years earlier. [NA]

Beckenham, Greater London
Baptist Church

Herbert D. Appleton and Edward W. Mountford aimed in 1883 at 'ecclesiastical character and dignity'. It is a cheerful church of yellow stock brick within and without, enlivened by dressings of red brick and Doulton stone. The style is Early English and the chief external feature is a NW saddleback tower bearing a slender spirelet. There are narrow passage-aisles beneath clerestory lancets. In the E end a vast brick arch contains the organ. [REH]

Beech Hill, Berkshire
*St Mary**

Delightfully situated in a rural hamlet, this is one of William Butterfield's most colourful and lovable churches. Built in 1866–7, it consists of nave and chancel under one roof. The exterior is of flint and brick with stone dressings: the bell-turret is of tile-hung timber, and the S porch is also timber. The interior is wonderfully polychrome, and has excellent fittings, notably the powerful wooden screen, beyond which hangs a vast two-storey corona of painted iron. On the E wall the tall reredos of stone and tiles rises between three windows filled with rich glass by Gibbs, who also made the windows on the S side of the church. The sanctuary has a tiled dado with diagonal bands. The wooden pulpit and glorious font of pink and grey marble are also notable. The aisle has a lean-to roof resting on quaint brick corbels. [PH]

Belmont, Herefordshire
St Michael and All Angels (RC)

Built as a Benedictine abbey by E. W. Pugin. Work began on the nave and aisles (1854–6), then came the crossing, transepts and choir (1859–60) and finally the sanctuary (1865). The crossing-tower was completed in 1882. The W parts are in a style closer to the older Pugin, the E more High Victorian. Most of the original furnishings have gone, but the Hardman E window of 1860 and the R. L. Boulton reredos of 1865 remain. [RO'D]

Bentley Common (Brentwood), Essex
St Paul

An elegant and carefully detailed church, founded in 1878, by E. C. Lee. In a park-like coniferous setting, it is severely Early English in style, of flint with stone dressings. A shingled broach-spire rises on the N side. The large chancel has grand quintuple lancets at the E end, ingeniously framed within by rere-arches which group the three middle ones together. The chancel-arch corbels consist of seated figures in niches. The splendidly rich fittings include the reredos with the Way of the Cross in high relief. [PH]

Bersham, Clwyd
St Mary

Bersham has the character of a Victorian estate village. In 1873 T. L. Fitzhugh commissioned the church from John Gibson. It is a lavish Romanesque effort, in red sandstone, in a setting of shrubs and conifers. The tower, added in 1890–2, was Gibson's last work. The plan is cruciform, with apsidal chancel and the vaults have bands of red and white stone. [PH]

Bettisfield, Clwyd
St John the Baptist

The grey stone church was built in 1872–4 by G. E. Street, in his mature Early Decorated manner. Approached from the SE through a stone lych-gate, its forms unravel marvellously angular and vertical, the tower ascending rocket-like from buttressed square by exceedingly steep broaches into a tall octagon, pierced only on the cardinal sides with elongated belfry-lancets; a low stone spire is kept sheer and sharp with no projections. This is a distilled variation of St Mary Magdalene, Paddington, but carried through in monochrome. The chancel is square-ended with a high traceried E window and brief lean-to S aisle, the broad nave marginally taller with SW porch. Roofs are open timber, but the interior is made cunningly spatial by treating the big N chapel and opposing tower as transepts to the nave, their arches dying into its E wall on either side of a lofty chancel arch. Street's furnishings are all in accord, his reredos set in a Minton majolica-tile dado below Clayton and Bell's E window. [PJ]

Betws-y-coed, Gwynedd
St Mary the Virgin

This church of 1870–3 was a competition winner for Paley and Austin. It was conceived as a series of steeply pitched roofs cascading from a pyramidal central tower roof, down the chancel roof and, again, down the S transept and vestry roof almost to the ground. The steep pitches are accentuated by the plate tracery of the five-light E window and two tiny lucarnes set into the gable above the string-course. Not executed until 1907, the tower as built omits the pyramidal roof and has a stepped parapet instead of the single line proposed. Internally a grand sense of space is achieved by the quadripartite vaults of the tower and the lower chancel. The W window is a single rose of plate tracery with a central buttress under. The drama of the S transept roof is matched on the N by the tower staircase snuggling up between two large lancets. [DM]

Beulah, Powys
Eglwys Oen Duw (Church of the Lamb of God)

Built by John Norton in 1867, this little church is externally of blue and grey stone, in severe Early English, but enlivened by a remarkable Germanic flèche over the junction of nave and chancel. The interior is rich and colourful, in polychrome brick banded with tiles. The E wall has a mosaic reredos. Elaborate fittings include carved stalls, an iron and brass pulpit, brass coronae, and brass candle-sconces representing water-lily leaves with frogs. [PH]

Bexleyheath, Greater London
Christ Church

The design is by William Knight of Nottingham but Burges advised the committee. In 1877 the project was abandoned for lack of funds, sorrily stumpy and spireless. So it remains, a massive cruciform church in Early French Gothic, of sandstone with slated roofs. Plate tracery is used to good effect in the high clerestory and W end and there are fine rose windows in the transepts. Within, arcades are of four arches and the crossing inspires, but the interior is barren of fittings. [REH]

Bickley, Greater London
St George

Sir Ernest Newton's 1905–6 upper tower and spire are a landmark across Bromley Common but are less imposing than the original spire of this vast Decorated building erected at considerable cost in 1863–5 to designs by F. Barnes on the land of the Wythes family, who repose in the crypt beneath Butterfield's 1871 monument in the N transept. The interior is expansive; the aisles are of five bays borne by slender granite columns. [REH]

Bicton, Devon
St Mary

A fascinating site on the perimeter of the grounds of Bicton House and comprising no less than three ecclesiastical buildings: the ruin of the medieval church of Holy Trinity, the Rolle mausoleum of 1849–50, and the church of St Mary of 1850. In the 1840s Louisa, Lady Rolle, employed A. W. N. Pugin to remodel the old S chancel chapel as a mausoleum for her late husband. Steeply gabled, heavily buttressed, its external severity contrasts with the ornate interior; floor tiles by Minton, glass by Hardman, the elaborately accomplished tomb carving by Myers, a panelled roof painted with formal and heraldic patterns; everything to Pugin's designs. To the E of the mausoleum is the new church of St Mary, by John Hayward. A well-conceived building in the best Geometrical Decorated, with nave, chancel, transept and transeptal tower, St Mary's shows Hayward's handling of space and mass at its most accomplished, and his preference for hard edges and clean surfaces at its most pronounced. It also has an engagingly original iconographic programme – all the English monarchy on the external dripstone terminals, with heads of Anglican divines for the nave roof-corbels – and an important set of windows by William Warrington. [CB]

Birmingham, West Midlands
St Agatha, Sparkbrook

The masterpiece of W. H. Bidlake, consecrated in 1901, and one of the most successful churches of the period in the country. Of thin red bricks in bold simple forms, relieved by the most delicately detailed stone arches, tracery and sculpture. It is in the Perpendicular Gothic style transformed by the Arts and Crafts. The composition is formal, the W front with a tall tower supported by a low baptistery apse and transverse porches with W entrances. Both porches and tower are contained by polygonal angle-buttresses, the only areas of wall being supported on broad arches spanning between them. At high level the wall face dissolves into twin belfry-openings with deep louvres and the tower is crowned by a pierced parapet, open lanterns and a tall spike. In the interior, of cream brick with stone dressings, the nave arcades have diagonally placed square piers, which allow the space to flow and lead up to arches which fly across both clerestory and nave to give a vaulted effect. [DH]

Birmingham, West Midlands
St Alban, Bordesley

Designed by John Loughborough Pearson and built in 1879–81, but for the tower and spire. The church is built of red brick with Bath stone dressings, and with Early English and Normandy Gothic details. W entrances lead to an aisled nave, a crossing and apsidal chancel with an ambulatory passage and a S chapel, itself treated like a miniature church in Pearson's characteristic way, with a nave, chancel and sanctuary of its own. Set beside the open chancel, it provides a contrasting vista of intricately planned spaces welded together by Pearson's effortless vaulting that at once gives his interiors individual points of excitement but an overwhelming sense of calm. The only part of the fittings designed by Pearson is the wrought-iron screen made by White and Son in 1897. The tower was completed to a new design with a saddleback by E. F. Reynolds in 1938. [AQ]

Birmingham, West Midlands
Cathedral of St Chad (RC)*

St Chad's cathedral (1839–41) marks an early and very important commission in Pugin's dramatic rise to the leadership of the Gothic Revival movement. Both the style and the material are unusual in Pugin's *oeuvre*. The red brick, however, was eminently suitable for industrial Birmingham and the style, that of 14th-century Baltic Germany, where brick facing, two W towers with spires and E apses are common features, matches the material. The external composition with chapels and transepts climbing up the hill, together with the triangular-shaped projection which forms the entrance to the crypt, is excellent and imaginative. This is paralleled in the interior, where the space is handled very effectively though by most economical means. The steeply pitched roof, painted with stencil patterns, has a continuous slope over nave and aisles. As so often in Pugin's churches, the fittings have been greatly changed for the worse. Here almost everything in the chancel belongs to the drastic reordering of 1967 when the great screen was removed. The high altar, incorporating the shrine containing the relics of St Chad which were discovered *c.* 1840, alone remains as the climax of Pugin's design. His original intentions, which included incorporating medieval work, may still be seen in the Lady Chapel. There is much good stained glass, particularly in the chancel and Lady Chapel, designed by Pugin and made by W. Warrington, and in the N transept made by Hardman in 1868. [AW]

Birmingham, West Midlands
St James, Edgbaston

One of the very best remaining examples of S. S. Teulon's adoption of the Franciscan ground-plan – cruciform but without nave arcading and designed to accommodate as many people as possible. St James, of 1851–2, was founded to serve the fashionable Calthorpe Estate, then being developed. The dominating feature inside is the schematized hammer-beam roof that weighs heavily over the otherwise simple space. Galleries in the transepts were removed in 1889. The church has been declared redundant. [MS]

Birmingham, West Midlands
St John the Evangelist, Sparkhill

Venetian Gothic in orange brick, St John's was built in 1888 to the designs of Martin and Chamberlain, the local exponents of Ruskin's teaching. The nave was extended and the steeple added in 1895. The large tiled roof results from the unusually broad aisleless nave, transepts and crossing all spanned by cast-iron arches, as used by the architects in their board schools, but on low clustered wall-shafts and encased in varnished pine. Apsidal chancel with gabled stone reredos, 1896, and rich Arts and Crafts windows by Benjamin J. Warren. Original furnishings include an excellent oak pulpit on a stone base carved with lilies. [DH]

Birmingham, West Midlands
St Mary, Selly Oak

Unremarkable externally apart from the steeply pitched patterned tile roof, soaring Lincolnshire-type steeple and braced oak lych-gate. Built in 1861 to the design of Edward Holmes, St Mary's is in his characteristic brand of Gothic which shows an admiration for the work of Butterfield. The well-considered interior is dignified yet intimate, the white plastered walls, divided by broad bands of buff stone, set with jewel-like glass by Hardman. The many treasures include an arcaded red-sandstone font by Butterfield, a delicately carved stone pulpit and several brasses by Hardman. [DH]

Birmingham, West Midlands
St Oswald of Worcester, Small Heath

The first church by W. H. Bidlake; the design, in an Early English/Decorated style, was exhibited at the Royal Academy in 1891. Bidlake was a pupil of Bodley and there are many signs of his influence including the positioning of the E window at high level. Of Leicestershire sand brick with Bath stone dressing, the W front, added in 1899, is reminiscent of Pearson's work in composition. The tower and spire were never built. The spacious interior, painted up to the clerestory level to lighten the effect of the brickwork, is divided by an impressive oak rood-screen, a First World War memorial designed by the architect to frame a large painting of the Crucifixion by S. Meteyard in the centre of the reredos. Pulpit and font are also by Bidlake. [DH]

Birmingham, West Midlands
St Peter and St Paul, Aston

The mature work of Birmingham's most prolific Victorian church architect, Julius Alfred Chatwin, and built between 1879 and 1890, replacing a less ambitious structure, the powerful 15th-century W tower of which survives together with the 18th-century spire. It is of red sandstone ashlar, in Chatwin's favourite 14th-century style, the broad nave with alternating octagonal and round columns supporting simply splayed arches and the apsidal chancel with richly carved ogee arches and large windows. Nave and chancel are one uninterrupted space covered by a fine hammer-beam roof derived from

Westminster Hall – Chatwin was articled to Barry and worked on the Victoria Tower. The Feeney monument by Sir George Frampton is a worthy addition to many excellent earlier ones. [DH]

Birmingham, West Midlands
St Thomas and St Edmund of Canterbury, Erdington (RC)

Resembling a large English parish church of the 14th century and of local red sandstone, St Thomas and St Edmund was built between 1848 and 1850 to the designs of Charles Hansom. The exterior is dominated by a well-proportioned broached steeple which now marks the entrance, the lower stage forming a lofty vaulted porch. A large W window, filled with scenes from the Life of Christ in clear bright colours, lights the tall nave and the comparatively light chancel, lined with large figures of popes and bishops, is terminated by a massive gilded reredos with many canopied niches. The stone rood-screen has been removed and a steeply roofed timber reliquary with painted panels relocated in the cloister. [DH]

Biscovey, Cornwall
St Mary the Virgin*

G. E. Street obtained this, his first independent commission, at the end of 1846. Built in 1847–8 of rough pink slate-stone with freestone dressings, it was supervised during holidays from Gilbert Scott's office where he was employed as an assistant until 1849. Biscovey church shows remarkable justification of the act of faith placed in a twenty-two-year-old beginner. Here in remote and impoverished Cornwall, Street was, from the first, willing to suspend the elaborate Camdenian formula in his use of the starkest lancet style of Early English, although the asymmetric layout agrees with established rules of Picturesque utility and expresses each internal compartment by a separate gabled roof. The nave is low and wide with no clerestory, the long chancel slightly lower. The S and only aisle is abruptly stopped short of the W end by a porch-entrance rising into a square tower with broached octagonal belfry and stone spire of almost primitive force, a brilliant adaptation of forms observed in two rare medieval Cornish steeples at Cubert and Lostwithiel. Broad well-textured wall-planes sliced through with grouped openings of varied proportions quite without superficial embellishment,

and craftsmanlike integrity in the use of simple materials, provide a striking foretaste of Street's mature practice in High Victorian design. Contemporary stained glass of medallion work in the chancel lancets is by Wailes, produced under the vigilant eye of the architect. [PJ]

Blackburn, Lancashire
Holy Trinity

1837–46. A remarkable building, by an even more remarkable architect, Edmund Sharpe. At first there were galleries all round, in the nave and both transepts but not in the chancel. With a huge W tower and full-height transepts the church has the massing of a Perpendicular church like Tattershall but the detail is intensely Decorated, particularly the Geometrical tracery and the original leaded glass (no figures) in the great three-light E window. The Gothic organ-case and the church have been incongruously painted blue and white. The flat timber ceiling made of over forty heraldic panels, like a mass of hatchments, divided by ribs is uniquely spectacular. It shows the arms of the queen and ecclesiastical, civic and local dignitaries. Now vested in the Redundant Churches Fund. [DB]

Blackburn, Lancashire
St Thomas

By E. G. Paley, of 1864–5, in a severe, yellow rock-faced, coursed random rubble sandstone with a band of nailhead ornament at the eaves and Geometrical and plate tracery. The N porch is set curiously close to the E end of the nave. A large S aisle is set off from the nave by an arcade of round piers. The chancel windows sit high on a string-course and project through the low roof with their own gables. Internally this results in a riot of exposed roof carpentry. [DM]

Blackheath, Surrey
St Martin

A strange, squat, rather individual and quite inexpensive little Arts and Crafts Italianate church built in 1895 from designs by Charles Harrison Townsend. Its simple exterior, with rough-plastered concrete walls, low-pitched pantiled roof and quirky Hispanic bell-cote, is solid and unprepossessing. Entered through a deep round-arched W doorway of roughly dressed Ham Hill stone, the low barrel-ceiled interior comes as a surprise. Judicious use of painted decoration worked directly onto wet plaster by the American painter Mrs Anna Lea-Merritt (celebrated for her picture *Love Locked Out*) relieves bareness, while a Renaissance-style screen half-conceals a marble-lined sanctuary. Original features include a semi-circular pulpit bay (lit by a pale Crucifixion window by F. Hamilton Jackson), and the subtle hidden lighting of the sanctuary. [RMH]

Blackmoor, Hampshire
*St Matthew**

Alfred Waterhouse designed this church in 1868. Though aisleless it is not small. It has a distinctive W tower with boldly projecting diagonal buttresses and steeply pyramidal tiled roof with parapet and large animal gargoyles. Inside, the broad nave is covered with an open timber roof of angular design and is separated from the lower chancel, which has a boarded ceiling, by a boldly chamfered arch springing from corbels. The chancel is richly furnished. Some of the windows are filled with patterned glass in the grey and madder tints of which Waterhouse was fond. [MM]

Blubberhouses, North Yorkshire
*St Andrew**

Built in 1849–50 by E. B. Lamb, this tiny church commands its steep moorside setting with absolute aplomb. Its compact geometrical form is dominated by a small but assertive tower and is invigorated by emphatically overscaled copings, corbels, and dripstones: its style is a pared-down Early English. The interior, dark and intimate, consists only of a chancel, nave, and a single N aisle. But these constricted spaces are opened up through a brilliant stroke: eliminating the conventional masonry nave arcade, Lamb rests the roof directly on top of the square piers, spanning the openings with arch-braced timber plates. This innovation, suggested by medieval barns, was to become the basis for his most remarkable timber roofs. The font (with a subtly Jacobean flavour) is by Lamb, as are the stained-glass windows. [ENK]

Bodelwyddan, Clwyd
St Margaret

When its 202-foot spire, built out of local white limestone, gleams in the sun across the coastal plain against a dark sky, one can see how this has come to be known as the 'Marble Church'. Everything about it is of the greatest elaboration. It was built, in Decorated Gothic, in 1856–60 by the Dowager Lady Willoughby de Broke in memory of her husband. Her architect was John Gibson. Inside there is plenty of red and black marble, as well as alabaster and Caen stone, richly carved, as is the woodwork, including the hammer-beam roof. Lavish pulpit, chancel bosses and stall ends were carved by Earp, the lectern (1882) by Kendall of Warwick. The Carrara marble font, representing the donor's daughters holding a shell, is by Peter Hollins. The E and other windows are by O'Connor. [PH]

Booton, Norfolk
*St Michael**

'Very naughty but built in the right spirit.' So said Lutyens of this whimsical though scholarly church designed by a talented amateur, the Revd Whitwell Elwin, who was the incumbent for fifty-one years. Rebuilding began around 1875 and was completed just before Elwin's death in 1900. The church is of local knapped flint and stone. It presents a lavish display of scholarly Gothic details, mainly Early English Geometric and Decorated, including exact copies of medieval originals, but the end result is a delightful and unscholarly pastiche of elements dominated by the two diagonally placed W towers with open upper parts and between them a curious elongated three-tier pinnacle. The interior has an open spherical triangle over the chancel arch and a roof with enormous angels. The stained glass is a rare complete scheme filling every window. It was begun by Cox and Sons and completed independently by two of their assistants, Booker and Purchase. The colours are pale and the forms influenced by the Aesthetic Movement. [NA]

Bothenhampton, Dorset
*Holy Trinity**

The only Victorian church by the dedicated Arts and Crafts architect E. S. Prior, who had local family connections. Prior designed and built this towerless church between 1884 and 1889, demonstrating his preference for the simplicity and economy of the Early English style. His commitment to indigenous materials and the qualities of texture and colour are apparent in the thick rough walls of Bothenhampton stone, which also forms the three transverse arches of the aisleless nave. Touches of Arts and Crafts collaboration are found in the Neo-Jacobean altar table, designed by Prior and decorated by W. R. Lethaby, and in the E window designed by Christopher Whall, which was executed in glass made up to Prior's own formula. [LW]

Bournemouth, Dorset
St Clement

Designed in 1871 this church was the first major work of John Dando Sedding, a founder member of the Arts and Crafts Movement, and a passionate admirer of the Perpendicular architecture of the West of England. Its tower, finished after his death in 1891 by his assistant, Henry Wilson, was in its final form one of his last works. Inside, the arcade between the nave and the N aisle is of very high, unusually moulded pointed arches. Font, pulpit, screens and reredos are all of exquisite form and workmanship in stone and alabaster. Throughout, furnishings in wood and metal are of the highest quality. Much good glass, including, in the unusual tracery of the W window of the tower, a design by Henry Holiday. Sedding's reputation as one of the pioneers in the use of Late Gothic styles in the 1870s, along with Bodley and Garner, Norman Shaw and George Gilbert Scott junior, rests on St Clement's. Of it, Bodley remarked that it was 'the best church I know – after ours'. [MM]

Bournemouth, Dorset
St Peter

Affluent, stately and essentially English in character, this famous Tractarian minster sprawls like an epic through its author's career. Bournemouth's first church comprised a plain hall of 1841–4 by John Tulloch, to which Edmund Pearce added the still existing S aisle in 1851. G. E. Street planned the rebuilding in 1854 and commenced with the N aisle 1855–6, next replacing Tulloch's shell by a lofty clerestoried five-bay nave in 1859; the S porch partly veiled Pearce's dull aisle-wall at the same time. Then

in 1863–4 followed the elaborate chancel-complex with transepts, short aisles and N vestries; and so to a big buttressed W tower in 1869–70. That, however, was cunningly placed 20 feet from the nave, allowing a spacious transeptal W vestibule to be inserted in 1874; ultimately, during 1878–9, the tower parapet, pinnacles and recessed broach-spire were achieved. All is in fluent Early Geometrical, built of local stone with some discreet polychromy. Bath stone and Purbeck marble columns, as well as coloured marble and alabaster shafts, enrich vistaed arcades. In spite of admitted stylistic disturbances within its hydra-like plan, inevitable effects of an accretive history, the composition remains firmly anchored by the commanding W steeple 202 feet high. This splendid paraphrase of Midland English Gothic shows Street's mastery of subtle proportions and delicate outline; four Latin Doctors by Earp adorn the pinnacles, and the spire has ingenious flying buttresses. Lengthily, but without hiatus, the solemn interior proceeds to its proper climax at the E wall; here the high altar and sculptured alabaster reredos are surmounted by a vast traceried window glittering darkly with Clayton and Bell glass. Roofs symbolically descend in level from high, timber hammer-beam over vestibule and nave, through boarded choir ceiling, to the ribbed stone vault of the sanctuary, each compartment having its own distinctive arch. In the deep tympanum of the chancel arch Clayton and Bell later painted a rood fresco. Font, pulpit and reredos by Thomas Earp, wrought-iron screens by James Leaver, sculptured churchyard cross and shapely timber lych-gate, all emanate from the architect's drawings. [PJ]

Bournemouth, Dorset
St Stephen*

Designed by John Loughborough Pearson at the peak of his creativity in 1881–3. The nave was completed in 1885; the chancel was added in 1897–8, the NW tower without its intended spire in 1907–8. The church is of stone in Pearson's characteristic Gothic style, vaulted throughout, and with numerous lancets and other memories of his beloved northern England and Normandy. The nave has inner and outer aisles, and cants inwards slightly to meet the chancel, which has a polygonal apse and narrow, full-height ambulatory. This is the finest apse Pearson ever designed: little bridges on pointed arches span the ambulatory, bay by bay, and high above is a narrow vault. The triple-light windows in the upper part of the ambulatory appear from the chancel through pointed arches above the arcade round the apse. The view of all this through the chancel's wrought-iron screen is wonderfully mysterious; nevertheless everything is clarified by a reading of the vaulting that crowns each part. The exterior is fine too, especially the E end where a vestry and clergy room act as a foil to the pinnacles and turrets of the church. [AQ]

Bournmoor, County Durham
St Barnabas

In cream-coloured brick extensively patterned with stripes and diapers of buff and red and mostly Early English in style, this small estate church without a tower is deceptively simple on the exterior. It was built in 1867–8 by Johnson and Hicks, but it is the subsequent enrichment of the church which is most compelling. In 1881–2 the chancel roof was carved, gilded and filled with motifs in red, green and cream. The oak screen, carved and gilded reredos, panelling and patternwork were completed by 1888. Memorials to the Lambton family include the arresting Angel of Victory (1894) by the American sculptor Waldo Story. [LW]

Bowdon, Greater Manchester
St Mary

The large, crumbling old church was rebuilt by W. H. Brakspear in 1856–60. He cleverly salvaged and adapted some existing features and then inflated the scale of the original by the addition of transepts. The aisle windows were rebuilt with similar square tops (a Cheshire feature) and substantial sections of the old nave ceiling were stretched and reused in the aisles. The clerestory is much grander; so also is the hammer-beam roof of the nave. The tower was enlarged and given an extra stage. There are four notable windows by Charles Clutterbuck and others by Kempe. Chancel stalls by Temple Moore are all that was completed of an ambitious proposal (*c.* 1920) to enlarge the E end. [DB]

Boyne Hill (Maidenhead), Berkshire
All Saints*

G. E. Street's early masterwork in polychrome brick and marble was designed in 1854–5 as the nucleus of a complete sequence of linked parochial buildings. It forms the N range of an enchantingly picturesque quadrangle, constructed in sections between 1855 and 1865. The combination of materials, orange-red brick with black brick courses and stone banding, yellow Bath stone dressings and applied marbles, reflects Street's recent studies in Italy and Germany. But the plan is thoroughly English and the style a highly personalized Geometrical Decorated. The tall nave with vast tile roof has a narrow clerestory and lean-to N and S aisles, originally of four bays. A gabled porch is compressed into the S aisle, and there is a stone sanctus bell-cote over the chancel-arch wall. Slightly lower than the nave, the short square-ended chancel has a lean-to vestry on the S side. Street intended that his superbly modelled steeple, the last element of the composition to be designed, should stand practically detached at the NW angle. Open-arched and buttressed at the base, it has a cylindrical newel-turret half submerged in its W face, and rises to an astonishing striated belfry crowned by a stone broach-spire. Exotic effects characterize the taut interior, made elaborately sombre by the deep shades of painted timber-cradle roofs, the reds, browns and golds of the structural coloration, and the glowing primary tints of Hardman's E and W glass. The chancel is a unique display, its high walls entirely encrusted with unequal bands of black and white bricks, green, red and buff tiles, all interspersed with slabs of veined alabaster. Marble inlay and sculpture are by Thomas Earp, wrought ironwork by James Leaver. In 1909–11 A. E. Street ill-advisedly extended the nave westward, thus negating the tower's important relationship to the quadrangle. [PJ]

Bradford, West Yorkshire
All Saints

Mallinson and Healey, 1861–4: the grandest Victorian church in Bradford, this is a major work by the leading local church practice of the 19th century. The influence of Scott, and particularly of All Souls, Halifax, is apparent in its lavish 13th-century detailing and noble spire. The interior is richly fitted, with an especially fine pulpit of brass and iron, probably by Skidmore. The chief glory of the church is the overall scheme of stained glass by Clayton and Bell, mostly of the late 1870s. A window in the S transept depicts the founder, Francis Sharp Powell, and his wife, kneeling at prayer-desks. [KP]

Bradford, West Yorkshire
St Clement

By E. P. Warren, 1892–4. Externally restrained, its interior possesses the high degree of refinement expected from one of Bodley's many talented pupils. The decorative scheme was supervised by Morris and Co., the chancel arch and roof being decorated to their designs. Reredos of mosaic by Salviati. Good glass by Kempe. [KP]

Bradford, West Yorkshire
St Mary (RC)

Edward Simpson built up a large Roman Catholic practice in the West Riding and St Mary's, of 1874–6, is one of his best churches: large, economical, a little gaunt, but also honest and inventive. The exterior is restrainedly vigorous, the interior huge and open, with a fine roof. Of the contents, the elaborate canopied pulpit is probably the finest item. The sanctuary was refitted early in this century and the original decorations considerably toned down. [KP]

Braemar, Grampian
St Margaret of Scotland

The best and most confident church of J. N. Comper's early period. Designed in 1898 in the Late Decorated style verging on Perpendicular, Braemar has a simple plan: chancel and aisleless nave, with an extensive S transept intended for use in winter, and a low central tower rising from a vaulted crossing, intended to have a lead or shingle spire. It is powerfully massed and expressed in terms of materials: warm, weathered granite lying in the glens was collected, and the roof is of old stone slates removed by the Duke of Fife from Mar Lodge. So convincing is it that when the nave was under construction in 1907 visitors asked in indignation 'what they were doing with the old church'. The interior is equally strong, cool and spacious with moulded arches dying into wall-piers, reticulated tracery in the E and W windows, and a wooden wagon roof with moulded beams. The chancel is lower than the nave and has a delicate rood-screen and loft (intended to house an organ) veiling a long medieval high altar with gilded riddel-posts, surmounted by angels holding tapers, and embroidered hangings. There is much exquisite glass: the E window is a memorial to Queen Victoria who highly disapproved of the church. [ANS]

Brampton, Cumbria
St Martin

The only completed church (1874–8) by the celebrated Arts and Crafts architect Philip Webb. It contains magnificent stained glass by Burne-Jones and the Morris firm, the outstanding example being the five-light E window (1881) which centres on an elaborate image of the Pelican, symbol of the sufferings of Christ. The church, of red sandstone, is an idiosyncratic interpretation of various Gothic styles in combination with vernacular forms; it has a large W tower (completed in 1905) and there is a strong contrast between N and S sides. Webb's bias to domestic architecture is seen in the over-emphasized vestry to the NE and in the effect of painted timber-work and whitewashed stone inside. The interior is surprisingly wide and spacious, with aisles only slightly lower than the nave. [TEF]

Brechin, Tayside
Baptist Church (former West and St Columba, Church of Scotland)*

A very individual Middle Pointed church designed by J., J. M. and W. H. Hay for Lord Panmure who had joined the Free Church. Five-bay buttressed rectangle of sophisticated random rubble, orientated N–S, windows of S bay raised high in gablets. Sturdy tower and tall stone spire of very original design at S gable, doorway with cusped inner order, four-light window, unusual semi-decagonal profile at belfry-stage resulting from the broaches of the spire being brought down into it. Single-span interior with arched laminated braces, big kerb roof with very large slates. [DW]

Brechin, Tayside
Southesk (Gardner Memorial) Church*

The most elaborate of the churches Sir John Burnet developed from his 1887 church at Shiskine, built

1896–1900. Right-angled group round enclosed garden, in mixed Romanesque, Early English and Late Gothic with richly sculptured detail. Church comprises a low nave with single N aisle of almost equal size, a chancel on W divided off by rood-beam and squat pyramid-roofed and bartizaned E tower containing gallery reached by flanking apsidal stair. Very low hall with cantilever-roofed open cloister extends northwards, cusped archway with Art Nouveau gate leads to vestibule serving both church and hall. [DW]

Brentwood, Essex
St Thomas

The masterpiece of the little-known E. C. Lee. Built in 1882–90, of flint and stone, in the Early English style, it has a tall NW spire with pinnacles and rich lucarnes, which, like the church as a whole, has a strongly individual flavour. The W front, flanked by turrets, has four grouped lancets over a triple arcade; the W door has rich sculpture. The interior is grand and spacious: the clerestoried nave and well-raised chancel have roofs at the same height, but of different designs. [PH]

Brighton, East Sussex
St Bartholomew*

Rising over what was once terraced housing in one of the poorer parts of Brighton, this church follows a familiar policy of the Victorian High Church – a deliberately impressive building placed amid the slums. It owes its existence to the passionate conviction of a rich High Churchman, Father Arthur Wagner, who also provided four other churches in Brighton. His architect here was a local man, Edmund Scott. Begun in 1872 and furnished during the next thirty years and never finished (chancel unbuilt), it is higher than any English cathedral, 135 feet to the nave roof. Plain brick is used and there are few Gothic features save the huge rose window at the W end. The enormous height is internally buttressed, some of the recesses so formed having side altars. Ciborium, candlesticks, altar, communion rail, pulpit and font are by Henry Wilson in a rich Arts and Crafts style of high quality. [DRE]

Brighton, East Sussex
St Joseph (RC)

A well-positioned Early English stone building fitted into a difficult triangular site, St Joseph's is architecturally the most ambitious church erected by the Roman Catholics in Brighton. It is a composite building, begun in 1866 (nave and transepts) by W. K. Brodo. To this J. S. Hansom added (1881–3) the E end with apsidal chancel and polygonal transept chapels either side. Finally a provisional W end, which was to be extended to support a large spired tower, was added by F. A. Walters in 1900. The lofty interior is vaulted throughout with narrow aisles. [DRE]

Brighton, East Sussex
St Martin

The largest church in Brighton, a massive Early English composition in Sussex brick. An intended saddleback tower with pitched roof was never completed. St Martin's was built in 1874–5 by A. D. Wagner and his half-brothers as a memorial to their father H. M. Wagner. The architect was a local man, Somers Clarke, who had been both a pupil of Sir Gilbert Scott and friend of H. M. Wagner. The interior is very impressive – a sombre atmosphere intensified by the windowless aisles and the huge octagonal arcade-piers. Wall columns run up to a decorated wagon roof. The vaulted chancel has a rood-beam and a very large gilded reredos containing twenty paintings and sixty-nine statues designed by H. Ellis Wooldridge and executed by Josef Mayer. The distinctive canopied pulpit by Somers Clarke is based on the sacrament house in St Sebald's, Nuremberg. [DRE]

Brighton, East Sussex
St Mary and St James

One of the most impressive Victorian interiors in Sussex. Designed in 1877–9 by Sir William Emerson. The large red-brick and terracotta building is Gothic in style, and the interior, especially the spacious vaulted chancel, transepts, and the arcade, possesses a distinctively French feeling. A massive tower was intended to rise above the main porch. [DRE]

Brighton, East Sussex
*St Michael and All Angels**

This early church by G. F. Bodley, built 1859–61, is a small polychromatic building of red and black brick with bands of sandstone, in the N Italian Gothic style of the 13th century. It has a steeply pitched roof and plate tracery. The interior is remarkable for the sculptural restraint of the powerful lily-leaf capitals to the low cylindrical columns, the sculpture and the mineral riches of the choir-screen and sanctuary. Here Morris and Co. were given their first significant ecclesiastical commission. There is much early glass by Morris himself, Burne-Jones and Ford Madox Brown. Morris and Philip Webb painted the chancel ceiling in flowing diapers in a dull red and black. None of this could have been achieved without the founder, the Revd Charles Beanlands, a curate of St Paul's, Brighton, for whom the church was built by two maiden ladies, the Misses Windle. He brought in Burges to design a pulpit, choir stalls and heavily jewelled plate and embroidery. Bodley was then dismissed and Burges commissioned to design an enormous extension in the French Gothic style of the 13th century, a virtuoso exercise with a triforium and clerestory, relegating Bodley's church to a chapel. It was executed posthumously in 1893 by J. S. Chapple and furnished in a spectacular but unsuitable Late Gothic style by W. Romaine-Walker who designed a towering gilded reredos and Spanish screens of wrought iron. [ANS]

Brighton, East Sussex
St Paul

A key building in the development of High Anglican worship in the S of England and architecturally one of the most striking churches resulting from that movement. St Paul's was erected in 1848 by H. M. Wagner and soon became notorious for the 'ritual' services introduced by his son Arthur D. Wagner. The Early English design in stone and knapped flint by R. C. Carpenter was later modified, a highly original Gothic timber octagonal bell-stage by R. H. Carpenter replacing a projected stone spire. The narthex by Bodley was added in 1874. The interior is modest in feeling but enriched by Pugin and Kempe stained glass, a fine screen by Bodley and an ornate lectern by Hardman. The reredos triptych by Burne-Jones is now displayed at Brighton Museum. The chancel roof has Bodley decoration and the wall above the chancel arch has paintings by Bell. [DRE]

Brightwalton, Berkshire
*All Saints**

Considering his obsessive exploration of the 'Vigorous' style in the years around 1860 it might come as a shock to find this quite unashamedly English Home Counties design on G. E. Street's drawing board in 1862. Yet in spite of its strongly traditional effect, his personal integrity pervades the whole, happily informal composition. Built together with the adjacent school in 1862–3, it has a tall nave with S aisle only; sturdy buttressed SW tower capped by a decisively big shingled broach-spire; independently stone-roofed S porch hugging the E side of the tower; and normal square-ended chancel with N vestry. The style is Early Decorated and the materials hammer-dressed Bisley Common stone, with excellent arch-braced timber roofs of enormous scale covered with tiles laid in diaper patterns. A narrow clerestory on the S side has six tiny foiled circles tucked under the eaves; the porch entrance is also cusped. Inside, the splendid S arcade has robust stylized capitals on low slim columns of blue lias; in contrast the chancel arch is wide and high. There is a first-rate ensemble of furnishings: stone pulpit and cancelli, and a gorgeous alabaster reredos with sculptured Majesty by Thomas Earp. Glass in the traceried E window is by Clayton and Bell, 1863. Beneath the tower stands a font from the previous church, but its flat wooden cover has one of Street's most imaginative metalwork designs in boldly conventionalized foliation. [PJ]

Bristol, Avon
St Mary on the Quay (RC)

A classical temple church built in 1839 by R. S. Pope. Though similar to contemporary Catholic churches in Ireland, it was not built for the Catholics, merely acquired in 1843 from the over-ambitious Catholic Apostolic or Irvingite Church. A full Corinthian portico comes forward to the street line, the columns on a high base. The church is distanced from its neighbours by high rusticated screen-walls enclosing the approach steps. The two columns of the entry are echoed inside at the chancel of the otherwise plain interior. [JO]

Brithdir, Gwynedd
*St Mark**

The foothills of Cadair Idris are an improbable place to find one of the few complete buildings by the great Arts and Crafts architect and metalworker Henry Wilson. Wilson wanted the church to look 'as if it had sprung out of the soil'. It was built in 1895–7 of local granite, and is very simple outside. The roof of local slates sweeps down over the porch. The interior is a surprise: the lofty white nave contrasts with the barrel-vaulted, apsed chancel, decorated in dark red, pale blue, and pale green. Not all the fittings Wilson designed were executed, but there are the copper altar-front showing the Annunciation, the copper pulpit, stalls carved with animals, inlaid altar-rails, a lead font modelled by Arthur Grove, and doors inset with mother-of-pearl. Note the door handles. [PH]

Bromborough, Merseyside
St Barnabas

Built in 1862–4 by George Gilbert Scott, in severe Early French Gothic, enlivened by the warm red sandstone and lush foliage carving. The nave aisles have gables over the windows, and the chancel is apsidal. The fine, stone broach-spire stands at the NE. Inside, the nave-arcades have square abaci (regarded as 'manly'). The apse has rib-vaulting and rich arcading on either side of the carved reredos. The wooden pulpit and stone font are characteristic of Scott. [PH]

Bryanston, Dorset
St Martin

An expensive stone late-Victorian estate church, built in 1895–8 by E. P. Warren. Perpendicular Gothic with a stately W tower carefully detailed in the manner of G. F. Bodley. The square proportions, panelled parapet and neat triangular shafts rising above the buttresses to frame the bell-openings show an elegant hand at work. Stone-faced interior with timber roofs and broad, effusively traceried E window. Contemporary stained glass. [JO]

Bryn-y-maen, Clwyd
Christ Church

Beautifully sited up above Colwyn Bay, this is sentimentally known as 'The Cathedral of the Hills'. A local girl vowed that if she became rich she would build a church. She went into service with the Frosts of Colwyn Bay, married the heir, and after his death built her church (1897–9) in his memory. Her architects were Douglas and Fordham. The compact and tough little building, in late Perpendicular, limestone outside, red sandstone within, has richly carved oak fittings. The central tower's arches frame the E window. [PH]

Buckland St Mary, Somerset
St Mary

A most unSomerset church in flint with Ham stone dressings built in 1853–63 by Benjamin Ferrey. The church stands high and has a big tower with pyramid roof and full complement of aisles, transepts and porch in the Decorated style. The interior is a complete example of mid-century Gothic. All the detail is of high quality, with hammer-beam roofs, carved foliage capitals, figures of the apostles in the nave by Thomas Earp, and carved angels in the chancel. The fittings, mostly by Forsyth, display lavish coloured marbles and alabaster with carved figures. In the chancel are a reredos with marble Pietà (1888) and a marble altar-tomb, both by Forsyth, E and W windows of 1857, the W window modelled on the 16th-century glass at Fairford, Gloucestershire. [JO]

Buckley, Clwyd
St Matthew

This church has a complicated building history. A Gothic church with nave, chancel and tower was built in 1821–2 by John Oates of Halifax. Altered several times, it was completely, and brilliantly transformed in 1897–1904 by John Douglas. The chancel was built in 1902 as a memorial to Gladstone, whose daughter's husband was vicar. The nave has a half-timbered clerestory. The interior is spacious, but here the odd effect of the remodelling is apparent in the arcade-piers of oak (encasing steel), supporting arches also of oak. The glass in the chancel and baptistery is by Henry Holiday. [PH]

Burringham, Humberside
*St John the Baptist**

S. S. Teulon designed more churches in Lincolnshire than in any other county. Burringham shows the most distinctive use of polychromy, particularly in the internal diapering. The capriciously elaborate outline to the base of the chimney which clasps the massively squat tower is typical of the architect in the effort to make at least one feature self-consciously difficult in design. Although all on a small scale (the seating capacity was just 197) the church is the main incident in the long straggling village and a landmark from the river Trent. It is now vested in the Redundant Churches Fund. [MS]

Bury, Greater Manchester
St Mary

J. S. Crowther favoured the English High Gothic style of the mid-14th century but in 1876 he was passing through a French phase. At Bury he had the task of enlarging an earlier church, retaining a tower of 1842. His transition from the smaller scale to that of his greatly enlarged new church is masterly if slightly bizarre. He introduced a lateral westwork, ingeniously turning it into a SW porch at one end and an apsed baptistery at the other. The liturgical pre-eminence of the chancel is marked off from the nave by the addition of a pinnacled parapet and a characteristic spire-topped rood-staircase. The choir finishes with a majestic polygonal apse. There is a notable iron screen, fine Hardman glass and a few souvenirs of the earlier churches on the site. [DB]

Bwlch-y-cibau, Powys
Christ Church

This delightful little church of 1862–3 by George Gilbert Scott admirably suits its setting in the Montgomeryshire hills. Early English, it has an apse and W bell-cote, above a rose window. There is good carving on the chancel arch corbels and Caen stone pulpit. The tiles are by Maw. The chancel windows are by Wailes, while those at the W were designed by J. W. Brown for Powell's (1877). [PH]

Caerdeon, (Bontddu), Gwynedd
St Philip

Up a steep and winding lane, above the glorious Mawddach estuary, stands this most unusual church. It was built in 1862 as a result of a dispute between the Revd W. E. Jelf, who settled here and coached undergraduates in classics, and the rector of Llanbedr, who refused to provide English services (this led to the English Services in Wales Act of 1863). It was even odder as first built – just a rectangle of rough local stone, with plain rectangular windows, and a rough loggia over the entrance, supported on square piers. A tablet over the door commemorates the Revd John Louis Petit, 'Founder and Benefactor', who was also the architect. He was well known as a writer on architecture and an artist. According to the *Ecclesiologist*, 'the object of the building . . . is to exhibit to the world the notions of picturesque appropriateness entertained by that clever amateur. Mr Petit . . . is always drawing and denouncing Gothic, while seeking his practical model in the rustic Italian of hillside chapels on the flanks of the Southern Alps.' The critic called the church 'something between a large lodge gate and a lady's rustic dairy', producing an effect 'like that of the Swiss chalet on the Barnet Road' (i.e. Swiss Cottage). The chancel and transept, and massive bell-cote, are remarkably sensitive later additions. The altar was originally at the opposite end. [PH]

Calverhall, Salop
Holy Trinity

The chancel, with its double-gabled N transept, was built in Decorated style in 1872. Nave and tower, in Perpendicular, followed in 1878. The architect was William Eden Nesfield. The grand SW tower, the bottom of which forms the porch, and the W front, flanked by pretty brick almshouses of 1724, form a striking group on the village street. The stone-carving inside and out is well conceived and executed: note the pots of flowers as stops to the transept window mouldings. Interestingly varied glass includes the chancel S window of 1875 by Morris and Co. [PH]

Cambridge
*All Saints, Jesus Lane**

At All Saints G. F. Bodley made two designs: the first in 1861 in his Continental manner, the second in the following year in a pure English Decorated idiom, distinguished by height, elegance and asymmetry. It was consecrated in 1864 and completed in 1870. The church is recognized (with St Salvador, Dundee) as marking the turning point from Continental influence back to the English Gothic of the 14th century first revived by Pugin, but executed in a calmer spirit, bringing the Gothic Revival full circle. It has a nave and S aisle divided by a central arcade; the chancel forms the base of the tower and spire. The interior has a richness of painted wall surfaces in flowing diaper patterns by Bodley and C. E. Kempe, executed by F. R. Leach. There is much early glass by Morris and Co. and later glass by Kempe. Here Bodley was moving towards the cool, restrained and elegant style of his maturity, governed by beauty and tender grace. [ANS]

Cambridge
Our Lady and the English Martyrs (RC)

The result of a competition held by Mrs Yoland Lyne-Stephens, former dancer at the Paris Opera and widow of the patentee of glass dolls'-eyes ('built with glass eyes to house idols', it was said). The winning entry was a conservative design in the Decorated style by A. M. Dunn and E. Hansom of Newcastle and the church was built from 1885 to 1890. It is on a major scale, elaborately planned and richly detailed and furnished. The plan includes a W narthex and a spire, transepts, crossing, and an E apse. It is vaulted throughout. Furnishings include a baldacchino by Boulton, sculpture and woodwork by Rattee and Kett, metalwork and glass by Hardman (narthex), and Lavers, Barraud and Westlake (clerestory), and painting by N. H. J. Westlake (baldacchino and Glory over the chancel arch). The wooden figure of St Andrew is by A. W. N. Pugin, from his replaced church of St Andrew (1841–3). [RO'D]

Cambridge
St John's College Chapel

A new chapel by George Gilbert Scott was built in 1863–9 to replace the old one, which it was not considered practicable to retain. It is T-shaped (an Oxford device), with the great tower (163 feet high) rising over the centre of the antechapel. The whole chapel is 193 feet long, and is in the style of the late 13th century (the date of the original chapel), with an apse. Crossing piers are of Peterhead granite, and British marbles are also used. The stone carving is by Farmer and Brindley, the wood carving by Rattee and Kett, and the painted decoration by Clayton and Bell, who also made most of the stained glass. [PH]

Capel-y-ffin, Powys
Monastery Church

An unusual instance of a Victorian ruin, that of the chancel (which was all that was built) of the church of the Anglican monastery founded here in 1869 by the extraordinary Father Ignatius. His architect was Charles Buckeridge, and the style was taken from its medieval neighbour – Transitional. Building began in 1872, and after Buckeridge's death in 1873 was supervised until it ceased in 1882 by J. L. Pearson. The vaults fell *c.* 1920. Father Ignatius' tiled tomb is in the centre. One has to imagine the exotic and melodramatic services held there. [PH]

Cardiff, South Glamorgan
Capel Pembroke Terrace

This exceptionally sophisticated chapel was built in 1877 by Henry C. Harris. He must have been influenced by the nearby work of William Burges, at the Castle and Park House, for the style is French Early Gothic, powerfully handled. The façade has a row of four linked lancets, with two deep-set traceried windows above. On either side are semicircular staircase projections with Burges-like conical roofs. The T-shaped interior has red-brick walls and cream and black diapering. [PH]

Cardiff, South Glamorgan
Eglwys Dewi Sant

Formerly St Andrew's Church, this is not prepossessing externally. It has a difficult building history, but is significant as the first-known example of the use of 'passage-aisles' – narrow aisles intended only as means of access. The point was to provide a wide nave giving unimpeded views of the chancel. The church was designed in 1859 by Prichard and Seddon.

The nave was to have been spanned by polychrome brick arches. At the crossing, arches would be canted towards the apsidal, vaulted chancel. Unfortunately, when the nave had been built up as far as the clerestory (which is framed within the pier-arches), money ran out. Col. A. Roos was called in to complete the church within the original cost-limit, which is why the chancel is the plainest, not the richest, part. The intended central tower and spire were never built. In 1884–6 William Butterfield added transepts, vestries, and also good choir-stalls and a tiled floor. [PH]

Cardiff, South Glamorgan
English Presbyterian Chapel

This is a rare example of a church by F. T. Pilkington outside Scotland. Built in 1866 of red and yellow stone, in a fancifully elaborate and very individual Gothic style, it has a spire on which steep gables strain upwards. From the sides of the church project broad bulges, whose purpose only becomes clear inside: they house curved galleries, the idea being to seat the maximum number close to the pulpit. The floor slopes, as in a theatre. The church was extended to the W in 1893. In 1910 it was burnt out, and restored by Col. E. M. Bruce Vaughan. [PH]

Cardiff, South Glamorgan
St Margaret, Roath

Built by John Prichard on earlier foundations in 1869–72. The exterior is plain, and lacks the intended octagonal central tower and spire (the low square tower was added in 1918). But the interior is gloriously polychromatic. The materials include several kinds of stone, from near and far, Penarth alabaster for the chancel, and patterns of red, white and blue bricks. The detailing is excellent (carving by E. Clarke of Llandaff). The low chancel screen and pulpit are original. The reredos is by Sir Ninian Comper. [PH]

Cardiff
St German, Roath. See **Roath**.

Carlisle, Cumbria
Our Lady and St Joseph (RC)

A rather angular design by Dunn and Hansom of Newcastle (1891–3), making substantial use of Per-

pendicular motifs and with a large battlemented tower to the W. Red sandstone is contrasted with Bath stone for tracery and internal facings and the interior – virtually a continuous space 122 feet in length – has a wagon roof of carved and gilded wood; there are hints of Lincoln Cathedral in the sculpted angels adorning the nave arcade, and in the E window, modelled on the Bishop's Eye. [TEF]

Carno, Powys
St John the Baptist

This rural village has a remarkably colourful church, built in 1863 of lumpy grey stone with red and yellow dressings. The architect was J. W. Poundley. The division between nave and chancel is marked outside by frilly ironwork, and inside by a big timber arch. The windows have vigorous plate tracery. The idiosyncratic little tower recently lost its maroon-painted wooden belfry. [PH]

Carnsalloch, Dumfries and Galloway
Johnston Mortuary Chapel

In 1847, Sir Alexander Johnston (the former governor of Ceylon) commissioned E. B. Lamb to build this family mortuary chapel on his estate at Carnsalloch. It is essentially a large gable-roofed Gothic mausoleum set upon a terrace, its only ornaments being overscaled buttresses and a flamboyant window over the W door. What is remarkable is the interior, a tightly defined space bound by a skeletal structure of arches and piers standing just within the walls. Above it all rests a ponderously sepulchral roof of red sandstone slabs. Now unfortunately the chapel is derelict. [ENK]

Castle Douglas, Dumfries and Galloway
St Ninian

The building, begun in 1856 by E. B. Lamb, is of local granite, and ruggedly picturesque, even without its original steeple. Inside is a space of great simplicity, roofed with an austere open timber truss. The roughcast walls and chancel panelling are later additions, but the nave benches, altar, and font are Lamb's. Lamb intended a stone pulpit: the present wooden pulpit appears to have been placed at some later date atop his granite base. [ENK]

Castle Howard, North Yorkshire
The Chapel

The chapel at Castle Howard provides a striking, and perhaps surprising, Victorian climax to the visitor's progress through this great Baroque palace. In 1875–8 it was transformed by R. J. Johnson into one of the richest and most specifically Aesthetic ecclesiastical interiors of the age. Structural alterations were confined to the lowering of the floor and the creation of a new entrance. The original ceiling by C. H. Tatham was richly decorated. Glass by Burne-Jones (in curious swivelling panels) filled the windows, and frescoes were executed by Kempe, who also painted the panel which fills the Baroque reredos. The fittings were designed by Johnson in an Italian Renaissance manner and include splendid stalls and organ-case. The whole ensemble demonstrates both the learned versatility of the best of the younger Goths and the way in which the best decorative artists were rapidly forsaking strict Gothic conventions. [KP]

Cattistock, Dorset
SS Peter and Paul*

Cattistock church is of particular interest for combining the work of two generations of Gilbert Scotts and so demonstrating the difference between High and Late Victorian approaches to Gothic. In 1855–7 the church was 'restored' or virtually rebuilt by Gilbert Scott the elder, who added a S aisle and a polygonal apse. The style of his work was the conventional 13th-century Geometrical, which seems crude and stiff compared with the spectacular additions made to the church by George Gilbert Scott junior in 1872–6. The younger Scott replaced the old tower – which had been spared by his father – with a tall and rich Perpendicular Gothic one inspired by the splendid medieval church towers of Somerset. The range of vestries placed along the W end of the church are also in the Perpendicular Gothic which most mid-Victorians considered debased and unworthy compared with 13th-century work. Under the tower is a baptistery, but the tall font cover and the richly stencilled wall decoration were not added until 1904–6 and are the work of Temple Moore. [GS]

Chantry, Somerset
Holy Trinity*

An early work of G. G. Scott built in 1844–6, no more than nave and chancel but in a finely detailed Decorated style enhanced by the crispness of the stone. The roof looks as if it is of sheets of lead but in fact is of slabs of slate of remarkable size. The decoration is chiefly well-worked ball-flower ornament, especially good on the porch. West bell-turret over a central buttress. Good timber roof and vaulted chancel. [JO]

Cheadle, Staffordshire
St Giles (RC)*

St Giles' is undoubtedly Pugin's most famous church and one of the few buildings with which he himself was really satisfied. The reason for its success was that the Earl of Shrewsbury, at whose expense it was built, was in sympathy with Pugin's aims and allowed him a relatively free hand. Pugin worked intensively on the church between 1840 and 1846, an unusual length of time for such a fast worker, and there were many revisions of the plans. It was built of the local red sandstone by Lord Shrewsbury's estate workers and the main feature of the exterior is the beautiful W tower and magnificent steeple. The interior is amazing, with every surface painted. The plan is simple, with N and S aisles and chapels, and a projecting chancel, but every possible decorative embellishment and fitting appropriate to a model parish church in the Decorated style has been included. It is a place to ponder Pugin's extraordinary ability to design countless vivid and suitable Gothic details. Laus Deo! little has been altered, and the elaborate rood-screen is still in position. There are many encaustic tiles by Minton and much good stained glass by W. Wailes. [AW]

Cheltenham, Gloucestershire
All Saints

The most lavish of several churches in the town by the local architect John Middleton, whose speciality was richly modelled and carved stonework and polychrome stone interiors. Tall exterior, quite conventional with plate tracery and complex E end. A great spire was intended. At the W end a rose window over heavily carved doorway. Inside two-coloured arches on thick granite piers with carved capitals and statues over. The richness increases in the chancel with tall chancel arch, alabaster reredos and painted apse roof. Alabaster, granite and stone pulpit and font. The chancel screen is very fine wrought ironwork of 1894 by H. A. Prothero, who also designed the organ-case and font cover. Complete scheme of stained glass of Old Testament figures and pious Christians including Wesley and Keble. W window 1897 by Sir W. Richmond. [JO]

Cheltenham, Gloucestershire
St Gregory (RC)

Built by C. F. Hansom of Bristol in 1856–9. The style is an elegant Decorated Gothic, the tower well proportioned with a pair of openings on each face, big corner-pinnacles and the spire rising to 200 feet behind battlements. Stone carving extends throughout the church including the high altar by Farmer and the pulpit and Stations of the Cross by Boulton. [JO]

Cheltenham, Gloucestershire
St Peter

Built 1847–9 by S. W. Daukes, this is a particularly successful example of the Neo-Norman. The chief feature is the tall circular crossing-tower with its tiled conical roof but the detail in smoothly carved ashlar stone is good throughout. Inside, good carved capitals and Neo-Norman plasterwork under the tower and in the apse. [JO]

Chester, Cheshire
St Paul, Boughton

Improbably perched on a steep site between road and river, this colourful brick church is a lovable landmark. The main part was built in 1876 by John Douglas, to replace an earlier church: he added the brick-nogged S aisle in 1902 and the spirelet in 1905. The interior is delightful, with timber arcades and broad apse, a wrought-iron screen, and pretty painted decoration in a rather Art Nouveau style (presumably *c.* 1902). In the N aisle is a window by Kempe (1887), and the baptistery glass is by Frampton. The rest is by Morris and Co., the E window of 1881 particularly fine. [PH]

Chichester, West Sussex
St Peter the Great

This subdeanery chapel was designed by R. C. Carpenter in 1850–2, and consists of an aisled nave, with large S aisle separately gabled and extending to form a chapel alongside the chancel. The fabric is ashlar limestone and the style Curvilinear, the interior having excellent detail and elegant proportions. In 1881, the present SW porch by Dunn and Hansom was erected on the site of a projected tower. St Peter's has been in use as a market since 1983. [DRE]

Chiddingstone Causeway, Kent
St Luke

This is the only Anglican church by J. F. Bentley. It was built in 1897–8 by the Hills family, to whom he was recommended by J. S. Sargent. Its presence is remarkable considering its small size. It has a stout little tower on the N, and the Hills pew and organ-chamber flank the chancel. The interior is broad and open, beneath a wagon roof. The Late Gothic style is freely handled and the detailing exquisite. Bentley designed the altar, chancel paving, altar-rails, and the striking font of cipollino from Euboea (a by-product of the current work on Westminster Cathedral). Pulpit and stalls were designed after his death by his firm. The incongruous stained glass in the E and sanctuary S windows is by von Glehn (1906). [PH]

Chingford, Greater London
St Peter and St Paul

Built in 1844 on what was the village green, to the design of Lewis Vulliamy; the E part was rebuilt and enlarged in 1902–3 by Charles Blomfield. Vulliamy's church was remarkable; in form a latter-day Georgian preaching box, but with serious Gothic features. The W tower, crowned by a spire with flying buttresses, is especially good. The body of the church is broad and aisleless, with chequerwork and Gothic patterns between the windows brought out in light-buff brick and flint, almost convincingly like medieval East Anglian flushwork. Inside, the low-pitched roof is supported by a series of very broad trusses of complicated pattern, with three hoops of timber in the space above each truss, to extraordinary effect. Blomfield's chancel and chapels are cool and conventional, seen through a trio of arches from the nave, making altogether a very effective whole of contrasting parts. [DL]

Chislehurst, Greater London
Annunciation of the Blessed Virgin Mary

A bold church of 1868–70 by James Brooks. The plan is unusual: the SW corner touches the street and the canted and pinnacled tower (1885, completed by E. J. May in 1930) stands cornerwise to the S wall like a detached campanile. Clerestory lights are of coupled lancets surmounted by small circles and the great wheel-window in the W is composed of nineteen circles in plate tracery. Brooks's aisles are low. The vaulted S chapel is an extension of 1885. Salviati's 1890 mosaic above the chancel arch forms part of an ensemble of enrichments to the dark E end that included Brooks's rood-screen and loft, the original figures of which are incorporated in the modern post-Blitz replacement. Wall paintings by Westlake (1882 and 1892) survive; he also executed the reredos (and sedilia?) to the design of Brooks in 1877. [REH]

Christleton, Cheshire
St James

Attractively sited in a quiet village, this sandstone Perpendicular church hardly suggests at once the name of Butterfield, who was in fact responding to the style of the 15th-century tower. He argued strongly for its retention: 'This country is an old country, but if we don't take care it will soon be as new a one as America . . . You had better keep the old tower and so look a little different to the modern new churches which are generally so noisy and pretentious.' In 1876–7 he added the pyramidal roof to the tower, and built the aisled nave and chancel, under one continuous roof, and transepts. The interior is harmonious, with its gentle polychromy of red and white stone (chequered in the chancel). As usual different types of roof differentiate nave, choir, and sanctuary. The excellent fittings include the wooden pulpit, lectern, altar-rails, pews and stalls, tiled floors, and the reredos (added in 1893) of carved stone with Minton mosaics and marble cross. [PH]

Chute Forest, Wiltshire
*St Mary**

A small estate church of 1870–5 by John Loughborough Pearson. Outwardly the church is in his characteristic Early English Gothic, executed in red brick with stone dressings. The interior is remarkably severe with lancet windows set in deep reveals, plain arches for the arcades and only moulded stone strips for capitals. Nave and chancel are treated as a single space, articulated by three plain transverse brick arches that carry the timber roof, an unusual form for Pearson. As one expects of him, the arches give the church an unusual grandeur. [AQ]

Clanfield, Hampshire
St James

In the disposition of its nave and porch, chancel, vestry and bell-cote, this small and extremely simple village church follows to the letter the recommendations of the *Ecclesiologist*. Very small single lancets set in roughly knapped flint walling, in combination with the very large heavily buttressed double-arched saddle-coped bell-cote at the W end, create an illusion of it being much larger than its true size. Inside, a scheme of polychromy in yellow, vermilion and blue brick suggests that its designer R. J. Jones was not unaware in 1875 of the work of William Butterfield and William White. [MM]

Clearwell, Gloucestershire
St Peter

A memorial church built in 1866 by J. Middleton of Cheltenham. The decoration is rich and effective use is made of contrasting coloured stones. Outside red sandstone contrasts with Bath stone details, Early French in style, with a SW tower and spire. Inside blue and red stone contrasts with the Bath stone laid in bands. Lavish marbles in the chancel with carved reredos by Hardman, stained glass by Hardman, and good encaustic tiles. Painted roofs. The pulpit and font are characteristically elaborate Middleton designs, mixing stone and marbles. [JO]

Cleator, Cumbria
Our Lady (RC)

In an iron-ore mining village, a lofty church in rusticated sandstone by E. W. Pugin (1856). More Continental than English in design it combines a variety of Gothic forms and has a large bell-cote above triple lancets to the W, nave and choir with continuous roof-line, aisles, transepts and W porch. The interior is ornate, with elaborately carved columns, reredos, and good stained glass. [TEF]

Cleckheaton, West Yorkshire
Providence Place United Reformed Church

Lockwood and Mawson 1857–9. Providence Place Chapel proudly proclaims the dominance of dissent in the Spen Valley. It is by far the finest building in this small mill town. The body of the chapel, externally austere, contains a vast galleried auditorium, inevitably focusing on an immense organ, and a sea of box pews, with the usual Sunday School below. In a shameless display of Nonconformist façadism, the architects applied a street frontage of the utmost grandeur. The great pediment rests on giant, unfluted Corinthian columns which support Brunelleschian arches. Heavily vermiculated quoins form a stop on each side. [KP]

Clewer (New Windsor), Berkshire
Chapel, Convent of St John the Baptist*

Clewer Convent was founded by Thomas Thellusson Carter and Harriet Monsell, and from 1854 until his death in 1896 Henry Woodyer designed all its buildings free of charge. A small chapel with Decorated tracery in the E window came in 1856–8, but the much larger, grand chapel that superseded it in 1878–81 is one of Woodyer's most important works. It has a wide but short aisled nave of four bays with very tall round piers, and a long ornate choir of five bays with a polygonal apse. An elaborate bell-turret is carried over the choir arch, and a stair-turret rises beside the roof to the S of it. The windows, which contain fine glass by Hardman (choir) and Clayton and Bell (nave), have typical Woodyer Decorated tracery, those in the choir having gables that emphatically break through the arcaded parapet in the way he liked. The blind E window carries a Crucifix on the outside. The interior has patterned brickwork that becomes very stripy in the choir. The floor is ornately tiled and this is echoed by the wooden rib-vault, which is painted with patterns of foliage. [AQ]

Clifford, West Yorkshire
St Edward the Confessor (RC)

One of the grandest Roman Catholic churches in Yorkshire. The plans are said to have been bought from a dying architect called Ramsay by one of the local Catholic gentry, who handed them over to J. A. Hansom to realize. It is a fine and vigorous example of the often-undervalued Neo-Norman style. Built in 1845–8 it was inspired both by the Norman churches of northern England (especially Durham) and by the Romanesque of France. The interior, with massive cylindrical piers and much spirited carved decoration, has a strongly French character. Much of the stained glass was imported from France. There are also windows by Mayer, Barnett and, in the Lady Chapel, Pugin (four windows of 1848–51). The central feature of the chapel is the statue of Our Lady by K. Hoffmann of Rome (1844). The fittings of the church (including the high altar, probably another foreign import) have remained mercifully undisturbed by liturgical changes. Hansom's projected tower was never built and in 1859–66 the present tower was constructed to a new French Romanesque design by George Goldie. [KP]

Clumber Park, Nottinghamshire
St Mary the Virgin*

By 1886, the year St Mary's was designed, Bodley and Garner had stopped their close collaboration. Built for the 7th Duke of Newcastle, a passionate Anglo-Catholic, to celebrate his coming of age and marriage, Clumber Chapel was Bodley's favourite work, designed by him alone. Cruciform in plan, with an aisleless nave, chancel with S chapel and N sacristies, short transepts, a central tower and octagonal spire, it is in Bodley's characteristic flowing Decorated style, built of Steetley stone from an earlier chapel with dressings of red Runcorn stone, the interior being entirely of Runcorn. The main space is the choir which is of four bays. It demonstrates Bodley's superb structural command: thick walls relieved by delicate detail, with the piers and arcades of the choir of accomplished scale and depth, richly moulded. Slender vaulting shafts rise to support the groining ribs. Some of C. E. Kempe's most successful stained glass is here, and there is furniture of comparable distinction by Bodley, notably the chancel screens and high altar of white alabaster, and early statuary by Comper. The duke quarrelled with Bodley over the accounts, and regrettably the Revd Ernest Geldart was commissioned to design much etiolated furniture and statuary in pear wood and oak. Nevertheless the chapel is a 'complete and sacred monument' of ducal opulence, determined to leave nothing to improvement. [ANS]

Coalpit Heath, Avon
*St Saviour**

William Butterfield's first parish church built in an area of scattered coal-mining settlements 'proverbial for vice and irreligion'. Built 1844–5 it follows Pugin's theories on church building closely. The style is Decorated Gothic, the parts each with their own roof, with a W tower and S porch, the angles and walls supported by ample buttresses. The local rubble stone is used with Bath stone for the details which are simple as appropriate to a village church. Notably plain is the W tower, which barely rises over the nave ridge and is quite without the pinnacles and battlements that the earlier Gothicists applied to any church however humble. Inside, a panelled stone pulpit and E window by Willement. The church is picturesquely grouped with a massive stone lych-gate and the vicarage. [JO]

Colehill, Dorset
St Michael

For this church of 1893–5, W. D. Caröe used the free Gothic taken up by architects looking for a lighter vein than the serious work of the mid-Victorian period. Here, where funds for expensive stonework were not available, Caröe took the red brick and half timber of contemporary domestic work to build a church that is picturesque in an unmonumental way. Low outline, building up to a central short brick tower carrying a timber top, pyramid-roofed with pretty dormers. The nave is half-timbered over brick with more dormers, while the chancel is hierarchically distinguished by being of brick. Timbered interior, including the arcade posts. [JO]

Collaton St Mary, Devon
St Mary

Designed with the adjoining school and parsonage in 1865 by J. W. Rowell of Newton Abbot, who used a muscular Decorated, somewhat eccentric in detail. The interior, largely unaltered, has important fittings designed by J. F. Bentley; these are the fine polychromatic font, of 1866, executed by Earp, and the reredos and E-wall decoration of 1865, the former with a relief of the Last Supper by Theodore Phyffers. The chancel stained glass, dating from 1868, was also designed by Bentley. [CB]

Colwyn Bay, Clwyd
St Paul

This large and grand church was begun in 1886, and completed in 1911, to the design of John Douglas. In Decorated style, it has a wide nave and chancel, light and spacious, and a tall NW tower. The reredos is by W. D. Caröe, carved by Boulton (1935). The adjoining Welsh Church (St David's) is also by Douglas (1902), as is St John's, Old Colwyn (1899–1903), smaller than St Paul's, but possibly even finer, Perpendicular, with a broad tower (added in 1912) and characteristic fittings. [PH]

Copley, West Yorkshire
St Stephen

By W. H. Crossland, 1863–5. Built to serve Edward Akroyd's factory village, this tough and original building, reflecting the influence of Pearson and especially St Peter, Vauxhall, is French in inspiration, a single volume internally, ending in an apse. Crossland's fittings, notably the reredos and pulpit, are inventive and strongly modelled and there is good glass. [KP]

Cowick, Humberside
Holy Trinity

This church, with those of Hensall and Pollington, is one of a group of three modest churches by William Butterfield, 1853–4, each accompanied by a school and parsonage, built by that conscientious churchman Lord Downe to serve neighbouring villages on his estate. All are built of brick, with a concentration on the effective use of the material and of simple

Gothic forms which exemplifies the proper use of limited resources. Massive roofs, broken by bell-cotes and chimneys (given a prominence they would not have in grander designs), characterize all three buildings. Such polychromy as there is is very restrained, and stone dressings are used economically. Hensall has the most notable fittings, including a fine reredos of encaustic tiles. These buildings demonstrate Butterfield's Gothic 'functionalism' – actually his ability to adapt his approach to the means available and to give dignity to cheap structures. [KP]

Cowley, Oxfordshire
St John the Evangelist

The Society of St John the Evangelist, a community of Anglican monks, was founded by the Revd Richard Meux Benson at Cowley in 1865. The church is one of Bodley's best late works and his only monastic building; it was the first conventual church for an order of men built for the use of the Church of England on any considerable scale. It is founded upon Cistercian models: built of golden Bath stone, broad and long with an unbroken wagon roof decorated with painted flowers; flying buttresses support transverse arches, four-clustered shafts support a deeply moulded arcade of four bays and a clerestory with severe tracery; the choir is longer than the nave. At the W end is a strong tower with a crenellated parapet, supported by thin buttresses and enriched with sculpture. All is austere dignity and ordered reticence with a note of calm severity. There is nothing to distract the eye: a wooden screen with a loft and attenuated rood divides the choir from the nave, the former paved diagonally in black and white marble; there is glass by Kempe. Few buildings so fully evoke the cold austerity which characterized Anglican monasticism in the last decade of the 19th century. The buildings and church are now occupied by St Stephen's House, an Anglican theological college. [ANS]

Crawshawbooth, Lancashire
St John the Evangelist

This large church with its great N transept tower was built 1890–2 to the designs of Paley, Austin and Paley. The chancel roof with its collar and gently curved tie-beam trusses heightens the drama of the chancel with Austin's ambitious handling of differing elements to the N and S. The deeply moulded pointed arches of the S chancel arcade die gently into their piers, a feature which, along with that noticeably turn-of-the-century look to the furnishings with delicately carved free-flowing tracery set within rectangular panels and bench ends, is so characteristic of Austin at this time. [DM]

Crewe Green, Cheshire
St Michael

This richly detailed and merrily colourful little estate church (to Crewe Hall) is, perhaps surprisingly, by G. G. Scott (1856–8). It has nave and apsed chancel, in late-13th-century style, with a spirelet at the NW and a S porch. The exterior is of red and blue brick, the interior of red and yellow brick, both enlivened with bands of tiles at the top, and with plenty of naturalistic carving. The buttresses have quirky tops, and arcading runs around the apse. Pulpit and font are of carved stone. The glass in the E and W windows is first-rate: note the Days of Creation in the W rose. [PH]

Crosby-on-Eden, Cumbria
St John the Evangelist

A small church in red sandstone by R. W. Billings (1854). Eccentric in design, it consists of nave and chancel without aisles, a small vestry to the NE, and an unusual W tower which rises to a kind of cruciform spire, stumpy and with crockets and lucarnes. The nave is lit by five windows on each side, Geometrical in style but hooded within arches of vaguely Perpendicular design. [TEF]

Croydon, Greater London
St John the Evangelist, Upper Norwood*

Designed by John Loughborough Pearson in 1878, and built in stages in 1881–2 and 1886–7. The tower was left unfinished. This is one of Pearson's great brick town churches, characteristically spacious and vaulted throughout. A W porch leads to entrances directly into the nave under a gallery. The nave has inner and outer aisles. Beyond the crossing are the aisled chancel and an apsidal side chapel. The chancel has an unusual vault of a type originating in Normandy; radiating ribs as though for an apse rise from a screen placed before the square E end, and between the screen and the E wall are two tiers of five tiny quadripartite vaults, one over each lancet that makes up the E window. It shows Pearson's remarkably imaginative use of vaulting to create special effects, here to emphasize the altar and reredos at the E end. [AQ]

Croydon, Greater London
St Michael, Poplar Walk

The third of John Loughborough Pearson's great brick town churches of the 1870s. It was designed in 1876-7 and built in 1880-1, except for the tower and spire, which remain a stump. The church has a five-bay aisled nave, the W bay having a complex arrangement of entrances and baptismal space beneath a gallery; beyond the crossing is an apsidal chancel with a narrow ambulatory and side chapels, the one to the S treated like a tiny church with its own nave and chancel. The body of the church is serenely calm, thanks to the overall quadripartite rib-vaulting and the use of the Golden Section in the proportions. The side chapels provide a contrasting intricacy with their proliferation of shafts and half-hidden spaces. Characteristically of Pearson, the vaulting resolves it all in its effortless progress from bay to bay, spanning the sweep of the apse or the tight corners of the side chapels. Many artists contributed the designs of the fittings: G. F. Bodley the font, pulpit and organ-case; Frank Loughborough Pearson the font cover and nave seats (and also extra vestries); Temple Moore the choir stalls; Cecil Hare the hanging rood and lectern. The stained glass is by Lavers, Westlake and Barraud, by Clayton and Bell, and by Kempe. [AQ]

Cullercoats, Tyne and Wear
*St George**

Designed in 1878-81 by John Loughborough Pearson, and built 1882-4. The church is Pearson's sternest design, admirably suited to defying the cold winds coming off the North Sea at its feet. Built of hard Coal Measures Sandstone, it is sparsely decorated but boldly massed. A tall unbuttressed polygonal apse at the E, entrances tucked into the shelter of the aisle ends at the W, and a dramatically tall steeple over the S transept make the church an instantly recognizable landmark. The interior is similarly uncompromising. The only decoration is the moulding of arches and shafts. The effect is entirely produced by harmonious

proportions and resolved clear-cut spaces, all of them rib-vaulted. [AQ]

Cumbrae, Millport, Strathclyde
Cathedral of the Holy Spirit (Cathedral of the Isles)*

A collegiate foundation financed by the Hon. G. F. Boyle, later Earl of Glasgow, and built to designs by William Butterfield from 1849 onwards (cf. St Ninian's, Perth). Parish-church sized, flanked at right angles by a canons' house and a choristers' house to form a T-plan group on an elaborately terraced plateau which is an integral part of the composition. Aisleless three-bay nave with tall slim SW tower and pyramidal spire, two-bay choir with N aisle extending into broader NE chapel. Traceried three-light screen filling the whole of the chancel arch, chancel walls patterned in green, black and red tile, roof picked out in ferns and roses. L-plan cloister abuts E elevation of the canons' house. [DW]

Daisy Hill (Westhoughton), Greater Manchester
St James

Built between 1879 and 1881 by Paley and Austin. The bell-turret is a wide soaring slab of solid brickwork, its width running E-W parallel to the body of the church and forming a gable end to the S transept. The panelled brickwork of the turret itself, with its three punched openings for the bells, sits high on a windowed sheer wall and terminates in its own series of gablets. At the W end, the transomed Perpendicular window is set between buttresses with its own outer shafts rising up to a gridded gable with decorated spandrels. The hood mould of the E reticulated window (with 1897 glass by Morris and Co.) sweeps up to a central square termination high on the gable immediately under a single lucarne. [DM]

Dalkeith, Lothian
St Mary (Episcopal)

Built for the 5th Duke of Buccleuch as Dalkeith House Chapel to designs by William Burn and David Bryce in 1843. Early English, heavily buttressed nave with paired lancets, gable front with doorway of three orders set in cusped blind arcading, wheel-window and bell-cote; lower chancel, N transept and S vestry.

Impressive interior with high, double hammer-beam roof, pulpit modelled on that at Beaulieu. Font by Benjamin Ferrey; stalls by William Butterfield, 1846; heraldic tiled floor by Minton. Memorial chapel to the 5th Duke added to N transept by Sir Arthur Blomfield, 1890, with decoration by S. Gambier Parry, 1913; tomb begun by Sir Edward Boehm and finished by Sir Alfred Gilbert, 1892. [DW]

Dalton-in-Furness, Cumbria
St Mary

By Paley and Austin, 1882–5. Externally, the familiar red sandstone is sprinkled with white limestone not only in the diapering over the E window – where it incorporates the gable lucarne – and in the parapets of the S aisle chapel and W tower, but also in the parapet of the SW porch. Here the diapering of the parapet is separated into the five facets of the attached half-octagon plan of the porch with slim, diagonal stepped buttresses. The interior has that asymmetrical composition of chancel, transept, and chancel chapels or aisles that is a hallmark of Paley and Austin's work. [DM]

Darlington, County Durham
St Hilda, Parkgate

A remarkably cheap church built by John Loughborough Pearson for £4,500 in 1887–8, and a fine demonstration of how much can be achieved with so little money. It is not a small church, having a spacious aisled four-bay nave, a narrow chancel and N chapel tucked into a constricted corner site. There is naturally little decoration. Pearson gave the church very narrow, tall lancets, especially at the E and W ends and in the clerestory. The chancel arch is finely proportioned but otherwise plain; and there is a characteristic view diagonally across the church into the side chapel. These at once raise it out of the ordinary and, despite a lack of vaulting, give it the sense of harmonious grandeur that is Pearson's hallmark. [AQ]

Datchet, Berkshire
St Mary

In 1857 a new nave and aisles were built, the medieval chancel being retained. The architect was John Raphael Brandon, known for his scholarly works on Gothic architecture. Here the style is predictably Decorated, but with some odd quirks. In 1859, as the church was already too small, the N transept aisle, vestry and tower were added. In 1864 – the church again being too small – the nave and N aisle were extended to the W, and the S aisle extended to the E. Finally, in 1867 the attractive timber S porch was added. The result of all this is a decidedly odd plan, but the massing is effective, and the spire (at the NE) is highly original – octagonal, with eight tall lucarnes. The N aisle is cross-gabled. The interior is rather sprawling, with a narrow chancel arch on fancy corbels, and a double arcade with granite columns S of the chancel. The stained glass is mostly by O'Connor (1860–5), and is very striking. [PH]

Daylesford, Gloucestershire
*St Peter**

Designed in 1857–9 by John Loughborough Pearson and completed in 1863. It is as vigorously High Victorian Gothic as anything Pearson built, its cruciform plan of nave, short transepts and chancel seemingly designed to buttress a remarkably massive central tower; it has deeply set bell-openings with tall gabled roofs breaking across the junction with a short pyramidal spire. The E end has three cusped lights with heavily foliated and cusped decoration around them; the other parts take up these forms in a less ornate way. Two surviving doorways from the earlier Norman church are incorporated into the nave. The interior is mildly polychromatic, with a variety of grey and soft-pink stones. The N transept has a wooden barrel-vault with a herring-bone pattern of boarding, and the chancel has a stone barrel-vault. Stained glass is by Clayton and Bell. [AQ]

Deeping St Nicholas, Lincolnshire
St Nicholas

A rich mid-14th-century Lincolnshire Decorated style church, tightly composed. Built in 1845–6 on reclaimed fenland by Charles Kirk of Sleaford. The church has nave and N aisle and a lower chancel, and a soaring pinnacled N tower and broach-spire, all in rubblestone with ashlar dressings. The tower acts as the porch. Rich detail and window tracery, much of which can be traced to nearby medieval churches. [NA]

Deganwy, Gwynedd
All Saints

This church was built in 1898–9 by Lady Augusta Mostyn (of Gloddaeth) in memory of her parents. It shows Douglas and Fordham's happy gift of responding to the *genius loci*: the long, low, clerestoried nave and aisles lie between the higher chancel and the W tower with its broad low spire, set against the steep, rocky hillside. [PH]

Denstone, Staffordshire
*All Saints**

Perhaps the most idiosyncratic of G. E. Street's rural churches to be designed in his 'Vigorous' manner, Denstone was built in 1860–2, of pale-brown and cream Hollington stone with red-sandstone bands and tiled roofs. It is in a rich Geometrical style and forms the central feature of a complete parochial arrangement including vicarage, school, lych-gate and churchyard cross. Street's handling is nothing if not dramatic. The long low nave is abruptly run up against a towering, high-roofed chancel with clean-cut polygonal apse, whose sharp outlines soar above crouching angle-buttresses. On the N the two compartments are linked by a tall cylindrical turret with tiled conical spire, which grows quaintly out of the lean-to vestry composition. But on the S, which is the principal side and contains the porch, the jagged conjunction is left to tell its own story. Subtle polychromy pervades the entire walls, with alternating cream and red voussoirs over varied tracery windows – plate in the chancel, bar in the nave. Derbyshire marble shafts are used to enhance the elevated apse interior, which glows in iridescent splendour beyond an elaborate chancel arch, an effect intensified by the shadowy timber nave roof with its huge stilted arch-braces. In contrast, the chancel roof is boarded and panelled. The three long apse windows sparkle like jewels, as do the rest, with some of the finest early glass by Clayton and Bell. Lavish fittings are of equal quality: Thomas Earp made the magnificent alabaster font with the Four Rivers of Paradise, the drum pulpit with spar inlay, and the reredos containing a Crucifixion. Wrought-iron screens are by James Leaver, and tiles by Minton. [PJ]

Derby
St Luke

The finest and most original church by Stevens and Robinson of Derby. Nave with an array of gables, SW tower and polygonal-apsed chancel. Rock-faced with a pronounced fortress-like batter to the lower parts. Nave and chancel were complete in 1870–1 and the dramatic soaring tower with saddleback roof was finished in 1875. The sloping site made possible a crypt chapel beneath the chancel. The interior in contrast is broad, with aisles reduced to narrow passages. Boarded ceilings and sumptuous marble and alabaster font and pulpit. [NA]

Derby
St Mary (RC)

The style of the Gothic Revival in the 1830s was the Perpendicular, and it was with this style that A. W. Pugin began his career as an architect. St Mary's may be considered Pugin's first large parish church. He made the drawings for it in 1837 and it was opened in 1839. The exterior was designed to be seen frontally from the W end, where the rather thin tower would not be seen in competition with the massive 16th-century one of the cathedral. The tower was intended to have a spire, and to be balanced by a school and a presbytery, now demolished. Inside, the tall nave has N and S arcades of slender piers without capitals. The climax of the church is the vaulted choir with an apse, containing splendid glass by W. Warrington in three great three-light windows. The rood is supported on a slight arch. [AW]

Ditton, Cheshire
St Michael (RC)*

This amazing great church – a notable landmark in the flat Mersey landscape – was built in 1876–9 for a large community of Jesuits expelled from Germany. The architect was Henry Clutton. In red sandstone, and lancet style, it has a tremendous W tower with saddleback top. The interior is tall and open: the lofty aisles are divided off by arcades with pairs of coupled shafts which run across the transepts. The chancel is very shallow. The richly carved tester from the destroyed pulpit now hangs over the tabernacle. Stained glass and hanging lamps are strongly Germanic. [PH]

Doncaster, South Yorkshire
St George

One of the largest of Victorian parish churches, this grand and splendid building by Sir George Gilbert Scott, of 1854–8, replaced the ancient church destroyed by fire in 1853. The new building echoed the form of the old with its great central tower, but Scott amended the style to the favoured Middle Pointed. The interior is extremely impressive: tall, finely proportioned and richly garnished. The fittings and glass were installed according to Scott's directions and include work by some of his favourite craftsmen. Much of the carving was done by J. Birnie Philip, including the excellent reredos. The general decoration of the sanctuary was carried out by Clayton and Bell. The E window, in memory of the great vicar Dr Sharpe (who rebuilt the church), is by Hardman, while Clayton and Bell, Wailes and other firms are well represented. [KP]

Dorchester, Oxfordshire
St Birinus (RC)

This charming little church of 1849 by W. W. Wardell was paid for by John Davey. In 14th-century style, it is very elaborate. On the W wall is a statue of St Birinus. The rich interior has polychrome decoration, wooden rood-screen, carved altar, and canopied sedile. The stained glass is by Ward and Nixon. [PH]

Dorking, Surrey
St Martin*

This is Henry Woodyer's grandest town church. Built in 1866–77, it has a W tower, aisled nave, and chancel with N vestries and organ-chamber; the short S chapel was extended in 1912. The junction of the tower and spire is excellently detailed, with angle-buttresses rising up to pinnacles that hide the broaches of the tall octagonal spire. The Decorated tracery is especially prominent in the triple windows of the clerestory. By comparison the interior is plain, though Woodyer's quirkiness shows through in the acutely pointed arches of the nave arcades, set on short, round piers, and in the clustered shafting of the chancel arch. Over the arch is a mosaic by Powell depicting the Crucifixion (*c.* 1890); the wooden chancel screen has been removed. [AQ]

Dover, Kent
SS Peter and Paul

The soaring parish church of Charlton-in-Dover is by James Brooks 1893. The Early English exterior in Kentish rag is perhaps the building's best aspect: lancets are tall throughout and are found in tiers in the N and S transept walls. A tall spirelet rises from the lofty crossing. Within are lofty nave, chancel, transepts, chapels, bays divided by low octagonal piers and a high clerestory. The walls are lined with ashlar or rendered. [REH]

Down St Mary, Devon
St Mary

Small and remote, St Mary's retains a medieval W tower and nave arcade; the rest was progressively remodelled under the aegis of the Revd W. T. A. Radford between 1848 and 1890. John Hayward rearranged the choir in 1848; the reredos and sanctuary enrichments were designed by G. E. Street in 1866, with carving by Earp and mosaics by Salviati; the nave and aisle were rebuilt 1870–2 by J. F. Gould of Barnstaple, who designed the pulpit and – in collaboration with Radford – the very attractive polychromy of the internal walls; the rood-screen, closely modelled on late medieval precedents, was commenced in 1881 by the village carpenters, William and Zachariah Bushell. The E window of 1854 is by Hardman; the rest of the glass, variously dated, is all by Clayton and Bell. The interior of St Mary's forms an ensemble of great richness, instructive for its successful fusion of work drawn from both national and local sources. [CB]

Downside, Somerset
Abbey Church of St Gregory the Great

The English Benedictine monks of the monastery founded at Douai in 1606 had to leave France in 1795, and settled in Somerset in 1814. Their first chapel, a pretty Gothic building of 1823, by H. E. Goodridge, still survives. In 1870 a great scheme for a church, monastery, and additions to the school was produced by the Newcastle firm of Archibald Dunn and Edward Hansom (whose father Charles had earlier erected school buildings). They planned a vast cruciform church with a tall spire up against the S transept and an apsidal choir with a chevet of chapels, all very

French. The first part built (opened 1882) was the transept, used as a temporary church – hence the elaborate N altar, beneath a rose window. Then came the chevet, from N transept round to the grand Lady Chapel. From there on the chapels are square-ended and Perpendicular (1887–9). In 1895 Hansom resigned, and the choir was built in 1902–5 by Thomas Garner, who substituted a square end for Hansom's apse, and a more English style. The great sacristy was built in 1915 by F. A. Walters. The nave (still unfinished) was built in 1922–5 by Sir Giles Gilbert Scott: he also (1938) altered and finished off Hansom's 1884 tower, in a Somerset manner. The result of this complex history is a soaring and noble church whose complexities and inconsistencies, as in many medieval buildings, serve to add spice without detracting from the overall effect. The rich collection of fittings and works of art, both ancient and modern, includes the superb altar, reredos and tester, and glass of the Lady Chapel by Sir Ninian Comper (1898–1929). The choir-stalls, by F. Stüflesser of Ortisei (1932), are based on those of Chester Cathedral. Garner's tomb (N choir aisle) has a crucifix designed by his former partner Bodley. [PH]

Dropmore, Buckinghamshire
St Anne

This charmingly colourful little church among the beechwoods is by Butterfield (1864–6). Built of flint, brick and half-timber, with a tile-hung timber bell-turret and timber porch, it has an unbroken roof-line. In the richly polychrome interior nave and chancel are divided by a tall cusped screen. Note the standard candlesticks, the striking font of coloured marbles, and the fine E window by Alexander Gibbs (c. 1866). [PH]

Dukinfield, Greater Manchester
Dukinfield Old Chapel

The shiningly scrubbed and sandblasted chapel which presides aloofly over the town at the head of Chapel Street conceals behind its W front of 1892 a delightfully complete and as yet unspoilt Gothic building of 1840 by Richard Tattersall of Manchester in a lancet style on a cruciform plan. Tall and slender piers rising to pointed arches carry the inevitable gallery, furnished with the largest and most luxurious box pews that early Victorian families could desire.

Overhead stretches a ribbed plaster vault, and across the eastern arm on a choir-screen worthy of a cathedral stands the great organ. The octagonal wooden pulpit, resting on a corbel in front of the screen and sufficiently old fashioned still to have a canopy, is approached from the vestry up a steep flight of steps. [CS]

Dumbarton, Strathclyde
St Augustine's (Episcopal)

Early Decorated, designed by Sir R. Rowand Anderson, 1872–3, on a tight site with only a gable front and the base of an intended tower to High Street. Uncommonly good interior: nave with alternately circular and octagonal piers and ceiled wagon roof, chancel arch with clustered shafts, richly detailed chancel with clustered piers, shafted clerestory of paired lights and ribbed barrel-roof, good sculpture at capitals and a large stone reredos, completed in 1893; good furnishings, delicately traceried screen with central gablet. [DW]

Dumfries, Dumfries and Galloway
*Crichton Memorial Church**

A huge non-denominational hospital church, designed by Sydney Mitchell in late-13th-century Gothic, 1890–7. Red sandstone, cruciform plan, nave with tall clerestory of three-light windows, aisleless transepts and apsed chancel, big central tower with pairs of belfry-openings, pinnacled and battlemented parapet. Mortuary crypt in the fall of the ground under W end of nave, flat-roofed battlemented narthex containing a vaulted stairhall with keeled quatrefoil piers. Tall and impressive interior, with shafted square-plan compound piers with rounded angles, flying-buttress-type transverse arches in aisles and multangular wagon roof ribbed with carved bosses. Elaborate sculptured detail throughout by William Vickers. [DW]

Dumfries, Dumfries and Galloway
Greyfriars Church (Church of Scotland)

An ambitious Middle Pointed church of red sandstone with a richly pinnacled profile by John Starforth, 1866. Complex galleried plan on D-shaped corner site, basically a short T, the angles being filled out by diagonal sub-transepts, pavilion-roofed towerlets and circular stairhalls with raking windows flanking the tower and broach-spire. [DW]

Dundee, Tayside
St Mark (formerly Church of Scotland)

Sizeable Ruskinian Gothic church by F. T. Pilkington 1868, simpler in plan than his earlier churches, but similarly detailed. Gable front with elaborate four-light window over deeply recessed double doorway flanked by NE tower progressively splayed and broached to octagonal belfry-stage with very tall gabled openings and stone spire, unequally gabled flank elevations with central bowed features. Galleried cross-plan interior with angles recessed behind columns, hammer-beam roof with tie-rods, extended by Ireland and Maclaren, 1879. Farther along Perth Road the same architect's McCheyne Memorial Church, similar size and profile with slimmer spire but different plan, aisled with iron columns and plaster groin-vaults between hammer-beams. [DW]

Dundee, Tayside
St Mary, Lochee (RC)*

A very original Early Decorated church and presbytery-house group on an obtuse-angled site, designed by J. A. Hansom, 1865. Long low nave with triplets of diminutive trefoiled clerestory lights and aisles clasped in small transeptal features with pairs of small plate-traceried windows divided off by buttresses. Tall octagonal tower-chancel in the angle of the site with prismatic roof; small flanking apse terminating the S aisle; all similar to his St Wilfrid's, Ripon. On the N side the composition extends E into a large two-storeyed presbytery house with an open porch. Subtle masonry, rubble in very thin courses emphasizing the low horizontality of the design. Low intimate brick-lined interior with elaborated corbelling at the aisles, arcades ending in half arches with short compound piers on high plinths; Late Gothic reredos by A. B. Wall, 1897. [DW]

Dundee, Tayside
St Paul's Cathedral (Episcopal)*

Built in 1852–5 on a historic urban hilltop by Alexander Penrose Forbes, Bishop of Brechin, to Middle Pointed designs by George Gilbert Scott, his first large commission in Scotland. Although not built as a cathedral it was planned on a scale comparable with Butterfield's cathedral at Perth: aisled hall-church nave, transepts, chancel with side chapels ending in a three-sided apse, and a giant spire, 220 feet high, containing a vaulted open porch at the head of a long flight of steps. The spire is of unusual design, the tower being of four stages with a narrow quatrefoiled parapet over the second stage, skilfully composed with a tall broach-spire. Within, tall arcades with slim quatrefoil piers, open roof with scissors roof-truss which does not acknowledge the transepts, and a rib-vaulted apse. Arched and gabled reredos with a gold mosaic by Salviati of Venice and other undisturbed Scott furnishings. [DW]

Dundee, Tayside
St Salvador (Episcopal)*

Founded by Alexander Penrose Forbes, Bishop of Brechin, and his chaplain James Nicholson, in 1856. Bodley designed the school as a temporary church in 1857, tall simple Early French with mincer-plate tracery. In 1865–8 the English mid-Decorated nave was built, aisled with tall clerestory and a low lean-to narthex, and in 1874 the chancel which has a S chapel and a blind E wall, all still in conformity with the 1865 design. Externally the church is very simple, though not without subtleties, e.g. the widening of the W gable into the buttresses. Spacious interior, with chamfered piers running straight into the arches which are moulded at the E bays only; but the whole was elaborately stencilled by Burlison and Grylls with diapers. By the same firm also is the reredos with its tiers of apostles painted on copper panels and the stained glass of the choir with its fine Holbeinesque drawing. [DW]

Dunecht, Grampian
Dunecht House Chapel

Romanesque and quite large (100 feet long, 50 feet high internally) by G. E. Street, *c.* 1866–77, entered off the same architect's vast cast-iron galleried library. Tall proportions; W front with circular towerlet and diapered porch of Italian type acknowledging Italianate style of main house (William Smith, 1859), aisleless wagon-roofed nave with tall clerestory, transeptal projection and narrow passage on courtyard flank, two-bay aisle and mortuary chapel on N, short sanctuary and semicircular apse. Inlaid stalls of Florentine walnut (Street, 1877) with further woodwork by William Kelly, 1920s. [DW]

Dunstall, Staffordshire
St Mary

This estate church was built in 1852–3 by Henry Clutton. Its correct Decorated is enlivened by quirks. Proportions both overall and of the porch and windows are steep, and details often original (especially the carved animals). The spire stands at the SW: both tower and porch are stone-vaulted. The reredos of 1890 incorporates an excellent alabaster Annunciation carved by Farmer and Brindley. The chancel E and one S window are by Willement; the W and the other chancel S window are by Burlison and Grylls. [PH]

Durham
Our Lady of Mercy and St Godric (RC)

Begun in 1863 by E. W. Pugin in the Early Decorated style, St Godric's was not completed until 1909 when its prominent tower was added but without Pugin's spire. The exterior of the apse is crowned with seven gablets and crosses, and the exterior enrichment reflects the elaboration of ornament and use of local references in the chancel, which contains painted panels depicting the life of St Godric. [LW]

Durham
*St Cuthbert**

A quirky but substantial church of 1858 by E. R. Robson. Modelled on early-13th-century English Gothic with French details. The nave, S aisle, vestry, and semicircular apse are all subordinated to the composition of the W front. This is dominated by a peculiar lofty tower covered by a saddleback roof. In the tympanum above the doorway is Christ in Majesty surrounded by symbols of the four Evangelists. Inside, the constructional polychromy has been obliterated by whitewash. [LW]

Ealing, Greater London
St Mary

Perhaps the most triumphant of S. S. Teulon's 'recastings' involving, in the words of the Archbishop of Canterbury, the transformation of St Mary's 'from a Georgian monstrosity into a Constantinopolitan basilica'. Teulon in 1863–6 added the chancel and aisles and transformed the W front by the addition of a narthex and two turrets. An elaborate and lofty spire intended for the Georgian tower was a victim of economies. What stands out inside is the use of horseshoe arches and the quite breathtaking roofs, that to the nave consisting of minimal Gothic-shaped apertures in wood suspended on both the EW and NS axes looking much like huge stencil moulds or plate tracery or even lace on elephantine scale. Much of the carving is by Earp, the mosaic in the reredos is by Salviati and the tiling by Maw and Company. The windows in the chancel and clerestory were designed by the local worthy Thomas Boddington of Gunnersbury Lodge and executed by Heaton, Butler and Bayne. The yellow-tinted glass with outline figures in the semicircular baptistery off the S aisle is by Lavers and Barraud but to the designs of Teulon. There is a memorial window to the architect himself in the N porch entrance. [MS]

Ealing, Greater London
St Peter

Designed in 1889 for the affluent new suburb of North Ealing by J. D. Sedding, executed after his death in 1891 by his partner Henry Wilson. Sedding aimed to 'attain a picturesqueness and breadth of effect by arrangement of simple masses, thickness of walls and variety of arched forms'. The result is an original and satisfying building despite the lack of both the intended N transeptal tower and the interior decoration. The curvaceous forms and generous spaces of Late Gothic are combined with Sedding's own novel ideas: a huge Curvilinear W window mysteriously recessed behind external flying buttresses; the long roof-line of the nave enlivened by a chain of shallow stone arches linking the projecting turrets which cap the nave piers. Inside the comfortably broad nave, the bulky panelled piers are eclectically combined with a Gothic gallery producing an effective play of light and shade. [BC]

East Grinstead, West Sussex
*Convent Chapel of St Margaret**

Apart from the Royal Courts of Justice, George Edmund Street's most extensive community of buildings was for the Society of St Margaret, designed

1864–5 but carried out in sections between 1865 and 1890 with numerous modifications in plan. This is the finest conventual house of its period in England; none can rival its elaborate homogeneity, let alone its sheer romantic splendour. Constructed of iron-tinged white sandstone quarried on site, with Bath stone dressings and red-tiled roofs, the main quadrangular blocks exploit a cumulative theme of gabled forms of ever-shifting scale against high roof-lines and slim brick chimney-shafts. The W entrance-front poises asymmetrical extremes in perfect balance culminating off-centre, beyond a big refectory gable, in the straight SW chapel tower with geometrically panelled saddleback top. Its design having been significantly recast in 1878, St Margaret's Chapel is one of the noblest creations of Street's latest phase. Internally, this soaring spatial triumph has the dynamic power of a compressed medieval cathedral. Not one feature is literally borrowed from elsewhere, yet the concept of enclosing a vaulted and passage-aisled sanctuary of such airborne delicacy within one end of a lofty timber-roofed nave was doubtless the outcome of Street's deep fascination with the revolutionary form of Gerona. Here he paraphrased it in High English with a monumental square chevet, and gave it lines of slender Irish black-marble columns to support the stone rib-vaulting. Tripartite entrance to a lower apsed sacrament chapel at the E end, also aisled and rib-vaulted, is discreetly guarded from view behind the sumptuous marble and alabaster reredos carved by Earp and Hobbs. Suspended aloft, the great Geometrical E rose has stained glass by Bell and Beckham, who also did the retrochapel lancets and tall traceried nave windows. Sadly depleted in number, the sisters have long abandoned their magnificent premises to private residential use; the chapel remains complete but deserted. [PJ]

East Heslerton, North Yorkshire
St Andrew*

The unfettered economy of Sir Tatton Sykes' patronage allowed G. E. Street's six Wolds churches extreme variety of form. As the last of the series, East Heslerton is the most ambitiously conceived and exploits its opportunities to the limits. Designed in 1873 and built 1874–7, it is of dressed stone in a well-developed Anglo-French lancet style. Around the rectangle of the nave, Street assembles a battery of familiar motifs: the elevated curved apse derived from Fawley; a noble

variation of the octagonal stone steeple of Bettisfield; and a regularized version of the open W narthex at Howsham. Subordinate to these are a transversely gabled SW baptistery with lean-to sexton's shed on its E; a similarly gabled N organ-recess; and outside that a longitudinal vestry abutting the N tower. All elements are individually stressed with their own independent roofs; a superb composition from most points of view, the tendency comes perhaps too dangerously near disintegration. Internally, the plan's logic is disconcertingly reflected in the progression of roofs. Kept at one level, they go through three separate phases: open timber wagon to the nave; boarded and ribbed where the tower forms a transept; and rib-vaulted in stone over the chancel. Nor is this all, however, as the two northern projections are made to disrupt the rib formations, giving them a slightly uncomfortable lopsided appearance. One turns instead to the splendid apse with its brass and iron screen by Thomas Potter, and harmonious glass by Clayton and Bell. Street's contemporary reredos polyptych, painted by the same artists, was transferred here from Bishop Wilton in 1883. [PJ]

Eastbourne, East Sussex
All Saints' Hospital Chapel

An unexpectedly fine chapel hidden away in a rather remote district. It was completed by Henry Woodyer in 1874, and clearly shows the influence of the architect's friend and master, William Butterfield. The rich polychrome detail of the interior, employing brick and stone banding, geometrical tiling and marble, forms a beautifully proportioned composition. [DRE]

Eastbourne, East Sussex
All Souls

A spectacular building, and the only Victorian church in Sussex furnished with a free-standing campanile. Designed in an Italian Romanesque style by A. P. Strong in 1882, the church is of yellow brick, with red-brick and terracotta dressings. The basilican aisled nave has monumental proportions emphasized by the seven-bayed arcade of Horsham stone, each column being embellished with a capital of varying Byzantine design, set off against walls decorated with red and yellow brick banding. The solemn vista of the nave is closed by a massive apsidal chancel pierced by seven tall round-headed windows. [DRE]

Eastbourne, East Sussex
St Saviour

Amidst dignified Italianate terraces, G. E. Street reared one of his awesome polychrome Tractarian churches capable of holding a vast congregation. Designed 1865 in Early Decorated style, the essential fabric was built of red brick with Bath stone dressings 1865–7, leaving the steeple until 1870–2. Street's spatial organization is impressive: a nave of exceptional span has a high clerestory of traceried lights, and a pointed timber wagon-vault braced by iron tie-rods; six-bay arcades supported on quatrefoiled piers divide off the lean-to aisles. So far all is regular, but taking a cue from North Oxford the last bay of each component cants inwards to make a three-sided apse with the tall chancel arch. Beyond this the real chancel apse is curved, its ribbed brick vault springing from Devon marble shafts unconventionally arranged so that one of the ribs falls central to the altar, with two high tracery windows spaced out on either side. Externally at the E the collision of differently scaled elements is adroitly resolved, building up to the steep polygonal end of the nave roof; at aisle level, diagonal gabled projections N and S were for organ and vestry. Below the arched W window composition is a lean-to narthex, the massive tower with stone broach-spire being placed to advantage outside the western bay of the N aisle where it forms an imposing porch. Later alterations have compromised Street's intentions, particularly in the chancel which has been colour-washed. His reredos and cancelli were removed in 1928, and war damage did away with Clayton and Bell's glass. [PJ]

Eastmoors, North Yorkshire
St Mary Magdalen

By George Gilbert Scott junior. The first designs were made in 1876 but the church was not built until 1882. It was designed for an exposed site in a little hamlet. There are no windows in the N wall and the S aisle can be divided off to make a schoolroom. All the details are both sturdy and sophisticated. The font of 1900 and the reredos of 1903 are by Temple Moore but the church is essentially a little masterpiece by Scott. [GS]

Eaton, Cheshire
Eaton Hall Chapel

The chapel and adjacent bell-tower and stables fortunately survived the demolition of the Hall in 1961. All were designed by Alfred Waterhouse and built in 1870–83. The apsed chapel is tall, as it needs to be so as not to be dominated by the tower with its fanciful top, and in French 13th-century style. The rib-vaulted interior is entered beneath a timber gallery. The stained glass was commissioned in 1876 from Frederic Shields, and made by Heaton, Butler and Bayne. He was also responsible for the mosaics filling the blank arches on the stable side. In the sanctuary is J. E. Boehm's superb effigy of the 1st Duchess of Westminster (died 1880). [PH]

Ecchinswell, Hampshire
St Lawrence

Designed in 1886 by the most highly regarded church architects of the Late Gothic Revival, Bodley and Garner, this small church manages to combine an effect of rustic charm externally and sophisticated refinement internally. Outside, the finely knapped, tightly jointed black-flint walling and the design of the tower with weatherboarded belfry and shingled spire are noteworthy. Inside, the exquisite proportions and mouldings of the arcade columns and arches, the open roof running the length of the church to a painted ceiure over the sanctuary and the screens and furnishings of the chancel reward study. [MM]

Eccles, Greater Manchester
Monton Church, Monton Green

On rebuilding the old chapel in 1873–5, Thomas Worthington, who like his clients was a Unitarian, designed a building of traditional Gothic appearance with a nave and aisles of five bays, transepts and chancel; the tall almost free-standing steeple at the SW corner, though not part of the original design, is indispensable to its success. The clerestory windows are of particular interest containing glass of the 1890s with a marvellously ecumenical collection of 'saints' both pagan and Christian, ranging from Homer and Trajan to Sir Thomas More and William Carey. [CS]

Eccleston, Cheshire
*St Mary**

Bodley's two favourite churches were designed for dukes: Clumber for the Duke of Newcastle, and Eccleston for the 1st Duke of Westminster; ten years divide them and the contrast is telling. Completed in 1899, Eccleston was built as an estate church for one of the richest patrons in England. It has a simple, uncomplicated plan of chancel, nave and aisles with a W tower. But, in comparison with Clumber, it is less inspired, stiffer and more formal, colder and given an abstract quality by nerveless mouldings. It is in the abstraction of his late work that Bodley's smile begins to freeze, casting a chill on many of his imitators who adopted his final mannerisms without compensating sensitivity. [ANS]

Edensor, Derbyshire
St Peter

The church, seen across parkland, is the centrepiece of the model village for Chatsworth built by the 6th Duke of Devonshire out of sight of the 'big house'. The village was built between 1848 and 1852, but the old church had to suffice until 1867 when the 7th Duke commissioned George Gilbert Scott senior to rebuild it. Grand and ashlar-faced and thoroughly competent, with a soaring Early English tower and broach-spire. The nave has narrow aisles and tiny clerestory windows. Here as well as in the chancel and S chapel (built to house the 17th-century monuments), the details are Decorated and Scott incorporated some genuine medieval fabric from the previous church. [NA]

Edinburgh, Lothian
Barclay Bruntsfield Church (Church of Scotland)*

One of the most astonishing churches of the whole 19th century. It was the result of a competition won by F. T. Pilkington in the wake of his success at Irvine, built in 1862–4. Like Irvine it consists of a large central space opening into a higher gable-fronted gallery outshot containing the main entrance, but it is appreciably more complex in plan: the main auditorium is apple-shaped and the gable-front gallery appendage T-shaped with two tiers of galleries. In the apse formed by the narrower end of the apple is a segment-fronted platform pulpit backed by arcading, now the base of an organ-case added in 1898. Again as at Irvine the plan form is changed at the upper level, this time to a trefoil, the angles of which are carried on circular piers with French capitals. These angles, with the detached square piers which rise up through the galleries, support a square-plan roof with intersecting king-and-queen post trusses. From the main roof rib-vaults fill out the E and W apses and radial struts the roof of the S apse, all stencilled in primary colours by Sydney Mitchell in 1898. Externally the main roof is again cruciform, apsed on S, E and W, the ridges from the gablets of the latter being raked up to produce an unprecedented cluster of prismatic sections: at the N arm the roof is steeply raked up over the gallery to the kerb roof of the N appendage which has a circular stair with a huge patterned candlesnuffer roof at its E arm. Gargantuan elevations in a thorough-going Ruskinian style with richly sculptured plate-traceried windows: huge NW broach-spire with giant double doorway set forward from the N gable front which has stilted arches at the lower tier and a Lincoln rose window sheltered by a cusped arch at the upper. Most of the sculpture is left in huge rough-hewn blocks, exaggerating the fantastic scale of the design, but some details carved by Pearce show what was intended. [DW]

Edinburgh, Lothian
Catholic Apostolic (now *Reformed Baptist*) *Church**

The result of a competition won in 1872 by Sir R. Rowand Anderson. A huge towerless church in the Neo-Norman style, built up to street level on a substructure of hall, library and offices. Tall wide nave with pyramid-capped angle-turrets and a big wheel-window above the narthex and circular baptistery at the W end, the latter revisions of 1884 substituting for the W tower originally planned. At the E a narrow choir in Gerona-type arrangement with aisles at the two W bays only and a towering semicircular apse with clerestory windows high up in a blind arcade. The nave is broad and simple, the chancel richly shafted with a huge arched and spired baldacchino added by Anderson in 1893. Both have simple tunnel-roofs. In 1893–7 the walls of the nave were painted by Phoebe Traquair with scenes from the Book of Revelation and the Life of Christ, all with moulded and gilded haloes, crowns and trumpets and overtones of the supernatural. The main church is now disused and the furnishings dispersed. [DW]

Edinburgh, Lothian
Highland Tolbooth St John (Church of Scotland)*

Built as the Victoria Hall in 1842–4, designed by A. W. N. Pugin for James Gillespie Graham, whose contribution was presumably limited to the razor-sharp Georgian masonry and the unusual plan-form devised to house both the General Assembly and the Tolbooth congregation. It consists of a buttressed and pinnacled rectangle with a great spire at the E gable, its design adapted from Pugin's second scheme for St George's, Southwark and the ideal parish church in *The True Principles*. A masonry rib-vaulted vestibule at its base opens into a long corridor which leads to a big top-lit imperial staircase, rebuilt in enlarged form by Hardy and Wight in 1893. Above is the auditorium, a vast space with a very flat rib-vault of plaster. The platform with its richly spired commissioner's throne-cum-pulpit is by Gillespie Graham and Pugin executed by William Nixon, while the shallow cantilevered U-plan gallery proudly bearing the royal arms was inserted by Robert Matheson in 1858–9. Secularized. [DW]

Edinburgh, Lothian
Old St Paul (Episcopal)

Early Pointed, orientated N and S on a steeply sloping hemmed-in Old Town site, its triple-lancet chancel gable towering high above Jeffrey Street. It was designed by an ex-assistant of G. G. Scott's, William Hay: the chancel and N half of the nave were built in 1880–3, the S half in 1889–90, and the Seabury Chapel in 1904–5, the latter to designs by George Henderson, Hay's partner. Dark but very spacious nave. Roof of arched trusses with beasts' heads holding the tie-rods in their teeth: chancel in the Gerona arrangement much favoured in Scotland at the time, delicate iron rood-screen and a huge and richly pinnacled Late Gothic triptych altarpiece by Henderson. [DW]

Edinburgh, Lothian
St Mary's Cathedral (Episcopal)*

Triple-spired northern Early Pointed, by Sir G. G. Scott, 1874–9, W spires completed 1913–17, chapter house 1890–1. Nave transepts and choir, aisled with clerestory and triforium throughout. Transept fronts have wheel-windows of Lincoln-Chartres type over lancets, and E end tall triple lancets, octagonal central tower and Chartres-type spire developed from Burges's at Cork. Nave has alternately circular and octagonal piers of Shoreham type and timber barrel-roof with sexpartite ribs, Transitional vaulted choir with details of Lincoln–Holyrood type. The square-plan chapter house has an octagonal vault on a central shaft of Shap granite. Furnishings intact except for font: reredos sculpted by Mary Grant, wrought-iron screens by Skidmore, glass by Clayton and Bell, Burlison and Grylls, and C. E. Kempe, some of it badly replaced in recent years. [DW]

Edinburgh, Lothian
St Michael, Slateford (Church of Scotland)

By John Honeyman, 1881–3, Early English similar in character to his Glasgow Lansdowne Church twenty years earlier with its very correct shafted and dog-toothed detail; but something of a landmark in Presbyterian church design, renouncing the iron-columned interior then in vogue in favour of correct Ecclesiological forms. Continuous nave and chancel with circular piers and tall shafted clerestory. Open roof of purlin trusses, and furnishings painted by Gertrude Hope. [DW]

Edinburgh, Lothian
St Michael and All Saints (Episcopal)*

London mission church-type group with parsonage house, hall, school and sisters' house picturesquely composed on oblique-angled site: church designed by Rowand Anderson, 1865, completion of W end and ancillary buildings 1876–8, all Early Pointed. Church is cruciform with nave of three wide bays, aisled with clerestory and lean-to narthex, aisleless transepts and apsidal chancel. Short cylindrical piers of red sandstone with chunky foliate capitals and an open timber roof; original polychrome and gilt reredos by William Burges now in side chapel, present reredos by C. E. Kempe, glass by Wailes, Kempe and Comper. [DW]

Edinburgh, Lothian
St Peter (Episcopal)

A sizeable Early Geometrical church by William Slater, 1857–65. Broad nave with lean-to aisles and no clerestory, continuous with semi-octagonal chancel which has one-bay aisles. Flat-roofed cloister-like narthex entered by a porch in the tall unbuttressed tower with diapered spire; circular vaulted baptistery projecting from the centre of the narthex. The arcades have circular granite piers with stiff-leaf capitals. There is a braced collar-beam roof, with stencilling by G. H. Potts; walls and roof of chancel have decorative scheme by George Dobie and Son 1890. Good furnishings of 1865, circular pulpit of Caen stone, glass mainly by Clayton and Bell 1865–90. [DW]

Edvin Loach, Hereford and Worcester
*St Mary**

Magnificently sited on a prominent hill-top in rolling country, this church was built in 1859 by G. G. Scott to replace a humble Early Norman building, which was left intact, but later fell into roofless ruin. The new church is small, but has great presence, with its polygonal apse and broach-spire. The tower is embraced, and rests inside on two fat columns with foliage capitals. The roofs are excellent, the chancel being marked off by a timber arch. Fittings, in stone and wood, are typical of Scott, and the E lancets contain good Hardman glass. [PH]

Elerch, Dyfed
St Peter

One would hardly expect to find a fine church by William Butterfield in the remote pastoral setting of the Cardiganshire hills. It was built in 1865–8 by the Revd Lewis Gilbertson, vice-principal of Jesus College, Oxford, who had spent his youth here. Not large, it has great dignity and strength. The pyramid-roofed central tower forms the focus around which the picturesquely irregular outline is composed. The rough local stone has unfortunately been mostly rendered. The interior is severe but well proportioned. The awful colour scheme detracts from the excellent E window, by A. Gibbs, and tiled reredos. [PH]

Ellerker, Humberside
*St Ann's Chapel**

John Loughborough Pearson's first church built in 1843–4. It is a simple two-cell building with Decorated Gothic tracery for the windows and a bell-cote on the W gable. The design is clearly influenced by Pugin, as much of Pearson's work in the 1840s was to be, but the chancel arch already shows the preoccupation with proportion that became one of his specialities. [AQ]

Ellon, Grampian
St Mary on the Rock (Episcopal)

A small but very original Early Middle Pointed church by G. E. Street, 1870–1. Granite-built with freestone windows and string-courses, broad nave with lean-to narthex canted into narrower apsidal chancel, with a N spirelet at the junction cleverly broached from square to octagonal and thence to circular. Interesting interior, differing treatment of N and S walls, wagon roof with tie-rods, apsidally treated towards chancel arch, stone pulpit, sedilia and marble reredos. Glass by Clayton and Bell, and Lavers and Barraud. [DW]

Englefield Green, Surrey
*St Jude**

This church offers proof that E. B. Lamb's architecture was not exclusively associated with Low Church views. Designed in 1856 for a moderate Tractarian vicar, St Jude's great glory is its polychromatic interior, which couples brick (laid horizontally, vertically, and diagonally) with stone (both warm-toned and cool, quarry-faced and smooth) in a vibrant yet controlled array of stripes. The exterior, by contrast, is grey and rugged, dominated by a blocky tower placed oddly where the S transept ought to be. When the church opened in 1859, it consisted of a nave, chancel, S tower, and short N transept. The nave-benches, choir-stalls, and the suavely Curvilinear font were also provided by Lamb. In 1867–8, he enlarged the church, extending the N transept to a great length and crossing it with a gabled projection to westward. This left the curious branching plan seen today. The reason for this arrangement had something to do with stained glass. Lamb had to accommodate new E and W memorial windows (by

O'Connor), but he could not discard the original E window, which had been so recently donated (and which he himself had designed). Accordingly, he moved the old E window into the lengthened transept and shifted the transept wheel-window into the new cross-gable. These windows are among Lamb's best, and the tracery is both beautiful and ingenious. Still, one problem remained. The new three-light E window was narrower than the original five-light window. Lamb cusped the windowhead on the exterior so that it bells out over the former outside lights (now walled in), thereby gracefully picking up the line of the original windowhead. [ENK]

Epping, Essex
St John the Baptist

One of a distinguished group of Bodley's late parish churches, designed in 1889 and completed in stages, culminating in the tower in 1909. It was erected during one of the architect's most prolific periods and is typical of his large suburban churches demonstrating features characteristic of his late manner. Built of Bath stone, there is no chancel arch, a comparatively low and wide nave, lean-to aisles, and tall stone arcades with the arches dying into the capitals, carried nearly up to the roof plates. There is no clerestory, but the church is lit from the aisle windows and those of the E and W walls; it has a round barrel-vault divided by ribs and decorated in soft, rich colour, with painted texts in black letters running horizontally above the cornice, and there are flush end-walls, divided by buttresses. At the SE end there is a sturdy tower decorated with figures of saints with double bell-openings and triple buttresses at the level of the ringing chamber. Most of the furniture is by Bodley's last partner, Cecil Hare, and there is glass by Kempe, and by Burlison and Grylls. [ANS]

Everingham, Humberside
The Virgin Mary and St Everilda (RC)

Pugin described this remarkable building as 'a plaster imitation of Italian design'. Yet it strongly reflects both the growing confidence of English Roman Catholics in the years after Emancipation and the conservative tastes of the recusant landed class. This great classical church is unrepentantly foreign in character. The designs were indeed supplied by a Rome architect, Agostino Giorgioli, and executed by J. Harper of York in 1836–9. The basilican interior, lined with Corinthian columns and large statues of the apostles, was mostly decorated by Leopoldo Bozzoni of Carrara. The high altar was imported from Rome. Splendid organ made by Charles Allen, mounted in the W gallery. The font, contemporary with the building, is perhaps the finest piece of all. To the N of the sanctuary, a delightful side chapel with very good encaustic tiles and housing various relics. The character of the interior is rich, thoroughly ultramontane yet more sober than showy. Though always parochial in use, the church was originally attached to Everingham Hall, but the wing which linked it to the house has now been demolished. [KP]

Exeter, Devon
St David

Built in 1897–1900 to the designs of W. D. Caröe and probably his finest church. Because the ground area was restricted, its highly varied constituent masses appear dramatically compressed, most evidently in Caröe's handling of the E end exterior with its robust and angular NE tower. Internally, the generous volume of the nave, its vaulting boldly simplified to a sequence of big transverse arches, is counterpoised to narrow passage-aisles which convert the aisle arcades into a series of spatially discrete recessed bays. In keeping with the rather mannerist free Gothic of the architecture, decorative details are everywhere widely eclectic, from the Art Nouveau-influenced Perpendicular of the sanctuary to the Flemish and Renaissance exuberance of the choir-stall carving. [CB]

Exeter, Devon
St Michael and All Angels

One of a number of High Anglican buildings – including Keble College chapel – financed by William Gibbs of Tyntesfield, and built in 1865–8, this is the only major church surviving by Rhode Hawkins. Impressively massed externally, with clerestoried nave, transepts, and a tall chancel, the ensemble is dominated by the 220-foot-high crossing-tower and spire, the whole design exploiting the site on a bluff above the Exe with supreme confidence. The style is Early French, handled with a strong sense of plasticity and with some lively detail. The mural decorations and stained glass of the chancel, all 1883 by Frederick

Drake of Exeter, were a memorial to William Gibbs whose startlingly life-like effigy, carved by H. H. Armstead, occupies a canopied niche in the sanctuary. The reredos, Byzantine rather than Gothic in inspiration, was designed by W. D. Caröe and erected in 1899. [CB]

Exwick, Devon
St Andrew

On its completion in 1842, the *Ecclesiologist* pronounced St Andrew's 'the best specimen of a modern church we have yet seen'. The architect was John Hayward, at the beginning of his long career. What is important is the assurance with which Hayward manages his Gothic vocabulary. Early Decorated details are correct; proportions are authentic, giving the whole a three-dimensional solidity; structure and function are unambiguously expressed. The significance of St Andrew's lies in the fact that it is the first example of the application of Pugin's principles to an Anglican church. In 1873–5, again under Hayward, a N aisle was added, the chancel lengthened, and the interior delightfully redecorated. Many fittings of the 1840s remain, however, including the liturgically daring stone altar and reredos, both carved by Simon Rowe of Exeter, the latter with a Salviati mosaic of 1875. [CB]

Farlam, Cumbria
St Thomas à Becket (Kirkhouse Village)

This assured, 13th-century-style design is by Anthony Salvin (1860). Modest in scale, it makes craftsmanlike use of local stone and has a nave, chancel, N aisle with gables, N and S porches and a heavily buttressed bell-tower to the W. The interior is simple and intimate with fine timber roof, triple lancets to the E, and good stained glass. [TEF]

Farlington, Hampshire
St Andrew

Although shelved for fourteen years, the design of 1856 by G. E. Street was adhered to in all respects when time came to begin the new chancel in 1872. The nave was rebuilt and its lean-to N aisle added 1874–5. Though extremely small, Farlington brings to mind such works as Fawley, with which it shares the distinction of a high stone-vaulted chancel over-topping a timber-roofed nave. Here, however, the sanctuary finishes square in the English mode, and is balanced at the W end by a lead-covered roof-turret with assertive shingled broach-spire. Walls are of knapped flint with Bath stone quoins and plate tracery; smooth white clunch inside with buff free-stone arches and dressings. These two colours alternate in the ribbed chancel vault which springs from long shafts of dark marble; similar shafts enrich the chancel arch, and quatrefoil piers to the N arcade are built in layers of two different marbles. The effect is completely enchanting. Stained glass is by Clayton and Bell. [PJ]

Farnham Royal, Buckinghamshire
St Mary

One of the comparatively few churches by W. E. Nesfield, it incorporates the medieval chancel of the old church, from which he took his materials – flint, with irregular streaks of brick. His church (1867–9) is large and dignified. The grand W tower, with pyramidal roof and oddly placed clock, was built in 1876. Inside the church, the details over the arcade springings are curious. The window in the N aisle to David Roxburgh of 1868 is by Morris and Co. (SS James and Peter by Morris; St John by F. M. Brown). In the S aisle is an unusually good window by Kempe. [PH]

Fawley, Berkshire
St Mary the Virgin*

Proudly reared above a spur of the Berkshire Downs, the semicircular apse and pyramid-capped tower of Fawley bear the challenging countenance of a small Continental fortress. It is one of the finest country churches of G. E. Street's maturity, designed 1864 and built 1865–6 in a rigorous Anglo-French Geometrical style. Its broad surfaces of rough hammer-dressed Bisley Common stone are dominated by immense tiled roofs. Nave and lean-to aisles without clerestory, and a S porch, have open rafters but the dramatically heightened levels of the chancel enclose a deeply ribbed stone vault. The blunt buttressed tower clasped against the S side of the chancel forms an organ-chamber within; opposite on the N is a lean-to vestry. The motif of the towering apse, used elsewhere by Street (cf. Denstone), was probably derived from medieval examples he had seen on the steep slopes of Switzerland. Dark red-veined Devon marble piers of glorious bulk support the low arcades, and there are slim shafts of the same marble to the high chancel arch and vaulting ribs. All emphasis is directed towards the altar and pedimental stone reredos containing a Crucifixion sculpture by Thomas Earp, who also carved the narrow capitals. A bold marble-mounted pulpit and cancelli, the circular stone font, and wrought-iron grilles, make up a very complete ensemble of furnishings. The E window has glass of 1868 by William Morris and Co. [PJ]

Field Broughton, Cumbria
St Peter

'The tower,' says Hermann Muthesius of this Paley, Austin and Paley church of 1893–4, 'which sits on four wide piers in the front part of the choir, buttressed on all sides, is remarkable, giving this part of the building a large spaciousness.' The solidity of it all is emphasized by the beautifully executed stonework of the interior with arches gently dying into piers and the low corbelling out of the chancel roof-trusses. Great stepped buttresses run diagonally from the W end of the nave. Both the tower openings and the nave windows are square-headed. The tower is crowned with a shingled spire. [DM]

Filkins, Oxfordshire
St Peter*

G. E. Street's grey stone church was built in 1855–7. The steep-roofed nave, with lean-to N aisle and S porch, proudly emphasizes its asymmetrical arrangement in a W front of scrupulous elegance crowned by a tall double-tier bell-gable. An essentially English, and local Early Decorated style is put to fine effect in the chancel which terminates in a lantern-like apse, Street's earliest executed design in this intrinsically French form. Outside, the five-sided polygon, with its three long close-set tracery windows, rises by subtle modulation from the sheer curve of the apse wall-base. It makes for a strongly vertical E-end composition. The interior, impressively high and light, has plastered walls and a severe four-bay arcade with circular columns, the wide chancel arch resting on small corbelled brackets. Roofs are kept as simple as possible, arch-braced in the nave and a single prominent tie-beam and king-post in the chancel.

Most of the plain fittings are of Street's devising, the apse glass being bright Clayton and Bell of 1868. In 1879 the ribbed and boarded apse ceiling was decorated with gold stars on a blue ground, and the tiny NE vestry enlarged. [PJ]

Finsthwaite, Cumbria
St Peter*

Built in 1874 by Paley and Austin, Finsthwaite, with its low central tower and series of slate roofs sweeping down towards the ground, nestling in a gentle bowl surrounded by lakeland hills, was just what its patron, Bishop Goodwin of Carlisle, had hoped for, '. . . a style of architecture for dale churches . . . in keeping with the old mountain chapel type . . .'. Both the quadripartite vault of the tower and the chancel, with its braced-collar rafter roof, are lavishly decorated. [DM]

Fleet, Hampshire
All Saints

Extended with great care to the W in 1934, this severe red-brick church no longer has the W narthex its designer William Burges intended. Now, with the exception of its apsidal chancel and bell-cote, all is gathered under the steeply cranked slopes of its roof, but the effect of massive simplicity Burges intended in 1861 is well preserved. Also of red brick inside, the massive square piers and broad arches of its interior form a ground for stencilled decoration in cream, indigo and red of abstract motifs. The wooden ceilings are also stencilled and painted with chevrons. About the church are several works, including the founder's tomb by Burges's favourite sculptor, Thomas Nicholls. [MM]

Fleetwood, Lancashire
Chapel of St John the Baptist, Rossall School

Designed by E. G. Paley in 1861, it followed straight on from his church at Singleton. The original cruciform plan has been much altered. With the gales from the Irish Sea battering the W doors, a narthex was added by Austin and Paley in 1902 which wraps round the end of the chapel and the base of the bell-tower to allow a sheltered N entrance. The Geometrical tracery and rangework is in a dark creamy-yellow sandstone. The nave roof is divided into six bays by principal rafters sitting on corbelled Decorated colonnettes with concave double wind bracing up to the purlins and scissor rafters above. Sir Robert Lorimer added a vast War Memorial Chapel to Paley's S transept in 1923; the outstanding timber reredos by Eric Gill was inserted against Lorimer's wishes. [DM]

Fonthill Gifford, Wiltshire
Holy Trinity

This estate church by T. H. Wyatt, 1866, has a High Victorian vigour, the spire flanked by plain pyramid pinnacles, the bell-openings with squat side columns, but best of all the build-up to the tower at the E end. The elements are a round apse with buttresses breaking through the eaves of the curved roof and capped with pyramid pinnacles as on the spire, and between the apse and the tower a round stair-turret with conical roof, taking the eye from the apse roof to the spire. Richly carved interior with squat pillars and vaulted chancel. Glass by Lavers and Barraud. [JO]

Ford End, Essex
St John the Evangelist

A surprisingly grand church in an obscure hamlet, by Frederic Chancellor; consecrated 1871. The materials are deep-red brick, with limited stone dressings, inside and out. The tower has a subtle and very effective outline, rising straight to the bottom of the belfry-stage, which is marked by statues of the Evangelists set diagonally at the corners, above which there is a more complex form, ending in a short spire with a marked entasis. A tiled 'catslide' roof sweeps over the S aisle; buttresses have long gradual slopes. The polygonal chancel, not added until 1883, has been demolished. [DL]

Fort William, Highland
St Andrew (Episcopal)*

A small but exceedingly richly detailed church, designed by Alexander Ross in 1879–80. Four-bay nave with W baptistery-narthex and N porch, lower chancel and spire of Scorborough type on the N; Early Decorated tracery and Early French doorways with granite shafts. The rib-vaulted baptistery-narthex has a mosaic floor by Salviati of Venice and a spired

and figured font cover made by Harry Hems of Exeter. The doors with relief panels in the N porch and the vestry and the choir-stalls were all carved by Hems; there is a stone pulpit with dwarf granite colonnettes. Hammer-beam roofed chancel reredos with dwarf granite colonnettes framing sculptured reliefs and central mosaic by Salviati. [DW]

Fosdyke, Lincolnshire
All Saints

1871–2, by Edward Browning of Stamford. A sizeable church with a porch tower S of the S aisle. With its fiery-red brick and copper-covered broach-spire the church stands out prominently in the flat landscape near the Wash. Early English with small quatrefoil clerestory windows but larger Perpendicular windows to the aisles. S porch entrance with trefoil arch and foliage capitals, a foretaste of the interior arcades which have rich stiff-leaf capitals. [NA]

France Lynch, Gloucestershire
*St John the Baptist**

Bodley's second complete church built in 1855–7, a small village church with bell-cote over the chancel arch all in excellent stone with stone tile roofs. Two deep-set W windows with sexfoiled circle heads. The sloping site is exploited in the massing of the E end, as at Selsey. Excellent carved capitals by Earp and chancel set high with lovely inlaid marblework to the pulpit, low screen and retable. Marble font. [JO]

Freeland, Oxfordshire
*St Mary**

Commissioned from John Loughborough Pearson, the church, of local limestone, was built in 1866–9, together with the linked parsonage; the neighbouring school and master's house, completing the design, were opened in 1871. The church is the last of Pearson's vigorously High Victorian Gothic designs: the three-bay nave leads into a vaulted chancel and semicircular apse, richly decorated by Clayton and Bell. The tower is placed beside the chancel, and has a saddleback roof. Despite its vigorous outline, church, vicarage and school form a picturesque group. [AQ]

Fylingdales, North Yorkshire
*St Stephen**

Exposed on the bleak moors' edge above Robin Hood's Bay, G. E. Street's large jagged church discharges its most effective broadside from the SE. The composition is gaunt, monochrome and fearless, in a laconic Early Decorated style embracing lancets and circles, plate and bar tracery. Designed in 1867–8, it was built 1868–70 in dark local stone. The bluff nave with lean-to S aisle and porch has only a narrow S clerestory, compensated for on the N by extremely long uplifted windows. It bears a lofty timber roof with tie-beams and king-posts and is pierced by a four-bay S arcade, whose octagonal columns with naturalistic carved caps foil the massively plain chancel arch. From low clasping buttresses, the S tower rises straight and stern to a steep saddleback top outside the E bay of the aisle, which is itself compromised within by a transverse strainer wall. Deeply rib-vaulted in stone, the chancel resolves into a buttressed semicircular apse and has its N organ-chamber balanced on the S by a short lean-to aisle, then for vestry a sharp-gabled outer S aisle running up against the tower-face. Angularity is the prevailing theme here. Sober furnishings are all of wood except the font; glass is by Powell of Whitefriars 1875 onwards, to designs of Henry Holiday. [PJ]

Galston, Strathclyde
St Sophia (RC)

Pioneer Neo-Byzantine church with matching presbytery house designed by Rowand Anderson for Lord Bute, 1885–6. Banded red brick, short cross-plan with aisles forming a simple rectangle, gable front with circular window and low circular crossing-tower with conical tiled roof. Plain domed interior; the planned mosaics and frescoes were never provided. [DW]

Gerrards Cross, Buckinghamshire
St James

A church (consecrated 1859) that demands attention more for its eccentricity than its merits. It was commissioned by two maiden ladies as a memorial to their brother, and they chose Sir William Tite as their architect because he had been a friend of the deceased. Tite adopted a vaguely Italian-Byzantine style with a campanile attached to the W front and an octagonal

dome with Gothic dormers over the crossing. The material is white brick with carefully contrived coloured bricks in the blank arches of the exterior. Flanking the dome are four turrets with concave-sided roofs. The original W door has been replaced by a window. Inside, the church has lost all its original decoration and furniture. The only dominant features are the four thick columns of porphyry-coloured scagliola with foliage capitals upon which the crossing rests. [IRS]

Giggleswick, North Yorkshire
School Chapel

This implausible edifice, whose green copper dome is a striking landmark up on its rocky knob in the Ribblesdale fells, was built in 1897–1901 to the design of Sir T. G. Jackson. The dome was suggested by the donor, Walter Morrison, because of his interest in Palestine, and Jackson relished the chance to combine it with Decorated Perpendicular Gothic. The chapel, in red and yellow stone, is tall, and the stumpy chancel and transepts only project slightly. The dome (over the crossing) is made of Pulham's terracotta, and is covered with mosaics designed by George Murray and made by Powell's, while the arches supporting it are decorated with sgraffito. The lavish furnishings include woodwork all in Argentinian cedar, glass by Burlison and Grylls, and excellent bronze figures of Edward VI and Victoria by Sir George Frampton. [PH]

Glasgow, Strathclyde
Barony Church (Church of Scotland)*

Built in 1886–90 to designs by Sir John Burnet which had won a competition assessed by J. L. Pearson. Red-sandstone Early Pointed, nave with a Dunblane front and a single transept on the E flank, and narrower presbytery following the Gerona arrangement rising high above the halls which flank it on the E and return transversely across the N gable to end in a small gatehouse. Bold porches at the SE and in the angle of the transept, bold buttresses at the gables, no tower, only an elaborate flèche over the crossing. Impressive interior, circular piers with the arch-mouldings dying into them in the nave, clustered piers and tall ring-shafted lancets in the presbytery, all with open timber roofs; rich triple-arched reredos added 1900, still to Burnet's design. [DW]

Glasgow, Strathclyde
former Barony North, now *Evangelical Church**

Italian Renaissance by John Honeyman, 1878–80, proudly Corinthian outside and in. Rectangular concert-hall plan with gallery on three sides, raised high on basement hall, and a pilastered apsidal stairhall at N end. Semi-symmetrical frontage to Cathedral Square, channelled lower tier and corner entrance-bays with pedimented niches carried up as towers. The five-arched windows at gallery level are framed by attached columns which break forward from pilasters to bear statuary on the balustraded parapet. The N tower is carried up as a tall Corinthian pilastered octagonal belfry with domelet and cupola. [DW]

Glasgow, Strathclyde
Belhaven-Westbourne Church

Italian Renaissance by John Honeyman 1880. Nave and aisles front with two-tier portico of coupled columns, Corinthian over Ionic, channelled lower tier extending into arched and pilastered hall frontage. Set-back flanking towerlets with arched top stages and ogee roofs. Galleried concert-hall type interior with coffered ceiling, now dominated by later organ-case by Whytock and Reid. [DW]

Glasgow, Strathclyde
Caledonia Road Church (formerly Church of Scotland)*

Only the ruined S end of the church now remains. It was designed by Alexander Thomson, 1856, in his characteristic Neo-Greek on an acute-angled corner site. Severe asymmetrical composition, the main body of church rectangular and galleried with window pilastrades down each flank at the upper level. The lower tier has banded pseudo-isodomic masonry on a cyclopean plinth; a blind vestibule with door-pieces at each end projects to form the podium of the hexastyle Ionic temple front above. Tall flanking tower of banded masonry, stepped back to a battered clock-stage at the top; pilastraded hall of triangular plan fills the remainder of the site. Tragically, the church was gutted by fire in 1965. Formerly it had richly stencilled temple roof, gallery and impressive organ-case with couch and box lectern-pulpit on a high stepped dais. [DW]

Glasgow, Strathclyde
Camphill, Queen's Park Church (Church of Scotland)*

Normandy Gothic, built 1875–6: William Leiper's second major church, still on a preaching church plan, but now at least with masonry rather than cast-iron arcades; three wide bays, well-detailed quatrefoil piers with stiff-leaf capitals supporting the galleries and a good roof. Impressive E gable-front with triple portals and twin windows treated as a single large window with a fine angel with outstretched wings carved by John Mossman at the spandrel area. Big 195-foot-high spire modelled on those in and around Caen. Central pulpit set in a chancel arch-like recess; stepped triple lancets behind with glass by Daniel Cottier whose mural decoration has unfortunately been painted out: at the roof his gold sunflowers still blossom. [DW]

Glasgow, Strathclyde
Dowanhill Church (formerly Church of Scotland)*

The result of a competition win by William Leiper 1864–5, then lately returned from the office of J. L. Pearson in London. Still a conventional preaching church internally, a rectangle with galleries under a wide single-span hammer-beam roof, the span of its roof masked by gablets down the flanks and a 195-foot spire. Excellent stone pulpit set high under a canopy with flanking arches, rose window above, all set in a chancel arch-like recess, glass by Cottier and decoration by Andrew M. Wells. Secularized. [DW]

Glasgow, Strathclyde
Govan Old Parish Church (Church of Scotland)*

A large Early Pointed ship-builders' church on an ancient site, more impressive within than without, designed by Sir R. Rowand Anderson in 1883–4. It was his first large Presbyterian church and is of unusual interest as a pioneer attempt to reconcile preaching church requirements with the more liturgical form of arrangement sought by the rising generation of Established Church ministers. Tall, wide nave with a gable front of stepped lancets over the deeply moulded doorway set in double arches, very tall buttressed clerestory rising from blind unbuttressed passage-aisles, lower and narrower choir in

Gerona arrangement with gable based on Pluscarden N transept. Brick-lined interior banded with stone dressings, moulded arcades dying into splayed piers without capitals, tall shafted clerestory windows, tied hammer-beam roof boarded into a trefoiled profile. On the W flank of the nave the two northmost bays open into a tall gallery to provide upper seating opposite the pulpit; in the chancel (lengthened to same design 1911) the S two bays open into another gallery to house the organ. The later N bay is of very unusual design, lit through the tribune with a blind clerestory area above. Flanking the choir on the W is a large chapel. [DW]

Glasgow, Strathclyde
Kelvingrove (originally *Finnieston*) *Church*

Neo-Greek church by James Sellars 1877–8, in both plan and elevation an update of late Georgian Greek Revival. Rectangular plan with fluted Ionic tetrastyle portico, tall Corinthian-columned octagonal cupola with Thomsonesque openwork screens rising from a skilfully stepped podium to the rear of the pediments, five-bay pilastrades between solid end-bays with pedimented windows on the flanks, banded masonry at the lower level. The internal finishings are of a very high order: gallery front on Ionic columns and drum-shaped pulpit in front of a panelled screen with anthemion detail. The church is now used as a recording studio. [DW]

Glasgow, Strathclyde
Hillhead Church, Kelvinside (Church of Scotland)

A tall Sainte Chapelle-type church designed by James Sellars in 1875–7. Undivided nave with three-light windows and polygonal apse; bold gable front, double doorway of four orders and Chartres-type wheel-window with angle spandrels set in a giant arch clasped between octagonal turrets of Normandy Gothic inspiration. Interior rib-vaulted in timber, furnishing remodelled 1921 and later, but two major windows by Cottier and one by Burne-Jones. [DW]

Glasgow, Strathclyde
Lansdowne Church (Church of Scotland)*

John Honeyman's first really large church in Glasgow, built in 1862–3, ashlar-faced Early English, richly shafted and dog-toothed, with sculpture by James Shanks and William Mossman. Nave with low aisles and very tall clerestory, transepts and semicircular apse, triple lancets at the gable fronts, those at the W gable stepped over the vaulted slab-roofed porch. A very slim spire, 218 feet high, links to the triple-lancet hall gable E of the transept. Internally the planning is very unusual. The body of the church has a straightforward Presbyterian arrangement with cantilevered galleries, but the outer pews are entered by doors from the aisles, screened off as foyers for the very well-to-do. Semicircular barrel-ceiling, vaulted apse originally containing a central pulpit, the ribs sprung from corbelled and clustered shafts of red marble; the stained glass in the lancet lights is by Ward and Hughes. [DW]

Glasgow, Strathclyde
Queen's Cross Church (formerly Church of Scotland)

By Charles Rennie Mackintosh, designed 1896, built 1898–9. Neo-Perpendicular in red sandstone; compact plan, wide nave and narrower shallow chancel at W flanked by a short steeply battered SW tower with an octagonal stair-turret based on Merriot Church, Somerset. Nave aisled on S, the two bays next the tower treated as a double transept with a gallery, two bays with low aisle and flying buttress to clerestory, stair-porch at E bay, all very individually detailed. Interior has pointed barrel-ceiling with steel tie-beams, square piers at aisle and gallery, vertically boarded panelling and pulpit; the rood-beam has unfortunately been removed but is currently being replaced. [DW]

Glasgow, Strathclyde
St Mary's Cathedral (Episcopal)*

Early English, by Sir George Gilbert Scott, 1870–1, built as an ambitious cruciform parish church with tower and spire in the S angle of nave and chancel. Nave with clerestory of cusped circular lights set in blind arcading, piers of arcades alternately octagonal and quatrefoil. Plate-traceried three-light windows at transepts, stepped triple lancet at E end. King-post roofs rise from triple wall-shafts except at the crossing which is rib-vaulted. The furnishings are original except for the oak reredos, replaced by Sir Robert Lorimer; glass by Hardman (1880), Clayton and Bell, and Heaton, Butler and Bayne. [DW]

Glasgow, Strathclyde
St Vincent Street Church (now Free Church)*

Designed by Alexander Thomson late in 1856, built 1857–9. Inspired by descriptions of the Solomonic temple, and conceived as a clerestoried hexastyle Ionic temple with flanking pilastraded aisles and porticoes at both ends, all set on a colossal podium rising from a steeply sloping site. The tall tower of banded masonry rises into a dwarf peristyle with a pierced and pointed top with detail of mixed Middle Eastern and possibly Indian character. Vestibule in podium under N portico. Ingenious plan, the Ionic temple structure housing only the upper church from back gallery level with the rake of the gallery and the main floor contained within the topmost tier of the podium. Superb iron-columned interior with capitals, temple roof and tiered dais with organ-case similar to Caledonia Road. The Pompeian red and biscuit colour-scheme is original, though not that intended by the architect. [DW]

Glasgow, Strathclyde
Wellington Church (Church of Scotland)*

The so-called Presbyterian Madeleine, designed by Thomas Lennox Watson, an ex-assistant of Waterhouse's, in 1883–4. Hexastyle portico of fluted Corinthian columns, the sloping bank of the elevated site exploited to create an arrangement of steps and podia on the model of Wilkins's London University College; recessed colonnades sheltering round-arched windows down the flanks, two-storeyed hall-annexe with pilastraded windows in the Thomson–Sellars manner at the rear. Spacious galleried interior, 60 feet by 90, roofed in a single span with longitudinal girders 7 feet deep, with segmental tunnel-vaults between them, that of the central division extending into a narrow S bay and into a semi-domed apse containing a pulpit and an organ-case at the N end. [DW]

Goathland, North Yorkshire
St Mary

This sturdy little gritstone church of 1894–6 is well suited to its situation on the North Yorkshire moors. The architect was Walter H. Brierley, better known as a domestic architect. Plain Perpendicular, it has a low tower set over the choir. Inside there is good simple timberwork in roofs and fittings. [PH]

Gosport, Hampshire
Our Lady of the Sacred Heart (RC)

Designed by a little-known architect named Phillips in 1855, the church and presbytery present an undistinguished façade to the High Street, but behind lies an attractive and ingenious interior. Beyond a narthex-like space below a gallery at the W end, a nave and S aisle lead to a sanctuary flanked by chapels having polygonal apsidal ends and delicately moulded plaster ceilings. [MM]

Grafham, Surrey
St Andrew

Grafham church was designed and built in 1860–1 by Henry Woodyer for himself (he lived here). Within a small compass it shows the originality of his architectural personality to the full. As at Hascombe nearby, there are two cells, a nave and an apsidal chancel, but here with a vestry on the N side under a continuation of the slope of the roof. The bell-cote at the W end of the nave roof this time has an exaggeratedly tall conical spire. It is endearingly playful rather than vigorous and earnest in the High Victorian way. The trefoiled heads of the chancel windows rise into charming dormers above the eaves. The interior is contrastingly rich. A tripartite screen of timber fills the chancel arch and it carries painted texts and foliage, with a rood and saints above. The chancel roof has tightly spaced rafters forming polygonal arches that turn round the apse. The E window, set within a vaulted niche and with the usual Hardman glass, is embraced by the reredos, which is carved and painted with angels and vines extending from the cross as though they were growing from it. On the outside the window is contained within a massive buttress. It is highly characteristic of the way Woodyer looked forward to the Arts and Crafts style of the following decades. There is an attractive font, but the most poignant decoration is carved over the sedilia. As Gordon Barnes discovered, it consists of portrait busts of Woodyer and his wife. She has a halo, for she had died after giving birth to the daughter whom Woodyer called his Chick. And indeed between the two busts is a nest with a chick in it, and an ear of wheat, a rebus for Woodyer. [AQ]

Great Bourton, Oxfordshire
All Saints

After the Reformation the 13th-century church of this attractive village became a school, two houses, and a shop. In 1863 it was rebuilt as a church by William White. Old work includes most of the chancel, and the W wall of the nave. White's work, which is sympathetic and quietly idiosyncratic, includes the arcade, font, pulpit, reredos, stalls, and tiled floor. What makes the church memorable is the spiffing lychgate-cum-belfry at the SW corner of the church-yard, built by White in 1882. [PH]

Greenham, Berkshire
St Mary*

Though small, Greenham church is a fine example of Henry Woodyer's work. Built in flint in 1875–6, it has lancet windows rather than his favourite Decor-ated. A S porch was added in 1883. The vertical effect of the windows is emphasized by the extremely steep, gabled roof of the W bell-cote. Beneath it is an unusually arranged baptistery, which Woodyer added in 1895–6 with a square font and pyramidal cover, and marble shafts carrying a pair of arches opening into the nave. His N aisle, with its arcade of stumpy marble columns, is an addition of 1892. The decoration of the chancel arch and the walls of the chancel with stencilling and painted figures of saints and biblical scenes was completed in 1890. The arch-braced timber roof is again painted. The carved marble reredos is Woodyer's design. [AQ]

Greenock, Strathclyde
St Paul (Church of Scotland)

Largest and best of Sir Rowand Anderson's later churches, designed 1890. Finely detailed red-sand-stone Late Decorated, tall and wide clerestoried nave with blind passage-aisles, lean-to narthex clasped between buttresses with sculptured frieze of angels and stone roof continuous with sill of W window which has central buttress mullion. Lower and nar-rower chancel with undercroft flanked by double-gabled aisle on S and unfinished tower on N, E gable with big octagonal pinnacles. Brick-lined Gerona-plan interior on the Govan model with W window by Douglas Strachan. [DW]

Hailey, Oxfordshire
St John the Evangelist

In 1866 the Revd G. C. Rolfe appointed as architect for the building of a new church his own twenty-one-year-old son, Clapton Crabb Rolfe. His first design was too eccentric for the diocesan architect, G. E. Street, and the church was built in 1868–9 to a revised, but still remarkably original, scheme. In 13th-century style, it has nave, well-raised chancel, and narrow N aisle. The NW bell-turret is delightfully cranky. The windows are groups of plain lancets. The interior is well detailed, including iron lamps, font, and sanctuary tiles. [PH]

Halifax, West Yorkshire
All Souls, Haley Hill*

'On the whole, my best church', wrote Sir George Gilbert Scott of All Souls, while the Ecclesiologist reckoned it 'among the most remarkable churches of the revival'. The church was built between 1856 and 1859 by Edward Akroyd, a local millowner and sometime Member of Parliament, as the crowning feature of his model village of Akroydon. It stands high above the town and the densely packed mills, proclaiming the revived splendours of the Established Church in a town where Dissent was strong. Scott's budget was virtually unlimited and, while the exterior, with the second tallest spire in Yorkshire, is rich and imposing, a vision of revived 13th-century splendour, the interior is a veritable treasure-house of church art. It is richly embellished with carved ornament (largely by J. Birnie Philip) and marble shafts, with fittings by Scott's favoured craftsmen. Birnie Philip executed the gorgeous pulpit, with its Cosmatesque panels, and the reredos. The woodwork is by Rattee and Kett, the metalwork by Skidmore, the painted decoration by Clayton and Bell (partly executed by H. Stacy Marks) and the tiles by Minton. The stained glass is of outstanding quality and includes E and W windows by Hardman, W window of the S aisle by Wailes and the clerestory lights by Clayton and Bell. All Souls, recently threatened with demolition but now vested in the Redundant Churches Fund and being repaired by a voluntary trust, represents Scott's vision of the ideal parish church. [KP]

Halkyn, Clwyd
St Mary*

Finely placed on the hillside overlooking the Dee estuary, this noble church was commissioned by the 1st Duke of Westminster from John Douglas. Built in 1878, it is superbly massed, the stout tower, with pyramidal roof, at the SW. The spacious interior has characteristically fine oak woodwork in roofs and fittings. The unusual monochrome (or grisaille) glass, delicately painted, is by Heaton, Butler and Bayne. [PH]

Hallow, Hereford and Worcester
SS Philip and James*

This surprisingly grand church by W. J. Hopkins dates from 1867–9, though the tower was not added until 1879. The stone broach-spire (150 feet high) was completed in 1900. Outside and in, the church, in the style of c. 1300, is of red sandstone with white stone tracery, capitals and carvings. The clerestory has varied patterns within circles. The curious stone flyers coming down across the aisles are explained inside: they support stone transverse arches. The interior is tall, light and colourful. The well-raised chancel has an effective reredos – an almost life-size Crucifixion scene (by R. Boulton of Cheltenham). The font (by Forsyth) has strips of stylized lilies of the valley in what looks like Ashford marblework. [PH]

Hanley Swan, Hereford and Worcester
Our Lady and St Alphonsus*

This delightful little church stands out in the country, in what was once the park of Blackmore Park, seat of T. C. Hornyold (of an old recusant family), at the expense of whose nephew and prospective heir, John Vincent Gandolfi, it was built in 1844–6. The architect was Charles Hansom, but it was his patron, Bishop Ullathorne, who suggested that the nave should be closely based upon the famous Early English church at Skelton, near York, and that the chancel should be a more elaborate Decorated, as being the more sacred part. The nave is rib-vaulted in plaster, as Skelton had been since 1818. The church happily retains its carved altars with reredoses, rood-screen, parclose-screens, font and painted decoration. The metalwork, including coronae, crucifixes, candle-sticks, and sanctuary lamp, was made by Hardman to the designs of Pugin, who also designed the splendid tiled floor (by Minton). The stained glass – all original – is by Wailes. The gabled presbytery (built for a community of Redemptorists) is linked to the church by a cloister, forming a picturesque group. [PH]

Hartlepool, Cleveland
Christ Church*

By E. B. Lamb, 1850, and at the time of its construction the most imposing structure in this explosively developing port town. A massively austere First Pointed design dominated by a ponderous tower, a sheer block of stone which rises directly over the W entrance and terminates in a strange, off-centre pinnacle. Lamb deviated from the conventional Gothic Revival church-plan of long, narrow nave and aisles, providing instead a Latin cross whose crossing seems to expand laterally into the transepts and diagonally into the corner bays, so that a strong central focus is developed which is quite at variance with the axiality of the nave. Today, the church is deconsecrated and stripped of almost all of its furnishings and stained glass. It is owned by the Grey Museum and Art Gallery, which plans to convert it to exhibition space. [ENK]

West Hartlepool, Cleveland
St Paul

Founded by former members of Christ Church, who had seceded from Lamb's parish church, this tall red-brick church was designed to great effect in 1885–6 by C. Hodgson Fowler, an ecclesiastical specialist. It consists of a tower, nave, lean-to aisles, chancel, vestries, and fine Lady Chapel. Inside, the red-brick gloom is vast and dignified. [LW]

Hascombe, Surrey
St Peter*

This is an excellent little church, built by Henry Woodyer in 1863–4. It has a nave with a S porch and a separate S chapel, and a lower apsidal chancel. The body of the church is treated in the simplest way, accented by very tall, narrow lancets, unusual for Woodyer, but most effective here. Set off against these are the porch, the chapel and shingled bell-turret. The turret is placed at the W end of the nave roof, and has three tiny openings on each face under an equally diminutive, but heavily overhanging broach-spire. The chapel, originally the squire's pew, is separately roofed and has prominent buttresses. Its E window has contrasting Decorated tracery, and the lancets in the flank wall are distinctively set under relieving arches linked by a string-course. The complete scheme of decoration inside is equally convincing and contrastingly rich, especially in the chancel. Its roof has closely spaced, gilded rafters, cusped to form a trefoiled section that turns round the apse. Rising into this roof in the centre of the apse is a panelled reredos, painted with saints and pierced by a trefoiled opening for the E lancet window. It is an extraordinarily inventive way of uniting wall, roof, reredos and window, all wonderfully adorned by Hardman and Powell with sombre paint and bright glass. The E lancet alone has glass by Clayton and Bell. [AQ]

Hastings, East Sussex
Holy Trinity

Holy Trinity by S. S. Teulon is in the words of the *Ecclesiologist* 'a bold adaptation to an awkward site'. The lack of the intended tower is unfortunate but the use of intricate, Flamboyant tracery and the enriched apse modelled on that of St Pierre at Caen and the fountain of 1862 at the E end, also by Teulon, make the exterior very busy. Romaine-Walker enriched the interior in the late 19th century and Thomas Earp who had been Teulon's carver was brought back in 1889–90 to carve twenty-two angels on the face of the chancel arch. [MS]

Hastings, East Sussex
St Mary Star of the Sea (RC)

A steeply sloping site adds considerably to the visual impact of this flint church, especially the buttressed apsidal E end with circular capped bell-turret rising prominently above the Bourne. The poet Coventry Patmore promoted the church in 1882, intending to make it a memorial to his second wife. The architect was his friend Basil Champneys. It is a convincing and richly furnished essay in the Perpendicular style. [DRE]

Hastings, East Sussex
St Peter

A large red-brick church with transepts by James Brooks who was at one time Diocesan architect for Canterbury. St Peter's was erected in 1884–5 and the style is Early English with lancets and plate tracery. There is a polygonal vaulted baptistery with conical roof at the NW corner. The brick interior has bold arcading, and the chancel is richly faced with alabaster. The striking reredos has a centrepiece based on the Volto Santo Crucifix at Lucca Cathedral. [DRE]

Hatherop, Gloucestershire
*St Nicholas**

Stone church built 1854–5 by Henry Clutton, distinguished mainly by the central tower with a steep saddleback roof, good tracery and heavily carved font. E window by O'Connor. What makes the church remarkable is the SE chapel in memory of Lady de Mauley who died in 1844. This is apparently by William Burges, Clutton's partner at the time. It has a French Gothic feel with rich pierced parapet and a splendid S doorway, the pointed arch starting low down and richly carved. Inside, a stone vault and beautifully carved stone frieze set low so that the deep ribs of the vault dominate. Lady de Mauley's effigy, by Raffaelle Monti (1848), is carved in the most natural detail. [JO]

Haugham, Lincolnshire
All Saints

A charming and unusually complete Gothick church, still Georgian in feel. It was built in 1840–1 by George Willoughby of Louth. W. A. Nicholson has also been named as the architect, and at nearby Biscathorpe the two worked together, so might also have done so here. Red-brick, cement-rendered, with Perpendicular-style tracery, battlements, crocketed pinnacles and a spire with openwork flying buttresses just like a miniature version of the famous spire at Louth. The interior has a plaster ceiling, pictorial stained glass and all its original fittings, including pews with cast-iron poppy-heads. [NA]

Haughton Green, Greater Manchester
St Anne

1874–6. Medland and Henry Taylor were 'rogue' architects. Their highly original style progressed from the bold and lumpy to later work combining High Victorian constructional ideals with all the decorative exuberance of the Art Nouveau. From Teulon, Medland absorbed an uncompromising vigour and sense of composition. St Anne is perhaps his most interesting church because it largely uses timber framing and gains its internal and external effect from a John Douglas-like concentration on roof forms. There are extraordinary traceried windows and a build-up of roof surfaces to the climax of an odd, perhaps funny, tile-clad tower and spire. [DB]

Havering-atte-Bower, Greater London
St John the Evangelist

Notable for its position beside a surprisingly unspoiled village green on the edge of suburban London, this is an early work of Basil Champneys, 1875–8, having much High Victorian hardness in its mottled flintwork (not a particularly local material) and Decorated windows; but the flanking tower, with a passageway through it at ground level, suggests something of the later, arty, Champneys, especially the three niches over the passageway and the perforated parapet. [DL]

Hawkhurst, Kent
All Saints

The church was built by G. G. Scott in yellow sandstone in 1861. In presenting the SE tower and broached spire as a fine landmark to the S, Scott neglected the approach from the road and the tower is not visible as we enter by the high-pitched NW porch as though by the tradesmen's entrance. Inside there is a broad nave with aisles of four bays on round piers and a chancel, darkened by Clayton and Bell's glass of *c.* 1861. There is Frenchy foliage on the capitals and bits of it are tucked here and there – even in the porch and on the font – as though it is harvest festival. [REH]

Hawkley, Hampshire
*SS Peter and Paul**

When S. S. Teulon rebuilt the medieval church at Hawkley in 1865 he gave the village an extraordinary design, Norman in its internal detailing but not in its composition and with a helm-roofed tower copied directly from the great Saxon exemplar at Sompting in Sussex. [MS]

Healey, North Yorkshire
St Paul

By E. B. Lamb, 1845–8; his first significant church. Many features show Lamb unexpectedly in sympathy with Puginian goals, such as the use of Decorated tracery motifs for windows and altar-rail, the sturdy open timber roof, the impressively plain wood furniture, and the exposed stone walling of the interior. Still, there is much here that is only Lamb's. The overscaled buttresses and supporting arches of the tower perform their structural roles with a thoroughly characteristic swagger, while the crudely hacked trefoil windows of the porch herald a vein of fierce primitivism. And the tight cruciform plan, with its spectacular shaft-like lantern tower, evinces an unsurpassed genius for spatial drama. The church's original furnishings are well preserved, including nave-seats, choir-stalls, pulpit, altar-rail, and font. All these are by Lamb, as is the stained-glass window bearing his cypher (and the date 1848) on the N side. The W window also probably by Lamb, the E by his frequent patron, Sir Robert Frankland-Russell. [ENK]

Heckmondwike, West Yorkshire
Upper Independent Chapel

This monumental classical building, now abandoned and facing an uncertain future, is the masterpiece of an obscure local architect, Arthur Stott, 1890. The façade, consisting of a grand portico between two towers, is as much municipal as ecclesiastical in character. The interior is perhaps the most striking Nonconformist auditorium remaining in Yorkshire: enormous galleries, organ in excellent case, fine woodwork, particularly in the elevated pulpit. The effect is again somewhat secular, like the concert hall of a great town hall. The chapel is surrounded by an evocative, vandalized graveyard. [KP]

Helperthorpe, North Yorkshire
St Peter

Designed 1870–1, this is the fourth and arguably the finest of the group of churches by G. E. Street for Sir Tatton Sykes. Built of Whitby stone, 1871–3, it is set above the village, surrounded by a churchyard wall with stone archway. Street's graceful building, in Early Decorated style, is given a distinctive profile by raising the square chancel slightly above nave level. A SW porch, NE boiler chimney, and as few buttresses as possible disturb the continuous wall-planes, but an odd projection on the S side lends extra room for the pulpit within. Left entirely unbuttressed, the W tower shows to the S a big off-centre stair-turret topped by a gabled statue-niche; belfry lights are filled with pierced panelling, and the low stone spire encircled with gables is massively broached – not in the conventional pyramid form, rather the splayed-off variety used in timber construction. Deeply revealed windows have simple bar tracery. Internally, the long rectangular plan yields an astonishing sequence of spatial effects. The nave roof has wide ogee arch-braces framing a strung chancel arch which disappears into the walls high up. Yet higher up, the steep chancel ceiling is panelled and slopes out of sight; all roofs received rich, painted decorations by Clayton and Bell. Beyond a low wrought-iron screen, the chancel floor ascends by eight steps to the altar and arcaded stone reredos. The elevated five-light E window has glass by Burlison and Grylls – a replacement of 1893 when Temple Moore added the over-refined N aisle and enlarged the vestry. [PJ]

Hereford, Hereford and Worcester
St Francis Xavier (RC)

In 1837–8 the Jesuits built this remarkable church, designed by Charles Day of Worcester. The stuccoed front, based on the Treasury of the Athenians at Delphi, has two Doric columns *in antis* and a pediment. Short towers were planned but not built. The inside is plain, but has a coved ceiling. Over the altar is a glazed dome. The impressive altar and tabernacle (the latter based on Bernini's in St Peter's) are by J. J. Scoles, *c.* 1850. [PH]

Hetton-le-Hole, Tyne and Wear
St Nicholas

This church, designed and built in 1898–1901 by the Sunderland architect, Stephen Piper, reflects the population growth in the heart of the Durham coalfield. The cosy gabled street-front belies the very large and very plain interior, barrel-vaulted throughout, which includes a baptistery and a morning chapel. [LW]

Heversham, Cumbria
St Peter

Although principally the rebuilding of an earlier church, with the only one major new work being a bold W tower in a convincing Early English style, this job of 1867–71 was Hubert James Austin's first job in partnership with E. G. Paley. [DM]

High Legh, Cheshire
St John

High Legh had two halls, E and W, both now demolished, and each had a chapel. The chastely Ionic chapel of West Hall, by Thomas Harrison (1814–16), was burnt in 1891. In 1893 it was rebuilt as the parish church by Edmund Kirby, in a picturesque mixture of half-timber, brick, and red tiles. Most windows have wooden tracery. The quaint W tower has two gables, one above the other, below the tiled spirelet. The narthex opens right up into the tower. The light and colourful interior is lined with brick, and has a good timber roof, supported on timber uprights. [PH]

Higham, Suffolk
St Stephen

Higham was a small hamlet without a church until 1861 when Robert Barclay commissioned G. G. Scott senior to design St Stephen's. A small church with a delightful round 'Suffolk' tower, with a conical roof set back behind a plain parapet above the arcaded bell-stage. Nave with N aisle, chancel and S porch, all in local flint with Ancaster stone dressings and some brick polychromatic details over the windows. The style is Early English, with plate tracery; the E window inside is shafted with shaft rings and dog-tooth in the arch. The ground stage of the tower is a rib-vaulted baptistery, the ribs supported on wall-shafts and leaf corbels. [NA]

Higher Walton (Warrington), Cheshire
St John the Evangelist

This small estate church with its magnificent central crossing-tower and spire was built between 1882 and 1885 by Paley and Austin. The tower is decorated with a whole band of diapering with flushwork below. Internally, the carefully cut mouldings of the red-sandstone walls and crossing-tower vault are beautifully contrasted with the painted timber panels of the nave. [DM]

Highnam, Gloucestershire
*Holy Innocents**

This sumptuous church was Henry Woodyer's first masterpiece. It was built in 1849–51 for the artist Thomas Gambier Parry. The plan is traditional, with W tower, aisled nave with S porch, and chancel with a S chapel; to its N is a highly complex arrangement of vestries. The style is Decorated. The 200-foot steeple, the lofty nave, the lavish carving, the tiled chancel, the stained glass, the wall painting and even the ironwork of the doors rival the best of Pugin's. Pugin in fact designed the glass made by Hardman in the S aisle, and there is more fine glass by Clayton and Bell (E window) and by Wailes of Newcastle (N aisle). The glory of the church is the wall painting. It is by Gambier Parry himself, executed over a long period from 1850 to 1871. He had invented a process called 'spirit fresco', which he used here to good effect. It has proved itself and allows his colours to glow nearly as richly today as when new. The chancel arch has a magnificent Last Judgement; and the Expulsion from Paradise, the Annunciation and the Entry into Jerusalem are shown elsewhere. Eastlake (*Gothic Revival*) called the church 'scholarlike' and 'genuine', but it has greater qualities, notably the extraordinarily fiery passion that Pugin and the Ecclesiologists could arouse in the 1840s. [AQ]

Hildenborough, Kent
St John the Evangelist

Ewan Christian was the most prolific designer of Kent's churches and Hildenborough represents his debut of 1843. It is an Early English project in sandstone with variegated tiled roofs, a broached SE spire with lucarnes and lancets throughout. The interior affords a broad uninterrupted preaching space, transepts and chancel beneath a great arch-braced roof. The church was restored in 1896 by F. W. Hunt and the nave was extended by one bay. The St John Evangelist window in the S transept is brilliant red by Burne-Jones 1881 and the Joy window in the N transept is by Morris 1876. [REH]

Hitchin, Hertfordshire
Holy Saviour, Radcliffe Road

By William Butterfield, 1863–5; aisles added 1880 (N) and 1882 (S); W façade to street with bell-cote. The interior is little spoiled, despite a new central altar, and whitening of the chancel inter-war by Martin Travers. The arcades are distinctive (were they designed from the start, with aisles to be added later?), springing, without capitals, from square, hollow-chamfered piers of alternate brick and stone; the wall surfaces in the spandrels have geometrical patterns in buff brick on a red background, with some black. Tall clerestory; simple scissors-beam roof; nice iron screen behind the new altar. Glass in the N aisle by Hardman. [DL]

Hoar Cross, Staffordshire
*Holy Angels**

The architects who pre-eminently realized the Pugi-nian ideal defined by scholarship and refinement were Bodley and Garner who brought it to the most sumptuous pitch of expression in the church of the Holy Angels, Hoar Cross. Built as a votive offering and memorial to her husband by the Hon. Emily Meynall Ingram in 1872–1900, it was conceived regardless of expense as an estate church for a small congregation. Standing among trees in a level church-yard close to her park gates 'it rises in the mellow harmony of warm red sandstone'. It has a massive square tower with deeply recessed faces, set on the crossing of a cruciform plan, elaborated at the E end by a complicated sequence of chapels and sacristies. The chancel is higher than the nave and forms the climax of the building. Within all is harmony and sensual, limpid beauty, 'the fervid almost passionate, realisation of an ideal . . . a visionary rehabilitation of the ancient glories of the Church'. Bodley and Garner worked closely on the design and later described it as 'the fruit of first enthusiasm'. Bodley was responsible for the stained glass and colour, Garner for the carved ornament in stone and wood; the plan, proportions and form they designed together. The exquisite furniture includes paintings, vestments and ornaments acquired abroad by the foundress, yet assimilated with the same effortless taste and distinction that governs the architects' own work. [ANS]

Hoarwithy, Hereford and Worcester
*St Catherine**

This idyllic village in the winding Wye valley owes its distinction to the remarkable beautification of the church carried out between about 1874 and 1903 by J. P. Seddon at the sole expense of the Revd William Poole, Vicar of Hentland with Hoarwithy for forty-six years. The church Poole found was 'a neat modern brick building' of 1843, with round-headed windows, perched up on the steep hillside above the village. The window-shapes prompted the choice of what Pevsner calls 'the South Italian Romanesque and semi-Byzantine style'. Seddon added the campanile, and the apse flanked by half-apses at the E end. The approach to the church is up steps, under the campanile, and along a loggia on the S side of the church. Inside, at the E end, four grey Devonshire marble columns with Byzantine capitals support an inner cupola. The E apse has a Pantocrator in gold mosaic. The pavements are of mosaic. All the capitals are richly carved. G. E. Fox (who also worked at Eastnor and Longleat) was responsible for the decoration. The ambo is in Cosmatesque work. The stalls (1883) and prayer-desk (1884) were carved by Harry Hems of Exeter in oak from Poole's estate with figures of saints and scriptural subjects. The stained glass is interesting: the best is in one of the N windows, designed *c.* 1880 by H. A. Kennedy, a pupil of Seddon, and made by S. Belham and Co. One W window is by H. G. Murray for Belham's, 1890. Seddon himself designed the five E windows erected in 1904 in memory of Poole. [PH]

Hockley Heath, West Midlands
St Thomas

A small red-brick church of 1879 in a brick-making village. By John Cotton, it is in the Early English style and full of vigour; the large belfry-openings rising into steep gables around the base of a short cream-brick pyramid spire, characteristic of the architect and here decorated with red brick; the W wall has three arrow-slit lancets below a rose window. [DH]

Holmbury St Mary, Surrey
St Mary the Virgin

On a wooded hillside near his half-finished country retreat at Holmdale, G. E. Street planned this church as a memorial to his young second wife Jessie. Designed 1877 and built in 1878–9, it is of Holmbury Hill green sandstone with Bath stone dressings and tiled timber roofs. Formally paraphrasing the Surrey vernacular, Street has created a paragon of disciplined virtuosity from an amalgam of Early English and Geometrical Decorated. Window types range from grouped lancets to plate and bar tracery. Nave and chancel are continuous beneath one long roof, brought down low to embrace N and S aisles. Taking advantage of the slope, the noble chancel builds up precipitously over a buttressed basement, and similarly a tall gabled N chapel rises from the low-level vestry block which is also buttressed. Against the hill, the broad W front has its gable sheered off by the square tile-hung belfry and shingled spire. This is supported inside on timber posts acting as framework for a glazed narthex-partition, to which entrance is by a NW porch enclosed in the aisle. Arcades are of three bays on piers of blue Pennant with attached marble shafts and moulded capitals. The roof is differentiated by tie-beams and king-posts over the nave and arch-braces over the chancel; in between, and above the high wooden screen, a cusped principal forms a vestigial chancel arch. Stained glass in the elaborate five-light E window is by Clayton and Bell; and Street gave from his own art collection the 14th-century Florentine reredos triptych attributed to Spinello Aretino, as well as the 12th-century Limoges enamel altar cross. Outside, the S chancel wall has a canopied arch recess for the tomb of Jessie Mary Anne Street (d. 1876). The stone churchyard cross is a personal memorial to the architect (d. 1881) by his son Arthur Edmund Street, who is also buried here. [PJ]

Honiton, Devon
St Paul

Erected 1836–8 by Charles Fowler. Built to seat 1,500 people, St Paul's originally had an iron roof, an experiment that proved a costly failure, another more conventional roof being erected by Carver and Giles in 1849. Stylistically, the church belongs to the Romanesque revival, its details and overall design showing little concern for historical accuracy – happily so in the case of the most imposing feature of the exterior, the three-stage tower to the street. The interior, an impressive single space not unlike that of a covered market, with side galleries set back behind the massive, very tall aisle arcades, has now been subdivided. [CB]

Hooton, Cheshire
St Paul

Beside the elegant Samuel Wyatt lodges to his house, Hooton Hall, the Liverpool banker R. C. Naylor commissioned James K. Colling to build, in 1858–62, a quite extraordinary church. Colling was the author of books on Gothic details, but this is in an extremely free Romanesque, of mainly Italian and French derivation. The exterior is in a mixture of red ashlar, white ashlar, and red rock-faced stone. The W front has a Lombardic frieze. The octagonal crossing-tower is curiously small. On the S side is an odd appendage with a pyramidal roof, linked to the church by a cloister: originally open, this formed a private entrance for the family. Inside, the arcades have Peterhead granite columns, but in the apsidal choir slimmer coupled shafts. The choir aisles continue as an ambulatory. Over the crossing is a stone dome, on pendentives, which turns, halfway up, into the lantern. The rich stained glass is in keeping. The green serpentine font was shown at the 1862 Exhibition. [PH]

Hopton, Suffolk
*St Margaret**

The tower of this church, of 1865–6, shows S. S. Teulon's much-favoured device of an octagon astride a four-sided spire. The main Teulon conceit is the N aisle where three wide double-coursed relieving arches in stone on the exterior clearly bear no functional relationship to the windows in each bay and give the impression of being ancient arches from an earlier building. Three enormous arches in brick reflect this conceit internally. The pulpit on a crystalline base and the lectern composed of a winged angel are very typical of the architect. [MS]

Hopwas, Staffordshire
St Chad

This charmingly picturesque church by John Douglas dates from 1879–81. Up on a hillside, it is approached from the E, and the composition of this end is most ingenious. The church is mostly of red brick, but the E gable is half-timbered, and so is the broad bell-chamber which rises above and behind it, crowned by a shingled spirelet and further diversified by a gabled stair-projection. The lean-to vestry completes the composition. The interior is less exciting: it is faced in yellow brick. The wide, open nave has a good roof, and the faintly Jacobean wooden fittings are characteristic of Douglas. [PH]

Hornblotton, Somerset
St Peter

A small country church by T. G. Jackson, 1872–6, that shows the reaction in church building to the vigour of the High Victorian Gothic, an ecclesiastical version of the Aesthetic Movement. The tower and spire are suggestive of Surrey with timber top, tile-hung at the bell-stage and carrying an oak-shingled spire. The interior is very prettily treated in sgraffito plaster. The ornament is characteristically Aesthetic with foliage and sunflowers. Derbyshire alabaster reredos with enamelled-tile blue-and-white figures by Powell and Sons, who also made the stained glass to Jackson's design and the mosaic chancel floor. Delicate inlay of satinwood, holly and ebony on the oak furniture. [JO]

Horton-cum-Studley, Oxfordshire
*St Barnabas**

This small church of 1867–8 by William Butterfield inevitably recalls Keble College in nearby Oxford. It consists of chancel, nave and N aisle, with a large belfry above the W end, and is built of yellow brick, banded with red and blue, with diaper patterns higher up, and stone dressings. The variations in tone of the handmade local bricks are particularly attractive.

The interior is similarly polychrome, with a zigzag brick cornice. The N arcade has wooden piers. The reredos of tile mosaic, the splendidly Geometrical font, and the glass by Alexander Gibbs are notable. [PH]

Hove, East Sussex
All Saints, Eaton Road*

The largest and the most expensive of John Loughborough Pearson's parish churches. The nave and aisles were built in 1889–91, the chancel and S chapel in 1898–1901; the W narthex and the stump of the proposed W tower were added in 1924. Unlike the majority of Pearson's great town churches of the 1880s, All Saints is not vaulted throughout, but has a fine, carved oak roof resting on stone transverse arches. The germ of the idea comes from Italy, but is here employed in an entirely English context. For instance, the clustered shafts of the nave arcade recall Exeter Cathedral and the detail, unusually profuse for Pearson, is similarly taken from 14th-century English Gothic. The nave's transverse arches frame a square-ended chancel; a triplet of two-light windows, the central one subtly wider, fills the E end and is framed within the arched bay of the sanctuary, whose height and width have the proportion of the Golden Section. The effect of the glowing E window seen through the gloom of the dark nave with only the framing arches catching the light is sublimely grand. The organ-case of 1905 is by Frank Loughborough Pearson, who completed the church after his father's death in 1897. The fine stained glass is by Clayton and Bell. [AQ]

Howe Bridge, Greater Manchester
St Michael and All Angels

Beautifully detailed by Paley and Austin and built 1875–7 in red Runcorn sandstone, this estate church builds up with alternating great circular and clustered piers of the arcade, supporting stone quadripartite vaults over the chancel corbelled out from the arcades on attached clustered colonnettes. The subtle play of light from the arcade clerestory with additional light from the taller transepts behind seems to punch through the plate-traceried windows, with their deep internal reveals emphasizing the massively thick stone walls. Externally the NW stair-turret with its blind arcading leads above the chancel vaults, and

a delicate two-stage flèche with great cantilevered rainwater chutes divides nave from chancel. [DM]

Howsham, North Yorkshire
St John the Evangelist*

Compact nave and chancel terminating in a smooth rounded apse make up the basic components of this Geometrical masterpiece by G. E. Street, 1859–60; a tiny vestry with chimney is tucked away at the NE. All display is reserved for the resourceful W front where the tall nave-gable and its high circular window appear behind a boldly asymmetric narthex porch of exotic provenance. This has thick red Mansfield stone shafts, corbelling out above the capitals to horizontal lintels and a deep lean-to roof. On the same plane a square NW turret restores the balance, though masking part of the W gable in its upward progress. At this point it develops a crossed gabled form out of which rises the piquant octagonal belfry of open columns supporting a short stone spire. The tooled grey Whitby stone is irregularly banded with pale brown throughout and alternates with coloured voussoirs over plate-tracery windows and arches. Inside, the two strongly differentiated spaces are marked off by a cusped chancel arch, the roofs being of two distinct forms of framed rafters, boarded in and painted over the apse. Font and pulpit, gorgeously inlaid with coloured marbles in abstract patterns, prepare one for the elaborate reredos carved by Thomas Earp, its three sunk bull's-eye panels of geometric inlay contained within rich foliated arches. Finally, there is an excellent scheme of stained glass by Clayton and Bell. [PJ]

Hunstanworth, County Durham
St James the Less*

Completed in 1863 by S. S. Teulon. The large tower with pyramid capping, the circular staircase turret and the great variety in the tracery are peculiarly expressive of the architect. The most striking internal feature is the pulpit approached through a two-bay Early English passageway set within the wall. The attention to detail is shown in the lock of the main door which has a little Gothic canopied surround to the keyhole. [MS]

Huntley, Gloucestershire
St John the Baptist*

The church, apart from the old tower, dates from 1862–3. The restful colour contrast between S. S. Teulon's pink sandstone for the shell and the grey Painswick stone of his octagonal broach-spire prepares the visitor for the lavishness of the interior, the architect's most sumptuous. The richly coloured marble lectern, pulpit and reredos are all by Earp. The reredos was exhibited in the medieval court of the 1862 Great Exhibition. The roundels of the four Evangelists and their symbols and the highly animated figures over the nave columns are very reminiscent of William Burges, as are the large capitals in the chancel composed of the symbols of the Passion banded by ribbons decorated with jewels. A notable feature is Teulon's very distinctive grisaille glass (probably by Lavers and Barraud) with biblical scenes rendered in outline only on a yellow background. [MS]

Hursley, Hampshire
All Saints

John Keble, the pioneer leader of the Oxford Movement, was vicar of Hursley from 1836 to 1866. He used the proceeds from his writings to pay for the reconstruction and enlargement of his church to the designs of J. P. Harrison of Oxford in 1846. A new nave with N and S aisles and chancel with N and S chapels all in the style of the mid-14th century were built onto the tower of the old church and covered with separate gabled roofs. Low and grey, it is unremarkable without (the spire has been removed) and within, except for the memorial brass to Keble designed by William Butterfield and the survival of all the original stained glass by William Wailes to a scheme by Butterfield which fills the traceried windows. [MM]

Hyde, Greater Manchester
Hyde Chapel, Gee Cross (Nonconformist)

The Unitarians of Hyde rebuilt the old Presbyterian chapel in 1846–8, when the passing of the Dissenters Chapels Act gave them security of possession in spite of doctrinal changes. The architects, Bowman and Crowther of Manchester, produced an archaeologically correct Middle Pointed chapel of parochial appearance set in a large graveyard close to the site of its predecessor. It has a long aisled nave with paired clerestory windows and open timber roof, a chancel with traceried E window, and a W tower with broach-spire. This is the first fully Gothic Nonconformist chapel. [CS]

Ilkley, West Yorkshire
St Margaret*

A large and prosperous church, built in 1878–9. Norman Shaw was the architect, and wrote: 'I am so sick of the everlasting modern church, with its orthodox pitched roof and its feeble spire . . . I should like to keep it all simple, but as large in *mass* as possible.' The result is a long, tower-less building, not nearly as low as it looks. In idiom it follows smartly on from the innovations in church-planning and style started by Bodley and G. G. Scott junior, with some special tricks of Shaw's own. The interior is spacious but a little dull. Fittings (mostly later) by Shaw with the help of assistants and others include the font, the hefty pulpit, some screens and the font cover. There is much glass by Powells. The focal point of the church is now a magnificent painted and gilded reredos of 1925 designed by J. Harold Gibbons. [AJS]

Inverness, Highland
St Andrew's Cathedral (Episcopal)

By Alexander Ross, 1866–9. English Middle Pointed with French general outline and some French Early Gothic details. Twin-towered liturgical W front with triplet belfry-windows and lateral entrance-porches, elaborate W door with high-relief tympanum sculptured by Earp in 1876. Narthex in bay between towers, full-height transepts, one-bay chancel with semi-hexagonal apse and octagonal chapter house. Richly sculptured and furnished interior with monolith circular piers of Peterhead granite, stencilled wagon roof of red pine, trefoil-plan pulpit sculptured by D. and A. Davidson, reredos by Earp and font by James Redfern after Thorwaldsen. Glass mainly by Hardman, 1869–87. [DW]

Irvine, Strathclyde
Trinity Church (Church of Scotland)*

The first of F. T. Pilkington's churches, built in 1861–3. In it the basic concept of all his earlier churches was established, that is a main central space (in this case a diamond truncated at the angles) opening into a higher and narrower gable-front building containing the gallery and flanked by a tower and spire containing the gallery-stair. An open narthex with a central door within its gable-front leads to the gallery-stair and not directly into the church. Detail all boldest Franco-Venetian Gothic, rich in sculpture, polychromy and contrasted textures of stonework. Cavernous gable-front with wheel-window recessed in cusped arch with voussoirs filling the whole of the tympanum; very original spire. The main roof is not the pyramid one would expect but is ingeniously brought to a cruciform triapsidal arrangement, its huge scale emphasized by the small prismatic roof of the vestry. This form is achieved by hefty circular piers carrying triangular masses of masonry within the church which bring the upper level to an orthodox cross-plan for roofing, but the carpentry of the crossing is of great complexity with radial tie-beams and twisted columnar struts. Some of the Daniel Cottier glass survives. The church is now secularized. [DW]

Itchen Stoke, Hampshire
St Mary*

Built in 1866 at the expense of its vicar, the Revd Charles Ranken Conybeare, to designs prepared by his brother Henry, this village church is unmistakably modelled on the then recently restored Sainte Chapelle in Paris. Its soaring interior, lit by richly coloured glass in every window, contains much of decorative interest, including a maze in the floor of the apse and patterned stone panelling finished with gold leaf behind the altar. [MM]

Kelso, Borders
St Andrew (Episcopal)

A modest-sized but neatly composed and well-detailed church by Rowand Anderson 1868–9. Early Geometrical, red sandstone with buff dressings; chancel with very original cylindrical belfry, conically corbelled from the buttresses at the junction of nave and chancel and capped by a banded candle-snuffer spirelet. Finely detailed interior with alternately circular and quartrefoil piers, open scissors roof, circular stone pulpit with paintings of saints, stencilled chancel ceiling and reredos. [DW]

Kelso, Borders
St John's Edenside and Ednam

By F. T. Pilkington 1865–7, it has a truncated diamond plan-form similar to Trinity Church, Irvine. Polychromy and foreign influences are, however, toned down to a highly individual interpretation of English Early Decorated with just a few Franco-Italian touches; the internal narthex is omitted and a projecting gabled entrance-porch with free-standing columns substituted. Above it the gable front has a pair of windows united by a vesica; the flanking spire again has tall gabled lucarne belfry-openings clasped in pinnacles, here two-tier open tabernacles with slated pyramid roofs as at Edinburgh's Barclay Church. Within, the roof structure is very remarkable, similar to that at Irvine with the radial struts at the crossing descending to a central boss held in place by tie-rods instead of tie-beams as at Irvine. Original pews and gallery fronts stripped to match wretched 20th-century Neo-Perpendicular fittings. [DW]

Kilndown, Kent
Christ Church

Envisaged as a simple chapel-of-ease to Goudhurst, commissioned by Viscount Beresford, and executed in local sandstone in 1839, possibly to a design by Salvin. But the Viscount's stepson, Alexander Beresford-Hope, sometime president of the Cambridge Camden Society, intercepted the project in 1840 and directed it according to Ecclesiological principles. It was too late to avoid a low-pitched roof so he had this masked with a parapet and embellished the spire with lucarnes. With adornments and fittings by the rising stars of the Ecclesiological movement, Beresford-Hope transformed an unpretentious chapel into what the *Ecclesiologist* regarded as the richest church in the country. Carpenter designed the stalls and screen, Butterfield the chandeliers, tapers and lectern: Franz Eggert of Munich produced the glass while Willement was responsible for the painted pulpit. Salvin complied with Beresford-Hope's direction to furnish a stone altar that was a copy of William of Wykeham's tomb in Winchester Cathedral. Unhappily the walls are now washed white and the former gilding shows through only in places. Beresford-Hope lies to the SW of the church in a tomb designed by Carpenter and Ingelow in 1882. [REH]

Kingsbury, Greater London
St Andrew

It is difficult to imagine that this church has not been here since 1847 when it was built, *not* in Kingsbury but in Wells Street, Marylebone. It was designed by Samuel Daukes in 1845 and attracted adverse criticism in the *Ecclesiologist* for its Perpendicular style. Built of ragstone on a conventional plan with a tower and spire, it might long have vanished and been forgotten had not Benjamin Webb, one of the founders of the Cambridge Camden Society, become vicar in 1862, remaining until his death in 1885. He developed it as a strong centre of Tractarian, but non-ceremonial, influence, famed for its music. He commissioned leading church architects to design expensive furniture and fittings. Pugin had already designed the E window and Butterfield the lectern; Street designed the superb reredos, carved by Redfern, which is a virtuoso statement of Victorian sculpture; he also designed the iron chancel screen, pulpit and the polychromatic marble font. Pearson designed the font cover and sedilia; Burges a litany desk of inlaid wood, altar plate and a monument to a former vicar, carved by Nicholls and decorated by Harland and Fisher, with a painting of Christ in Majesty by Smallfield and Poynter, exhibited in the International Exhibition of 1862; Bodley decorated the sacristy; Clayton and Bell provided more glass and decorated the wooden gallery fronts with paintings of saints on a gold ground. After the First World War the choral tradition was abandoned and the changed social conditions of Wells Street hastened decline. In 1932 it was closed and demolished but because of its fame strong influence was exerted and in 1933–4 it was rebuilt by W. A. Forsyth for a new and prosperous suburb. The plan was regularized, the N and S galleries were abandoned and some wall decoration was lost. Victorian architecture was then at the nadir of appreciation and it is astonishing for this reason that the reconstruction was so faithful, meticulous and sympathetic, including conventional monuments as well as the exemplary furniture and glass. [ANS]

Kingston, Dorset
*St James**

Faced with the severe agricultural recession of the early 1870s John Scott, 3rd Earl of Eldon, devised a unique building programme which might keep his Encombe estate labourers in employment. His scheme culminated in a magnificent church on the Isle of Purbeck, designed by G. E. Street in 1873–4 with no restrictions as to form or cost. Using materials hewn exclusively from the Encombe quarries, construction proceeded during 1874–80. Street unassumingly proclaimed Kingston the jolliest church he had built; it was certainly his most expensive. Cast in noble proportions and erudite language it achieves a deliberate, rare perfection. Apart from North Oxford, this is Street's only regular cruciform church with central tower. Like that earlier, but much larger work it adopts an idealized northern French massing and terminates in a buttressed semicircular apse at the E, although here compressed transepts are at full level with clerestoried nave, the powerful crossing-tower rising tall, four-square and terse; a fine sight on its ridge overlooking Corfe Castle. Lean-to aisles evenly flank the nave, and a two-storey vestry-block spreads out from the NE. That is the one part of the plan where symmetry is abandoned; between it and the N transept a thick cylindrical newel-turret has trellis patterning derived from Christchurch Priory. Above the lean-to narthex the W gable is perforated by a bold circular window; its singular Geometrical bar tracery – a reminiscence from Lausanne Cathedral – epitomizes the whole structure's monumental unity. Otherwise, openings are practically restricted to lancets, arranged singly, in couples or grouped. Impressively articulated walls are of close-jointed Purbeck ashlar, the deep roofs covered in graded Purbeck slates. Entrance is by a lavish W portal within the arcaded narthex. Of cathedral splendour, the white interior is enriched in Salisbury fashion by a system of grey Purbeck marble shafts and strings. Sumptuously moulded four-bay arcades have piers with clustered shafts and stiff-leaf capitals; the steep crossing-arches are equally elaborate but with moulded capitals, and they soar to a majestic height. Street's classic spatial progression from lofty timber-roofed nave to stone rib-vaulted choir and sanctuary is subtly reinforced by changes in light: shadowed beneath the high tower, luminous in the apse; seen through the diaphanous wrought-iron screen set on grey marble cancelli the effect is spectacular. Thomas Potter made the sinuous pulpit and all other metalwork, Thomas Earp did the carving, and Clayton and Bell the lucid stained glass. [PJ]

Kingston upon Thames, Greater London
St Raphael, Portsmouth Road (RC)

Built in 1846–7, this exotic church overlooking the Thames is an engaging hybrid of Italianate Early Christian and Renaissance styles, by the little-known Charles Parker. Its campanile-like W tower and tall clerestoried nave and chancel are in pale-yellow brick with smooth matching stone dressings. The lofty interior is strange and foreign with weird patterned glass in the aisles and a shrill Continental E window. [RMH]

Kingswood, Surrey
St Andrew

In a leafy outer suburban setting, this is a characteristic early work by Benjamin Ferrey of between 1848 and 1852. It is virtually a copy of the 14th-century church at Shottesbrooke in Berkshire, on which William Butterfield had published a book in 1844. The deep-coloured O'Connor E window to the founder, Thomas Alcock (d. 1866), has rich medallions below elaborate traceries. [RMH]

Kirkby, Merseyside
St Chad

Built 1869–71 by Paley and Austin, using red sandstone quarried within the parish. The large, square central tower with its saddleback roof dominates the church. Internally the tower soars to its sexpartite vault with ridge ribs plummeting down to a corbel between the pair of large lancet windows on the N and S tower walls. Nave piers, to the N octagonal and to the S circular, support a clerestory of coupled lancets with internal relieving arches over each pair. The short square-ended chancel has blind arcading at the E end with three large lancet windows surmounted by a large circular light. Below the arcading is the beautiful *opus sectile* 'Last Supper' by Henry Holiday who also did the stained glass. [DM]

Lampeter, Dyfed
St Peter

Dominating the town, this tall, strong church of 1867–8 is by R. J. Withers. The noble SW tower has a pyramidal roof. In rough grey stone with white dressings, the style is Early French Gothic. The E

window has striking plate tracery with three 'wheels'. The most remarkable feature inside is the glass of the W window, by Wilhelmina Geddes (1938), one of the best of the Irish 'Tower of Glass' artists. The colours are strong, the drawing firm. [PH]

Lamplugh, Cumbria
St Michael

A tiny rural church by William Butterfield (1870), aisleless and with a dominating bell-tower at the W. It is characteristically craftsmanlike, but untypically Perpendicular in style – to match a number of parts from an earlier church which have been integrated, rather eccentrically, into the new design. Thus the vestry window, and another inserted above the chancel arch, are original 15th-century forms. Other unexpected details include an 18th-century gravestone walling up what was once the chancel door, and prominent gargoyles to the E. [TEF]

Lancaster, Lancashire
St Peter (RC)

Elevated to cathedral status in 1924, St Peter's was built in 1857–9 to the design of E. G. Paley. It is a great town church with an elegantly slender broach-spire flanking the lofty gable of the W end, pierced by a Geometrical five-light window. To the N is the chapter-house-like baptistery, while the presbytery range runs to the S. The high altar and reredos (now displaced) are by Giles Gilbert Scott (1909). [DM]

Lancing, West Sussex
Lancing College Chapel

'A Gothic chapel as Turner might have imagined it . . .' and embodying in its noble proportions the aspirations of Nathaniel Woodard, founder of the college. This superbly sited chapel was begun in 1868 from designs by R. H. Carpenter, and erected in stages until dedicated in 1911. The last bay, incorporating the impressive rose window, was completed in 1977. The general style is French 13th-century. The height of the vaulted nave, 90 feet, is emphasized by the glazed triforium and the soaring clustered columns unfettered by capitals or string-courses. The apsidal chancel and nave have pinnacles and flying buttresses. The Chapel of St Nicholas has a reredos by Ninian Comper, and the Stations of the Cross are by Frank Brangwyn. The stall canopies (1851) by James Deason were originally presented to Eton College by the Prince Consort. [DRE]

Langleybury (Abbots Langley),
Hertfordshire
St Paul

This is an elaborate church built by Henry Woodyer in 1863–4. It is of flint and Bath stone, and ambitiously decorated inside. There is a W tower and timber broach-spire. The S porch has imaginatively designed iron gates treated like reticulated tracery. The arches of the N arcade are decorated with angels set between them, and more angels with shields between them adorn the chancel arch, the inner arch resting on corbels decorated with yet more angels, here carrying musical instruments. All were carved by Thomas Earp. Sharply cusped arches in the chancel divide off the S chapel and N organ-chamber, and surround the E window; and the arches of the braced timber roof are again strongly cusped. The plain Geometrical font of Cornish serpentine has a remarkable cover in the form of three storeys of arches set crosswise like buttresses supporting each other. [AQ]

Langton Green, Kent
All Saints

This is an Early English composition of 1862–4 by George Gilbert Scott: lancets throughout, and the standard bell-cote, rendered the more attractive and durable by the choice of local sandstone. Within, the aisles are divided by late-medieval arches spanning octagonal columns. The splendour of the church, however, is not Scott's, but the twin-lancet window of the four Evangelists in the W wall (1865–6) by Burne-Jones, Ford Madox Brown and William Morris. The exciting five-light E window is by Kempe, partly masked by the reredos, a fine work in alabaster, coloured marbles and mosaics by Powell. [REH]

Larbert, Central
Stenhousemuir and Carron Church (Church of Scotland)*

Designed by Sir John Burnet in 1897, a low-naved, squat-towered building with mixed Romanesque and Late Gothic motifs, roughcast with red-sandstone dressings. There is a single S aisle and a half-timbered porch, open-sided and integrated with an apsidal semi-octagonal stair-projection clasping the tower. Internally the nave has a low masonry arcade and an open timber roof; a rood-beam separates it from the single-bayed sanctuary. Interesting furnishings – stone pulpit, silvered-bronze font by Albert Hodge, communion table with sculpture by William Vickers and E windows by Douglas Strachan. [DW]

Largs, Strathclyde
Coats Memorial Church (Church of Scotland)

Built in 1890–2, and designed by an ex-assistant of Sir John Burnet's, William Kerr, then in association with T. Graham Abercrombie of Paisley. Very tall, red-sandstone Early Decorated church, aisleless, with a single N transept and a lower hall and semi-octagonal vestry projecting at right angles from the SE to link with a tall Normandy Gothic spire. High interior with hammer-beam roof, light fittings supported by angels, glass by Meikle (E window) and Stephen Adam (W and transept windows). [DW]

Leafield, Oxfordshire
*St Michael and All Angels**

A church whose spire is a landmark for miles. By George Gilbert Scott, it was built in 1858–60, but the octagonal tower and spire over the crossing were not completed until 1874. The style is Early English. The aisles have cross-gables, and the W front makes a fine show with its rich doorway, lancets, and rose window. The lofty clerestoried interior is austere but impressive. Only the tower-arch capitals are carved: the nave arcades have flat unchamfered arches, over which sacred texts are painted on metal strips. [PH]

Leamington, Warwickshire
St Mark

St Mark's is the principal surviving work of George Gilbert Scott junior, now that his London masterpieces, St Agnes, Kennington, and All Hallows', Southwark, have been destroyed. St Agnes was, in its day, a landmark in the move from High Victorian Gothic to a more refined revival of later Gothic styles. St Mark's is Decorated Gothic in style with strong hints of Perpendicular; like St Agnes, it has the mouldings of the arcades dying into the piers, which have panelled bases. The first designs were made in 1873, but construction of a modified design only began in 1876 and the finely modelled W tower is smaller than originally intended. St Mark's was consecrated in 1879 but never furnished as its architect wished. It was designed for Anglo-Catholic ritual but the tradition here has always been Low Church. A screen was eventually added in 1904, to the design of Scott's mentor and friend, G. F. Bodley, but the reredos of 1902 is quite unworthy of the building. The fine font and cover and the splendid painted and gilded organ-case in the N transept are, however, Scott's work. [GS]

Leckhampstead, Berkshire
*St James**

In this design of 1859–60 S. S. Teulon combined dazzling internal polychromatic effects with notable economy. The vitrified bricks turn out to be red bricks painted black, what looks like high-quality black mastic jointing is in fact tuck pointing. The impressive roof with two massively cusped trusses either side of the crossing has an ancient naive quality emphasized by the use of simple planks visibly jointed. Even the tiles are brought into the unity of composition by reflecting the spurred Renaissance cross-section of the nave columns. [MS]

Leeds, West Yorkshire
All Souls, Blackman Lane

One of Sir George Gilbert Scott's last works (1876–81), All Souls was built as a memorial to Dr Hook. It is a large, noble, austere building, standing amidst the desolation of the inner city, where the tower is a notable landmark. The ashlar-lined, partly stone-vaulted interior has something of a monastic character. Some of the fittings, most notably the stone pulpit and stalls, are typical of Scott, whilst others, including the fine font cover (with amusing paintings inside by Emily Ford) are by Scott's talented pupil R. J. Johnson (who also designed the adjacent vicarage). [KP]

Leeds, West Yorkshire
Mount St Mary, Richmond Hill (RC)

By J. A. Hansom and William Wardell, 1853–7. The exterior is massive but ungainly, with the stumps of Wardell's intended W towers clearly visible. The vast interior has real grandeur: very tall piers and the capitals mostly left uncarved. In 1866, E. W. Pugin gave the church its apsidal chancel and transepts, and the high altar is to his design, a typically rich Roman design of the period. There are many side altars, shrines and devotional objects, giving the church the character of a place of simple but definite faith. [KP]

Leeds, West Yorkshire
St Aidan, Roundhay Road*

This vast red-brick basilica, rising above the back-to-backs of Harehills, is well known for the huge, jaggedly Arts and Crafts mosaic of the life of St Aidan which adorns the apse, a major work by Frank Brangwyn and his only large-scale work in this medium. Designed in 1916 – the original scheme for a fresco was thought unsuitable for the city's polluted atmosphere – it was given to the church by R. H. Kitson. St Aidan's is, however, Brangwyn apart, one of the most remarkable churches of its period in the country, and is a striking product of the growing interest at that time in Byzantine and Early Christian architecture and decoration. Designed by R. J. Johnson and A. Crawford-Hick, 1891–4, it was intended as a large economical mission church but sumptuous fittings were eventually installed. Italian Romanesque in style, with Baroque touches; these include the pulpit, font, organ-case, lectern (with trumpeting angels) and gargantuan litany desk. [KP]

Leeds, West Yorkshire
St Bartholomew, Armley

By J. Athron and H. Walker, 1872–7; tower 1903–4. St Bartholomew's is a dominant feature of the West Leeds skyline: massive, black and slightly forbidding. The interior is very tall, culminating in the vaulted, apsidal chancel with its excellently carved reredos by Thomas Earp. The other fittings are good but conventional in their design. The organ is a famous instrument, built by Edmund Schulze c. 1870 for a private mansion at Meanwood, near Leeds, and brought here in 1879. The huge case is set on a vaulted arcade to the N of the chancel. The monuments of the Leeds woollen manufacturer Benjamin Gott (1762–1840) and two of his sons, by Joseph Gott, from the previous church, are major works of art. [KP]

Leeds, West Yorkshire
St Chad, Far Headingley

Built in 1868. Although severely restrained by Lord Grimthorpe's patronage and interference, W. H. Crossland produced a building of some vigour, with a fine spire and apsidal chancel of French inspiration. Grimthorpe had laid down the overall plan of the building: Crossland would probably have preferred something less conventional. St Chad's is lifted above the ordinary, however, by the work of Harold Gibbons, up to the standard of his master, Temple Moore. In 1910 the old chancel was demolished and the church extended eastwards with a long, square-ended chancel, aisles and large side chapel. Everything is beautifully detailed and the climax of the church is Gibbons's great polychromed wooden reredos, topped by a high E window containing glass of strongly Arts and Crafts character by Margaret Aldrich Rope (1923). [KP]

Leeds, West Yorkshire
St Hilda, Cross Green Lane

St Hilda's, by J. T. Micklethwaite, 1876–81, is an ideal town church. Outside it is plain, even severe, built of decent, common brick, with stone dressings. Inside, painted and gilded fittings stand in contrast to whitewashed walls. The fittings, executed in close accordance with Micklethwaite's original designs, were carried out by the Newcastle architect W. H. Wood and include the rood-screen (1921), reredos (1927) and the 25-foot-high font cover, completed as late as 1938. [KP]

Leeds, West Yorkshire
St Matthew, Chapel Allerton

St Matthew's is a model Late Victorian suburban church, constructed in 1897–1900 of fine Ancaster stone in G. F. Bodley's usual late-14th-century style. It is dominated externally by the beautifully proportioned, almost detached tower. Inside, the 'extreme slimness, the attenuation of detail' in Bodley's late work, to which E. P. Warren drew attention, is evident. The wooden roof, screen and pulpit are typical of the architect's style, though the reredos, painted by Jackson of Ealing, was probably designed by his less able successor, Cecil Hare. E window (1896) and some other glass by Bodley's usual firm of Burlison and Grylls. [KP]

Leeds, West Yorkshire
St Peter (Leeds Parish Church)*

The present church by R. D. Chantrell, 1837–41, was built by the great Vicar of Leeds, Walter Farquhar Hook, to replace the medieval St Peter's, itself a cruciform structure of some grandeur but internally 'like a conventicle built up in a church'. The new church reflected Hook's High Church views, particularly in its long and elevated E arm, providing accommodation for the first surpliced choir in any Anglican parish church and leading the eye to the altar. At the same time, accommodation for up to 3,000 worshippers was required and Chantrell provided much of this in capacious galleries of the sort so despised by Pugin and his followers. It is thus both a late example of the Georgian preaching-box and a landmark in the rise of the new Ecclesiology. Chantrell, a pupil of Soane, had no Puginian scruples about 'shams' and plaster, wood and iron are freely combined in the interior, whilst the planning owes little to medieval precedent. This highly atmospheric building is rich in stained glass, monuments (some brought from the old church) and fittings. Chantrell's extraordinary pulpit and organ-case survive, but the sanctuary was remodelled in the 1870s (with reredos by Street) and the font of 1883 was designed by Butterfield. The Lady Chapel was refitted as a First World War memorial by F. C. Eden, who designed the exquisite painted and gilded reredos. [KP]

Leeds, West Yorkshire
St Saviour, Ellerby Road

St Saviour's, founded by Dr Pusey and designed by one of the most promising Oxford architects of the day, J. M. Derick, 1842–5, was the pioneer Oxford Movement church of northern England. Its plan, virtually that of a miniature cathedral with transepts and long chancel, is neither typically Tractarian nor very convenient. Internally, the narrow height of the building is, however, very impressive. The chancel, intended for the use of a community of clergy and laymen, is now divided from the nave by a screen designed by G. F. Bodley. The reredos to the high altar, rood and Pusey Memorial Chapel are also by Bodley, the result of a 'renovation' scheme begun in 1888. The delicate colours of Bodley's decorative scheme sadly perished in G. G. Pace's redecoration of the 1960s. The most remarkable feature of St

Saviour's is the series of four windows with glass by O'Connor, three of them certainly designed by Pugin and that in the S transept (the 'Martyrs' window') the finest. O'Connor was also responsible for the clerestory glass; and there are two windows by Morris and Co. [KP]

Leek, Staffordshire
*All Saints**

Probably the finest of Norman Shaw's surviving churches, imposing, original, and handsomely decorated. Built in 1885–7, it is set into a slope and allows Shaw to indulge his later-found fondness for horizontality and strength. In style it follows the pattern of Bodley's churches, but the setting of a squat central tower on top of the easternmost bay of the nave makes the whole composition *sui generis*. Inside, Shaw contrives by means of side arches to carry the tower on thin piers, leaving the crossing uninterrupted and presenting a splendid breadth of effect from W end to E end. The very fine fittings include a reredos (painted by F. Hamilton Jackson but poorly restored), a pulpit and a font all attributable to W. R. Lethaby, Shaw's chief assistant, and other items by Gerald Horsley, who also decorated the chancel. Frontals by Shaw and by Horsley worked by the Leek Embroidery Society and one or two good windows show the strength of local Arts and Crafts ardour. [AJS]

Leicester
former *Baptist Chapel*, Belvoir Street*

The only Nonconformist chapel to be designed by Joseph Hansom was built in 1845. This most unusual building presents a rounded end to the street giving rise to its nickname 'Pork Pie Chapel'. At each end of the colonnaded front is a circular entrance pavilion enclosing a spiral staircase, the design clearly taken from the Choragic Monument of Lysicrates but with columns borrowed from the Tower of the Winds. The interior, now cleared of seating and forming part of an Adult Education Centre, comprises a horseshoe-shaped auditorium lit by a ring of clerestory windows set back from the main outer wall. The gallery is supported by cast-iron columns with leaf capitals which spill over below the gallery front to form lively scrolled and acanthus-leaved brackets. [CS]

Leicester
St Andrew

This very tough and radical church of 1860–2 by George Gilbert Scott is built of patterned red and blue brick. It has a wide nave, with a bell-cote over the junction with the apsed chancel, and a large S transept. The interior is broad and aisleless: although it could seat almost a thousand, it was claimed that 'the altar and pulpit can be seen from every part of the building'. Unfortunately the internal polychromy has been painted over. [PH]

Leicester
St Mark

Ewan Christian was prolific and normally pedestrian in his output. Occasionally, however, he found a client and a budget that allowed him to produce memorable and richly decorated churches, as at St Mark's, which was constructed in 1871–2, and extended one bay in 1903–4 by Edward Shearman. The facing material, Mountsorrel granite, offers a variegated and striking mixture of blue, green and brown. There is a full-blooded spire. The interior is sumptuous. The eye is caught by the huge murals in the apse executed in 1910 by J. Edie Reid representing The Travail and Triumph of Labour introduced during the incumbency of the Revd F. Lewis Donaldson who propounded a strong Christian socialist philosophy. But most of the remainder belongs to Ewan Christian. The columns of polished Shap granite with Ketton stone capitals contrast with the polychromatic brick shell and the huge timber vault which is plastered and painted with a series of geometric patterns and simple stylized flowers. In the spandrels of the arches are mosaic roundels with figures of Ezekiel and David and the twelve apostles. [MS]

Leigh Delamere, Wiltshire
St Margaret

Built in 1846 as part of the extensive estate building of Joseph Neeld of Grittleton House. His architect was James Thomson. The church is an intermediate stage between Picturesque and seriously archaeological Gothic, i.e. Thomson reproduced those parts of the previous building that took his fancy while the rest is quite theatrical. The splendid bell-cote is a copy, the original he moved down the road to Seving-ton schoolhouse. Inside, the almost windowless chancel is lit by a small round E window, a white dove in brilliant yellow clouds. Beneath is an elaborate Gothic reredos with Neo-classical statues by E. H. Baily after Thorwaldsen. Minton tile floor to the 'choir'. N arcade is of most odd design, apparently a copy of the original S arcade. At the W end an overwhelming, apocalyptically coloured Crucifixion window by T. Wilmshurst. [JO]

Leighton, Powys
Holy Trinity

This estate church, 1851–3, with its tall stone spire, is by the obscure W. H. Gee of Liverpool. It has flying buttresses, crocketed pinnacles, and much elaborate carving. The interior is high and narrow, with hammer-beam roof and rich chancel arch. There are varnished oak pews filling the whole centre of the church and narrowing triangularly towards the chancel, Minton tiles, and colourful glass by Forrest and Bromley of Liverpool. All the doors are covered in red baize. The octagonal mausoleum, reached via the family pew, contains a large marble angel carved by Georgina Naylor. [PH]

Leiston, Suffolk
*St Margaret**

E. B. Lamb designed this large Gothic church in 1853 (the tower is medieval). The exterior is dour, but the interior is magical. At West Hartlepool and Aldwark, Lamb had already balanced the axiality of a long nave with the centrality of a nine-square crossing area. Here, he implemented this scheme on a generous scale, roofing it over with one of the most fantastic of all Victorian timber roofs. This is a massive hammer-beam truss supplemented at the crossing by a lattice of soaring diagonal braces, which intersect in a sort of knop whose carpentry must be ferociously complex. At the W end of the nave is another virtuoso display of timberwork, a gallery in the form of a bowstring-arch bridge, all sheathed in heavily flowing Curvi-linear tracery. Furnishings by Lamb include the massive stone pulpit (also adorned with flowing tracery) and the small bull's-eye window bearing his cypher on the S side. [ENK]

Lever Bridge, Bolton, Greater Manchester
St Stephen and All Martyrs

This is an extravaganza in terracotta. The church is the realization of an idea by a local colliery owner to build a terracotta church to show the versatility of this material. The architect he chose was Edmund Sharpe, who, between 1842 and 1845, produced a 'very fruity' Decorated style church with much ornamentation – ball-flower, florid foliage, lettering – and a staggering openwork spire, now sadly dismantled as unsafe. A timber model of the spire was exhibited at the Great Exhibition of 1851. The communion table was also originally terracotta, but this was objected to as uncanonical and it was replaced by a wooden table. [DM]

Lincoln
St Swithin

Built in 1869–70, steeple 1884–7, by James Fowler of Louth, and his finest work. Lavish proportions, with a W tower and soaring 200-foot spire which competes with the cathedral in the Lincoln skyline. The style is that of the cathedral, i.e. mid- to late-13th-century. The spire has openwork flying buttresses reminiscent of those at Louth. The clerestory has a continuous arcade with windows grouped in triplets. The interior is broad and lofty but the fittings are disappointing. The pulpit of 1883 has tracery motifs like those of the chancel S windows. [NA]

Little Cawthorpe, Lincolnshire
St Helen

'A truly excellent design . . . for cheaply rebuilding a small rural church', wrote the *Ecclesiologist* in 1860 of R. J. Withers' design for St Helen's. The parts are well defined – nave, chancel, S porch and N vestry; over the W end of the nave, a shingled bell-turret and spire. The material is a hard red brick enlivened by bands of black brick. The steeply pitched roof is crowned by decorative ridge cresting and cross finials over the chancel arch and the E gable. The style is of the early 14th century, the Middle Pointed favoured by the Ecclesiologists. Plain lancets and bar tracery. Dark interior with polychromatic brickwork and richly coloured stained glass of a high quality. One N window is signed by Lavers and Barraud. The decorative scheme, in accordance with the

Ecclesiologist's principles, becomes progressively richer towards the altar. [NA]

Little Ilford, Greater London
St Michael, Romford Road/Toronto Avenue

Externally a brick church with some stone and a central flèche, by Charles Spooner, 1897–8. Inside it is spacious and impressive, with massive, simply detailed roof structures in various forms – hammerbeam over the nave. The nave arcades are partly of brick on stone piers; the chancel is notably narrower, and its height is emphasized by tall containing arches, within which are the clerestory windows, and low, segment-headed arches opening, on the S side, into a wide chapel. Nice fittings with arty details, e.g. the long canopies over the choir seats, with sinuous lacy edges, backed by plain glazing. The church supplements the tiny medieval St Mary's, half a mile to the south. [DL]

Little Petherick, Cornwall
St Petroc Minor

The small medieval church was extensively rebuilt to the designs of William White in 1857–8: the result is a pleasant enough exercise in Decorated, but without White's more distinctive characteristics. The remarkable feature of Little Petherick is its interior, remodelled in 1898–1901 for the ritualist patron, Athelstan Riley, by J. N. Comper. The intention was to re-create the church's appearance on the eve of the Reformation and the interior is dominated accordingly by a lavish rood-screen stretching across both sanctuary and Lady Chapel. Comper's design is based stylistically on West Country examples, the whole screen gilded and painted, with a full loft; the nave benches – the set only partly completed – similarly follow local woodwork traditions. Less historically determined are the Seraphim and Thrones which accompany the rood figures in the loft, and the decorations, fittings, altars and reredoses of sanctuary and Lady Chapel. [CB]

Liverpool, Merseyside
All Hallows, Allerton

This lavish suburban church of 1872–6, pleasantly set among trees, was built by John Bibby of Hart Hill. The architect was G. E. Grayson. The grand W tower (of Somerset type), nave and transepts are Perpendicular, but the chancel is Decorated; red stone outside, white within. At the NE corner is the Bibby 'vault', like a vaulted porch with iron grilles. Inside, the nave arcades ignore the transepts. The chancel is lined with red and green jasper squares with alabaster strips above, and its floor is of inlaid marble. In the S transept is the astonishing marble monument to Mrs Bibby, who floats up to heaven while an angel points the way. The sculptor was Federigo Fabiani, who did monuments at the Staglieno cemetery in Genoa. The glory of the church is the stained glass. All is by Morris and Co., and designed by Burne-Jones, except the E window of the N transept (David Mourning), which is by Heaton, Butler and Bayne (Burne-Jones refused to include portraits of two of Bibby's children). The E window (Adoration of the Lamb) and W window (Evangelists) date from 1875–6; S transept (Holy Men) 1877; N transept (Holy Women) 1880; chancel N windows (Angels) 1881; eight aisle windows (scenes from Our Lord's life) 1882–6. [PH]

Liverpool, Merseyside
Our Lady of Reconciliation de la Salette (RC)

Built in 1859–60 by E. W. Pugin for a large waterfront congregation on a low budget. The exterior is unadorned because of the restricted site. The interior, with nave and apsed sanctuary under one roof, is lit by a W rose window with plate tracery and circular clerestory windows. The nave, with its arcade of only four wide arches and no screens, is more open than the elder Pugin would have approved. Note too the arch-braced roof, partly panelled, partly exposed to reveal scissor braces and louvre. This begins the younger Pugin's decisively individual High Victorian style. [RO'D]

Liverpool, Merseyside
St Agnes, Ullet Road, Sefton Park

Designed in 1882 and built 1883–4. The architect was John Loughborough Pearson, and the church is in his characteristic Early English Gothic style. It is built of red Ruabon brick with local sandstone dressings; the interior is faced in Bath stone. Pearson eschewed the tower and spire that were so often left unbuilt in his other churches because funds were exhausted, and instead designed a remarkably symmetrical church with W transepts to form a huge narthex, and placed a flèche over the main crossing and a pair of tall, spired turrets in its E re-entrant angles. The church is given further vertical emphasis by tall lancets and prominent, tall angle-buttresses at all the corners. The W ends of the aisles form entrance porches, and the aisles continue after the narthex-transepts down the nave; the polygonal apse has a characteristically narrow ambulatory passage, and again, the church is vaulted throughout, right through to the aisled side chapel to the S of the chancel. The S chapel reredos and screen are by G. F. Bodley. [AQ]

Liverpool, Merseyside
St Bridget, Wavertree

This striking and unusual example of an Italianate basilica is by E. A. Heffer and dates from 1868–72. The plain, tall exterior is enlivened by red and purple brick. The slim NW campanile is placed by the main road, and on the W front the narthex is recessed behind a wide round-headed opening with a gable above. Inside, the arcade, which has foliated capitals, continues around the apsidal chancel as a blank arcade. The remarkably wide nave has a richly coffered ceiling. The altar stands free before a mosaic reredos of the Last Supper by Salviati (1886). [PH]

Liverpool, Merseyside
St Clare, Sefton Park (RC)

This memorable church of 1888–90 was a comparatively early work of its architect, Leonard Stokes, but shows his highly individual approach to style. With its long, tall proportions, its internal buttressing and passage-aisles, it recalls St Augustine's, Pendlebury, of 1874, by Bodley and Garner (whose pupil Stokes was). The brick exterior is quiet, but note, for example, the hood-mould stops on the door of the presbytery, which forms an L-shaped composition with the church. A spired turret is set in the angle. The striking interior has semicircular arches supporting the galleries which run beneath the tall clerestory windows. The E window tracery incorporates a cross. The arcading runs on past the chapels flanking the chancel. The pulpit and the font, with its iron railing, are characteristic original fittings. [PH]

Liverpool, Merseyside
St Dunstan, Wavertree

Well placed on the curve of a road, the flaming red Ruabon brick façade, crowned by a green copper-covered flèche, towers above the remains of close-packed terraced houses. Built in 1886–9 by Charles Aldridge and Charles E. Deacon. The W front has a group of five lancets above which are Christ and worshipping angels in relief. Below are the baptistery and NW porch, over which is a terracotta statue of St Dunstan. The fine, lofty interior is all of brick except for the stone piers. The rich wrought-iron lectern incorporates a statue. [PH]

Liverpool, Merseyside
St Francis Xavier (RC)

This church, which epitomizes the aspirations and achievements of Liverpool's 19th-century Catholics, was built by the Jesuits to serve what was then a densely populated area. The architect was J. J. Scoles who often worked for the order. He was appointed in 1844, and the church opened in 1848. In Geometrical Gothic, it has a remarkable plan, consisting basically of a long rectangle divided into nave and aisles by slender columns of polished Drogheda limestone, with a shallow apse for the sanctuary. The exterior is not too prepossessing, despite the tower over the SW porch, whose spire was only added by Edmund Kirby in 1883. But the richly furnished interior is impressive both for its spatial grandeur and its completeness. The high altar dates from 1856. The Sacred Heart Chapel and altar were redesigned by S. J. Nicholl. The carved panel of Christ and the Afflicted, after a painting by Ary Scheffer, includes a Greek, a Pole, a Negro, and Tasso. The fine hanging rood of 1866 is by Earley of Dublin. The bronze statue of St Peter came from the Gesù in Rome. In 1885–7 the tall, polygonal Sodality Chapel was added at the SE by Kirby: it has Purbeck marble shafts supporting a plaster vault. The tabernacle and marble panels of the Annunciation and Assumption are by Conrad Dressler. [PH]

Liverpool, Merseyside
St John the Baptist, Tue Brook*

At St John's, Tue Brook, consecrated in 1871, Bodley finally achieved the refined splendour of his mature style. Here he abandoned the boldness of detail and what he had come to regard as the coarseness of French and Italian Gothic and designed a faultless statement of 14th-century Decorated Gothic to whose delicacy, refinement and beauty of detail is added Bodley's personal vein of poetry, scholarship and elegance of design. Built of red and white sandstone, with a roof of red tiles, the plan is composed simply of nave, aisles, chancel, N chapel, W tower and spire. Bodley designed and supervised every detail. It is furnished gorgeously with a handsome reredos, and elaborate screen and organ-case. But if one feature is to be distinguished it is colour. The walls, roof and furniture are richly decorated with gilding, flowing diaper patterns, stencils of wreaths, monograms and flowers in fresh colours; the tympanum of the chancel arch is painted with a mural of the Tree of Life by C. E. Kempe, who was also responsible for the panels on the screen and reredos. Undecorated wood surfaces are stained dark, providing a sombre foil to the sandstone, gilding and colour. There is pale early glass by Morris. St John's established the form of the Late Victorian church. It has been faultlessly restored by S. E. Dykes Bower. [ANS]

Liverpool, Merseyside
*St Margaret**

Undoubtedly the most accomplished of George Edmund Street's six Lancashire churches, this is the only one to be built in brick or to make extensive use of internal polychromy. Designed in 1867 and constructed in 1868–9, it is a spacious suburban High Church *par excellence*. Here Street is shown to be moving away from the bold fundamentalism of High Victorian Gothic with its intense Continental overtones and, like Bodley, deriving fresh inspiration from the graceful forms of 14th-century England. St Margaret's takes up the theme of nave without clerestory, flanked by taut stone and coursed Devon marble arcades dividing off high-walled lean-to aisles, but breaks with convention in having no structurally distinct chancel and no tower. The clarity of outline produced by these elements dominates the external design so that it relies almost entirely on finely judged proportions and a grand regularity of features. The big roof is continuous from W to E without break, but nicely foiled at the point where nave and chancel meet by an octagonal flèche above a pair of cross-gabled dormers which create unexpected chiaroscuro within.

There, light streams down from boarded and painted roof between two canted arch-braces marking the place of a chancel arch. The crisply symmetrical W façade is given a thoroughly urban treatment with prominent central buttress and rose between two broad Decorated tracery windows, and there are gabled W entrances through the aisles. Set off at an angle N of the church, the tall brick vicarage is connected by means of a covered walk to the NE vestry. [PJ]

Liverpool, Merseyside
St Mary, West Derby

This large, stately church stands near the entrance to the park of Croxteth Hall. It was built in 1853–6. The style is G. G. Scott's favourite Gothic of the late 13th-century to early 14th, tall and cruciform, with a polygonal apse. There is lots of good foliage carving. The reredos is alabaster with incised work and gold mosaic. The striking iron cross-cum-sanctuary lamp is by G. G. Scott junior (1873–4). The chancel woodwork, paving and altar-rails (1889–1906), and the pulpit (1902), are by John Oldrid Scott. There is a varied assortment of stained glass: much, including the five apse windows and transept windows, is by Clayton and Bell. [PH]

Liverpool, Merseyside
SS Matthew and James, Mossley Hill

This mammoth church, with its great crossing-tower, was built between 1870 and 1875 to the designs of Paley and Austin in a late-13th-century style in alternating bands of red-sandstone ashlar and squared coursed rubble. The NW porch projects from the N aisle and lines up with the W end of the church to produce an asymmetrical W elevation. A five-light W window with intersecting bar tracery surmounts the deeply recessed W door set within flushwork arcading. The N transept is in line with the N aisle, but emphasizes the great height of the tower by rising above it. The twelve pairs of Geometrical traceried clerestory windows are set within an arcade of shallow buttresses below a parapet of blind quatrefoils. [DM]

Liverpool, Merseyside
St Vincent de Paul, Vincent Street (RC)

Built in 1856–7 for an Irish dockside congregation (literally this time with the 'pennies of the poor'). The architect was E. W. Pugin, now in mid-career and favouring Early English Geometrical. The interior is well lit from E and W and massive four-light cross-gable clerestory windows. Nave and chancel are under one roof, and there is a separate 'confessional aisle'. Elaborate high altar with alabaster reredos. [RO'D]

Liverpool, Merseyside
Unitarian Chapel, Ullet Road*

Thomas Worthington's son and successor Percy was responsible for the freedom seen here in the use of Gothic elements. Begun in 1896 and completed in 1899, with the addition of a hall a few years later, the chapel has a wide aisled nave with choir and sanctuary beyond, pulpit and reading-desk flanking the chancel arch in a thoroughly Anglican manner, Morris glass, doors of beaten copper in the best Art Nouveau manner at the entrance, and fresco paintings by Gerald Moira in the vestry and library – though naked 'Truth' was more than even Unitarians could accept and they ordered her to be clothed! [CS]

Llanbedr Dyffryn Clwyd, Clwyd
St Peter

Nestling under the Clwydian Hills stands this wonderfully vigorous little church, built in 1863 by J. W. Poundley and David Walker. In prickly High Victorian Gothic, it is built of grey and yellow stone, and the roof has slate patterns. Over the porch is a hexagonal spirelet with sprouting crockets. Elaborated carving includes gargoyles round the apse and a squirrel on the porch. Inside there is good glass, and a table with portrait of Edward Lloyd carved in 1863 at 'Rhufain' (Rome) by the Welsh sculptor John Gibson. [PH]

Llanberis, Gwynedd
St Padarn

A large and distinguished church, designed by Arthur Baker, and built mostly in 1885. The nave was completed and the aisle added in 1914–15 by Baker's son-in-law, Harold Hughes. In the Early English style, it has a tower over the wide crossing, which is supported on curious 'double arches' in pink and grey stone. [PH]

Llandegwning, Gwynedd
No dedication

Out in rural Lleyn this endearing little church seems quite at home, looking for all the world like a child's toy, or a china ornament. Built in 1840 by John Welch, it has an octagonal W tower, turning circular, with conical spire. All details are crude and simple. The windows have wooden tracery. Inside it is painted white, except for the box pews which are grained in green. There is a two-decker pulpit. [PH]

Llandogo, Gwent
St Dochau (Odoceus)

This pretty little church is of 1860–1, by J. P. Seddon. In Geometrical Decorated, the exterior is of red sandstone and yellow Bath stone, with a spire-like W bell-cote over a W porch which has a stone roof. The S porch and vestry were added in 1889 by Seddon and Carter. The interior is rich with polychrome stonework and excellent tiles. The marble and alabaster reredos and the painted decoration of lilies and angels date from 1889. [PH]

Llandwrog, Gwynedd
St Twrog

In the middle of this pleasant estate village stands the spired church built in 1858–64 by Henry Kennedy. It has some fanciful details outside, but the cruciform interior is astonishing. The seating consists of stalls running round the nave and N transept, like a college chapel. The W gallery is of stone. The chancel screen is a juicy example of High Victorian ironwork. In the N transept is an excellent Clayton and Bell window. [PH]

Llangasty Tal-y-llyn, Powys
*St Gastayn**

The church was rebuilt in 1848–50 by Robert Raikes of Treberfydd House, who came from Yorkshire to bring Tractarian worship to this remote vale. His architect was the family friend John Loughborough

Pearson, still a young man with only a handful of churches behind him. It provides for the needs of Tractarian ritual, with all those features stipulated by Pugin from incense burners and water stoups to painted texts and symbols. But its austere exterior, with plain chamfered openings for lancet windows as practically the only relief, is a promise of the way Pearson's style would develop. Typical of him is the skilled way the tower, nave, chancel, S porch and organ-chamber are massed together and pro-portioned, belying the simplicity of their geometrical forms. [AQ]

Llangorwen, Dyfed
All Saints

The land for the church was given by M. D. Williams of Cwmcynfelin, whose brother, the Revd Isaac Willi-ams, a Tractarian poet and theologian, had been J. H. Newman's first curate at Littlemore. Hence the choice of H. J. Underwood as architect, for he had built Littlemore Church in 1835–6, and the use of Littlemore as the model here in 1841, with the same simple lancet style. The striking W bell-turret and S porch (note the roof with boldly foliated principals) were added in 1849 by William Butterfield. The stone altar was the first erected in Wales since the Reformation. The wooden eagle-lectern was given by Keble, and the remarkable bronze chandeliers are said to have been given by Newman. The intended tower was never built. [PH]

Llanyblodwel, Salop
St Michael

This basically medieval church, in the pleasant Tanat Valley, owes its celebrity to the Revd John Parker, vicar from 1844 to 1860. He was an accomplished watercolourist, and toured Wales and Europe paint-ing rood-screens, fonts, flowers and mountains, and was also an author and amateur architect. His work looks dotty, but he was clearly quite sane: it must have been his artist's eye that led to such picturesque results. The octagonal tower has a curiously bulging stone spire (1855), based – according to Parker – on 'the German Fribourg': he claimed that such spires were stronger than straight ones. He sprinkled the exterior with gabled dormers, and added N and S porches and a funny 'helmeted' finial at the SW. He was fond of cusped arches. The S porch (1849) has a

crazy timber roof. The interior was lovingly restored in 1958–60, and is rich in elaborate woodwork, stencil-painted decoration, and painted texts. The screen is basically Perpendicular. The reredos was carved by Parker himself. There is what Pevsner calls a 'Wild West Gallery', and also a choir gallery in the N aisle. Pevsner thought the font was of *c.* 1660: in fact, Parker had it 'rewrought in Normanesque'. [PH]

Llanymynech, Powys and Salop
St Agatha

The Welsh–English border runs down the main street of this former mining village. Its remarkable church, built in 1843–4 by Thomas Penson, is in Shropshire. In the currently fashionable Norman style, it is built of local grey limestone, but all the mouldings, jambs and ornamental parts are of yellow terracotta. Both W and E fronts are elaborate compositions, with intersecting arches. At the SW stands the striking tower, crowned by a stumpy pyramidal spire. The clock has two huge faces, visible from the quarries where its maker Richard Roberts (a celebrated inven-tor) used to work. The chancel is arcaded internally, and the E window is by Wailes (*c.* 1853). The interior was refitted in 1879. [PH]

London

[*Churches in central London are listed not under their boroughs (which would require a knowledge of modern political bound-aries not possessed by most readers) but alphabetically by their dedication or by the name by which they are most generally known. Thus 'All Saints' is under A; 'St Martin' under S; the French Protestant Church under F; and Westminster Cathedral under W. Churches in areas outside the centre are distributed throughout the book under their towns, counting Greater London as a county like any other.*]

London
All Hallows, Gospel Oak, St Pancras*

James Brooks's last and, many consider, his best church. Begun in 1891, it is the culmination of a distinguished career. Bumpus summed it up as 'a union of simplicity and massiveness with refined study of form and proportion'. Refinement was new to Brooks yet he achieved it here by an abstract purity of conception achieved by ambitious scale, stone and sculpture. The windows are tall lancets and there is a generous wheel-window occupying the greater part of the W wall. The most distinctive features of the exterior are rows of battered buttresses to N and S rising from foundations to roof; inside, the lofty cylindrical columns are without capitals but instead culminate in the ribs of an unfinished vault. The nave was consecrated in 1901, the year of Brooks's death. For years the chancel walls remained unfinished; in 1908 Giles Gilbert Scott made plans for completing the E end and it is to him that we owe the noble high altar, sanctuary and chancel, the beautiful chapel of the Blessed Sacrament, the image of Our Lady and the font. Then came the First World War and plans for the completion of the vault were immediately arrested, never to be resumed. [ANS]

London
All Saints, Ennismore Gardens, Kensington

Designed by Lewis Vulliamy in 1837 and modelled upon San Zeno at Verona, it was not finished until 1844. It is an extraordinary design from the time before Ecclesiology was born and demonstrated an unhappy compromise between Italian basilican architecture and Low Church worship. It has an apsidal E end and galleries: the clerestory is supported by cast-iron pillars painted to represent stone. The W front has a large doorway and a wheel-window modelled on the columns and mouldings at San Zeno and the small porch is roofed in copper. A campanile was added at the SW corner in the 1870s. Owen Jones was responsible for much decoration acclaimed by the *Ecclesiologist* as 'another triumph of the principle of decorative colour' but this was swept away by a transformation of the interior by the Arts and Crafts architect, Heywood Sumner, in 1892. A very fine mosaic of the Good Shepherd was placed in the tympanum of the W door; a new font was provided from a single piece of marble, surmounted by a bronze cover of Italianate design. The chancel and sanctuary were paved and panelled in marble and mosaic. A mosaic rood decorated the chancel arch and the walls of the clerestory were covered with sgraffito executed by Italian craftsmen. Heavily leaded glass was put in the W windows. All Saints is now used as a Russian Orthodox cathedral and looks far more convincing in its present life than it did as an Anglican church. [ANS]

London
All Saints, Margaret Street, Westminster*

A key building in the history of the 19th-century Church, both ecclesiastically and architecturally. Supervised by the president of the Cambridge Camden Society, W. Beresford-Hope, this became its model church. Here William Butterfield threw off antiquarian restraint and built in his favourite polychrome brick. Begun in 1849 and finished ten years later, it was expensive, lavish and colourful, a 'high' church in every sense. From the outside it seems to be squeezed into a space too small to hold it, an effect emphasized by the surrounding buildings (also by Butterfield), the tiny courtyard and immensely tall spire. The interior consists of an aisled nave and an unaisled chancel, the surfaces covered with ceramic murals, coloured marbles, mosaics, patterns in inlaid mastic, and naturalistic sculpture. The windows are filled with stained glass by Gerente (W window) and O'Connor (S aisle), resembling 'a good hand at bridge'. Pulpit, font and screen show Butterfield at his strongest. The reredos covers the E wall in place of a window. It was originally painted by William Dyce; the frescoes deteriorated rapidly and attempts to restore them failed. In 1909 J. N. Comper covered the originals with faithfully executed copies on boards. He later decorated the chancel vault, lengthened and heightened the altar, refurnished the sanctuary for elaborate and sensuous ceremonial, and designed the exquisite Late Gothic Lady Chapel, executed in gilded wood and alabaster. [ANS]

London
All Saints, Notting Hill, Kensington*

In 1852, Dr Walker, of St Columb Major, in Cornwall, conceived an ambition of building a great church with a conventual establishment and cloisters in Notting Hill. Only the church was completed, designed by William White in the Middle Pointed style, and consecrated in 1861. Built of Bath Stone relieved by red, a conventional plan of a nave of four bays, aisles, S porch, transepts gabled from the E bay of the nave and chancel with N and S chapels, lends itself to much architectural ingenuity. The broad nave, for instance, is defined by arcades carried across the transepts with an open continuation of the clerestory, founded upon Italian models. An attenuated tower and the W end culminates in an octagonal lantern which itself was meant originally as the base for a lofty spire. Following severe bomb damage an ambitious scheme of refurnishing and glazing was undertaken, including existing work by Cecil Hare and Martin Travers and new work by Comper and A. K. Nicholson, all most beautiful, embodying the dying fall of Edwardian ecclesiastical taste. [ANS]

London
All Saints, Rosendale Road, Brixton*

Even in its incomplete state, and after war damage, this is a remarkable church, built in 1888–91 to the design of G. H. Fellowes Prynne. In Early English Decorated style, of brick and stone, it is impressively lofty. The aisled (and incomplete) nave is linked to the chancel by canted bays: the chancel arch is filled by a screen of stone tracery, an idea taken from the medieval church of Great Bardfield (Essex), later used several times elsewhere by Prynne. The apsidal chancel has aisles and an ambulatory, beneath which (owing to a fall in the ground) is an open arcade. Prynne planned a tower placed at an oblique angle between the chancel and the apsidal Lady Chapel on its N: in 1952 J. B. S. Comper erected a small, plain tower there. [PH]

London
The Ascension, Battersea

Begun in 1876 by James Brooks and completed in 1883 by J. T. Micklethwaite who faithfully executed Brooks's design with few alterations. Brooks was dismissed because of the great expense incurred by providing foundations on a sharply sloping site. He designed a church of monumental grandeur achieved simply by using plain materials: red brick with cylindrical stone piers in the Early French Gothic style. It follows his conception of a town church first worked out in his East End churches: a single vessel with an unbroken roof-line, lean-to aisles with thick unbroken walls, a clerestory of lancet windows carried round the apse. There is a well-massed Lady Chapel and two-storeyed sacristies to the N making maximum use of a difficult site. [ANS]

London
Brompton Oratory, Church of the Immaculate Heart of Mary, Kensington (RC)

The London Oratory was established in 1853, and the house and Little Oratory to the W of the church were built at that time by J. J. Scoles (decoration by Hungerford Pollen, 1872). The main church is the result of a competition held in 1878 to provide a 'Renaissance' design in accordance with the Oratorian Newman's anti-Puginian belief that the Counter Reformation offered a better model for English Catholics than the Middle Ages. The winner was Herbert Gribble and the building went up from 1880 to 1884 in a style that is essentially Italian Baroque: cruciform, with a dome over the crossing. The exterior is faced with Portland stone; inside, the vaults are of concrete. The façade, dating from 1892–4, lacks its intended towers. The lead outer dome is by George Sherrin (E. Rickards designer), 1895. The interior, using Devon and foreign marbles, is partly by other hands, although the altar of St Philip Neri and the chapels of the Sacred Heart, the Seven Dolours, St Mary Magdalene and St Patrick are all Gribble's. The St Wilfrid altar is from Maastricht in Holland, the Lady Altar from Brescia, and the large statues of the apostles in the nave are important Baroque works from Italy. [RO'D]

London
Catholic Apostolic Church, Maida Avenue, Paddington*

The church was built in 1891–3 to the design of John Loughborough Pearson for the Catholic Apostolic Church. The exterior is of red brick and stone, the interior of stone. The style is his favourite Early English Gothic with elements taken from Normandy as well. There is a characteristic yet entirely new arrangement of entrances and font at the W end, and short passages lead left and right to a caretaker's house and an unfinished tower with a meeting room behind it. The church itself is sparsely decorated and vaulted throughout. It has an aisled nave, crossing and chancel with a polygonal apse and narrow ambulatory; it is flanked by chapels, that to the S treated like a miniature hall church with narrow aisles and a semicircular apse. Its proliferation of columns and its tiny vaulted spaces are a miracle of compression: even here there is no sense of crowding between the grand chancel and S transept but, rather, a sense of effortless flow of spaces from large to small. This kind of treatment makes up for the lack of decoration, which is almost entirely confined to mouldings. Only the altar and reredos are ornate, and designed in the Early Christian style. [AQ]

London
Chapel of the Brompton Hospital, Fulham Road

Hidden behind the red-brick Tudor masses of the Brompton Hospital for Chest Diseases stands an important work by that most individual of Victorian church architects, E. B. Lamb. The chapel, designed in 1849, was Lamb's first significant London building. Its style (Perpendicular) was chosen to harmonize with the hospital, its material (Kentish rag) to contrast with it. Though standing apart from the hospital, it was linked to it by a long corridor which traversed the courtyard, allowing patients to travel comfortably between them. The chapel itself has been altered three times, most severely in 1892, when the N aisle was added and the chancel enlarged and reroofed. But the main features survive, above all the maniacally ingenious nave roof, a hammer-beam truss with doubled principals, scissor braces, matchboarding, and vaguely Elizabethan pendants. There is also a diverse and fascinating collection of furnishings – cancelli, choir-stalls, organ-case, pulpit, nave seating, encaustic tile floors, and stained-glass windows (porch, nave W, S, and N, both transepts), all designed by Lamb. [ENK]

London
Chapel of the Hospital of SS John and Elizabeth, St John's Wood

This chapel was originally built in 1864 in Great Ormond Street. Its classical style was unusual for its architect, George Goldie (described by the shocked J. F. Bentley as 'a rampant Gothicist'), but was explained by the fact that it was built for the Order of St John of Jerusalem. In 1898 the hospital moved to St John's Wood, and Goldie's son Edward rebuilt the chapel there, between large projecting wings. It has a pedimented front with Ionic and Corinthian pilasters, a dome, and a Corinthian baldacchino over the altar. [PH]

London
Christ Church, Streatham*

Christ Church has confused people ever since it was built in 1841. Nobody is quite sure about its style. As architect, James Wild regarded it as Byzantine but he included an Egyptian cornice and the tower is Italianate. It has also been called Romanesque, Lombardic, Neo-Romanesque, eclectic Romanesque and Rundbogenstil. It possesses all these elements but Basil Clarke seems to be right in describing it as 'Italian with Saracenic influence'. Hitchcock considers it as 'perhaps the most original of all early Victorian churches', and his admiration was shared by Ruskin, Goodhart-Rendel and Pevsner. It is a basilica of precisely laid red and yellow brick with thin joints and smooth unbroken surfaces with an apse and a thin and tall campanile at the SE. The interior was originally decorated by Owen Jones and in 1925 by Arthur Henderson but little of their work remains. The interior suffers for lack of colour. J. F. Bentley designed various fittings, including the pulpit and much stained glass, of which some rich windows of 1864 survive in the gallery. [ANS]

London
Christ the King, Gordon Square*

In 1850 the Catholic Apostolic Church, to which this building still legally belongs, engaged John Raphael Brandon to design a church suitable for their elaborate ritual. It was opened in 1854. Although still lacking the two W bays of the nave and the tall spire intended to rise above the crossing-tower it is a masterpiece of cathedral-like grandeur. The lofty nave flanked by aisles with a full triforium and clerestory above passes on unhindered by the arches of the tower to a vaulted choir and sanctuary in which the canopied Angel's throne, the seven hanging lamps, the tabernacle given by the architect himself, the sanctuary lamp by Pugin, and other original fittings, remain with little alteration. To the E, beyond the high altar, is what was called the 'English Chapel', more homely in size but of equal if not greater elaboration than the rest. This is the grandest, and most accessible, monument to a movement which rose to its peak in less than twenty years but which has now become little more than a legend. It is now used by the University Anglican Chaplaincy. [CS]

London
Congregational Church, Lyndhurst Road, Hampstead

Built by Alfred Waterhouse in 1883–4, this church makes an instructive contrast with his King's Weigh-house Chapel: it seated 1,100, as against the latter's 900, but cost less than half as much. Its plan is entirely practical and original – roughly hexagonal, with a 'tail' containing schoolrooms etc.: the seating is arranged on two levels so that it all faces pulpit and organ. Romanesque in style, the materials are purple brick and red terracotta. Three large gables face the street, with porches between them, and big windows to light the galleries. Its future is uncertain. [PH]

London
Corpus Christi, Brixton Hill (RC)

Towering above Brixton Hill, this mighty fragment is all that was built of what would have been J. F. Bentley's largest church, apart from Westminster Cathedral, whose materials (brick with bands of stone) it anticipates. The ambitious project was due to the Belgian Father Hendrik van Doorne. The church, in Early Decorated style, was to consist of nave, chancel with ambulatory, N aisle flanked by confessionals, S aisle flanked by a chapel and sacristies, transepts, a tower and spire 190 feet high, and clergy house, all contained within a rectangle 142 feet by 88. All that was built in Bentley's lifetime (in 1886–7) was the chancel with its flanking chapels and sacristies. After his death the transepts were added by his firm. The interior is movingly impressive, with its wooden vault rising 64 feet. The E wall has a double thickness, which produces three-dimensional effects echoing in miniature the vistas of arches in the rest of the church. The stone-carving is exquisite. The high altar and reredos, incorporating several types of marble, as well as *opus sectile* panels and tiles, were erected to Bentley's designs after his death. The copper gilt tabernacle is a superb example of his metalwork. [PH]

London
French Protestant Church, Soho Square, Westminster

Built in 1891–3 by Sir Aston Webb, the church presents a domestic front to the Square, in cheerful brick and terracotta, and Franco-Flemish style. The stone tympanum of 1950 commemorates 400 years of Huguenot connections with London. The spacious and dignified interior is in Romanesque style, with clerestoried nave, aisles, and apsidal chancel, roofed by a wooden wagon vault. [PH]

London
Good Shepherd, Stamford Hill

This remarkable building owes its existence to Henry James Prince whose 'Abode of Love' at Spaxton, Somerset, gained great notoriety in the 1860s. In 1896 his sect of Agapemonites built what was then called 'the Church of the Ark of the Covenant' in north Hackney. Almost from its erection the church was very little used; from 1956 it has served as the 'Cathedral' of the 'Ancient Catholic Church', a society of questionable antiquity formerly meeting in Chelsea. The architect was J. Morris of Reading. The W tower of the church with its tall spire carries a plentiful burden of imagery with the symbols of the Evangelists carved in stone on the base of the buttresses and cast in bronze with wings aloft around the parapet. Inside on stone, wood and glass the symbolism continues, but it is the glass which is of greatest note; a marvellous series of windows 'designed by Walter Crane, executed by J. S. Sparrow' – flowers, fruit, vine scrolls in the nave, and in the great W window the 'Sun of Righteousness' rising in splendour above the waters. [CS]

London
Greek Orthodox Cathedral of Hagia Sophia, Bayswater

Built to an orthodox Byzantine plan: a Greek cross, with a central dome, by John Oldrid Scott, 1877–82, for the Greek community in London. Heavily massed to support the dome, it is of polychromatic brick with Early Christian rather than Byzantine detail. The interior is spacious and rich with a wealth of coloured marble. Magnificent furniture: carved stalls and an iconostasis of inlaid wood and mother-of-pearl with icon paintings by Ludwig Thiersen of Munich, executed in 1880. The vaults and dome are filled with mosaics by A. G. Walker, 1893. Here Scott anticipated the fashion for Byzantine instigated by W. R. Lethaby in the 1890s. [ANS]

London
Holy Innocents, Hammersmith*

The Holy Innocents was begun in 1887 and finished in 1891. Here James Brooks is still loyal to Early French Gothic but he follows the experiments of Street and Bodley by making a wide nave with narrow passage-aisles, pierced through external rather than internal buttresses. He gives the church double transepts and takes a leaf from Street's All Saints, Clifton, by giving the chancel a low arch, S chapel and N vestries. He remains faithful to red brick with stone dressings but the scale and breadth are unmistakably Late Victorian. Chancel screen and furniture by Charles Spooner and Ernest Geldart. [ANS]

London
Holy Redeemer, Clerkenwell

In this church, John Dando Sedding went far in his rebellion against the stylistic orthodoxies of High Victorian Gothic. Here he dared to employ the forbidden Renaissance in a very pure form. The Church of the Redeemer was designed to look Italian and it is usually mistaken for a Roman Catholic church. Internally Sedding indulged in the Renaissance game of placing a cross within a square such as Wren played in the City churches while the colonnades of Corinthian columns retain a longitudinal emphasis. The church was consecrated in 1888 but was never completed as designed in 1887. Sedding intended that the walls should be painted in fresco, but this was never done and in 1894-5 the interior was lengthened with a Lady Chapel, leaving the baldacchino free-standing. This work was carried out by Sedding's assistant and successor, Henry Wilson, who also, in 1901-6, added the campanile and the buildings which flank the façade. These are more Romanesque than Renaissance in style. Wilson was also responsible for most of the furnishings. [GS]

London
Holy Trinity, Latimer Road (now Freston Road), Hammersmith

Now a youth club and divided internally, but still discernible as Norman Shaw's most original church. It was built in 1883-9 for the Harrow Mission. The mission room came first at the W end of the site (up against the M41), succeeded by the gaunt, barn-like church, a single splendidly vaulted space lit solely by huge thirteen-light windows at either end. The 'fraying' tracery of the windows was probably Lethaby's, as were a set of splendid fittings now dissipated or destroyed. [AJS]

London
Holy Trinity, Sloane Street, Chelsea*

Holy Trinity is the finest example of the application of Arts and Crafts ideals to church architecture. It was designed in 1888 by John Dando Sedding, who was anxious to liberate the Gothic Revival from strict dependence upon historical precedent. The exterior is in the Perpendicular Gothic style with unmistakable flavour of the coming Art Nouveau, but it is the wide and spacious interior which is most impressive. Sedding was a disciple of Ruskin and he had been Master of the Art Workers' Guild, believing that life could only be brought into architecture by collaboration with artists and craftsmen. Not much was achieved before Sedding's early death in 1891 but the work was carried on by Henry Wilson, who was himself responsible for the Byzantinesque beaten copperwork in the N aisle and other furnishings. The nave corbels were carved by Hamo Thornycroft and there is also sculpture by H. H. Armstead. The reredos of 1901 (not what Sedding envisaged) was carved by John Tweed and the stalls by F. W. Pomeroy. More sculptors – Onslow Ford and F. Boucher – were responsible for the font while the metalworker, J. Starkie Gardner, made the electroliers. The great E window was filled with glass by Burne-Jones and Morris, the clerestory windows by Christopher Whall – to whom Sedding said of the church, 'Well? Well, is it too naughty? I hope it's not too naughty' – and those in the N aisle by Sir William Richmond. Unfortunately, the spandrils of the nave arcade were not all carved, nor the frieze above filled with mosaic by Thornycroft, and in the 1920s the interior was whitened by F. C. Eden. Although, therefore, it remains incomplete and there is no real harmony between the work by different artists, the design is clever and impressive, and it is filled with gorgeous things. [GS]

London
Immaculate Conception, Farm Street,
Westminster (RC)

The architect of this Jesuit church, as of several others, was J. J. Scoles. Built in 1844–9, it is in correct Late Decorated. Originally it had clerestoried nave, aisles, and lofty chancel: the W front was especially rich, but was redesigned in 1951, after bomb damage, by A. G. Scott. The splendid high altar, of gilded Caen stone, is by A. W. N. Pugin (1848). In 1864 the sanctuary floor was raised, as was the E window (based on that of Carlisle Cathedral), by George Goldie: he also lined the chancel with green marble and alabaster. The Sacred Heart Chapel, S of the chancel, was rebuilt in 1858–9 by Henry Clutton. J. F. Bentley designed the alabaster angels in the arcading, carved by Theodore Phyffers. The gorgeous altar, made by Earp, incorporates gilded bronze reliefs also by Phyffers. The mural is by Peter Molitor. The outer S aisle was added in 1876–8 by Clutton, and has a series of chapels with rich decoration by Clutton and others. The outer N aisle was added in 1899–1903 by W. H. Romaine-Walker, who ingeniously hollowed out the internal buttresses to fit confessionals between the polygonal chapels. The remarkable statues are by Joseph Swynnerton and Charles Whiffen. [PH]

London
Our Lady Star of the Sea, Greenwich (RC)

The best surviving Catholic example of Pugin's style in London, but in fact not by Pugin but by W. W. Wardell. The date is 1846–51. Kentish ragstone on the outside, Purbeck marble piers in the interior. The high altar by Boulton and Swales was shown in the 1851 Great Exhibition, but its reredos has since been removed. Lavishly decorated rood-screen and pulpit, E window and richly furnished Blessed Sacrament Chapel by Pugin and Hardman. E. W. Pugin designed the tomb of the founder, Canon North (1861) and the Lady Altar. The effect of the interior, however, is marred by insensitive modern flooring, panelling to the roofs and W gallery. [RO'D]

London
Our Lady of Victories Clapham (RC)

Built 1849–51 by W. W. Wardell for the Redemptorist Order. Rock-faced in Kent ragstone with a vaulted porch beneath the spire and a vaulted chancel. There is a contemporary high altar by Wardell, an E window by Hardman and Pugin (1851) and a Doom over the chancel arch originally by Settegast of Koblenz (1854). Between 1882 and 1902, J. F. Bentley provided an exquisite Lady Chapel, complete with its glass, altar and polychromatic decoration, an additional transept, a tabernacle and the monastery building. [RO'D]

London
St Augustine, Kilburn Park Road, Kilburn*

The masterpiece of John Loughborough Pearson, designed in 1870. For it he took Gothic features widely scattered in Europe and welded them brilliantly together. The system of internal buttressing of Albi Cathedral, the galleried section of the hall church of St Barbara at Kutna Hora, the steeples and turrets of St Etienne at Caen, the bridges across the transepts of St Mark's at Venice, and from England, the arched W end of Peterborough Cathedral, the disposition of rose window and narthex of Byland Abbey, the piers supporting the arched entrances to the transepts of the Chapel of Nine Altars at Fountains are all integrated into a design at once taut in its complexity and noble in its spaciousness. From the outside the church appears as a single-aisled cell built of red brick with Bath stone dressings. Hardly projecting transepts mark the break between nave and chancel, and at the W are the lofty tower and spire, happily completed within a few days of Pearson's death in 1897. The interior forms an unbroken cell of ten bays covered by quadripartite rib-vaults running from W to E. The arcades carry a gallery round the church. They cross the transepts like bridges, blanking them from view, but still allowing a flood of light from their large lancet windows to illuminate the chancel screen. Beyond the arcades everything is mysterious: dark aisles, inner and outer; the obscured clerestory above the galleries; then, again obscured, the transepts and the apsidal morning chapel on the S side; and lastly, the windows at the E and W ends appearing from behind arcaded screens and the last ribs of the vaulting. The effect of all these is to give the church an impression of great size, though its dimensions are not large. As so often in Pearson's churches, the vaulting provides the unifying element and sublime vistas of its own. It makes up for the stiff character of the carved decoration, never Pearson's happiest feature; it was executed by Thomas Nicholls. The brickwork in the lower part of the church is painted with a series of biblical scenes by Clayton and Bell, and they did the fine stained glass. The body of the church was built in two stages, the E in 1871–2, the W in 1876–8; the steeple was added in 1897 and provides the church with a fine landmark. [AQ]

London
St Augustine, Queen's Gate, Kensington*

One of Butterfield's biggest and most mature churches, opened in 1871, which demonstrates fully his theory of constructional colour. Broad rather than high, it continues to embody Butterfield's formula for a town church: no windows at aisle level, light is admitted from the clerestory and W windows, built of brick. The W front is a violent and assertive statement of the architect's style, flanked by turrets foiling a central bell-cote over attenuated windows with plate tracery, all executed in strident materials. The culmination of the interior decoration is the sanctuary, finished in 1879, which is a marvel of mineral riches with a sumptuous pavement of marble and dull-red, black and yellow tiles. For many years the decoration was hidden beneath lime wash, making it 'like an organ played with half the stops missing' (Paul Thompson). Martin Travers has been blamed but the culprit was an assistant priest. In 1928 Travers designed his vivid Southern Baroque reredos and other furniture in the same style, making the church one of the most flamboyant examples of Anglo-Catholic Baroque. In 1974–5 Butterfield's colours were carefully reinstated, tile murals and mosaic exposed and the church returned as far as possible to its original appearance, while retaining Travers's furniture which blends surprisingly well in such a powerful mid-Victorian context. [ANS]

London
St Barnabas, Pimlico*

Designed by Thomas Cundy and consecrated in 1850 at the height of the papal aggression, no new church excited so much antagonism and misunderstanding from Protestant agitators, who saw it as a symbol of Anglo-Catholic treachery. The church, school, clergy house and choir school form a prim Tractarian group, built of ragstone in the Early English idiom. A simple plan of a nave, aisles, tower and spire at the NW corner, S porch, aisled chancel and crypt is said to have been improved on execution by Butterfield. No other Anglican church so fully demonstrates the development of the Puginian ideal in terms of Late Gothic furniture, plate, painted decoration and stained glass. Pugin himself designed the altar plate and ornaments; Bodley was brought in later to design the sombre Spanish Gothic reredos and rood-screen, the organ-case and the delicate painted decoration of wreaths and monograms on the chancel roof and the walls and vault of the crypt. His pupil, Comper, covered the arcading of the sanctuary with flowing diaper patterns in green and gold, provided much Late Gothic imagery and designed a Germanic sacrament house flanked by censing angels and a chantry with gilded screens and silver-stained glass in the S aisle. C. E. Kempe and W. E. Tower came last and added more than either Bodley or Comper: diapering in Indian red, grey and green on the upper walls of the chancel and gilded angels in song with entwined wings, carved in shallow relief, the rood figures, images, two heavily carved and gilded altars and reredoses and much opaque glass. St Barnabas is unrivalled in so successfully embodying the refining influences of the Gothic Revival, untouched by mid-Victorian vigour and 'go'. [ANS]

London
St Chad, Shoreditch*

Bringing the Gospel to the slums was one of the main objectives of the Anglo-Catholic movement. The Shoreditch and Haggerston Church Extension Fund was started in 1862 for the provision of churches in these densely crowded districts. By 1869 three stately churches had been built dedicated to the three British missionaries Augustine, Chad and Columba. James Brooks was given his major opportunity by designing the second and third; they were mission churches which had to be cheap, impressive and dignified. St Chad's fulfils these conditions: it is built powerfully of red brick, in the Early French style, on a cruciform plan with a vaulted apse separated from the nave by a light iron screen; the aisles have no windows, light is admitted through plate tracery from the W end and clerestory. There is stained glass by Clayton and Bell and a massive reredos filled with figures of saints. An Early French vicarage was built next door. [ANS]

London
St Columba, Kingsland Road, Shoreditch*

Of all Brooks's East London churches (he designed five) St Columba's is his masterpiece. It was the crowning achievement of the Shoreditch and Haggerston Church Extension Fund and was built in the most conspicuous position. It is on a very large scale and designed for elaborate quasi-medieval ceremonial. The plan is cruciform: a lofty nave with side aisles and lean-to roofs, a short NW transept; a central tower rising above the chancel and sanctuary and shallow transepts with galleries. It is built of red brick with stone dressings but the interior was whitewashed in the 1930s. Light is admitted through the clerestory and lancets at E and W; there are no windows in the aisles, thus preventing noise and distraction. In the windows Brooks broke with tradition and introduced square rather than diamond quarries, separated from the jambs by narrow borders of rectangular leading. There is a mortuary chapel by Ernest Geldart at the NW end, over a vaulted passage. To the NE is the clergy house and from there W a mission house and school, forming an internal courtyard, once full of plane trees, but linked externally with the church by a continuous wall surface. The church was made redundant in 1975 and is now used by Nigerian Pentecostalists. [ANS]

London
St Cuthbert, Philbeach Gardens, Kensington*

An unexpectedly successful fusion of opposing schools: the dying fall of the mid-Victorian sumptuary tradition gone bland and the first enthusiasm of the Arts and Crafts at its most lavish and original. St Cuthbert's was designed by H. Roumieu Gough in 1884–7; he was responsible for its generous scale and the wealth of marble but much of the furniture was designed by a member of the congregation, W. Bainbridge Reynolds, an outstanding craftsman and metalworker who loathed mass production and left the mark of human artistry on everything he touched. He designed the lectern of wrought iron, brass and beaten copper, altar-rails, the screens and organ-case, the royal arms, the altar crucifix, candlesticks,

tabernacle and much else. The font, rood, sedilia and pulpit are Gough's. The Revd Ernest Geldart was brought in to design the immense reredos in 1914 on the theme of the 'worship of the incarnate Son of God, with incense and lights'. Geldart also designed many sumptuous vestments and altar frontals, stiff with jewels and embroidery, executed by a parish guild, while another executed much of the sculptured diapering and wood carving which covers every surface. [ANS]

London
St Dominic, Gospel Oak (RC)

The church of this Dominican Priory was begun in 1863 by G. R. Blount, but not much had been built by the time he died in 1876. Charles Alban Buckler was appointed to redesign the church, which was opened in 1883. Enormously large (200 feet long, 80 feet wide, and 100 feet to the ridge of the roof), it has an unbroken roof-line, and no tower, according to Dominican tradition, though a pyramidal-roofed tower stands at the end of the L-shaped group of Priory buildings attached to the N side of the church. In Early English style, it is built of yellow brick with stone dressings. The vast, apsed interior is timber-vaulted. Fortunately the rich fittings survive intact. The elaborate high altar has a prickly reredos. There are no less than twenty-three side chapels, seven flanking each aisle, and the rest in the transepts. Fourteen of them represent the Mysteries of the Rosary. That of St Dominic has a reredos painted by Philip Westlake, and all the rest have richly carved stone reredoses. What with all the stained glass (by several different firms), the statues of saints, the iron screens and monuments and brasses to benefactors, the effect is more Continental than English. The Annunciation chapel (E end of N aisle) was founded by Buckler, who is commemorated by a large monument and stained glass above (by J. N. Pearce). The excellent Stations of the Cross, painted in Late Gothic style, are by N. H. J. Westlake (1887). [PH]

London
St Francis of Assisi, Kensington (RC)

Manning's newly founded Oblates of St Charles decided to build a church in the notorious slums of Notting Dale, and in 1859–60 Henry Clutton erected a small brick building in severe Early French Gothic.

J. F. Bentley was in charge of the work. The Oblate in charge, Fr Rawes, almost at once asked Bentley to design a Lady Chapel, baptistery, presbytery and school, as well as fittings and decorations. This encouraged Bentley to leave Clutton's office and set up on his own. The Lady Chapel was ingeniously made by prolonging the aisle round the apse. The altar was painted by N. H. J. Westlake, as was the altar of St John (1861). The baptistery also dates from 1861, and Bentley was the first person baptized in it. The splendidly rich high altar dates from 1863. Other excellent fittings include the statue of Our Lady by Phyffers (1870), the Stations of the Cross by Westlake (1865–70), and some stained glass designed by Bentley and Westlake (the best is the intense Annunciation window, made by Lavers and Barraud). The presbytery (1861–3) is ingeniously planned, and has marvellous iron finials. [PH]

London
St George's Cathedral, Southwark (RC)

This is, in ecclesiastical terms, A. W. N. Pugin's most important church in London, and as such has always attracted much criticism. It was built with great financial difficulties between 1841 and 1848 and was from the outset a compromise between Pugin's ambitious first designs and the needs of a large but poor congregation. It was badly damaged in the Blitz and the E end, the lowest part of the W tower, the long yellow-brick aisle walls and a few details inside are all that now remain of Pugin's church. The rest is a rebuilding and extension by Romilly Craze. The result, although essentially a 20th-century Gothic Revival building, still depends on Pugin's plans. The exterior, though it lacks its intended great W tower and spire, is still impressive. Inside there survive from Pugin's work the large Decorated E windows, the N aisle windows, some fittings in the Blessed Sacrament Chapel, and the enchanting and untouched Petre Chantry of 1848–9. The Knill Chantry of 1856–7 is by E. W. Pugin, a refinement of his father's work opposite. [AW]

London
St Giles, Camberwell*

Won in competition by Scott and Moffatt after the destruction of the medieval church by fire and built 1842–4, St Giles marks a culminating point in Scott's early life as a church architect. Here he flowered in his first Gothic building of any size, designed in his favourite Middle Pointed style. Built of Kentish ragstone on rising ground in a large churchyard, a cruciform plan was adopted with a bold broached spire rising over the crossing between nave, chancel and transepts; it is the first instance of one of Scott's churches having a central tower. The interior is a model of purity and orthodoxy: five bays with alternately round and octagonal piers with foliated capitals and an open timber roof. The furniture did not come up to the architecture. Much good stained glass, notably the E window by Ruskin and Oldfield, others by Lavers and Barraud, and Ward and Nixon. The 'wretched galleries on iron columns' were removed after the war. [ANS]

London
St James, Spanish Place (RC)

A large and stately stone church by Edward Goldie in Early French Gothic style, with apsidal chancel, galleried double aisles, and transepts which do not project. Begun in 1887, and opened in 1890, it only received the three W bays of the nave in 1918, and tower and spire remain unbuilt. The interior, with the vault rising to 60 feet, is very impressive. Pier-shafts are of Derbyshire marble. J. F. Bentley designed furnishings, which include some of his best, especially the Lady Chapel altar, its gilded triptych framing a copy of a Murillo. He also designed the altars of the Sacred Heart, St Joseph, and Our Lady of Victories, the wall-lining of marble and *opus sectile* of the chancel, the iron communion rails, and the high altar. The latter was removed in the reordering *c.* 1970, and its front is now on the W wall. The reredos, cross and candlesticks, and corona, all designed by Thomas Garner after Bentley's death, survive. [PH]

London
St James the Less, Westminster*

Three daughters of Bishop Monk of Gloucester, in devising a memorial to their father, gave George Edmund Street his first opportunity to design, in early 1859, a London church showing his mature powers at full stretch. Built 1859–61, the whole structure is particoloured in red and black brick with yellow Morpeth stone dressings and blue-slated roofs. The style is Street's personal interpretation of Early

Geometrical, adapting and co-ordinating English, French and Italian motifs to his own principles, an original and creative proclamation against the ties of insular archaeological precedent in the Gothic Revival. A sheer and stern campanile, perhaps the finest Ruskinian steeple ever to rise in Victorian England, stands detached N of the church and groups admirably with the Italianate arcaded school-block which Street added in 1863–6. Its elaborate belfry is crowned by a machicolated cornice and overhanging slated pyramid roof transmuting into a blunt octagonal spire and corner pinnacles. From the tower base a cloistered porch leads to the high broad nave with clerestory and narrow lean-to aisles, but from the E the semicircular sweep of the heavily buttressed apse dominates beyond a tall palisade of sumptuous wrought ironwork. Lower double transepts project N and S of the chancel, a vestry with hipped roof hinging on to the S. W windows show a variation between lancets and plate tracery. For the interior, the traditional Ecclesiological scheme of clearly defined spaces related according to their function is forcefully restated, but welded into a dramatic, harmonious crimson integrity. As at Oxford, Street states his preference for a painted timber canopy enveloping the nave, contrasting this with a lower, ribbed brick vault over choir and apse; a large mosaic after G. F. Watts fills the space above the chancel arch, and in order to light it the last bay of the clerestory is heightened into dormers. There is an exhilarating juxtaposition of deeply modelled carving and flat polychromatic surface enrichment; inlaid marble reredos and mastic decoration to the apse walls, and serrated brick edging to the arches. Weighty three-bay arcades are supported on squat granite columns, their capitals exuberantly sculptured by W. Pearce. William Farmer carved the ornate stone pulpit, and James Leaver wrought wonderful metalwork including a truly exotic baldaquin over the font. Maw's tiles and the superb stained glass by Clayton and Bell exactly complement the ensemble. [PJ]

London
St John, Hammersmith*

One of Butterfield's stateliest churches, built of yellow brick, thinly banded with red, in 1858–9, its plan is typical of the architect's structural articulation: a nave of five bays but the W bay is narrower to define the entrance and flows into a W narthex integrated by extended buttresses. The chancel is lower than the nave; the tall tower, whose base forms a S porch, is gabled at right angles to the nave roof. The interior was once full of rich polychromatic decoration but much has been effaced, most seriously in the chancel, and Butterfield's heavy wooden screen has been removed. Bentley was brought in to design the sumptuous and exquisite Lady Chapel, organ-case and other furniture, demonstrating his skill as a designer of church furniture and his tact in adding to a building of altogether different aspiration. [ANS]

London
St John the Divine, Kennington*

In early 1871 G. E. Street designed his third and largest church in London, capable of holding a congregation of 1,000. The chancel complex was built in 1871–3, nave and aisles following in 1873–4. After the architect's death A. E. Street superintended the tower and spire, erected in 1887–8 in exact accord with the original drawings. The style is a supple Geometrical Decorated, relying on fine red brick of narrow gauge, with Corsham Bath stone dressings and slated roofs to assert their own polychromy. Street's masterly plan incorporates the final development of his characteristic theme of broad nave with lean-to passage-aisles, the richly moulded five-bay arcades canting sharply inwards at the E bay to frame a wide and lofty chancel arch. It is a yet more majestically urban version of St Saviour's, Eastbourne, but doing without clerestory for the sake of a truly noble W steeple. In compensation the aisle walls are extremely high so that large tracery windows sufficiently light the interior, giving at the same time a mysterious suffused calm to the great spaces of the nave and its enveloping timber rib-vault. Like the other two London churches there is a brick-vaulted apsidal chancel, here with five-sided buttressed E end. Externally, the tremendous nave roof is carried on straight to the chancel cross-wall which is surmounted by a tall sanctus bell-gable. Subsidiary compartments are treated hierarchically, the vaulted SE chapel having a shallow polygonal apse, and the transversely gabled N organ-gallery a vaulted cloister beneath. Outside this, the NE vestry block finishes in a longitudinal pair of gabled roofs. Parapets and pinnacles crown buttressed aisles, interrupted at their W bay by a vaulted N porch and corresponding semicircular S baptistery. W of these the nave emerges clear as a half-bay vestibule, terminating in the magisterial W tower with cylindrical newel-turret clasped against its N side. Exceedingly long coupled louvres compose into narrow gabled panels all round the belfry, from which soars the massive octagonal broach-spire to a height of 212 feet; this is of stone with three diminishing tiers of lucarnes, and heavy square pinnacles springing above the broaches. Destroyed by incendiary bombs in 1941, the interior was faithfully restored from Street's plans, 1955–8, by H. S. Goodhart-Rendel. Not attempting to recreate G. F. Bodley's unsympathetic decorative scheme of the 1890s, he placed a free-standing altar forward in the nave apse, flanking it with neo-Streetian wrought-iron grilles. A. E. Street's curved iron baptistery-screen of 1889 had fortunately survived the fire; but the excellent stained glass in the chancel is all new, by W. T. Carter Shapland 1959–62. [PJ]

London
St John of Jerusalem, Hackney*

E. C. Hakewill emulated the style of Sir Gilbert Scott and he had a profound admiration for Butterfield. St John of Jerusalem is his biggest and most ambitious church and one of the largest churches built in London since the Reformation. Consecrated in 1848, it replaced a chapel-of-ease to Hackney built by Savage in 1810. Early English in style, cruciform in plan, built of Kentish ragstone dressed with Speldhurst stone, it soon fell victim to its soft, porous materials and much sculpture had to be removed from the tower and spire, spoiling their definition. The interior demonstrates considerable archaeological ambition and has richly carved capitals and corbels, an inner plane of tracery in the clerestory, arcaded walls in the apse and tentative wall paintings. [ANS]

London
St Mark, Battersea*

A Broad Church rector of Battersea instigated an ambitious scheme of church building in one of the most rapidly developing and drab suburbs of S London. William White was commissioned to design five churches. St Mark, Battersea Rise, completed in 1875, demonstrates how well White rose to a modest brief. Early English in style, its plan owes much to Brooks's contemporary church of the Ascension, rising on Lavender Hill nearby, but executed on a

miniature scale: nave and aisles, SW tower and porch, lofty clerestory and an elevated polygonal apse surrounded by an ambulatory leading down to a crypt and vestries. It is built of concrete faced in and out with stock brick dressed with red brick. Glass by Lavers and Barraud, chancel pavement of mosaic, tesserae and marble, by Minton, designed by Clayton and Bell. Font of Devonshire marbles containing pebbles from the Jordan. English altar in the Baroque style by W. Randoll Blacking. [ANS]

London
St Mark, Dalston*

The biggest and one of the most eccentric churches in London with one of the most animated building histories. Designed by a young, inexperienced architect, Chester Cheston junior, who had never built a church before and who had designed the strange, rather sinister houses surrounding the site as surveyor to the Amherst Estate. Disaster after disaster dogged the years between 1860 and 1870 when it was being built, obscured by misunderstandings and culminating, it is said, in the discovery that Cheston had forgotten to provide any drains. St Mark's seats 1,713 people and is designed as a vast Protestant auditorium in a rogue style with lancet windows filled with strident stained glass, internal polychromy in red, white, blue, black and yellow brick, strangely attenuated arcades of five bays with annulated iron columns and foliated capitals supporting a varnished oak roof, filled with stained glass in the crossing. In 1877 E. L. Blackburn superseded Cheston's design for a spire with an over-confident tower in the manner of S. S. Teulon which is more in the spirit of the interior of St Mark's than the exterior; it boasts a vast external thermometer. [ANS]

London
St Martin, Gospel Oak*

It is often supposed that E. B. Lamb worked for low-church, nouveau riche clients: here, at his most famous church (as almost nowhere else), it is true. The patron was John Derby Allcroft, a rich manufacturer and a strong Evangelical. The church was begun in 1864 and consecrated in 1866. It is a large church, and one of Lamb's most expensive. The exterior, with its nubbly Kentish ragstone and restlessly broken planes, is picturesque in an old-fashioned way, though every break and angle corresponds to some feature of the interior. There is much detailing of an idiosyncratically late medieval character. The strange and impressive tower, now unfortunately shorn of its corner pinnacles, projects out over the entrance, its base quarried away to form a cavernous porte-cochère – an effect somewhat weakened by the later addition of a chapel (by Lamb's son, Edward Beckitt Lamb). The interior is breathtaking. St Martin is the penultimate recension of a complex plan which Lamb had developed as early as 1850. It is basically cruciform, with a long aisleless nave and polygonal chancel, but Lamb inserts a spacious rectangular bay into each of the angles formed by the intersection of the cross-axes. The result is that the church seems to centre, like a nine-square plan, on the crossing. There is an almost magical flow and interpenetration of spaces, and this is emphasized by the magnificently daring timber roof, with its sinewy rafters and web-like surfaces. Under this voluminous covering, the stone walls are left unplastered. The square piers, also unplastered, sprout strange colonnettes which climb up into the roof. Lamb's seating furniture, altar-rails, font and pulpit remain. [ENK]

London
St Mary, Cadogan Street, Chelsea (RC)

The old chapel of 1812 was replaced in 1877–9 by the first complete church built by J. F Bentley, Early English in style. Externally, with its stock brick and stone dressings, and cramped site, and lacking its spire, it is not especially impressive, but the interior is of noble elegance. The nave is tall and clerestoried, while the chancel, almost as high, is enriched by the double tracery of the E lancets and the stone panelling below, with angels well carved by McCarthy. Unfortunately the magnificent high altar designed by Bentley in 1864 for the old chapel has been moved to the N chapel: it is of alabaster, marble and glass mosaic, the sculpture by Phyffers. The pulpit, with paintings by Westlake, was also designed for the old chapel in 1864. The hanging rood (1902) and the lovely shrine of Our Lady in the N transept are also by Bentley. The S chancel chapel – the former cemetery chapel of 1845 – is by A. W. N. Pugin, while the richly carved Blessed Sacrament Chapel, S of the S aisle, is by E. W. Pugin (1860). The presbytery is by Bentley (1879). [PH]

London
St Mary Abbots, Kensington

St Mary Abbots demanded a distinguished and fashionable architect: Sir Gilbert Scott was the obvious choice. He provided an expensive building, on a grand scale, using Kentish ragstone for the exterior and Corsham stone and Irish marble for the interior. Completed in 1872, it has a stateliness and repose which demonstrate the fruit of Scott's work in its maturity. The tower and spire were completed in 1874 and were the tallest in London until Pearson designed St Augustine's, Kilburn. Since the war, much of its Victorian splendour has been diminished, the uniform series of stained-glass windows by Clayton and Bell has been interfered with, and an unhappy colour scheme spoils the groined roof. Clayton and Bell also executed the high altar and reredos. The S chapel was designed by Scott's grandson, Giles, as a war memorial in 1921 and his younger son, J. O. Scott, added the vaulted cloister from the street in 1889–93. [ANS]

London
St Mary of Eton, Hackney*

In 1880 Eton College established a mission of the Church of England in Hackney Wick. The architect was G. F. Bodley whose aristocratic style was applied in 1890 to build a splendid, anachronistic set of buildings in the midst of main roads, railway lines and bad housing. Here he designed an ensemble emulating on a small scale and with refinement and great dignity the layout of Eton and the older public schools. The church is a long hall with narrow passage-aisles and an arcade with chamfered piers rising to the height of an unbroken barrel-vault but without a clerestory. It is a broad, horizontal building, bearing the marks of expensive simplicity with a plain abstract quality and nerveless mouldings, altogether different from Bodley's earlier work with Garner which was so dependent on mouldings in deep relief, sculpture and colour. The high altar is by one of Comper's assistants, W. Ellery Anderson. The tower, clergy house and a medley of subsidiary buildings are by Cecil Hare. [ANS]

London
St Mary Magdalene, Munster Square*

At St Mary Magdalene, begun in 1849, R. C. Carpenter was responsible for bringing Pugin's influence into the Church of England. It is in the flowing Decorated style, built of ragstone on a hall plan with nave and aisles of almost equal height, no clerestory, piers of four clustered shafts, graceful arcades, white plastered walls, and a large sanctuary intended for ceremonial. Much of the stained glass was destroyed in the war. On its consecration in 1852 the *Ecclesiologist* described it as 'the most artistically correct new church yet consecrated in London'. In 1883–4 Carpenter's son extended the church by adding a N aisle and crypt. The interior is unspoilt: the later roodbeam and screens by J. T. Micklethwaite and Somers Clarke and a carved and gilded reredos by Sir Charles Nicholson respect its intrinsic austerity; it retains a devotional spirit and still has a faint but pervasive odour of incense. [ANS]

London
St Mary Magdalene, Paddington*

G. E. Street designed his second London church in early 1867. The style is Geometrical Decorated with strong Continental inflexions, although with far less constructional coloration than at Westminster. Inevitably of red brick with pale-yellow Bath stone dressings, it was cleverly planned to take full advantage of an acute triangular piece of ground lying against the S bank of the Grand Junction Canal. This has resulted in a highly picturesque asymmetrical arrangement intended to soar above close-surrounding terrace houses, now swept away. Built by degrees 1867–73, the structure rises sheer from a deeply excavated crypt creating an impression of awesome verticality, a quality stressed by the tall clerestory and enormous blue-slated roofs. The E end is made powerfully dramatic by the juxtaposition of its unbuttressed polygonal apse and slim SE steeple with newel turret. High above the chancel roof this tower, of complex octagonal forms, culminates in a striated belfry built up in alternating layers of brick and stone; it is of such compacted richness that the sharp stone spire appears almost to float above it. Nearby, the chancel-arch gable terminates in a stone sanctus bell-cote. Entrance is by a shallow S transept placed W of the tower, or by the low lean-to narthex-cum-baptistery

at the W end. Of exceedingly lofty proportions, the nave has a boarded and painted wagon roof with iron tie-rods. Six-bay arcades support the clerestory with its elegant inner-plane tracery on long marble shafts; at first all seems comparatively regular, but the constrictions of the site allowed only one aisle – that on the S. Independently behind the differently detailed N arcade, but masked by its subdivided bays, stands the external nave wall. Sumptuously enriched with coloured marbles, mosaics and alabaster inlay, Crucifixion reredos executed by Thomas Earp and painted decorations by Daniel Bell, the high brick-vaulted chancel glitters with Henry Holiday's most wonderful early glass. It is a perfect summation of the 1860s polychrome aesthetic; but below, secreted within the crypt, Ninian Comper's radiant chapel of St Sepulchre spins a different sort of medievalist's dream in blue and gold, 1894–5. [PJ]

London
St Matthias, Stoke Newington*

Butterfield's first London church. Completed in 1853, it fully demonstrates the clarity and precision of his structural articulation. It is a town church, built of common yellow brick with stone dressings, and its high pitched roof, huge clerestory and gabled saddleback tower set over the chancel stand over rows of poor housing. The contrast between the vast nave and low, vaulted chancel is dramatic and the second is given emphasis by vigorously carved capitals in deep relief which challenge the prettiness of much contemporary sculpture. The church was restored after war damage by N. F. Cachemaille-Day who whitened the interior and redisposed the liturgical plan. [ANS]

London
St Michael, Bedford Park

A highly individual church by Norman Shaw (1879–82), tailor-made for Jonathan Carr's aesthetic suburb of Bedford Park, flagrantly mixing Gothic and Queen Anne motifs in an exhibition of daring, informality and whimsy entirely typical of Shaw. Outside, the impressive roof-line is perversely broken into by sunk clerestory windows and by the white Queen Anne 'trim' of the balconies, porch and bell-cote. The interior, with its revolutionary green woodwork, is relaxed and secular but spacious and has a well-elevated chancel. Benches take the place of the usual chairs. Some fittings are by Maurice B. Adams, who added the SE chapel and the hall in the NW corner. [AJS]

London
St Michael, Camden Town*

It is surprising that Bodley designed only three churches in London. This was his first, partly finished in 1880–1, with his partner Thomas Garner whose contribution was more extensive than Bodley's. An austere exterior of yellow brick gives little indication of the great height (increased by the floor being several steps lower than the Camden Road) and assured handling of the flowing Decorated style within. A continuous wagon roof, vaulted above the chancel, is broken by stone arches, requiring flying buttresses. All is cool, dignified and distinguished by repose. The chancel was built in 1892–4 but it has never been furnished adequately and the massive tower was never built. [ANS]

London
St Peter, Vauxhall*

First designed in 1860 by John Loughborough Pearson as part of a religious, educational and social centre in a desperately poor part of Lambeth. As built in 1863–4, the Decorated Gothic of the first design gave way to the stylistically earlier as well as cheaper plate tracery of the final design, in which much other carved decoration was abandoned as well as a fine, tall steeple. This is the first of Pearson's great, vaulted town churches, and a prototype for those of the 1870s and 1880s. The design is brutally plain: the yellow stock brick used throughout is only occasionally relieved by meagre diapering in red or black brick, or by carved stonework. The W front on the street is characterized by plate-traceried windows set between massive buttresses that rise from an entrance porch: only an Italianate turret relieves the overall massiveness and takes the place of the abandoned steeple. The E end is dominated by a plain, unbuttressed semicircular apse. The plain exterior does nothing to prepare one for the spacious interior. Despite the low cost, Pearson did not abandon the vaulting, which for the first time here he applied throughout the interior of a church. Nave and aisles, N transeptal chapel, chancel, sanctuary and apse are all finished with quadripartite or sexpartite vaults or variants of them, carried out with stone ribs and brick cells. For the first time Pearson employed the Golden Section for the proportions of many of the parts, like the blank panels over the nave arcades, and the length and width of the nave bays as well as many of their details. Some stained glass is by Lavers and Barraud, some by Clayton and Bell. Clayton and Bell also executed the painted decoration of the apse. The boldly Italianate reredos, Pearson's best, was carved by Poole of Westminster and has mosaics by Salviati of Venice. [AQ]

London
St Saviour, Aberdeen Park, Islington*

Surrounded by a broken circus of Italianate villas, St Saviour's, embowered in mature trees and dense verdure, is one of the most original and rare examples of the work of William White. Completed in 1866, built of red and buff brick, cruciform in plan with a central tower culminating in an octagonal lantern, it embodies a personal and deeply considered essay in the constructional theories of Butterfield and Street, mingling English and French 13th-century Gothic. The interior is defined by precisely articulated space culminating in a low chancel raised on gently graded steps, intensifying its mystery by shafts of light falling from the lantern at the crossing of nave and transepts. Polychromatic brickwork in geometrical patterns, sculpture and rich painted decoration in hard colours in the chancel and on the roof of the lantern, powerful glass by Lavers and Barraud. A jewelled and poignant shrine of mid-Victorian ritualistic aspiration, heightened by the forlorn decay of its setting. [ANS]

London
St Simon Zelotes, Chelsea*

Joseph Peacock designed relatively few churches but St Simon's, consecrated in 1858, is one of the most vivid examples of internal constructional polychromy applied on a small scale, on an insignificant site, enclosed by ragstone walls with an assertive gable at the W end which ill accords with the red-brick and terracotta refinements of the Cadogan Estate. Details of the Decorated period are piled up in riotous conglomeration, giving the impression that the illustrations in Parker's *Glossary* have been 'taken down, altered and used in evidence against him. Never can there have been more architecture in less space' (Goodhart-Rendel). [ANS]

London
St Stephen, Hampstead*

For S. S. Teulon this was 'my mighty church', the largest, the most expensive and one of the most sophisticated constructionally, supported on a system of brick arches on concrete bases. Sadly it was a climax not just to a career but to a life. Begun in 1869, the finishing touches were still being added in 1873 when Teulon died. There is an outstanding brick vault to the crossing but the nave is roofed in timber by massive trusses of arched braces, queen-posts and collar purlins. Much of the stone carving, including the scene depicting King David on the external gable of the N transept, is by Thomas Earp. The church has been declared redundant and has suffered from vandalism and theft. [MS]

London
St Stephen, Westminster*

Built as a Christian memorial to her father by the philanthropist, Angela, Baroness Burdett Coutts, designed in the flowing Decorated style by Pugin's pupil, Benjamin Ferrey, and built 1847–9, St Stephen's is one of the most complete and expensive churches of its time and one of the most graceful achievements of its architect. It has been sadly mistreated by conventional Anglican taste during the second half of the present century so that much of Ferrey's decoration has been lost. A stereotyped plan of chancel, nave and aisles is arrested by the placing of the tower and spire at the E end of the N aisle. The spire was lopped in 1967. The carving on the capitals of the nave piers represents the birds and beasts from the Benedicite. The pulpit is of Caen stone and the font has carvings of scenes from the Life of Christ. The bosses on the chancel roof proclaim the story of the Creation. Ferrey's painted decoration and the clustered piers of polished red granite have long disappeared under cream distemper. [ANS]

London
St Swithun, Hither Green, Lewisham

St Swithun's, built by Norman Shaw's pupil, Ernest Newton, in 1892–3, is a strong, cool and spacious church of red brick in the 14th-century style on a sloping site, greatly influenced by Gilbert Scott junior's St Agnes, Kennington Park. It is composed of three generous bays with arches dying into their piers and a spacious chancel meant for ceremonial; the S aisle is wider than the N with its own ridged roof and it flows into a wide and tall transept leading to an asymmetrically placed chapel. Lofty barrel and wagon vaults are borne on heavy, moulded beams; the walls are plastered and whitened. There is a narthex with a gallery above (taken from Sedding's Holy Trinity, Sloane Street) and the vestries are in a crypt beneath the chancel, a favourite Late Victorian device. W. R. Lethaby was brought in to detail the building and his influence is found in the crisp flowing tracery influenced by Shaw's web-like windows at Holy Trinity, Latimer Road. Here they are filled with yellow-green glass with naturalistic leading in the cusps in the form of leaves. A disappointing reredos by Wisepelaere, of Belgium, was erected without Newton's sanction in 1911. [ANS]

London
St Thomas of Canterbury, Fulham (RC)

This church, a typical design of A. W. N. Pugin in the Decorated style, was built quickly between 1847 and 1848. The exterior is built of nasty Kentish rag and stone, and the adjoining presbytery is in stock brick. It shows Pugin's favourite three-gabled E end, dominated by a NW tower and spire. Inside there is no division between nave and chancel, though Pugin had clearly intended that, as in all his churches, there should be a rood-screen. The original fittings have been much changed. [AW]

London
Ukrainian Catholic Cathedral of the Holy Family in Exile, Weighhouse Street

Until 1965 the King's Weighhouse Congregational Chapel, this was built between 1887 and 1891 by Alfred Waterhouse in 'Carolingian Romanesque'. Red brick and terracotta predominate in the outer walls, with a corner tower and short spire which would be at home in any northern university. The body of the chapel is oval with a continuous gallery later interrupted by the new chancel created in 1903 by John Burnet and Sons. In the period 1914–32 Congregational opinion was shocked or fascinated by the elaborate liturgical services conducted by the minister, William Orchard. [cs]

London
Union Chapel, Islington

James Cubitt, called upon to design a building suitable to seat 2,000 (it once had 3,365 within its door when Spurgeon preached), took the opportunity to put into practice his views on the design of buildings for Congregational worship. The chapel opened in 1887. Concealed at the front behind a lofty tower not finished until 1889, it is in essence a vast brick octagon with Gothic arches opening to galleries at each side and below the tower, all the seats facing towards the pulpit with the least possible interference from columns or piers. Behind the pulpit, unusually at ground level, is a fine 'Father Willis' organ, above it is a rose window and over all an elaborately detailed wooden ceiling. [cs]

London
Westminster Cathedral (RC)*

When Herbert Vaughan became Archbishop of Westminster in 1892, he decided that a cathedral must at last be built, and in July 1894 appointed J. F. Bentley as architect. He insisted on a wide nave, a building that could be constructed quickly and decorated later, and an avoidance of rivalry with Westminster Abbey. As a result, Bentley chose the Byzantine style, and travelled to Italy, returning in March 1895 with the design worked out. The cathedral was begun in July, and was structurally complete when he died in 1902. The nave is covered by three shallow domes, the sanctuary by a fourth. The nave aisles are flanked by chapels, all the buttressing being internal. The transepts do not project, and the nave arcades carry on across them. Beyond the sanctuary is an apse. The façade (not originally visible from Victoria Street) is flanked by a campanile 284 feet high. The exterior is in cheerful red brick with a granite plinth and Portland stone dressings. The domes and vaults are of concrete, cast *in situ*. The Byzantine style is mixed with other elements, especially of Renaissance character. The interior was to be decorated with marble and mosaic: most of the marblework had been completed, mainly to Bentley's designs, but little of the mosaic. His intentions are best appreciated in the Holy Souls' Chapel (first on the left), where the mosaics and *opus sectile* reredos were designed by his friend W. C. Symons and executed in 1902–4. The columns in the nave are of *verde antico*, and have wonderfully inventive capitals. The magnificent baldacchino over the high altar and the hanging rood (painted by Symons) are also to Bentley's designs. In the Lady and Blessed Sacrament Chapels, flanking the sanctuary, the marblework is to his designs, the metalwork by his firm, the mosaics later. St Andrew's Chapel, paid for by the 4th Marquis of Bute, was designed by Robert Weir Schultz, and is a fine example of Arts and Crafts collaboration (1910–15). The Stations of the Cross are the masterpiece of Eric Gill (1914–18). In the crypt chapel are buried the archbishops, Wiseman's tomb (by E. W. Pugin) being under the high altar. [PH]

Longham, Dorset
United Reformed Church

The formerly Congregational chapel was built in 1841 by W. Gollop of Poole. Grey brick walls and round-arched windows follow a distinctly Georgian pattern but the gabled front with three arched bays between Ionic pilasters surmounted by an octagonal wooden clock-turret with colonnaded belfry-stage and green copper-clad spire has all the appearance of having been transported from New England. The interior is light and cheerful, with a single gallery at the S end. [cs]

Loughton, Essex
St Mary the Virgin, High Road

Built in 1871–2 by T. H. Watson, externally in Bargate stone from Surrey, it is remarkable for the series of carvings on the arcade capitals and elsewhere by an unknown sculptor, displaying astonishing richness, liveliness and variety in foliage, flowers and other natural features; there are representations of wild and garden flowers, ferns, fruit, creeping plants and even wheat and barley, together with birds flying to their nests. They depict mainly the flora and fauna of Epping Forest and its fringes, though a few of the plants are exotic. [DL]

Low Marple, Greater Manchester
St Martin

An exceptionally interesting church, part of a group built in 1869–73. It was designed by Edmund Sedding, but executed after his death by his brother, John D. Sedding. At first there was just the nave and chancel. The Lady Chapel was added in 1895–6 by Henry Wilson, who in 1909 added the N aisle, which has a shallow plastered apse, with a reredos by Christopher Whall, and other magnificent fittings. Fine font cover and side-altar furniture. There is glass by Morris, Whall and Bryams and remains of mural decoration unhappily painted out. Whilst the Sedding screen exists, the rood figures have been dismantled. [DB]

Lower Kingswood, Surrey
The Wisdom of God*

A small, externally unprepossessing church of the Arts and Crafts Movement designed by Sidney Barnsley between 1890 and 1892, and more interesting for its extraordinary fittings and imported treasures than for its architecture. The church reflects a thorough understanding of Byzantium suffused with real progressive Arts and Crafts originality. The plan, derived from the ancient basilican church of St Eirene at Constantinople, consists of aisled nave under one sweeping roof, a projecting W narthex and apse. A rather strange timber bell-frame stands detached. The red-brick exterior, relieved with decorative Ham stone patterning, belies an interesting interior of bold simplicity in which stone, plaster, marble and mosaic combine to original and unusual effect. Circular iron hoops with candles hang from the timber barrel-ceiling whose beams are delicately hand-painted with spring flowers. Barnsley's beautifully made chancel fittings, including two ambones, are set below the apse rich with mosaics of 1903 by Powell of Whitefriars. Materials brought in from Balkan ruins in 1902 include two large 4th-century stone capitals from St John at Ephesus. [RMH]

Lower Shuckburgh, Warwickshire
St John the Baptist*

By the 'rogue' architect J. Croft and wilfully original with improbable combination of forms. Built in 1864, the church is basically Early English in style but exhibiting Eastern influence, following George Shuckburgh's return from the Crimea. Of yellow stone banded with lias, the exterior has an hexagonal steeple and numerous gables. Saracenic arches, lumpy and flat window tracery and purple gravel mosaic. The interior, of bright-red imitation brick, has serrated arches, an awkward nave roof and a structurally unsound chancel vault, restrained by later iron ties. The pews have Eastern-style finials. [DH]

Lowfield Heath, West Sussex
St Michael*

A successful, picturesquely composed church of 1867 in crisply detailed Early French Gothic style by William Burges, consisting of un-aisled nave and chancel with a tall pyramid-capped SW tower, now in an unfortunate position close to the runways of Gatwick Airport. The W front is superb, with a strong, thick wheel W window exquisitely enriched with sensitively placed and vigorously carved small panels, rising over a lean-to porch. The W door, enriched with radial ironwork of almost Art Nouveau patterns, opens into a simple and no less well-detailed interior replete with clear-speaking Clayton and Bell glass in the E windows and a characteristic Burges pulpit with painted naturalistic reliefs. [RMH]

Lyndhurst, Hampshire
St Michael and All Angels

This red and yellow brick church was begun in 1858 and completed in 1869 with the construction of its tower and spire, which rise to a height of 141 feet. It is widely regarded as the masterpiece of its architect, William White. While not obviously eccentric, many features make it clear that he was not trammelled by convention. On the outside one notices the unusual dormers lighting the nave. Inside the eye is almost overwhelmed. Pointed arches of exceptional scale in polychrome moulded brick rise from extraordinarily naturalistic capitals supported on Purbeck shafted piers; from corbels between them spring roof-trusses decorated with life-size wooden angels playing musical instruments. Each of the four main windows is filled with magnificent glass: the W end by Kempe, the E end and S transept by Morris and Co., and the N transept by Clayton and Bell. Many of the aisle windows are filled with Powell glass. Behind the altar is a fresco by Lord Leighton and there are notable memorials by Flaxman, S. P. Cockerell and G. E. Street. [MM]

Macclesfield, Cheshire
St Alban (RC)

St Alban's, built in 1839–41, was one of the first churches designed by A. W. N. Pugin and, like St Mary's, Derby, is in the Perpendicular style. It is of considerable size and grandeur, though the exterior would have been more imposing if the W tower, well placed on top of a little hill, had been completed. The interior remains a fine example of Pugin's ideals, because the chancel was not altered in a recent sensitive reordering. The raised high altar can therefore be seen through the dark, finely proportioned rood-screen. The E window is by W. Warrington. [AW]

Maentwrog, Gwynedd
St Twrog

Nestling down in the idyllic Vale of Ffestiniog, the barn-like churchwarden Gothic church of 1814 was completely transformed in 1896 by John Douglas for the slate-quarry owners Mr and Mrs Oakeley. He put tracery in the church windows, inserted timber arcades to form aisles, and added the lofty chancel, the tower with its characteristic slated spire, and the half-timbered porch. Above the arcades are prettily decorated panels. The superb carved woodwork is what one expects of Douglas, but the surprise here is that, according to her nice 18th-century-style monument, 'all the carving' was done by Mrs Oakeley. Up on the village street is the lych-gate of 1897, in half-timber infilled with big brown-slate slabs. [PH]

Malpas, Gwent
St Mary

There was a Cluniac cell here, but the present building is entirely of 1847–50, by John Prichard. Its Norman style is unusual for him. Even the 'lych-gate' consists of a Norman arch. The church is very elaborate, in red and yellow stone. The chancel arch has big dogtooth, and the remarkable lectern is of stone, richly carved. The stained glass is vigorous and in style with the church. That in the E triplet is by George Rogers of Worcester (1850). [PH]

Manchester
All Saints, Barton-upon-Irwell (RC)

Begun as a chantry in 1863 for Sir Humphrey de Trafford, later extended as a full-size church (1865–8) with the chantry forming the N chapel; cloister and presbytery to the S. The architect was E. W. Pugin, with his typical W front with a rose window, bellcote and flèche recently re-erected. Inside, the nave arcades and chancel arch are treated polychromatically by alternating bands of red Runcorn sandstone and white Painswick stone. There are vaulted passage-aisles and a double-framed roof with rich inlays. The chancel has an inlaid floor, a vaulted and painted roof, eleven windows under cross-gables with Hardman glass, a painting on the S wall showing the donors and the architect, and an altar carved by R. L. Boulton. The chantry is even richer, with a double screen to the chancel, its inner piers supporting vaults. More Hardman glass and metalwork and another Boulton altar. This was one of E. W. Pugin's most lavish commissions, though not his most important work stylistically. [RO'D]

Manchester
Holy Name, Oxford Road (RC)*

Of enormous size and French in style, this building by J. A. Hansom is of outstanding structural innovation, profoundly influenced by the contemporary theories of Viollet-le-Duc and the belief that by 1869/71 Gothic architecture could, indeed should, develop and not just imitate. Windows, pier details, the apse and the form of the vaults are adapted from Rheims or from Chartres but the nave is greatly widened in a very un-French way making the entrance to the sanctuary more Spanish or Italian. The use of terracotta blocks helps the wider spans, saving weight. The same material is used extensively for repeated surface redecoration. Hansom intended a great tower and spire, never built. The W front was completed in 1928 by the masterly octagonal tower added by Adrian Gilbert Scott which looks very much like a trial run for the central tower of Liverpool Cathedral. The Chapel of the Madonna della Strada (S of the nave) is by J. F. Bentley (1891–4). [DB]

Manchester
Holy Trinity, Platt Lane

Edmund Sharpe's second terracotta church. He based his design on a 14th-century Lincolnshire church with an extremely elegant buttressed tower and spire. He had just taken his pupil, Edward Graham Paley, into partnership, who had studied Lincolnshire churches for his brother Frederick's book on Gothic mouldings. Sharpe described the church built in 1845–6 to the RIBA in 1876: 'The whole has been treated as a work in masonry, and very few of those who live in the neighbourhood are aware that it is not so.' But the problems of warpage and shrinkage of terracotta, although not noticeable today, were highlighted by the criticism of the *Builder* in 1845. [DM]

Manchester
St Augustine, Pendlebury*

In 1869 Bodley formed a partnership with Thomas Garner, twelve years his junior and, like him, a pupil of Sir Gilbert Scott. They worked closely together in the 1870s and early 1880s and designed a sequence of outstanding churches, of which the first and most original is St Augustine's, built 1870–4. The importance and originality of this church cannot be overestimated, nor can its profound influence upon the future. Built by a rich industrialist, E. S. Hayward, for his millhands, it is modelled upon Albi Cathedral but translated into an English flowing Decorated idiom, using internal buttresses to form a high arcade which embraces a recessed clerestory; the buttresses are pierced to form narrow passage-aisles; above is an unbroken wooden barrel-vault, powdered with stars on a blue ground, rising to 80 feet. Its vast scale and simplicity of detail give it clarity, grandeur and repose. Built of red brick with dressings and horizontal bands of stone the external elevations, with a canted E bay, were deliberately kept austere to harmonize with the adjacent mills. The detached tower was never built. There is flowing tracery filled with exquisite early glass by Burlison and Grylls, sombre, fastidiously detailed furniture, including an altar and reredos raised on many steps and decorated in the style of Dürer, and walls painted with flowing diapers in muted half-tones. Restored by S. E. Dykes Bower. [ANS]

Manchester
St Benedict, Ardwick

This is one of J. S. Crowther's last churches, built in a poor populous district. It is his only adventure into terracotta, by 1880 becoming with brick a common material for the construction of a new generation of cheaper buildings in the outer suburbs, a tradition which went on until after the First World War. Stone is used only for the internal piers and a few details. Early English/Decorated in style, very large, impressive and quite original. The E end has a richly glazed seven-light Geometric window; the W end a very large rose window and a thin tall tower of Italian shape topped by a pyramidal roof and four overhanging pinnacles. The sickly classical baldacchino over the altar (*c.* 1950) is unworthy of its setting. [DB]

Manchester
St Cross, Clayton

Designed by William Butterfield, completed in 1866 but not consecrated until 1874 because the bishop would not countenance a Tractarian dedication to the Holy Cross and it became instead St Cross. Money was short and the church had to be large. It has all the usual characteristics of the architect's structural polychromy simply done on a large scale. The massing exhibits the accustomed vigour. In 1974 the lower walls and reredos were restored and repainted with riddel hangings woven to a Butterfield design by Marion Dorn. [DB]

Manchester
St Francis of Assisi, Gorton (RC)*

Begun by E. W. Pugin for a community of Belgian Franciscans, 1866–72, and finished by his brother P. P. Pugin, 1878–85. It is a massive church in red brick with much stone banding, its assertive polychrome W front of two windows, three buttresses (70 feet high), life-size Crucifixion, gable and flèche (of 1911) leading into an equally impressive interior 100 feet in height. The arcade and roof are by Puginian standards simple. There is a multi-pinnacled high altar of 1865, a prominent series of Stations of the Cross, and a 'confessional aisle' to the N. [RO'D]

Manchester
St John the Evangelist, Cheetham

By Paley and Austin in 1869–71, and showing Austin's enthusiasm for the gutsy European Gothic he had seen as a student in Belgium. The four spirelets project forward from the plane of the pyramidal spire, but at the height of their finials the whole spire is set gently forward again. The effect is magnificent as the shallow clasping buttresses reach up the tower to be crowned by the four spirelets. Built in an early Gothic style of the 13th century, the lofty church has nave aisles, and apsidal chancel. Lancet lights high on the walls give an atmosphere of mysterious gloom with detached shafts corbelled out at sill level of the clerestory supporting the nave roof. [DM]

Manchester
St Margaret, Burnage

This small church by Paley and Austin with a bellcote and apsidal baptistery in a free 13th-century Gothic style was built between 1874 and 1875 using a red sandstone. Austin's confident handling of both carving and lettering was to become a hallmark of his later work. This attention to detail can be seen here in the canopied figure of St Margaret over her emblematic dragon and in the segmental relieving arch over the baptistery. [DM]

Manchester
St Mark, Levenshulme

1884–5. Medland and Henry Taylor's later churches tend to be cheap, but all the better for that, built in the second generation of artisan suburbs. Those to the N of the city were usually of stone, those to the S frequently of brick with the maximum use of huge and deliberately tricky roof structures. Here stone is reserved for essential features such as columns and corbel. Tracery can be as minimal as brick or terracotta. Externally this one is superb, a wilful and deliberately asymmetrical composition of roof slopes, apses and a sharply pointed, straight-sided chancel of a kind only occasionally found in medieval work. There is much innovation inspired by E. B. Lamb and Teulon with an internal roof structure boldly supported on wall-brackets, leaping across wide brick arches and robustly laced together by a grid of exposed joists and diagonal boarding. [DB]

Manchester
St Mary, Hulme

J. S. Crowther was a scholar architect (Bowman and Crowther's *Churches of the Middle Ages* was published in parts between 1845 and 1853). St Mary's uses two kinds of masonry: ashlar for details with coursed rougher stone in between. The tower is placed at the NW corner, an unusual location in the Middle Ages, which allows a large and spectacular window of Geometrical tracery at each end of the church. This and the turrets between nave and chancel are typical Crowther features. The interior is now bereft of some of its fittings but the schools, house and church make up a fine group. [DB]

Mansfield, Nottinghamshire
St Mark

Built in 1897, this is a mature work by Temple Moore and one which demonstrates his originality within the dry Late Gothic style in which he chose to express himself. The exterior is long and low, with a typically bleak outline. There is an emphasis on smooth, plain ashlar stonework, which is unbroken by projections. This is achieved by the use of wide internal buttresses, pierced by the low passage-aisles which Moore favoured. The passages themselves are round-arched while the arcades are barely pointed. A further idiosyncrasy is that the lateral arches between the buttresses which form the aisles are placed lower than the main arcades which support the roof, leaving an intervening tympanum which is left blank. The interior seems austere yet is far from simple, and full of clever subtleties which all seem sensible and logical. [GS]

Marchwood, Hampshire
St John the Apostle

This stately church, designed in 1843 by John Macduff Derick, is an interesting example of the use of the Early English style before the influence of the Cambridge Camden Society led to the almost universal use of the Middle Pointed. Built of the pale-yellow local brick, its nave, S aisle transepts and chancel, all lit by lancets, rise to a considerable height and are overtopped by a SW corner tower supporting a sturdy stone broach-spire. Behind the tower the W end of the nave is galleried and the open roof is a curious combination of scissor truss and hammer-beam. [MM]

Marlow, Buckinghamshire
St Peter (RC)

Pugin designed this for C. R. Scott-Murray, a recent convert to Catholicism. The foundation stone was laid in July 1845 and only a year later the church was consecrated. The W façade has a taut design with NW tower and broach-spire in line with the W gable of the nave. The interior is charming, with a stone screen to the chancel and a built-in lectern. The splendid E window of St Peter (now blocked) was made by Hardman. A complete new church has been built to the E with a connecting link made through the former N Lady Chapel, which together with the organ-loft has been destroyed. [AW]

Marston Meysey, Wiltshire
St James

A remote country church of 1874–6 by James Brooks, known for his powerful town churches. Here the church is a simple stone vessel with a bold W rose window and an overall stone roof. Inside, a boarded, curved nave-roof leads the eye to a stone-vaulted chancel, divided off by a low stone screen with inset tiles. The screen connects to a rounded stone pulpit. The richness is concentrated at the E end, and achieved with strong mouldings and geometrical forms rather than profusion of carving. Fine ironwork and stained glass by Clayton and Bell. [JO]

Matlock, Derbyshire
St John the Baptist

1897 by Guy Dawber, built as a private chapel by Louisa Harris who favoured a more Tractarian form of worship than was offered at the parish church. Perched dramatically and picturesquely in the cliff-side from which it appears to grow. A modest domestic-looking chapel, its position and use of traditional local materials are indicative of Guy Dawber's Arts and Crafts style of architecture. Built of limestone with sandstone dressings, the interior of red brick. Mullioned windows with shallow-arched lights. The one prominent accent is an asymmetrically placed canted oriel with diminutive bell-turret. Along the entrance front is a verandah-like lean-to porch. Plain interior with simple Arts and Crafts fittings. Stained glass in the E window by Louis Davis. Plaster ceiling with birds and flowers in relief, by George Bankart. [NA]

Melplash, Dorset
Christ Church

Benjamin Ferrey was one of the more successful architects in the Neo-Norman style, which had its heyday in the 1840s, and Melplash is one of his most expensive works. Built in 1845–6, this is a fully articulated cruciform church with high central crossing-tower and apsed chancel. Norman-style carved detail throughout, mechanical in look, but well executed. Timber nave roof, unhistorically of hammer-beam type. [JO]

Meole Brace, Salop
Holy Trinity

This large and rather ungracious church of 1867–8 by Edward Haycock junior has one of the best sets of glass by Morris and Co. anywhere. The three apse windows date from 1870–2: each three-light window is divided horizontally into three tiers of panels, except for the Crucifixion in the centre light. The left-hand window is by Ford Madox Brown and Burne-Jones, the right-hand one is by William Morris and Burne-Jones, and the centre one is entirely Burne-Jones. The centre window of the S aisle, of 1873, is by Ford Madox Brown and Burne-Jones. There is later glass by the Morris firm (1894–1921), and some by Kempe. [PH]

Merthyr Mawr, Mid Glamorgan
St Teilo

The church is prettily situated. Built in 1849–51, evidence for its authorship is divided between Benjamin Ferrey and John Prichard. Probably they collaborated, but the exquisite detailing suggests the hand of Prichard. The style is Early English. The W bell-turret is very original. There is good contemporary glass. [PH]

Middleton, Lancashire
Wesleyan Methodist Church

Designed by Edgar Wood in 1897, and built in 1897–1901, this brick and stone church shows what a remarkable effect can be achieved with simple forms if massing and detailing are truly sensitive. The style is free Gothic, and the exterior effect comes chiefly from the grouping of the church with the lecture room and school surrounding a court on the N side, which is entered from the street through a boldly original archway. Inside, the carved stone pulpit and wooden stalls are striking Arts and Crafts pieces. [PH]

Midgham, Berkshire
St Matthew

Grandly sited up on a hill over the Kennet valley, this church by John Johnson was built in 1869, though outside it could almost be of 1849, in its correct Decorated, flint with stone dressings, with a stone-roofed S porch and a SW spire whose broaches are ornamented with the symbols of the Evangelists. The rich interior is more High Victorian, in a charmingly batty way. The arcades have polished granite columns, and an extra fat one supports the tower. Above them are large well-carved heads, and there is plenty of naturalistic carving especially on the crowded corbels of the chancel arch. The carving is by Farmer and Brindley. The chancel has a splendid tiled floor, and a poor E window by Ward and Hughes. [PH]

Millom, Cumbria
St George

Built in attractive pink sandstone by Paley and Austin (1874–7), the church dominates a small industrial town. This Decorated-style design is characteristically assured, based on largeness of scale, fine proportions and careful embellishments such as the blind arcade, with roundels and tracery, of the N transept wall. Over the crossing is a splendid tower and spire of traditional English type. Inside, the nave, with wooden wagon roof, is divided from the almost equally spacious N aisle by a crisply shaped arcade. [TEF]

Milton, Oxfordshire
St Mary*

This small early work of Butterfield (1854–6) is built of the local brown stone, with white dressings and red-tiled roof. Between nave and chancel rises the pyramidal-roofed tower: the tower stair is within what looks like a huge buttress. The S porch and lych-gate are striking exercises in stone and timberwork. In the light, white interior the original fittings include a typical reredos, simple iron altar-rails, font, wooden pulpit and stalls, and pews which include smaller ones for children. [PH]

Milton-under-Wychwood, Oxfordshire
SS Simon and Jude*

An imposing village church by G. E. Street, intended to serve a scattered group of hamlets in Wychwood Forest. Although remote and rural, the church is nevertheless quite a large one of high-roofed, clerestoried nave with shorter balancing lean-to aisles, the square chancel having an important-looking S chapel and cross-gabled N vestry. The style is a free interpretation of Early Decorated where sheer close-knit rubble surfaces and abrupt freestone profiles form a dynamic framework for the concentrated details. Almost aggressively sharp and vertical, the tense outlines culminate in a forceful central buttress cutting up the W front between two close-set tracery windows. From its apex rises an elegantly slender bell-turret with octagonal stone spire. Near the W end a large porch curtails the S aisle, its transverse gable breaking into the narrow clerestory zone of tiny foiled circles. The interior is tall and gaunt but full of light, with large traceried E window and wide stone arches defined by ample mouldings. Otherwise, the walls are plastered and whitened to contrast with the dark-stained open timber roofs. Stone pulpit and cancelli, font with spired wooden cover, form part of Street's design. So, too, do the churchyard walls and timber lych-gate, as well as the adjacent stone school and teacher's house. [PJ]

Moffat, Dumfries and Galloway
St Andrew (Church of Scotland)

Large and ambitious Early Pointed church of red sandstone by John Starforth, 1885–7. Rectangular galleried plan with octagonal angle-buttresses rising into big pinnacles, tall triple lancets at the upper level, paired beneath, double transepts. Boldly buttressed tower with octagonal stair-turret, doorway of four orders with tympanum and trumeau, triple belfry-openings and crenellated parapet with angle rounds, clasping cylindrical stairhalls with conical roofs. Interesting interior with galleries cantilevered off columns set close to the wall; glass by Starforth himself and Meikle and Son. [DW]

Monkton Wyld, Dorset
St Andrew

Built 1848–9 by R. C. Carpenter, this church is a model of Puginian ideals. Everything is rational, each part distinct, nave and chancel roofs of equal pitch divided by a firm and unornamented square tower carrying a strongly detailed Northamptonshire broach-spire, whose smooth ashlar contrasts with the flint walls of the church. Low aisles run from the nave to embrace the tower base. Inside, carefully detailed arch mouldings and octagonal piers, a high nave roof and more enclosing, boarded chancel roof. The chancel divided from the nave by a wooden screen as Pugin recommended. The other fittings are of *c.* 1888 and there is excellent, richly coloured stained glass of *c.* 1875 by G. E. Cook. [JO]

Moorhouse, Nottinghamshire
Chapel

A small building in the middle of a field, designed by Henry Clutton and built in 1860–1. It is in a muscular 12th-century Gothic style. Nave and chancel in one, but the division marked externally by buttressing and a twin bell-cote. Plain painted interior with a sturdy chancel arch on stumpy shafts and a stone rib-vault in the chancel. [NA]

Morriston, West Glamorgan
Capel Tabernacl

The so-called 'Cathedral of Welsh Nonconformity' was built in 1870–2 by John Humphreys of Morriston, to seat 1,800. The lofty front has tall round arches and a slender spire, but – considering its size – the interior is surprisingly intimate, with its rich but elegant decoration, curving galleries, panelled roof, and stained glass. [PH]

Murston, Kent
All Saints

By William Burges in knapped flint with crisp stone dressings. The style is 13th-century French and the date 1873–4. It consists of nave and N aisle, apsidal chancel and vestry in the base of the short tower which was heightened in 1959. There is a huge tie-beam and king-posted nave roof but the plate-traceried rose window in the W is regarded by some

as the church's best feature. Some medieval features from the previous church are incorporated. [REH]

Neath, West Glamorgan
St David

The town is dominated by the great tower, 152 feet high, with a Germanic pinnacled cap, of this church, built in 1864–6 by John Norton. The exterior is of blue sandstone, with Bath dressings, and bands of red sandstone, while the interior is in geometrically patterned red and black brick. Large and lofty, it has transepts and an apsidal chancel, with windows by Clayton and Bell. [PH]

Netherfield, East Sussex
St John the Baptist

This church, consecrated in 1855, forms a charming group with the adjacent school and schoolmaster's house. All were designed by S. S. Teulon. Although the intended octagonal broach-spire was never built, the church remains an attractive design in Middle Pointed, constructed in the local stone. The foliated capitals on the chancel arch are by Earp. [MS]

Newbury, Berkshire
Methodist Chapel, Northbrook Street*

Built in 1837–8, this employs Gothic elements in a theatrical rather than in an architecturally academic manner. The front wall is divided into three parts by substantial buttresses, a solution frequently adopted for gabled fronts throughout the 19th century. Here the central bay projects to give prominence to the main entrance; side porches were added later. The simple rectangular plan with a continuous gallery follows a traditional pattern and has a recessed communion area behind the tall stone central pulpit in conformity with 18th-century Anglican practice. [CS]

Newcastle upon Tyne, Tyne and Wear
Cathedral of St Mary (RC)

St Mary's, begun in 1841 and opened in 1844, belongs to the period in which A. W. N. Pugin was at his most prolific. It is in confident Decorated style with good and varied tracery. The site is a fine one, and the external composition is particularly successful, especially from the E, where the three big, gabled E windows are given the necessary vertical accent by the splendid SW tower and spire. Pugin intended his church to have a spire, but the present one was designed by J. A. Hansom and built between 1860 and 1873. The entrance, originally under the tower, is now through what was built in 1902 as the baptistery. The interior is very straightforward: nave and aisles, with a short chancel and N and S chapels, no clerestory and no chancel arch. The stained glass in the E window made by W. Wailes, who was a local man, is especially good. [AW]

Newcastle upon Tyne, Tyne and Wear
Jesmond Parish Church

An essay in the Decorated Gothic style by John Dobson, the leading classical architect of central Newcastle, and completed in 1861. Dobson was instructed to prepare galleries, an old-fashioned feature. [LW]

Newcastle upon Tyne, Tyne and Wear
St George, Jesmond

A large 13th-century-style church with an Italianate bell-tower at the SE, consecrated in 1888. It is by T. R. Spence, an Arts and Crafts designer who used local stone, finely carved. In the interior, intricate metalwork and elaborate woodcarving complement the glowing colours of stained glass, marble, mosaic and other materials and are fused into a complex scheme of decoration, rich in symbolism and based on Art Nouveau motifs. [TEF]

Newcastle upon Tyne, Tyne and Wear
St Matthew

This noble church, which towers over the surrounding terraced housing, is one of the finest works of R. J. Johnson. Begun in 1877, it got its tower in 1888, but the W end of the S aisle was only completed by Hicks and Charlewood in 1904. The grand tower has a pair of tall bell-openings on each side, and rich pinnacles. The lofty interior has great poise and refinement, building up to a sumptuous stone reredos below the richly traceried E window. [PH]

Newport, Gwent
Congregational Chapel, Victoria Road

In its pleasantly Victorian context up on the hill overlooking the town, the stone façade of this chapel, built in 1858 by A. O. Watkins, cannot fail to amaze. Basically classical, with an attached portico, the lavish decorative carving is highly original. The semi-columns are striated. After this, the interior, with the usual galleries and pitch-pine, seems quite tame. [PH]

Newport, Isle of Wight
St Thomas

Built 1854–5 by the under-rated S. W. Daukes. It stands beside the small market place, with no church-yard and alleys on two sides – a situation more characteristic of France than England. Assertive but not aggressive, in rough Island limestone with elaborate fine stone dressings; Geometrical to Flamboyant tracery, and a strong tower crowned by a pierced parapet and a prominent angle-turret. Inside, some of the most interesting features are from the previous church, but there are a royal arms of Queen Victoria, and a monument, given by the Queen, in memory of Princess Elizabeth, daughter of Charles I, supposedly buried here. The sculptor was Baron Marochetti. [DL]

Newtown, Hampshire
St Mary and St John the Baptist

This small flint and stone church was built in 1864–5 by Henry Woodyer. It consists of a nave with N aisle terminating at the W in a tower with a timber broach-spire, and a chancel with S vestry. Typical of Woodyer is the way that carved sprays of wild flowers and leaves are attached like specimens to the capitals of the fat columns of the nave arcade. It is as though the naturalistic medieval carving of Southwell Minster and Ruskin's delight in nature had been fused in the most fanciful and indeed forward-looking manner. [AQ]

Nicholaston, West Glamorgan
St Nicholas

This delightful and elaborately detailed little church is an unexpected find in rural Gower. Built in 1892–4 by G. E. Halliday and Anderson of Cardiff, it incorporates a few medieval fragments, including one roof principal. The rich carving is by Clarke of Llandaff. The pulpit has statues of Keble, Liddon and Pusey, which reveal the sympathies of the founders. The reredos is of pink alabaster, with figures of Christ and the Virgin in white Portuguese lias. [PH]

Nocton, Lincolnshire
All Saints

1860–3 by G. G. Scott and one of his best churches. An ambitious and expensive estate church. A compact plan of nave with S aisle and porch, chancel, and a NW tower with octagonal bell-stage and spire; all in warm Ancaster stone. Early English in style with plate tracery. The clerestory on the S side with a continuous arcade. The S porch is vaulted and has figures in niches around the entrance. Interior with sumptuous foliage carving, shafting to the windows, and painted friezes and decoration. In the chapel the monument to the 1st Earl of Ripon, by Scott, with a marble effigy by Matthew Noble, 1862. [NA]

Northampton
St Matthew

This magnificent great church, designed by Matthew Holding, was built in 1891–4. Lofty and elaborate, of local brown ironstone with white dressings, it has transepts and a polygonal apse flanked by turrets. The grand NW spire is 170 feet high. The clerestoried interior, faced in white stone, has a timber roof set on high diaphragm arches. Chancel and apse are vaulted in stone. The big alabaster reredos was designed by Holding. The Lady Chapel reredos was painted by C. E. Buckeridge. The glass is varied in character and merit. The organ is by Walker, and the church has a notable musical tradition. Walter Hussey (vicar 1937–55) commissioned the Horton stone Madonna by Henry Moore in the N transept (1944), and the Crucifixion by Graham Sutherland in the S transept (1946), as well as Britten's *Rejoice in the Lamb*. [PH]

Norwich, Norfolk
Cathedral of St John the Baptist (RC)

This huge church designed by George Gilbert Scott junior was entirely paid for by the 15th Duke of Norfolk. Never furnished as elaborately as its architect intended, it has always had the character of a small Anglican cathedral but has only been a cathedral – as its donor clearly intended – since 1977. Scott owed the commission to Cardinal Newman, who had been instrumental in his conversion to Roman Catholicism in 1880. Construction began in 1882 and the nave was commenced in 1884. Scott continued to supervise the work despite his mental breakdown, lunacy trial and flight to France, but the duke was obliged to ask his brother, John Oldrid Scott, to take over in 1891 following Scott's third incarceration in an asylum. J. O. Scott made modifications to the design of the E end and transepts but the nave and the noble crossing-tower are as his brother designed. The church was consecrated in 1910. The incomplete furnishings are by J. O. Scott; the glass in the nave by John Powell of Hardman and Powell and that in the E parts of the building by Dunstan Powell. The style of the building – Early English – was the choice of the client and what originality there is is in the handling of detail and precedent. Although the use of this period of Gothic was untypical of the Late Victorian decades, this great church exposes the dilemma faced by all Victorian architects when asked to design a large and expensive church. Originality seems to have been more possible in a cheap urban building than in a great cathedral, in which precedents were too obvious and inescapable. [GS]

Nottingham
All Saints

1863–4 by T. C. Hine (Hine and Evans) of Nottingham. A lavish 13th-century-style church with parsonage and school designed simultaneously and forming a courtyard to the SW. Rock-faced with bands of ashlar. W tower with large triplet bell-openings, a stair-turret and broach-spire. Plate tracery throughout. The polygonal apse has unfortunately been shorn of its gables. Inside, the nave roof exhibits an impressive network of timbers. [NA]

Nottingham
Baptist Chapel, Woodborough Road

A huge chapel and poignant lone survivor in an area redeveloped in the 1970s. Built in 1893–4 by Watson Fothergill in his own inimitable style, on a sloping site, with a rock-faced basement and harsh red brick above with bands of blue brick. Eccentric, thin, octagonal SW tower turning at the top into a rectangle with hipped roof and spiky iron cresting. The plan is as eccentric as the detailing, with a semicircular apse at the S end to which one face of the tower is attached. Entry is by way of the tower and immediately up a flight of stairs to the main nave of the church which has round-arched cast-iron arcades and galleries, the arcades with crudely detailed capitals. It is now used by the Pakistani League of Friends. [NA]

Nottingham
Cathedral of St Barnabas (RC)

The church of St Barnabas represents one of Pugin's most ambitious designs: a large cruciform building in the Early English style with very little decoration, begun in 1841 and opened in 1844. It became a cathedral in 1850. The external composition is most satisfying with good stonework building up to a proud steeple above the crossing. There are nice changes of level in the interior, as there is a three-bay crypt below the chancel, which has an ambulatory and three E chapels beyond. Sadly few of the original fittings remain, except in the Blessed Sacrament Chapel, which is covered with splendid patterns. The stained glass was all made by Wailes. [AW]

Oare, Wiltshire
Holy Trinity

This small chapel was built in 1857–8 as a memorial church to the Revd Maurice Hiller Goodman of Oare House and was largely paid for by his widow. It was she who told Teulon that the church had to be in brick and that the style was to be Romanesque. The effect of reasonably accurate Norman scallop capitals in the apse and circular font decorated by blind interlacing arches is somewhat offset by his self-indulgence in notching and nicking his round-headed arches and introducing a schematized corbel table onto the rainwater heads. And yet his love of brick-work comes through particularly in the herring-bone blind panels on the apse which contrast with the rest of the shell in a simple header bond. [MS]

Odd Rode, Cheshire
All Saints

Built in 1864 by Sir George Gilbert Scott. Very English and suggesting how a medieval church might have looked in about 1250, after the building of one aisle and before the addition of a tower or later Gothic refenestration. Goodhart-Rendel thought it 'a triumph of the academic type of good Gothic design'. The use of a brown Staffordshire plain tile is unusual. There is a W bell-cote, a nave, chancel, S aisle and the Wilbraham Chapel, each under a separate roof. Good restrained fittings and typical Scott open benches. Excellent glass, some by Kempe and Tower, but the E window is probably by Heaton, Butler and Bayne. [DB]

Old Hall Green, Hertfordshire
Chapel of St Edmund's College (RC)

St Edmund's College, now only a school, was, after Oscott and Ushaw, the third RC seminary in England where Pugin worked. The chapel was commissioned in 1844, with the foundation stone laid in 1845, and, though it was substantially finished by 1848, it was not opened until 1853. The entrance to the chapel is confusing, as it has been lapped around by later buildings. The plan provides an antechapel and a long main chapel, and the style is *c.* 1300–30. Inside there are two great glories: the stone rood-screen, two bays deep, vaulted, and containing two altars, and the seven-light E window with its wonderful tracery and Hardman glass. The N Lady Chapel was built in 1861, and, further N, the Shrine Chapel was added in 1904. In 1922 the Galilee Chapel was built at the W end, and E. W. Pugin designed the Scholefield Chantry to the S of the main chapel in 1862. [AW]

Oxford
Exeter College Chapel

G. G. Scott intended to site his new chapel of 1856–9 in the middle of the E range of the quadrangle, on axis with the main gate, but was obliged to put it where its 17th-century predecessor had stood. As a result it dramatically overpowers the quadrangle. It is very French, with its great height, apse and flèche. The interior has mild polychromy in the vaulting, whose shafts are of Devon and Cornwall marble. The stone-carving is by J. Birnie Philip, including fine capitals, but the credence shelf is by O'Shea. The mosaics are by Salviati, and the stained glass is mostly by Clayton and Bell, the earliest and best in the apse (1859–61). The superb screen-gates are by Skidmore.

The stall canopies were added by Bodley in 1884. [PH]

Oxford
Keble College Chapel

It is appropriate that a college founded in memory of John Keble should be dominated by its chapel. Like the rest of this college, it was designed by Butterfield and built (in 1873–6) of polychrome patterned brick. The cost (£40,000) was borne by William Gibbs of Tyntesfield. It consists of a tall single vessel, subtly divided into bays and elegantly vaulted, 'gloriously adventurous in its proportions' (Summerson). The rich and harmonious scheme of decoration is based on an iconography of 'the successive dealings of God with his church', worked out by Butterfield, and executed in mosaics and stained glass by Alexander Gibbs (no relation). The seats face the altar, unusually for a college chapel, but in accordance with Tractarian emphasis on the Eucharist. The metalwork lectern and candlesticks are especially fine. Unfortunately the organ was raised (obscuring a window) in 1892, by J. T. Micklethwaite, so as to form a chapel for the display of Holman Hunt's *Light of the World* (1853). [PH]

Oxford
St Barnabas, Jericho*

The brick terraces of Jericho housed most of the workers at the University Press, and St Barnabas was built in 1869 to serve them at the expense of Thomas Combe, Printer to the University, Pre-Raphaelite patron, and devoted Tractarian. He demanded from his architect, Arthur Blomfield, 'strength, solidity, and thoroughly sound construction', but no expense on decoration, which could be added later. The walls are of rubble, mostly rendered, with brick banding, and a substantial amount of concrete (for example, for the lintels). The church is in the style of an Italian Romanesque basilica, unusual for its time, but well suited for Tractarian ritual. The sanctuary has a shallow apse, and the raised choir projects W into the nave. The great gilded baldacchino is Trecento Gothic. Blomfield also designed the decoration of the E end (1893) and the pulpit (executed by Heaton, Butler and Bayne). The N aisle has a Morning Chapel at the E end. Only the N wall of the nave was decorated in Powell's *opus sectile*. A small W apse

houses the font. The tall campanile, built in 1872, originally had a steep-pitched roof covered in patterned slates. [PH]

Oxford
St John, see **Cowley**.

Oxford
SS Philip and James

This noble building occupies a crucial position in the progress of High Victorian Gothic, not only for its radical stylistic innovations but also by reason of its experimental Tractarian planning. The design, by G. E. Street, was evolved during 1859, construction proceeding piecemeal over 1860–2 although the belfry and spire were delayed until 1864–5. Street improvised a plan of monumental symmetry centred on a mighty oblong crossing-tower, broader across the main axis, capable of stabilizing the forceful nave arcades and clerestory as their final bay veers off the parallel and converges towards a majestic chancel arch. Here on the W face of the tower the apparently flexible arches are caught up unresolved and become absorbed into the bare wall-plane. A curved rib-vaulted apse, steeply buttressed, is clamped onto the E face of the tower to define the sanctuary, riveting focus beyond the tent-like space of the nave and its billowing timber wagon-vault. Brief transepts off the ribbed crossing are lower than this vast vessel of a nave. Thick columns of polished red granite with burgeoning caps support elemental four-bay arcades, from which the six-bay alternating rhythm of the clerestory is eerily independent above an emphatic string-course. Lean-to passage-aisles and S porch provide general access, but an impressive symmetrical W front is displayed to the road with high flanking buttresses and protruding gabled entrance. Strong Early French influence pervades the aptly named 'Vigorous' style of which this church is the paramount exemplar; lancets, plate tracery and rose windows are strictly adhered to. Especially idiomatic is the powerful S transept façade where Street excavates his austere geometric forms by cutting back the wall-plane layer by layer. External textures partake of the discipline too; pink-sandstone bands in lieu of string-courses, intermittent pink voussoirs, freestone quoins and openings, all set off against the variegated courses of rough Gibraltar stone walling and, originally, harmonious Stonesfield slate roofs. Inside, contrasts are achieved with Devon marble vaulting-shafts and particoloured arch voussoirs. Northern France is undoubtedly not far behind the central steeple, a *tour de force* of almost Mannerist intensity. Accompanied by a heavily spiked newel-turret, its oblong belfry with deeply recessed paired louvres rises into a massive, irregularly banded octagonal broach-spire bearing far-projecting shafted lucarnes, but the unique logic of its elongated plan conjures up strange and memorable effects. No longer parochial, SS Philip and James' is used as the Oxford Centre for Mission Studies. Of Street's fittings, font and cover, pulpit and cancelli survive, the latter with wrought ironwork by James Leaver who also made lectern, standards and door-hinges. Carving of capitals was by Thomas Earp and, above huge tie-beams and king-posts, the painted nave-roof decoration by Haynes of Oxford. Glass in the apse is by Clayton and Bell 1861–74. [PJ]

Oxford
Worcester College Chapel

The chapel was begun in 1720 to designs by Clarke and Hawksmoor, and its interior was given elegant Neo-classical decoration by James Wyatt *c.* 1776–91. In 1864–70 it was completely transformed by William Burges, who overlaid Wyatt's plasterwork with coloured embellishment, in Renaissance style and to an elaborate iconographical scheme – 'Man in the Te Deum, and Nature in the Benedicite', combining in the worship of God. Hence the animals (including a dodo) on the inlaid stalls. The magnificent marble lectern-cum-candlestick proclaims 'Thy Word is a lantern unto my feet.' Most of the sculpture was by Thomas Nicholls. The floors are of marble mosaic. In the antechapel, painted in Pompeian style, the organ-bench has leopards' heads. The painted decoration was supervised by Henry Holiday, who also designed the glass, made by Lavers and Barraud in 1864–5. [PH]

Oxton, Merseyside
St Saviour

Built in 1889–92 by C. W. Harvey, Pennington and Bridgen, the church is finely sited up on a ridge, but its exterior is crude and uninviting, with its rock-faced sandstone, and even the broad pinnacled crossing-tower is ungainly. The interior, by contrast, is finely proportioned, rich and warm, in red brick with sandstone dressings and timber roof. A large, gilded wooden reredos of 1906 is by G. F. Bodley, but is outshone by the strikingly original woodwork (chancel screen, choir-stalls, and S transept altar) designed by Edward Rae to commemorate various members of his family, and executed by Heath and Co. The W window commemorates his father George, a notable Pre-Raphaelite patron: it is by Morris and Co. (1903), as is the N transept window. The war memorial of 1920 is by Sir Giles Gilbert Scott. [PH]

Paisley, Strathclyde
Thomas Coats Memorial Church (Baptist)*

In 1885 the Coats family of thread fame held a competition won by Hippolyte Jean Blanc who conceived this vast memorial church as an Early Decorated cathedral with a central crown-tower. To provide a wide preaching church for a Baptist congregation Blanc adopted the Gerona arrangement of Anderson's church at Govan, adding transepts, which resulted in an oblong crossing. To produce the desired cathedral proportions he set the church into a hillside with a choir room beneath, masked the extremities of his nave-gable with octagonal stair-turrets, and extended the apparent length with a huge perron and three boldly projecting portals: the proportions of the tower were equally skilfully adjusted by some daring construction which took it into the square at the second stage. The interior is of breath-taking richness: a transverse rib-vaulted narthex with a mosaic floor, fountains and painted decoration opens into a nave with clustered piers, diapered spandrels and a ribbed barrel-roof. The crossing, transepts and presbytery are rib-vaulted with painted decoration and much sculpture in alabaster and marble by William Vickers. An ambulatory round the presbytery leads to sumptuous vestries and retiring rooms: all the furnishings and fittings exhibit craftwork of the highest quality, even down to the umbrella stands. [DW]

Parbold, Lancashire
Our Lady and All Saints (RC)

This very grand church, set in a spacious churchyard, was built in 1878–84. The architect was Edmund Kirby. The fine W spire turns octagonal and pinnacled. The interior is light and well proportioned. The chancel has gabled dormers to provide extra light, since most of the E wall, below the rose window, is taken up by an elaborate reredos with eight angels in niches. The side chapels also have sculpted reredoses. [PH]

Penarth, South Glamorgan
St Augustine

One of William Butterfield's best churches, of 1844–66. As the previous tower had been a sea-mark, the tall new one also has a saddleback. The exterior is in grey limestone, with Bath dressings, while the noble interior is a dramatic exercise in geometrical polychromy – red brick diapered in white and black brick, combined with the cream and pink stone of the severely simple arcades, in the spandrels of which are cinquefoil panels. The E window, by A. Gibbs, surmounts a splendid reredos. [PH]

Penicuik, Lothian
South Church (Church of Scotland)

By F. T. Pilkington, 1862, similar to Irvine and equally richly detailed though without polychromy, but much reduced in scale. It has the same truncated diamond plan, again brought to a cruciform triapsidal form at the upper level, and has a similar open recessed narthex at the gable front of the gallery outshot, here giving access directly to the church. At the NE angle a square tower rises into a tall octagonal belfry-stage which lacks the slated spire intended for it. [DW]

Penrhyncoch, Dyfed
St John the Divine

This compact little Early English church of 1880 is by R. J. Withers, who did a great deal of excellent church work in South Wales. It has a square timber belfry at the W end. The interior is rich in effect, with good fittings. The most striking is the lectern, a brightly coloured eagle and dragon in pottery. [PH]

Pentre, Rhondda, Mid Glamorgan
St Peter

Far the grandest church in Rhondda. Like Baglan, it was built at the expense of Griffith Llewellyn. Unfortunately, by the time it was built in 1888–91 Prichard was dead, so the architects here were his

successors, F. R. Kempson and J. B. Fowler. In 13th-century style, it has a W tower, and a lofty and dignified interior, with constructional colour. The rich fittings include a large alabaster reredos. [PH]

Pentrobin (or Penymynydd), Clwyd
St John

This rather gawky Early English church was designed in 1843 by John Buckler. It has a thin spire and an octagonal vestry with stone vault. It is chiefly remarkable for the elaborate scheme of decoration, including painting, stained glass and sculpture, carried out by the Revd J. E. Troughton, curate-in-charge between 1843 and 1864, and designed by R. P. Pullan, brother-in-law of William Burges. Some of the paintings have been crudely restored. The sedilia are especially rich. [PH]

Peplow, Salop
Epiphany Chapel

A picturesque little building of 1877–9 set quietly in the fields, by Norman Shaw in one of his simpler moods. The exterior, of plain brick, rises to timberwork with brick-and-tile infilling under a continuous tile roof with a little bell-cote. The interior is equally pleasing. Screen, pulpit and font are all by Shaw, and there is an exceptionally satisfying E window by Heaton, Butler and Bayne. The chancel was redecorated in 1903 by Douglas Strachan. [AJS]

Perlethorpe, Nottinghamshire
St John

An estate church in the 'Dukeries' paid for by the 3rd Earl Manvers of Thoresby. Designed by Anthony Salvin and built in 1876. W tower and spire, all ashlar faced, and in a conventional Nottinghamshire Decorated style. The outline is enlivened by pinnacles to nave and chancel and decorative ridge-cresting along the roofs. The chancel has a sumptuous reredos with figures in niches with cusped and crocketed ogee arches on marble shafts. [NA]

Perth, Tayside
St Leonard's in the Fields (Church of Scotland)

By J. J. Stevenson, 1885, the first church in which the late Scots Gothic forms of the mid to late 15th and early 16th centuries were revived. Six bays, aisled with clerestory, extending into an aisleless tower-bay which rises into a belfry-stage capped by a crown of four fliers, three-sided apse with short pinnacles, crenellated parapets, crenellated hall and vestry block with cap-house. Internally, galleried aisles, the galleries lit by small square upper lights. [DW]

Perth, Tayside
St Ninian's Cathedral (Episcopal)

An interesting composite church, begun by William Butterfield in 1849, the chancel, transepts, central ironwork and lead flèche, one bay of the nave and its aisle walls being built at that date. Completion of nave to four bays and lower part of W tower, new reredos, still to Butterfield's design 1888–90. Early Middle Pointed, with wheel-windows at the transepts and wide arched nave-bays with clerestory of pairs of spheric triangles. Redesigned by J. L. Pearson 1896–7 for Bishop Wilkinson, executed by F. L. Pearson from 1899, tower rebuilt as extension of nave with buttressed octagonal angle-turrets, answering turrets added at E end, sacristy raised and apsed Lady Chapel added; chancel completely refurnished with large baldacchino, Butterfield's reredos being divided and set up in the new vestries; triple-arched rood-screen replaced by Sir J. Ninian Comper, 1924. [DW]

Peterborough, Cambridgeshire
All Saints

All Saints is an early work by Temple Moore and shows his debt to his master, George Gilbert Scott junior. It has a wagon roof and arcades with the mouldings dying into the piers very similar to those in Scott's now destroyed masterpiece, St Agnes, Kennington, which Moore completed following Scott's conversion to Roman Catholicism in 1880. The church was built in 1885–1903 and has reticulated Decorated tracery and an almost detached SE tower. The design has the refinement and austerity typical of the architect. [GS]

Petersham, Greater London
All Saints

Built at the expense of Mrs Lionel Warde in 1907–8, this robust and rubicund exercise in Italian Romanesque is by John Kelly. It is an extraordinary demonstration of dark-russet brick and terracotta with a tall S campanile and big octagonal baptistery grouping with separate hall and institute. The large interior consisting of clerestoried nave and aisles, raised chancel and chapels is lavishly lined with assorted marbles and partly glazed with oddly pallid Ward and Hughes glass. [RMH]

Petworth, West Sussex
The Sacred Heart (RC)

A Curvilinear-style church in stone by F. A. Walters erected in 1896. The long nave continues at the same pitch into an apsed chancel and an octagonal bell-turret rises in the angle of the chancel and S transept. The interior of the church is superior in proportion and effect to the outside: the rib-vaulted chancel is the *chef-d'oeuvre* and has a fine stone reredos. [DRE]

Plumbland, Cumbria
St Cuthbert, Arkleby Village

This complex, well-articulated design by J. A. Cory and C. J. Ferguson, 1870–1, culminates in an unusual gabled tower at the SW, only slightly higher than the nave. It has a prominent N transept and clerestory windows of contrasting type. The style is Early English with some Decorated features, but effective use is made of elements from the previous church: the transept window is 13th century, a small window in the E wall of the tower 14th century, while contrasting with a typically Victorian nave arcade is an inserted Norman chancel arch of red sandstone, much increased in height. [TEF]

Pontypool, Gwent
English Baptist Church

Built in 1846–7, this Grecian chapel was 'designed by Aaron Crossfield Esq., improved and perfected by Mr Langdon, architect' (probably J. H. Langdon of London). It has a grand Doric porch, with pediment and columns *in antis*. Originally the interior was lit only by the huge coved roof-light, decorated with an anthemion frieze, in accordance with the erroneous theory that Greek temples were top-lit. Much of the original decoration survives, as does the magnificent mahogany reading-desk, with Doric columns, but the galleries with rich bulgy ironwork are later. About

1900 side windows were inserted, in Perpendicular Gothic with Art Nouveau glass. [PH]

Port Talbot, West Glamorgan
St Theodore

Built in 1895–7 to the designs of John Loughborough Pearson, the church follows the tradition of his large Gothic town churches, though it is unusual in being designed to have a W tower, which was never built, and having timber roofs in the nave, crossing and transepts, although the aisles, chancel and apsidal S chapel all have rib-vaults. There is an attractive bell-turret over the chancel arch. [AQ]

Portsmouth, Hampshire
St Agatha

Intended to bring grandeur and beauty into the heart of one of the city's most squalid slums, this startling church was built in 1893 by J. Henry Ball for the controversial Anglo-Catholic mission priest Robert R. Dolling. Designed at Dolling's request in the form of an Early Christian basilica, it contained interior decorations and furnishings by Heywood Sumner and others. Having been used until recently as a naval store since its deconsecration in 1955, it stands today isolated and deprived of its Lady Chapel in an urban wasteland. By a miracle Sumner's majestic sgraffito murals and mosaics still adorn the E wall of the nave, and the apse and the brick arcades of impressive scale supported on alternate columns of polished granite and panelled marble with exquisitely carved stone capitals remain undamaged. [MM]

Portsmouth, Hampshire
Cathedral of St John the Evangelist (RC)

J. A. Crawley won the competition for the design of this cathedral in 1877 but died shortly after construction began in 1881. Work continued under J. A. Hansom and was completed under A. J. C. Scoles in 1906. The high spire at the SW corner intended by Crawley was not built. The massing and external treatment of the cathedral is undistinguished, so the spaciousness and dignity of its interior come as a surprise. The nave rises to a great height and closes overhead in a vaulted wooden ceiling. Its well-proportioned arcades lead to a crossing flanked by short transepts and continue along the chancel beyond to

sweep around the apsidal E end. In the S transept is a vast window of prickly curves. [MM]

Portsmouth, Hampshire
St Mary, Portsea, Fratton Road

By Sir Arthur Blomfield 1887–9. A Victorian version of a great late-medieval town church. Tall aisles and clerestory with Perpendicular windows; spacious interior suitable for a large congregation. Tall, thinly pinnacled tower. [DL]

Prenton, Merseyside
St Stephen

This church makes less of an impression in its prosperous leafy suburb than was originally intended. As designed by C. E. Deacon, and begun, with the building of the nave, in 1897, it was to have had a tower and spire over the choir, but when it was completed in 1909 by Deacon and Horsbrugh, they were omitted, and the nave was given an extra bay. The sandstone exterior has lancets grouped under blank arches. The interior is long, spacious and warm, with well-varied pressed red brick and sandstone. The detailing is original and successful. [PH]

Preston, Lancashire
St Walburge (RC)*

This is one of the most extraordinary churches in Britain. The main body, dating from 1850–4, consists of a vast rectangle of red sandstone, 165 feet by 55 feet, covered with a hammer-beam roof so large that it reaches up as high again as the side walls. The style is Early Decorated. The architect, J. A. Hansom, was providing his Jesuit clients with a Counter-Reformation church in Gothic form. The *Ecclesiologist* attacked it as 'this flaunting offspring of the unhappy nuptials of Oratorianism and true Christian ecclesiology'. Originally the altars stood in screened 'pens', but in 1872 S. J. Nicholl added the apsidal sanctuary. The corbelled-out pulpit is reached by an arcaded stairway in the wall. The W gallery is a wild piece of carpentry. The large windows are filled with glass by Hardman, Mayer, and other makers. On the S side of the church stands the immensely tall and strongly modelled spire, in white limestone, completed in 1869. Its height, 300 feet, is exaggerated by the railway cutting. [PH]

Preston, Lancashire
St Wilfred (RC)*

This rich and colourful Jesuit church has a complicated building history. The original church of 1793 was completely remodelled in 1878–80 by Fr Ignatius Scoles, SJ, and S. J. Nicholl, who added an extra aisle. In 1892 the exterior was recast by S. J. Nicholl in brick and terracotta, in North Italian Renaissance style. The W front is especially splendid. The lavish interior has Corinthian columns of pink Shap granite, and a tunnel vault. The apsidal sanctuary contains the high altar by Fr Scoles. Everywhere are marble, alabaster, mosaics, and gilding. The Lady Altar was designed by Pugin and Pugin and carved by R. L. Boulton. The grandiose baptistery was added in 1902 by Edmund Kirby. [PH]

Preston Patrick, Cumbria
St Patrick

On an isolated hilltop overlooking fields this rugged church of rock-faced stone by Sharpe and Paley, 1852, with its large battlemented tower at the NW, is reminiscent of border vernacular forms. It was built on the site of a late-15th-century chapel (from which a number of elements have been reused), the chancel being a compatible addition by Paley and Austin in 1892. The interior is austere, a simple three-bay arcade dividing nave from N aisle, but window tracery is Perpendicular in style. [TEF]

Prestwood, Buckinghamshire
Holy Trinity

By E. B. Lamb, 1846–9, and controversial despite its unpretentious Gothic rusticity. The controversy concerned its unorthodox disposition – the nave bracketed between a chancel to the E and an identical projection to the W. Today, later alterations to the E end (including the addition of a vestry and the raising of the chancel roof) have destroyed the original symmetry, but the puzzling W pseudo-chancel remains. So does the porch, designed in 1848 – significantly, for its violent collision with the aisle wall, in which its E buttress appears permanently embedded, antedates Butterfield's very similar handling of the porch at All Saints, Margaret Street, London. Inside, the space is cosily Gothic, but Lamb is at his most playful in the large roof-corbel poised

precariously over the porch door, and in the quaintly down-scaled arches of the E nave bay. By Lamb are the pulpit and the very fine font (modelled after the early-14th-century font at St Mary Magdalene, Oxford) as well as the small saint in the S chancel window, the remains of a much larger stained-glass programme. In the N aisle, a window by Oliphant. [ENK]

Privett, Hampshire
Holy Trinity

Sited near the edge of a shallow escarpment, this large church enjoys a commanding position. Designed in 1876 by Sir Arthur Blomfield, it is a convincing essay in the Early English style. High clerestoried nave flanked by low, very narrow aisles, and chancel with vestry and S chapel arranged as transepts are lit by double, triple and stepped lancets and plate tracery. At the W end a magnificent cross-buttressed tower supports a stone broach-spire which rises to 160 feet. Notable features of the interior are the clerestory arcades over aisle arcades, a bold open roof with cusped arched braces, much good wrought ironwork and the rich materials and detailing of the sanctuary. [MM]

Pulford, Cheshire
St Mary

Beside an entrance to Eaton Hall Park (now closed) the 1st Duke of Westminster erected a new church in 1881–4 to replace the old one. Though not a large building, it has tremendous presence. The stately shingled spire at the NW is typical of John Douglas, as is the broad aisleless nave. The exterior is in red sandstone with bands of lighter stone. The style is Decorated, but the traceried nave-windows have straight heads. The interior has a fine oak roof. The stained glass is by Heaton, Butler and Bayne, and the reredos and charming alms-box are by Shrigley and Hunt. [PH]

Rainhill, Merseyside
St Bartholomew (RC)

This exceptionally fine classical church was built in 1838–40 at the expense of Bartholomew Bretherton of Rainhill Hall, who was a retired stagecoach proprietor. The architect was Joshua Dawson of Preston, but the 'idea' is said to have been due to Mr Carter, a painter and glass-stainer also of Preston. It has a temple exterior in red sandstone, with hexastyle Ionic portico, pilasters round sides and apse, and no windows visible at all. The Italianate campanile on the N was added in 1849. The gorgeous Roman basilican interior is in striking contrast. The coffered barrel-vault is supported on Corinthian columns, whose entablature breaks forward over fluted columns to mark out the apse. Light comes from windows above the entablature. The decorative painting and glazing was originally by Carter, but by 1855 the painting had been redone by J. T. Bulmer. It was done over again in 1984 during a sadly unsympathetic reordering, when the Siena marble altar was moved forward and made narrower, and the only other original fitting that remained, the organ, was burnt. The packed churchyard is entered through a triple archway of the 1850s. [PH]

Ramsgate, Kent
St Augustine (RC)*

Built lovingly and slowly, at his own expense and next to his own house, the Grange, but as a parish church, St Augustine's is one of A. W. N. Pugin's most successful and most individual churches. It is also an impressive example of Pugin's belief in the 'true principles' of the Gothic Revival, and contains excellent work by his close friends and colleagues, George Myers, who was also the builder, John Hardman and Herbert Minton. Begun late in 1845, it was opened in 1850, but was still unfinished at Pugin's death in 1852. The Benedictine monks came to Ramsgate in 1856 and it became the abbey church to their monastery, which was built opposite from 1860. Pugin began his building with the bell-tower by the road and the E range of the cloister, beyond which the church lies. Its exterior, with carefully placed knapped flints and narrow bands of Whitby stone, can only be seen from two directions: a complicated composition from the E, and a severe one from the S. The intended spire was never added to the central tower. The plan is most unusual, with a nave and chancel of almost equal length, divided by central tower, a S aisle almost as wide as the nave, S Lady Chapel, a S transept and porch. The interior of Whitby stone is splendid, full of strong mouldings and excellent carvings in an early-14th-century style. Pugin was generous with his fittings. Sadly, those in

the chancel have all been moved. They included the tabernacle which, together with the font and cover at the W end of the S aisle, was made by George Myers and exhibited at the Great Exhibition of 1851. The rood-screen is now in the Lady Chapel, as well as the fine metal screen designed by J. H. Powell for the International Exhibition of 1862. All the stained glass is good and by Hardman, but not all dating from Pugin's lifetime. The finest is the E window by Pugin. The S transept forms the Pugin chantry chapel. E. W. Pugin, Pugin's eldest son, designed his father's deeply felt monument and the Minton tiles, and J. H. Powell, Pugin's son-in-law, designed the S window. The N and W ranges of the cloister with their chapels were added later by E. W. Pugin and P. P. Pugin. [AW]

Ranmore, Surrey
St Bartholomew

A splendid, richly detailed church built from designs by Sir Gilbert Scott in 1859. With plentiful money available, Scott raised one of his best, most carefully ornamented churches, worthy of its prominent position by a breezy hilltop common. It is a solid, thick mixture of Early English and French Gothic styles with a tall impressive central spire over the crossing. Its little-changed interior with suitably sumptuous, if slightly barbaric, furnishings including a splendid dark-maroon and black marble font is memorable for the elaborately vaulted crossing-space luxuriantly enriched with an abundance of naturalistic carving. [RMH]

Reading, Berkshire
Christ Church*

This is one of Henry Woodyer's finest churches. It was built in 1861–2 and enlarged in 1874–5 to comprise an aisled nave with a SW tower and spire, and a chancel with S chapel and N vestry and organ-chamber. The tower has corner pinnacles and flying buttresses rising to a tall, inset octagonal spire. The windows have typical Woodyer Decorated tracery, and the clerestory windows are joined into continuous rows by blind tracery. The nave arcade is especially interesting: the piers have clustered shafts rising to support curious but most imaginative capitals consisting of canopies with cusped gables, set over the shafts and decorated with naturalistic flowers and foliage. The chancel arch has its head filled with open reticulated tracery to form a screen. The pulpit, carved by J. Birnie Philip, has steps with panels decorated with carved flowers. The sedilia have a vaulted canopy with odd detail. The excellent glass is by Hardman. [AQ]

Reddish, Greater Manchester
St Elizabeth

Built in 1882–3 as part of a model village layout of houses, mill, institute and rectory, the last two like the church by Alfred Waterhouse. The hand of Waterhouse is clear, with hard surfaces of brick and bands of contrasting stone and an open-cradled timber roof of great simplicity. Short, fat columns of granite and the marble facing of the apsed sanctuary add richness where necessary, as also the Venetian marble screen, with four figures on top, and the vaulted chancel. Unusually the tower stands on the S site outside the aisle at the junction of nave and sanctuary. The patron Sir William Houldsworth's memorial is a small chapel on the N side separated by a thin incongruous Perpendicular screen. [DB]

Revelstoke, Noss Mayo, Devon
St Peter

Designed by James Piers St Aubyn and erected in 1881–2 on a fine, steeply sloping site overlooking the Yealm estuary, the church was entirely financed by the banker, Edward Baring, 1st Baron Revelstoke. The conventional Perpendicular exterior hardly prepares one for the rich elaboration of the interior, completed in the ten years after the church's erection. All the carved work is by Hems of Exeter, including an imaginatively varied set of bench ends. The stencil patterns on the walls of the nave are by Fouracre and Watson of Plymouth, as also is the decorative scheme of the E end, where stencil patterns are combined with mural tiles and a sequence of pictorial panels in gesso, heavily gilded. There is a full set of stained glass, again designed by Fouracre and Watson. [CB]

Rhyl, Clwyd
St Thomas

Begun in 1861 and consecrated in 1869. The architect was Sir Gilbert Scott, and the style a severe but handsome Early English. The strong square tower

(erected in 1874) is surmounted by a striking broach-spire with gabled clock-faces, reaching 203 feet – a fine landmark on the flat estuary. The interior is richly fitted: the arcades have marble shafts. [PH]

Richards Castle, Salop
All Saints*

A grand, rather lonely church, set away from the village on an eminence overlooking the Leominster to Ludlow road. It was built in 1890–3 by Norman Shaw. The S elevation is masterly in its massing and notable particularly for its powerful tower, approached up an avenue of yews. The building is calmer within and lacks the rich decoration which Shaw hoped would come in time. An exception is the broad reredos, made by Farmer and Brindley and painted by C. E. Buckeridge. [AJS]

Richmond, Greater London
St Matthias

A grand Gothic church in Sir Gilbert Scott's most confident style. It was built in 1858 and dominates the neighbourhood with its NW tower and spire. The interior is lofty, with Dec tracery in the aisles, but has been spoilt by subdivision. [IRS]

Ridgmont, Bedfordshire
All Saints

By Sir Gilbert Scott, 1854–5, for the Duke of Bedford. A fine, confident Ecclesiological church, of roughly dressed stone, with a prominent broach-spire rising from a tower with geometrical patterns in dark-brown ironstone round the parapet. The interior is little altered, with original chancel fittings, panelled chancel roof, openwork nave roof, strong foliage carvings on the arcades and generally buff decor. [DL]

Ripon, North Yorkshire
St Wilfrid

By J. A. Hansom, 1860–2; completed by E. W. Pugin. A remarkable design, culminating in the extraordinary, tall chancel, virtually an octagonal tower. The interior is relatively little altered. Amongst the fittings Pugin's fine high altar is most notable. The glass in the nave is of special interest having been designed by John Hungerford Pollen for the 1st Marquis of

Ripon. The eleven windows of assorted saints were moved here from the chapel at Studley Royal in 1909. [KP]

Roath, Cardiff, South Glamorgan
St German

The three major churches of Bodley and Garner's partnership are Pendlebury, Hoar Cross, and St German's. The third was built in 1884–5 and was the last significant building designed by them together before they began to work independently, though still in partnership. It is a marvel of collaboration, possessing breadth of effect, spaciousness and grace, 'simple, sheer and unaffected'. High rather than long, it demonstrates a brilliant handling of scale on a restricted site. Built of stone, its delicate grace is created by slender clustered columns, supporting a wooden wagon roof interspaced with ribs. It has an elevated chancel and sanctuary with a wooden roof divided into three bays by stone arches. The attenuated E window is given ingenuity by double tracery, filled with sombre glass by Burlison and Grylls, foiling Cecil Hare's dignified triptych, heavily carved and coloured, carried across the width of the E wall. The organ is raised on a tribune on the S side of the chancel. Bodley defined architecture as 'power held in restraint' and that is fully exemplified here. [ANS]

Rochdale, Greater Manchester
St Edmund, Fallinge

This must be one of the most unusual and extraordinary churches built in the 19th century. Medland Taylor often indulged in architectural gymnastics and bizarre detail, but here in 1873 he rose to the unique opportunity given to him by the extravagant patronage of Albert Hudson Royds, a leading and even fanatical Freemason. Centrally planned, it has a massive tower supported on four gigantic granite piers. The same material is used throughout for other columns. Externally there is a mixture of ashlar dressings and coursed rubble; inside the finest dressed stone. Dimensions are said to be based on those of Solomon's Temple. References to the traditions and lore of Masonry are everywhere, in the weathervane and the lectern in particular. The detailed construction of the timber roofs is remarkable, with boards laid to the most effective structural patterns. Exuberantly carved capitals and corbels are outdone by the intri-

cate splendour of the reredos in which five pointed arches burst into leafy growth interwoven with vines, fruit and other flowers emblematic of the Passion. There is nothing quite like St Edmund's anywhere else. [DB]

Rugby, Warwickshire
St Andrew

The 14th/15th-century parish church having become too small, William Butterfield enlarged it in 1875–9. He retained the old building, as the N aisle and outer N aisle of his own much grander church. The old tower remains at the W end, but in 1894–6 Butterfield added the tall spire at the NE. All of this produces a highly picturesque effect towards the main street on the N. The exterior is quiet, except for the top of the new steeple, so that the lofty and colourful interior comes as a surprise. The colour comes from the alternating red and yellow stone, with grey marble for shafts etc., and the painted roofs, less so from the disappointing stained glass. The great cross above the chancel arch is wonderfully effective. The chancel fittings are gorgeously elaborate, including the altar-rails and chunky, brass, standing candlesticks (1885). Unfortunately the reredos was filled in 1909 with Alec Miller's adaptations of Fra Angelico. Pulpit and font are splendid. [PH]

Rugby, Warwickshire
School Chapel

The fine site and unusual brief here led William Butterfield to produce, in 1870–2, one of his most striking and original buildings. It is cruciform, with broad, shallow transepts. Over the choir rises the bold octagonal tower, with stone pyramidal roof: with the canted apse of the sanctuary it forms a powerfully dramatic composition towards the older school buildings and the Close. The nave and low aisles were completed in 1897 by T. G. Jackson. The polychromy of brick and stone is glorious outside and in. The lofty roofs, supported on slender piers, are cheerily painted. The apse has mosaics of 1882. The seats face each other lengthwise. The stained glass includes 16th-century work from Belgium, as well as new glass by Willement, Gibbs, Hardman, Kempe, and Morris. [PH]

Ryde, Isle of Wight
All Saints

One of Sir Gilbert Scott's more ambitious churches, built 1869–72 on a prominent site in a wholly 19th-century town; the flanking tower and spire, designed by his son J. Oldrid Scott, were added in 1882. In 14th-century style with three W gables, corner pinnacles and Gothic perforated parapets; the polygonal-ended vestry of 1891 adds a nice touch at a corner of the church. The interior is broad and spacious; a clerestory originally intended by Scott was not built; there are an elaborate font and pulpit by Scott, and originally brilliant decorations in the chancel by Clayton and Bell, who also designed the fine glass in the E window and elsewhere. [DL]

Ryde, Isle of Wight
St Michael, Swanmore

Mainly built in 1861–3 by an amateur architect and Hampshire rector, Revd William Grey, together with the local professional architect R. J. Jones. It is externally austere, of grey local limestone, but the interior is astonishing – a free and varied adaptation of Gothic to serve what was then a controversially ritualistic congregation. The nave arcades rise, without capitals, from octagonal piers; the walls above them are decorated with red, blue and black brick patterns against a buff brick background. The arches of the crossing rise from ornate, almost Corinthian capitals, and the climax is a rich, vaulted polygonal chancel with Purbeck stone shafting, completed in 1874. [DL]

St Leonards, East Sussex
Congregational Church (URC)

This handsome building of 1863 with lofty spire is among the most ambitious Nonconformist buildings in Sussex. Early English in style, the architects were Habershon, Spalding and Brock. The tower has a copper steeple and is approached by matching curved flights of steps. A striking feature is the bold cross-gabling of the aisles, each bay having a large window with wheel tracery. [DRE]

Salford, Greater Manchester
St Clement

A great town church carefully done in brickwork by Paley and Austin between 1877 and 1878. Its towering slate-clad flèche and panelled brick-gabled buttresses, which project beyond and above the clerestory walls, divide the timber-roofed nave from the brick-vaulted chancel. A pinnacled circular turret of lancet panels of brickwork rising from a square base at the NE junction of the N transept and chancel leads to the vaults above the chancel. Internally the sensitive and bold 1980 church hall by Donald Buttress is set in the westernmost bays of the nave with their great circular piers of red Runcorn sandstone. [DM]

Salford, Greater Manchester
St John's Cathedral (RC)

J. G. Weightman, and particularly his partner M. E. Hadfield, were in the 1840s building many good mock-medieval Roman Catholic churches. All of them are good and they often have more architectural substance than those of Pugin himself, even if they lack his elegance in detailed design. At Salford, built in 1844–8, the texture of the external masonry is convincing and the details of the tracery and mouldings equally so. The central tower is clearly based on Newark, the nave owes something to Howden and the choir to that at Selby. It is as if the designers felt that the sum of good parts would inevitably mean an even better amalgam, or Gothic improved. The internal effect is a bit of a let-down; plaster is no substitute for ashlar and the recent reorderings hardly help. The Wailes glass of the E window (1854) contains a particularly repellent portrait of Henry VIII. The E parts were furnished and decorated in 1853–5 by Weightman, Hadfield and Goldie. [DB]

Salford, Greater Manchester
United Reformed Church, Broughton Park

For the Congregationalists, S. W. Daukes produced a building in the Decorated style, 1872–5, which in its external features continues the Anglican pattern with which he was most familiar. The nave and aisles, with a tall steeple at the S end of one aisle, terminate abruptly to the N in short transepts beyond which outward appearances are deceptive. There is no chancel and the whole of the N (ritual E) end is in two storeys with vestries below a large lecture-hall approached by a staircase in an 'apse'. The hall was made open towards the nave forming a large but discreet gallery behind the central pulpit. [cs]

Saltaire, West Yorkshire
United Reformed Church

In 1853 Titus Salt (created a baronet in 1869) removed his manufacture of alpaca cloth to a new factory away from the crowded streets of Bradford. Around it he built a model village for his workpeople reserving the best site for a place of worship of his own denomination. The Congregational chapel designed by Lockwood and Mawson and opened in 1859 stands in a park-like setting facing the mill. The slender domed tower rises above the ring of Corinthian columns encircling the E vestibule. The interior has all the magnificence of a Victorian town hall with two enormous lanterns suspended from a richly decorated vaulted ceiling. In the vestibule is a statue of Titus Salt by Thomas Milnes and at one side in a later mausoleum is a memorial sculpture by John Adams-Acton. [cs]

Sandbach Heath, Cheshire
St John the Evangelist

This excellent church by G. G. Scott (1861) makes a fine show from the M6. The exterior is in rough yellow stone with pinky-brown dressings. Cruciform, its crossing-tower has an octagonal spire. The style is mid- to late-13th-century Gothic. Everything is well detailed and beautifully proportioned. The interior, of brownish ashlar, has real grandeur despite its small scale, the well-lit crossing especially impressive. Big inscriptions cut in the stone record benefactions. Original fittings include choir-stalls, pulpit, and font. The E window is first-rate Clayton and Bell. The extraordinary wood-carving in the chancel, which includes giant hollyhocks and lilies in three dimensions, is by Jessie Barbara Kennedy, a local lady. [PH]

Scarborough, North Yorkshire
St Martin on the Hill

An expensive church in Bodley's early manner, 13th-century Gothic with a flavour of France. Consecrated in 1864, it consists of nave, aisles and chancel with a NE chapel, a W narthex and gabled tower; it has short, sturdy octagonal piers supporting an arcade of tall acutely pointed arches with simple mouldings; there is plate tracery. Here Bodley reached the fullest expression of his collaboration with the Pre-Raphaelites and even joined them in painting the tympanum of the chancel arch himself and part of the E wall. Morris carried out the stained glass, Rossetti, Burne-Jones, Philip Webb and Campfield painted the pulpit and reredos, accomplishing the most complete Pre-Raphaelite church interior in England. There is later stencilling and furniture in the chapel, a rood-screen in Bodley's mature style and glass by Burlison and Grylls. [ANS]

Scorborough, Humberside
St Leonard

Built in 1857–9, this was John Loughborough Pearson's first successful High Victorian Gothic church. The prominent W steeple has deep-set lucarnes and corner pinnacles at the junction of tower and spire. The body of the church is treated as a single cell, the interior resplendent with highly carved corbels, capitals and cornices, and the constructional poly-chromy of various grey, yellow, red and black stones. These are all used to emphasize the articulation of the parts, bay from bay, nave from chancel, wall-shaft from nook-shaft, and draw them together into a unified whole. The stained glass is by Clayton and Bell. [AQ]

Scotforth, Lancaster
St Paul

Designed in 1874 by Edmund Sharpe, who had abandoned architectural practice in 1851 to take up railway engineering. He used mass brickwork for the tower, with its Geometrical tracery and saddleback roof. But, for the round arcade piers and architectural details internally and externally, terracotta is used. After the drying and firing problems of terracotta Sharpe experienced in his earlier work, did he con-sciously choose the simplicity of Neo-Norman detailing? [DM]

Scunthorpe, Humberside
St John the Evangelist

By J. S. Crowther, 1891; it is large and ambitious, with a soaring W tower, clerestoried and aisled nave and chancel. All is Perpendicular Gothic, richly and consistently handled. The openwork parapets and complex arrangement of pinnacles on the tower are straight from Manchester cathedral, which Crowther had just restored. Two clerestory windows to each aisle window, and tall three-light chancel windows. Battlements and fleuron friezes. Lofty interior with hammer-beam roofs and fittings by Crowther. [NA]

Selsley, Gloucestershire
All Saints*

An early work of G. F. Bodley, designed in 1858 and built in 1862 for the millowner Sir S. S. Marling. The church is superbly set high over the valley and is of powerfully simple outline, a single roof steeply hipped at the apse and, to one side, a sheer tower with leaded saddleback roof echoing the line of the main roof. Bodley is here High Victorian in this severe geometry and the plate-traceried rose window but the elegance of his later work shows in the fine traceried side-windows and the well-detailed buttress dividing nave and chancel. Good High Victorian carving and fittings inside. The glory of the church is the complete scheme of Morris glass, one of the firm's earliest commissions, with work by Morris, Burne-Jones, Rossetti, Madox Brown, Campfield and Webb. The W Creation window of nine circles, six by Morris, three by Webb, is a triumph of rich colour and swirling design. The apse has lovely panels including the Visitation by Rossetti, the Annunciation by Morris and Nativity by Brown. Good lych-gate based on Butterfield's at Coalpit Heath, Avon. [JO]

Shackleford, Surrey
St Mary

A satisfying, well-proportioned and especially finely modelled design of 1865 in local yellow Bargate sandstone by Sir Gilbert Scott. Aisled and clerestoried nave, transepts and large apse are carefully grouped round a commanding central tower, relieved by a strong lower stair-turret and crowned by a shingled broach-spire. Inside, the detail is rather mechanical, but contemporary Clayton and Bell glass in the apse completes the High Victorian effect. [RMH]

Sheerness, Kent
SS Henry and Elizabeth (RC)

Typical of its architect Edward Welby Pugin but on a grander scale than most of his projects. It was constructed in 1863–4, in Early English and Decorated, of yellow brick banded with black and dressed with stone. The apsidal chancel and sanctuary are gabled without and canted within. The W end is of five lancets and a rose window and supports the tall bell-gable that is almost E. W. Pugin's signature. [REH]

Sheffield, South Yorkshire
St Matthew, Carver Street

By Flockton and Son, 1854–5, St Matthew's is a decent and pleasing building, reminiscent of the medieval churches of York, but its chief interest derives from its fittings. J. D. Sedding refitted the chancel in 1884–6 and the high altar, altar cross and reredos are his, the latter gorgeously carved and gilded. The excellent stalls, beautifully carved and inlaid, are an early work by Sir Charles Nicholson. Font and pulpit in corresponding style were added by H. J. Potter in the 1900s. [KP]

Sherbourne, Warwickshire
All Saints*

A splendid estate church designed by Sir George Gilbert Scott and built in 1862–4, All Saints has a soaring slender steeple which is reflected in a lake. Entered through the vaulted tower-space, the nave has elegant stone arcades with marble shafts and an impressive inlaid marble font. Alabaster reredos and a dado carved by F. W. Pomeroy, who worked on site from real flowers and leaves. Pulpit stair by Skidmore of Coventry and stained glass by Clayton and Bell, Powell and Hardman. The vaulted Ryland Chapel, rebuilt around an 1843 tomb-chest by Pugin, is balanced by an organ-chamber by John Oldrid Scott. [DH]

Shiskine, Strathclyde
St Molio (Church of Scotland)

A very original church by Sir John Burnet, 1887. William Kerr worked on the drawings with Alexander MacGibbon and A. R. Scott. Mixed Gothic and

Romanesque motifs, very low nave with a big broad-eaved roof spreading down over an even lower S aisle, all with narrow round-headed slit windows. Squat W tower with twin round-arched belfry-openings, corbelled parapet and pyramid roof; a medieval tomb-slab is incorporated into a single W buttress and a half-timbered Neo-Tudor porch projects from its S flank. Internally the church has a timber arcade, wide-arched splays to the windows and a ceiled wagon roof with the bay divisions emphasized. [DW]

Shotton, Clywd
St Ethelwold

This grand red-sandstone church, built by John Douglas in 1898–1902, is in the Early English style he sometimes favoured. The aisled interior is lofty and refined. The pentagonal chancel rises higher than the nave. Unfortunately the tower and spire proposed for the NW corner were never built. [PH]

Shrewsbury, Salop
Cathedral of Our Lady and St Peter of Alcantara (RC)

Built by E. W. Pugin in 1853–6 for the Earl of Shrewsbury as the cathedral of the new diocese. The original scheme was more ambitious. It now consists of nave and aisles with a straight-ended chancel, large E and W windows and triangular clerestory windows. Pugin designed the font and high altar. The E window is by Hardman. In 1891 Edmund Kirby added the vaulted chapel of St Winefrid and in 1906 the fiery-red brick porch. Much excellent glass by Margaret Rope. Regrettable reordering in 1985. [RO'D]

Silvertown, Greater London
St Mark*

St Mark's is quintessential Teulon. Although closed since 1974 and its roof lost in a fire in 1981, the shell remains a triumph of decorative brickwork varied by the use of terracotta drainage bricks. The effect is heightened by a poetic contrast with the neighbourhood, industrial Essex at its most infernal. The composition is the one most favoured by Teulon: a nave (with passage aisles) a crossing-tower over the chancel and an apsidal sanctuary beyond. The tracery throughout the building is consistently square-sectioned and the four differing clerestory windows in the tower appear to owe more to Islam than to Christian Gothic. The church, now converted into a museum, is fully repaired and the roof faithfully reinstated by Julian Harrap. [MS]

Singleton, Lancashire
St Anne

E. G. Paley designed this estate church in 1860. It has a tall NE steeple. The simple cruciform plan echoes Paley's Rossall School Chapel at Fleetwood and, as at the Rossall Chapel, the construction of the nave roof is very much part of the overall design. Here a scissor-and-collar rafter roof is used. The three-light E chancel window with its traceried eight-light rose window contains glass designed by Frederick Preedy in 1859. [DM]

Skelton, North Yorkshire
Christ the Consoler*

One of the most memorable of all Victorian churches. It was built in 1871–6 by Lady Mary Vyner, mother of the Marchioness of Ripon, in memory of her son Frederick Vyner, who had been murdered by Greek brigands. Her architect was William Burges. The intense quality of the interior derives partly from the combination of a tall nave with a low-vaulted chancel, the chancel arch being filled with rich carving. As at Studley, the Gothic style is strongly French in influence, though used in a typically original way. The nave is cool and relatively austere, with long shafts of black marble from floor to roof. The chancel is lavishly decorated, with carving by Nicholls, glass by Saunders and Co., painting by Campbell and metalwork by Barkentin and Krall. The fittings of this church are strikingly original. The organ is fixed to the N wall, with an elaborate gallery for the organist. The font canopy is a magnified version of a Gothic reliquary with figures of Christ and John the Baptist. The pulpit is more Byzantine than Gothic, a huge marble affair approached from the vestry. [KP]

Sledmere, Humberside
St Mary*

St Mary's seems less typical of Temple Moore than his other Yorkshire churches as the client demanded elaboration while Moore was best when aiming for a certain gaunt austerity and grandeur. It does, however, have that bleak outline of which the architect was fond. It was built in 1897–8 by that munificent builder of churches, Sir Tatton Sykes of Sledmere. While arcades, window tracery and furnishings are all richly carved and modelled, Sir Tatton imposed the condition that all internal woodwork was to be of unstained oak without colour or gilding. This creates an unfortunate balance of colour but, nevertheless, as Goodhart-Rendel noted, 'nowhere can Moore's great virtuosity in the management of architectural riches be better studied than here'. The stained glass is by H. V. Milner and by Burlison and Grylls. [GS]

Slindon, Staffordshire
St Chad

This charming little toy church was designed in 1894 by Basil Champneys, and built by Bridgeman of Lichfield, at the expense of the banker J. C. Salt. In warm-red local sandstone, it has a low tower over the choir, and all the details are meticulous and personal. Both choir and sanctuary are vaulted. The carved stone reredos is rich in miniature detail. The E window glass is by Kempe. [PH]

Slinfold, West Sussex
St Peter

The exterior of this Victorian country church has been much spoilt by the removal of the elegant broach-spire in 1970. Begun in 1861 from designs by Benjamin Ferrey, it uses an individual version of the late-13th-century style, carefully worked out to harmonize with a rural setting. The S aisle is separately gabled and the spacious interior has a massive arcade. [DRE]

South Dalton, Humberside
St Mary, Dalton Holme*

Designed by John Loughborough Pearson for Lord Hotham of Dalton Hall, who wanted an estate church to eclipse his neighbour's work at Scorborough (q.v.), the church was built in 1858–61, and extended in 1868–70. It is a lavish example of Middle Pointed Gothic, with much carving in and out, and varied tracery in all the windows. The verticals are accentuated, especially by the slender, 200-foot steeple at the W end, and they contrast with broad bands of carving. The aisleless nave opens out into a crossing, and a chancel flanked by an organ-chamber and a mortuary chapel seen through traceried openings with wrought-iron screens by Skidmore of Coventry. The ornately arcaded sanctuary has a fine E window with Decorated tracery and splendid stained glass by Clayton and Bell, a glow of colour against the white Holdenby stone of the interior. [AQ]

South Norwood, Greater London
St Alban

Designed in 1888 by William Bucknall, few churches have had such a long and complicated building history. Bucknall's first design was for an Early Christian basilica; in the same year he formed a partnership with a colleague in Bodley and Garner's office, J. N. Comper, and under his influence changed the style to flowing Decorated, although the design remained much more Bucknall's than Comper's. An ambitious church, built of rubbed red brick with Bath stone dressings, it rises from a gently sloping site, with complicated massing, and flying buttresses at the SE, strongly defining the elevation. It was built for ceremonial and has a wide and tall chancel of three bays, raised on steps above a vaulted crypt containing vestries, with a seven-light E window with double-ogival tracery linked by enriched cusping, a nave of six contracted bays of Bath stone with arches dying into their piers, narrow passage-aisles with transverse arches similarly treated, a high clerestory of four-light windows and an elaborate tie- and hammer-beam roof, painted white. The walls are plastered and whitened and the aisles flow into narrow choir-aisles containing chapels with painted and gilded ceilings. The main part was built 1889–1901 but thereafter it was finished in stages from 1912 to 1939. Bucknall and Comper's partnership was broken in 1905; four years earlier Comper wrote: 'It is the function of the building to lead up to the ornaments, which it is raised on purpose to contain.' Hardly any were executed, making its lines and scale far more austere than was intended. There is a window by Comper in the Lady Chapel, stone walls in the sanctuary and his earliest altar ornaments, of surprising robustness. After the Second World War, Bucknall's nephew, Arthur, added a hanging rood and a classical sounding-board to the Gothic pulpit. If it had been furnished, coloured and filled with painted glass it would be a marvel. [ANS]

South Tidworth, Hampshire
*St Mary**

A small but sumptuous church designed by John
Johnson in 1879. A massive central buttress divides
its W front to support a cantilevered belfry and conical
stout spire. The interior is astonishing. From the
outer walls, finished inside in ashlar, the open timber
roof rises to cover nave and aisles in a single slope
supported by arcades borne aloft on quatrefoil polished grey-marble piers. Behind open stone screens,
chapels lie to N and S of the finely furnished chancel
and richly elaborate sanctuary which has an arcaded
reredos against the E wall flanked by trumpeting
angels. Woodwork, metalwork and glass in plate
tracery are of striking design and remarkable workmanship throughout. [MM]

Southend-on-Sea, Essex
All Saints, Queensway/Sutton Road

A brick church of 1889 by James Brooks, with a plain
W front of 1934 facing a huge traffic roundabout. The
interior is exciting – a broad, plain aisled nave with
lofty curved-braced wooden roof, a chancel arch
surmounted by an upper tier of three open arches,
and a climactic Pearson-like chancel with two tiers of
lancets. [DL]

Southend-on-Sea, Essex
St Alban, St John's Road

A beautiful church, in some ways eccentric; an early
work of Sir Charles Nicholson. Nave and aisles
1898–9; rest completed 1904. Exterior of rough stone
with thick brick bandings and dressings; low tower,
with chamfered angles, at the SE corner. The interior
is surprisingly spacious, with simple arcades on
square piers; barrel roofs painted with increasing
richness towards the E; screen with delicate upper
tracery but open below (a good arrangement); early-
20th-century chancel fittings with Art Nouveau lean-
ings. The wall surfaces are whitened, but because of
the colour and fittings this does not give a cold effect.
There is fascinating spatial complexity when one
looks through the two transeptal S chapels towards a
prominent many-recessed arch which leads into the
space under the tower. [DL]

Spalding, Lincolnshire
St Paul, Fulney

Built in 1877–80 to the designs of G. G. Scott senior
and carried out by G. G. Scott junior after his father's
death in 1878. A large townish-looking church,
impressive both in its composition – with aisled nave
and chancel and detached SW steeple – and in the
richness of detail. Early English style with lancets
and groups of lancets, with shafts and shaft-rings in
the chancel. Especially impressive E window of three
stepped lancets. Harshly red brick with Ancaster
stone dressings. Lavish tower with lots of arcading
and broach-spire; connected to the church by an
arcade. Inside, unusual nave arcades (based on
Boxgrove Priory) consisting of two pointed arches
within a single round arch. Polychromatic effect of
two shades of Ancaster stone. [NA]

Sproxton, North Yorkshire
St Chad

The early-17th-century chapel at West Newton
Grange, then in use as a barn, was taken down
and re-erected at Sproxton in 1878–9. Despite the
unfashionable date of the building, both the patron
Lord Feversham and the architect, George Gilbert
Scott junior, were anxious that it should be rebuilt
exactly as it was. The only alterations were the
addition of a lead-covered wooden bell-turret and a
chimney for the heating apparatus. The deliberately
overblown provincial Baroque style of the furnishings
– pews, screen and reredos – was probably Scott's
idea. The plaster panels on the reredos were made by
Mr Fry. The glass in the E window is by Burlison and
Grylls. [GS]

Staines, Surrey
St Peter

A large suburban church in red brick, built from
designs by Fellowes Prynne in 1893–4. The spreading
exterior with a low SW tower is elaborate Decorated
in style with rich window tracery. The capacious red-
brick interior culminates in a stone-traceried chancel
arch. Elaborate glass by J. Jennings from designs by
the architect's brother, Edward Prynne RA, fills the
big E and W windows to scintillating effect. [RMH]

Stansted Mountfitchet, Essex
St John the Evangelist

An early work of W. D. Caröe. Built 1889 in red brick with stone dressings; the tower, added 1896, is the best feature. It rises, with pinnacled buttresses, and a series of string-courses, to an elaborate parapet with crocketed corner-turrets, pinnacles supported by gargoyles, and crowning spirelet in the Herts–Essex border tradition. [DL]

Steppingley, Bedfordshire
St Lawrence

Rebuilt by Henry Clutton for the Duke of Bedford, 1859–60, in a small Victorian estate village with Gothic school and model cottages. Externally it is in local sandstone with freestone dressings and embattled W tower, very much in the local vernacular manner. Internally it seems grand for its size, with a tall chancel arch setting the scale. Alas, in 1968, the church was denuded of Clutton's pulpit and stained glass, and the whole was whitewashed internally, including the Bath stonework of piers and window frames. But the boldness of the mouldings and the clarity of the proportions still tell. [DL]

Stockport, Greater Manchester
St George*

A massive church of 'cathedral-like grandeur' built in 'outspoken late Gothic' between 1892 and 1897 to the designs of Paley, Austin and Paley and undoubtedly Hubert Austin's major work. The seven-light E window ascends in a mass of reticulated tracery. Above and below it the stonework is panelled; so too is the parapet. This element is used also on the tower and spire with its four flying buttresses coupling the corner pinnacles to the spire. Inside, clustered piers march down the six bays of the nave supporting the panelled stone spandrels of the galleried clerestory. The soaring arches of the great crossing-tower rise grandly from great panelled piers. Below the crossing-tower the choir is raised from the nave and divided from it by a low screen wall which projects out to the S as the pulpit. Underneath the great E window with its glass by Shrigley and Hunt, the chancel is terminated by the beautifully detailed alabaster reredos of the Crucifixion. [DM]

Stockton-on-Tees, Cleveland
St Mary (RC)

The first Catholic church built on Teesside after Catholic Emancipation. A. W. N. Pugin's design of 1841 best survives in the Early English W front and nave to which the N aisle, Lady Chapel and tower, first envisaged by Pugin, were added in 1866 in response to the influx of Irish residents. In 1870, Goldie and Child added the S aisle, baptistery, and chancel with semicircular apse; their rich decorative scheme is fully preserved in the Lady Chapel. The tower was completed along with the clerestory by C. and C. M. Hadfield in 1909. [LW]

Stoke-on-Trent, Staffordshire
Holy Trinity

Built in 1841–2 at the expense of the potter Herbert Minton, this church, high up on the site of a windmill, was designed by Scott and Moffatt. In correct Decorated, it has a pinnacled W spire, and the clerestoried nave has a plaster vault. After a fire in 1872 Scott rebuilt the chancel with a stone-vaulted apse and S chapel. The side windows of the apse are excellent early Hardman. The church is – predictably – lavishly tiled; not just the floors, as a tiled dado runs all round, incorporating memorial panels. The rich W window is by Leonard Walker (1936). [PH]

Stretton, Staffordshire
St Mary

This tremendously grand church, soaring above nondescript Burton-on-Trent suburbia in its open churchyard, was built in 1895–7 at the expense of John Gretton (of the brewers Bass, Ratcliff and Gretton). The architects were Micklethwaite and Somers Clarke: it is said that Micklethwaite executed a design by Clarke. The aisled nave and chancel are of the same height, and between them rises the noble buttressed tower, which has a pyramidal roof. S of the chancel is a chapel, and on the N the vestry with organ-chamber above. The interior is light and dignified. All the roofs are prettily painted. Excellent woodwork includes pews, pulpit, rood-screen, organ-case, and the cover of the splendid marble font. The stained glass of the chancel and chapel was designed by Sir William Richmond and executed by James Powell and Sons *c.* 1897: the E window, showing

Christ in glory among angels, is particularly rich and intense. [PH]

Studley Royal, North Yorkshire
St Mary*

Long redundant and now cared for by the National Trust, St Mary's has one of the most striking settings of any Victorian church – on the edge of the Studley Royal park, which has Fountains Abbey as its climax, and at the end of a long avenue from Ripon Cathedral. Built in 1871–8 at the expense of the Marquis and Marchioness of Ripon, William Burges's church, said to have been designed 'at a moment's notice', is worthy of its setting. The exterior is rich and exotic, patently French in inspiration and culminating in the luxuriant decoration of the E end. Even this, however, fails to prepare one adequately for the splendours of the interior and of the chancel in particular. Here Burges's exoticism ran riot. The walls are lined with marble, there are shafts of coloured marbles, double tracery to the windows, and a splendid inlaid mosaic floor with the four rivers flowing around the Garden of Eden. The walls of the chancel are decorated with painted and carved ornament, while the roof is a barrel-roof turning into a dome over the sanctuary, gilded and painted. There is a remarkable brass door between the sanctuary and the vestry. The entire building is full of the symbolism beloved of the architect. The sculptural work was executed by Thomas Nicholls, the stained glass by Saunders and Co., the designers W. H. Lonsdale and Fred Weekes working closely with Burges. The fittings throughout are appropriately lavish. [KP]

Sunderland, Tyne and Wear
Christ Church

The best Victorian church in an architecturally well-endowed suburb of Sunderland. The designer was the young Coventry architect, James Murray, who won the commission in competition in 1862 but died during its erection. Completed in 1864 under his partner, J. Cundall, it is a large, rugged church, built of limestone, having nave, aisles, chancel, transepts and tower with spire which is set at the NE. The nave arcade of five bays has good stiff-leaf capitals and round pillars which rest on octagonal bases. The most notable feature of the interior is a Morris and Co. E window inserted by E. R. Robson. [LW]

Sutton Veny, Wiltshire
St John the Evangelist*

Designed in 1865–6 by John Loughborough Pearson and built in 1866–8, this fine stone church marks Pearson's move away from the vigour of his High Victorian Gothic style and towards the refinement of his town churches of the 1870s and 1880s. In many ways it returns to the correct Middle Pointed or Decorated Gothic of Pugin and the Ecclesiologists, fashionable in the 1840s, but it is immaculately finished, the plain stonework of the nave contrasting with the ornate, vaulted choir, chancel and sanctuary. The church is cruciform with a central tower and broached spire with slight entasis typical of Pearson. The stained glass is by Clayton and Bell. [AQ]

Tanworth, Warwickshire
Christ Church, Umberslade (Baptist)*

In 1877, G. F. Muntz, the Baptist squire of Umberslade Hall, employed George Insall of Birmingham to design a Gothic chapel which stands in solitary splendour in the midst of fields. Muntz allowed himself the luxury of a polygonal chancel and shallow transepts besides a large preaching nave, and in the spired SW tower, for the orientation is entirely orthodox, a carillon of eight bells, sadly no longer in working order. [CS]

Tarfside, Tayside
Maule Memorial Church (Church of Scotland)

Small Anglo-Saxon church with convincing herring-bone banded masonry by J., J. M. and W. H. Hay, 1857. Simple rectangle lit by small round-arch windows with long imposts. Three-stage tower with paired belfry-openings and pyramid roof. [DW]

Tavistock, Devon
St Mary Magdalene (RC)

Originally an Anglican chapel of ease, built in 1865–8 as part of the Duke of Bedford's town improvements. Designed by the duke's architect, Henry Clutton, the church is dramatically sited on a steep hill. It is French Transitional in style, the masonry of Tavistock greenstone, and comprises a tall clerestoried nave, N and S aisles, chancel, a two-storeyed SE vestry with separate pyramidal roof, and – standing free from the main body – a N bell-tower with large, louvred belfry-windows and a short, square spire. The interior is impressively lofty, but similarly severe, with stilted arcades, idiosyncratic in profile, and an open timber roof. [CB]

Tebay, Cumbria
St James

This church (1878–80) serves a small 19th-century railway town and is of local rock-faced granite on a steeply sloping site. A compact, unpretentious design by the scholarly C. J. Ferguson of Carlisle, it has an unusual round tower at the NW, with nave, chancel, N porch and a W apse with meeting room below. It is basically Early English in style but the interior is a surprise, faced in brick and more High than Late Victorian with cream and red patterns and bands. The nave roof resembles the upturned hull of a ship. [TEF]

Tenbury, Hereford and Worcester
*St Michael and All Angels**

The parish church of Tenbury St Michael was built in 1854–6. Until 1985 it served the College of St Michael and All Angels, founded by the musician and composer, Sir Frederick Gore Ouseley, chiefly for education in music. His architect for all the works was Henry Woodyer. The church is large and cruciform, with an aisled nave, and chancel with a polygonal apse and side chapels. The high apse and steep roofs give the church a strong vertical emphasis. The windows, including the large three-light clerestory windows, have Decorated tracery in the Woodyer manner, and there are roses in both transepts. The nave arcade has round piers and capitals carved with ornate foliage. The side chapels open into the chancel through double arches set under large relieving arches with foiled roundels in the spandrels. There is a wooden vault. The high altar, characteristically of Woodyer, is emphasized by being set under a canopy with triple gables and a curious rib-vault. The glorious sanctuary glass is by Hardman. A timber cloister leads to the college buildings, which are more strongly characterized by Woodyer's quirkiness. [AQ]

Thirkleby, North Yorkshire
*All Saints**

Designed by E. B. Lamb in 1849, All Saints was the first and grandest of a series of churches commissioned by Lady Louisa Frankland-Russell (see also Aldwark, Bagby and Blubberhouses). The grandeur is due to the fact that it was built as a family mausoleum and memorial to her husband, Sir Robert, 7th Baronet of Thirkleby Park. Dominated by a tower and spire, the church forms a commanding asymmetrical silhouette both from the road to the E and the fields to the W. Inside, despite some quirky Gothic details (like the amusingly truncated arches of the W nave bay), the general effect is ample, serious, and surprisingly 'correct' in the Ecclesiological sense – surprisingly, that is, for Lamb. This is partly due to the strongly axial plan, which is among Lamb's most conventional, but also to a sumptuous decorative scheme: the richly traceried pulpit, the sturdy wood altar table, and the remarkable font with its hanging Curvilinear tracery, are all by Lamb, as are the prayer-desk, nave-seats, choir-stalls, and a varied array of bright-coloured encaustic tiles. The stained glass was largely designed by female members of the Frankland-Russell family and is amateurish, but there is a small window by Lamb in the chancel (N side). [ENK]

Thurstaston, Merseyside
St Bartholomew

A small church designed in 1883 by John Loughborough Pearson, and completed in 1886. Externally it is a fine if conventionally detailed Early Decorated Gothic church, dominated by a tower and spire centrally placed over the choir between the nave and the higher chancel. The interior is no less conventional in its decoration, but within small dimensions encompasses a wonderful progression of spaces, from the nave through a tripartite, traceried screen to the taller, square choir, and the still taller chancel. All these are united by stone quadripartite vaulting that serves to define each part in Pearson's characteristic way. Some stained glass is by Clayton and Bell, and the organ-case of 1905 is by Norman Shaw. [AQ]

Titsey, Surrey
St James*

Designed in 1859 by John Loughborough Pearson and built 1860–1. It is a vigorously massed church: a fine tower and broached spire mark its site at the foot of the scarp of the North Downs. The church is built of local Greensand with Bath stone dressings and mild constructional polychromy inside, using local Firestone and red and green marble. The Gothic details are early, with lancet windows or plate tracery. These are abruptly changed inside the church for the mortuary chapel, seen on the N side of the chancel through a heavily cusped and traceried opening with shields and a seated angel set within cusped foils. Coloured foils, bands and texts enliven the chancel walls and reredos, and there are bright encaustic tiles by Minton on the floor. The mortuary chapel and vestry project on the N side of the chancel; the outside doorway is curiously placed diagonally across one corner, the roof continuing over it to be supported by a shaft with a boldly carved capital and tightly pointed arches. [AQ]

Toddington, Gloucestershire
St Andrew*

This parish church was commissioned from G. E. Street by Lord Sudeley in 1868 and built between 1869 and Sudeley's death in 1877, when it was still not quite finished. Its esoteric quasi-transeptal plan reflects the former modest structure on this site. Even so the exceptional purity of its serene English Geometrical Gothic represents, for Street, an extreme statement of national historicism. It is of orange-gold local stone faced inside with white ashlar. Purbeck marble is used for shafts to the rib-vaulting, arches and windows. The scale is ambitious for an estate church, its nave with hammer-beam roof having a remarkable tunnel-vaulted W narthex-bay screened by a huge stone arcade, SW porch, and a heavily buttressed S tower with tall stone broach-spire of Lincolnshire type. In consequence of its noble ribbed vault the chancel rises above the nave and has a shorter, vaulted S aisle, N vestry, and continuous arcading to the sanctuary walls below a large tracery window. This contains glass by Hardman. Double transept-wise on the N, overlapping choir and nave, is the monumental funerary chapel, again vaulted,

containing the altar-tomb of Charles, 1st Baron Sudeley, by John Graham Lough 1865. [PJ]

Todmorden, West Yorkshire
Unitarian Chapel*

This splendid Gothic chapel by John Gibson of Westminster, begun in 1865 and opened in 1869, stands at the highest point of a steeply sloping site; it is dominated by a transeptal tower rising to a tall pinnacled spire. The nave and aisles of seven bays have piers of Devonshire marble; the chancel, more elaborate than the rest, is spanned by two stone arches with ball-flower ornament, the choir-stalls have carved bench ends and the windows are filled with stained glass by Capronnier of Brussels. The font and the pulpit are of comparable magnificence. This is a worthy memorial to John Fielden, one of the most enlightened of Victorian factory masters, and represents the highest achievement of Nonconformist Gothic. [CS]

Torquay, Devon
St John the Apostle

Unsurpassed among seaside High Churches for its picturesque setting above Torquay Harbour, St John's was raised direct from the quarry out of the steep limestone cliff-face. G. E. Street produced designs in 1862–3. Construction spread over four campaigns, at first around the old chapel of 1822–3 to which a chancel with aisles and NE vestry were appended in 1863–4; then a N aisle abutting the Tor's wooded eminence 1865–6; the new nave with S aisle and tower-base was brought sheer to the road edge 1870–1; and finally in 1884–5 A. E. Street dutifully completed the tower to his father's revised drawings of 1870. Despite a long programme the original plan was adhered to, allowing for deviations only in the superstructure. The work is thus cohesive, splendidly proportioned and regular, in a Geometrical style assimilating grouped lancets, plate and bar tracery. Walls of the indigenous silver-grey stone are massively carried up in random blocks, with buff Ham Hill stone dressings and Caen stone openings; the square chancel with its own clerestory and heavy flying buttresses clasped over short lean-to aisles presenting a calculated foil to the severe tall-clerestoried nave and its plain lean-to aisles. Engaged with the aisle wall to serve as a porch, the elegant unbuttressed SW tower has recessed belfry-lights under a big arch on each face and splinters into a transverse saddleback top with corner-pinnacles, rich geometric panelling filling the gables; it is the one obvious asymmetrical motif. Roofs sail high but cleanly demarcated, and are covered in blue-grey slates. The stately, grey-stone interior has a luxurious plenitude of coloured Devon marbles. Nave arcades spring from clusters built up in alternating thick and thin layers, and long marble shafts support inner-plane arcading to clerestory lights; chancel arch and choir arcades have the additional distinction of stone and marble voussoirs. Blank arcading to the sanctuary walls, inlaid with a kaleidoscopic display of different coloured marbles, forms a sumptuous framework for the marble and alabaster reredos containing Thomas Earp's Crucifixion sculpture. Over this, the great traceried E window has brilliant glass by Morris and Co. 1864. Roofs too join in the finely controlled polychromy: bold painted chequers to the nave's timber tunnel-vault; delicate three-colour stone banding in the chancel rib-vaulting. Of a great wealth of fittings the cancelli, polygonal stone pulpit and font were inlaid with marble by A. W. Blackler; wrought-brass and iron chancel screens executed by James Leaver; tiles by Minton. Edward Burne-Jones designed the W window 1890. [PJ]

Trefnant, Clwyd
Holy Trinity

Built in 1853–5 to designs by G. G. Scott, the church is in an elegant Decorated style, with a bell-cote over the chancel arch, and gables over the aisle windows. In the rich interior, the arcade piers have shafts of Anglesey marble, the capitals carved by J. Blinstone of Chester, from natural specimens gathered from the woods and hedges around, an early application of Ruskin's teaching. [PH]

Truro, Cornwall
Cathedral*

The see of Cornwall was revived in 1876, and in the following year the formidable Edward White Benson was appointed bishop. He determined to build a new cathedral to rival the achievements of the Middle Ages. That for him meant Lincoln Cathedral, where he had been chancellor. His building committee chose John Loughborough Pearson, who had been restoring

Lincoln since 1875 and was willing to consider it as a starting point for his design, but he took away the quirks of its long history of building and imposed both his own rather stern logic, taken from an understanding of classical architecture as well as French Gothic, and his delight in the forms of the Gothic of Normandy and northern England. Consequently the design has all the Englishness of a central tower and twin W towers, E as well as central transepts, and a square E end, as at Lincoln; but it also has spires such as one might see at Caen or Bayeux, massed lancet windows as at Whitby, and a completely vaulted interior with quadripartite and sexpartite rib-vaults, which, though French, were Pearson's speciality. The site was awkwardly placed in the heart of Truro. Pearson resolved to keep the S aisle of the decayed parish church that lay there. This caused problems, but Pearson's brilliant solution of them gives the cathedral its greatest touch of genius. He had to build two aisles between the choir and the parish church aisle, which retained its parochial use, so that the high vaults of the choir could be properly buttressed. The proliferation of aisles and the columns that support their arcades provide one of the most exciting views within the interior. The arcading of the old aisle set the rhythm of the arcading in the choir and, with it, the pattern of the quadripartite vaulting over it. The old aisle also determined the alignment of the choir and necessitated the marked change in alignment between it and the nave because of the constricted site. The interior is severely grand, thanks to Pearson's use of the Golden Section to proportion many of its parts, and to the ubiquitous vaulting that crowns them. The design was completed in 1879, the E parts were built in 1880–7, the nave and crossing-tower in 1897–1903, the W towers in 1910. The stained glass and many of the fittings are by Clayton and Bell; Nathaniel Hitch carved the reredos and much else. The cathedral is built of Cornish granite and Bath stone, a compromise forced on Pearson after the design had been accepted because local people wanted their own stone to be used. [AQ]

Tuckingmill, Cornwall
All Saints

For this church, built 1843–4 in the middle of a then booming tin-mining area, John Hayward of Exeter used Romanesque for the only time in his career. The design, though unarchaeological in detail and disposition, is impressive: local freestone masonry with granite dressings, large nave and chancel with plain round-headed windows. S aisle, and a pyramidally roofed W tower to the aisle complementing a strongly simplified W front to the nave. Internally, ruggedness is again the keynote: the walls random-coursed and whitewashed, a big open timber roof, granite chancel arch and a monolithic arcade – again in granite – between nave and aisle. In the chancel, the triple E window has stained glass contemporary with the building, by Robert Beer of Exeter. [CB]

Tunbridge Wells, Kent
St Barnabas

A lofty complex building which alone has served the ritualistic tradition in Tunbridge Wells since 1890. It was designed by the brothers J. E. K. and J. P. Cutts and both without and within is of rich red brick banded and dressed with sandstone. The intended tower was never built and a slender shingled flèche suffices. The nave is clerestoried, the aisles marked by broad arches on octagonal columns continuing into an arcaded E end. After the Second World War, Martin Travers was commissioned to work in both Gothic and Baroque: by him the Lady Chapel was transformed in the Ultramontane taste while his high altar and the reredos of St Stephen's chapel are disciplined Gothic. The statue of St Barnabas in the N aisle is of 1952 by Sir Ninian Comper; the unusual baldacchino above the font in the W end is of the same period. [REH]

Tunbridge Wells, Kent
St Mark, Broadwater Down

A French Gothic project by R. L. Roumieu, 1864–6. The plan is an exciting one: a lucarned and buttressed spire of 140 feet surmounts the NW tower; there are transepts, a polygonal apse and clerestories of tiny quatrefoils. Within, Roumieu has provided a broad auditorium: the arcading directs us upwards to the choir and on to the canted stone reredos. There is glass by O'Connor and by Clayton and Bell. [REH]

Tutshill (Tidenham), Gloucestershire
St Luke

Tutshill church was built in 1852–3 by Henry Woodyer. The N aisle was added by him in 1873. A pretty bell-cote with three openings rises unusually over the S side of the chancel arch. The window tracery, typically of Woodyer, is Decorated and heavily cusped. Otherwise the church is plain. Inside, the N arcade has piers with mouldings rising directly into the arches without capitals. The chancel glass is of 1853, by Wailes. [AQ]

Twinstead, Essex
St John the Evangelist

Twinstead church was built by Henry Woodyer in 1859–60. It has a nave and chancel, with a S porch and N vestry. The W bell-cote is placed over a large window in the form of a spherical triangle. It and all the other main windows are low and broad, and filled with spiky Decorated tracery of such elaboration that they seem overlarge for the church. This and the restless yellow and black decoration of the red brick-work give the church the vigour of appearance that so pleased High Victorian taste. More typical of Woodyer, however, is the elaborate triple-arched opening into the chancel and the font standing on a clustered central shaft and eight peripheral shafts. [AQ]

Ullenhall, Warwickshire
*St Mary**

An unusual design in the Early English style, but strangely Romanesque in character, St Mary's was designed by J. P. Seddon and built in 1875. Of yellow stone, it has an apsidal E end and a slender SW steeple. Aisle and apse walls are arcaded internally and the nave arcades have alternate triple and single columns of grey marble. Stencilled wagon roof with half-wagons in the aisles and, beneath the altar, a circular mosaic pavement with rings of crosses, crowns, leaves, fish and water. [DH]

Ushaw, County Durham
Chapel of St Cuthbert's College (RC)

A. W. N. Pugin designed a chapel here with a T-shaped plan of antechapel and choir, and excellent stained glass and metalwork by Hardman, which was built between 1844 and 1848. By the 1880s the college had outgrown this and a new chapel by Dunn and Hansom replaced it between 1882 and 1884. It followed the former plan but was twice as large, and incorporated most of the Decorated style features and fittings from the earlier building, so that the overall impression is still that of Pugin. The high altar and reredos of 1890 and 1891 were added by P. P. Pugin, and the screen, Lady Chapel and Chapel of the Venerable Bede were decorated by J. F. Bentley in 1896–9. Two fan-vaulted W bays of the antechapel were added in 1925–8 by S. P. Powell, Pugin's grandson. [AW]

Waresley, Cambridgeshire
*St James the Great**

By William Butterfield, 1855–7, standing in the middle of a village of heavily picturesque Early Victorian estate cottages (not by Butterfield). The beautiful slender tower, capped by a simple broach-spire, flanks the N side of the nave. Like the rest of the church it is faced in sheer, smooth stone, with half-height stepped buttresses projecting diagonally from the two outer corners. The rest of the church is a carefully massed composition with steep, sweeping roofs at varying angles and alignments, a boldly geometrical E window and, on the N side, a transeptal chapel or mausoleum (evidently added shortly after the church itself was finished); this has curious vesica windows. In the chancel is geometrical stencil work in pink, buff and two shades of green. The simple, subtle pew-ends are typical of Butterfield, with their play of curves, as are the font, its wooden cover and the king-post roof with curved braces. A double-arched well-head under a broad gable, also Butterfield's, stands on the edge of the churchyard. [DL]

Warrington, Cheshire
St Luke

One of the most unregarded late buildings by Bodley, of such assertive originality and surprising experimentation that its unorthodoxy probably offended his pupils' canons of taste. Built in 1892–3, it is a small stone building in a poor suburb, composed of a double nave divided by a very large arcade of five bays rising from the middle of the nave-passage to the ridge of the roof, 'like some monstrosity crammed into a barn for storage' (Goodhart-Rendel). There is a wide N aisle in a later style with its own barrel-roof, square piers and a low arcade. The chancel arch terminates in a boldly carved angel at its apex and leads to a tall, narrow chancel and elevated sanctuary

(freely visible from the nave) with a flowing Decorated window high in the E. If St Luke's had been built in the south, there is little doubt that it would have been widely illustrated, lectured on and visited and would not now be redundant and used as a builders' store. [ANS]

Warwick Bridge, Cumbria
Our Lady and St Wilfrid (RC)

Though tiny, this church is a perfect and unaltered example of Pugin's ideals as they are revealed in his most important book, *The True Principles of Pointed or Christian Architecture*, which was published in 1841, the same year in which the church was built. Everything was designed with the utmost care. It consists of a nave with a bell-cote and a chancel, in the local sandstone, with diagonal buttresses at E and W ends. The interior is a delight, with a rood-screen surmounted by six brass candlesticks, hinged so that it can form communion rails. The chancel has stencilled walls and a painted ceiling, sedilia and piscina in the S wall, and opposite, in an Easter-sepulchre-like recess, the tomb of the founder, Henry Howard of Corby Castle, who died in 1842. [AW]

Washford Pyne, Devon
St Peter

A very small church in remote countryside, entirely rebuilt – except the stump of the W tower – to the designs of Robert Medley Fulford, 1883–4. Its inventiveness, despite the small scale, is entirely characteristic of his work: component masses – tower and spire, S porch, S transept, chancel – are carefully proportioned and picturesquely varied; varied too are the window forms, strikingly so in the transept S face; windows on the N side are asymmetrically grouped. The walling is local brownstone, varied by purple-red sandstone and ochre Ham Hill, the upper stage of the tower, like the stubby spire, is tile-hung, the belfry wooden. The interior, equally delightful and equally clever in its varied handling, is entirely of a piece, with fittings, tiling, stained glass by Drake, and even brass oil-lamps, holders and standards. [CB]

Watchfield, Oxfordshire
St Thomas

A small-scale rural church by G. E. Street, 1857–8. From poor resources he created a proud barn-like structure with closely embraced NW entrance and fierce central buttress to the W front dying out beneath a steep gabled bell-cote – a distillation of the Milton-under-Wychwood theme but here no less forceful. A pair of high, narrow, tracery windows flank the great buttress which throws out its own sharp-gabled set-off level with their heads. Walls are constructed of the rough local rubble stone with emphatic freestone dressings, and the style chosen is Early Decorated imbued with regional characteristics as interpreted by Street's highly personal sense of proportions. The plan is simplicity itself: heavily buttressed nave of four bays with an enormous, open timber roof sweeping down over the low-walled N aisle at a slightly less acute pitch, square unbuttressed chancel with its own marginally lower roof, and a W porch contrived in the westernmost bay of the aisle without interrupting its external form. There is therefore only a low three-bay arcade inside, and the walls are plastered. Cinquefoiled arch-braces to the nave roof, a favourite Street motif, make satisfying contrast with the curved tied rafters beyond the wide chancel arch. Good simple furnishings are also by Street. [PJ]

Waterford (Stapleford), Hertfordshire
St Michael

Waterford church was built in 1871–2 to the design of Henry Woodyer. It has a nave and S porch, and a chancel with N vestry and organ-chamber under a continuation of the slope of the roof. A large timber bell-turret with a shingled broach-spire marks the W end in the emphatic way Woodyer liked, and the same is true of the gabled window on the S side of the sanctuary. The ornate chancel is decorated with gilded mosaics of vines and angels by Powell and Sons, who also executed the reredos. The candlesticks and vases are by Omar Ramsden (1909). The stained glass is remarkable: most is by Morris and Co. (1872–1917), almost all from cartoons by Burne-Jones. Other glass includes St Cecilia by Karl Parsons (1929); the Road to Emmaus by Douglas Strachan (1920s); and Wise Virgins designed by Selwyn Image and made by Clayton and Bell. [AQ]

Watford, Hertfordshire
Holy Rood (RC)

In his *English Architecture since the Regency* Goodhart-Rendel illustrated this church with the caption 'Perfection'. It was the only chance J. F. Bentley ever had completely to build and furnish a church without stint. The result gives an idea of what Westminster Cathedral might have been like had he been allowed to use his beloved Gothic. Paid for by Mr S. Taprell Holland, of the building firm, it was erected in 1889–1900. In late Perpendicular style, its plan, tightly fitted onto its corner site, includes wide nave and large chancel, with transepts across which the arcades continue (a favourite device of Bentley's). The aisles are short, the N one halved to form the founder's chantry. Beneath the tower is the vaulted baptistery, and at the NE is attached the charming little presbytery. The exterior is in the local mixture of flint and stone. The massive tower combines strength and refinement. Inside, the fittings and decoration are gorgeous in colour, detail and materials. The sanctuary, seen beneath the red-painted rood-loft, is wondrously rich. Electric light-fittings, pulpit, shrines, altar-rails, side altars, stained glass – all are by Bentley. Almost the only exceptions are the glass of the W window, by Burlison and Grylls (1904), and the Stations of the Cross, by Westlake. Over the SW door is a memorial to Bentley, carved by McCarthy. [PH]

Wells, Somerset
*St Thomas**

This lavish church by S. S. Teulon dates from 1856–7. The exterior is commanded by the very fine octagonal spire banded in local stone of two colours. The interior is rich and enjoys ironwork by Skidmore and windows by Wailes. The green-tinted glass with patterns formed by the lead cames and vines drawn in outline is typical of the architect. The S aisle dates from 1864. [MS]

Welshampton, Salop
*St Michael**

This little jewel was built in 1863 by G. G. Scott at the expense of the Mainwarings of Oteley Park. It consists of nave with S aisle, apsidal chancel, and N porch. The bell-turret is over the chancel arch. There are lancets and also windows with plate tracery. The roofs are of gaily patterned blue and green slates. Inside, all is rich and well detailed. The arcade pillars are of polished Aber marble. Pulpit and font are of Caen stone with marble columns. All the carving is by William Farmer of London: it includes many naturalistic forms – lilies on the font, convolvulus in the chancel cornice, and passion flowers on the splendid alabaster reredos, which incorporates a panel representing the Crucifixion. The excellent chancel glass is by Heaton, Butler and Bayne. [PH]

Welshpool, Powys
Christ Church

This aggressively Norman church was built in 1839–44 by 'voluntary public subscription' to commemorate the coming-of-age of Viscount Clive, and designed by Thomas Penson. The spiky exterior, with apse and NW tower, is of rough grey granite. Inside terracotta is used for the nave arches, the rich arcading and vaulting ribs of the chancel, and the elaborate font. The apse glass is probably by David Evans. [PH]

Wentworth, South Yorkshire
Holy Trinity

A grand estate church, designed in 1872 by John Loughborough Pearson, completed in 1877. It is lavishly built in a conventional but immaculately carried out Decorated Gothic with varied tracery for the windows and an imposing steeple rising to 183 feet over the crossing of its cruciform plan. The whole of the interior is rib-vaulted. The chancel has an elaborate marble floor of a type Pearson had recently seen in Early Christian churches in Italy, and the stained glass adds a further glow of colour to the finely traceried windows. The E window is by Clayton and Bell, and the W by C. E. Kempe. [AQ]

West Kirby, Merseyside
St Andrew

Begun in 1889–1901 by Douglas and Fordham, and completed, with the building of the chancel in 1907–9, by Douglas and Minshull. It is large and well massed, with clerestoried nave, transepts, and a very tall chancel with great square-headed windows on the sides. The slate-hung flèche set diagonally over the crossing is highly original. Inside, the progression in

height and light towards the E is striking. The reredos of 1911 is by Geoffrey Webb. [PH]

West Lavington, West Sussex
St Mary Magdalene

William Butterfield's only Sussex church, erected in 1850–1, St Mary's is modest in size but designed in stone with careful attention to the traditional style of the locality – the 'Sussex cap' bell-turret and the pitch of the aisle roofs. The Middle Pointed detail is presented with the architect's characteristic stylization and intellectual vigour, setting off the simple furnishing to advantage, especially the sedilia and choir stalls and above all the beautiful Sussex marble chancel screen. [DRE]

West Lutton, North Yorkshire
*St Mary the Virgin**

Penultimate of the six Wolds churches designed by G. E. Street for Sir Tatton Sykes of Sledmere, West Lutton matches proliferation of incident with skilful invention. Planned in 1871 and built in 1872–3, it was elaborately fitted out during 1874–5. It is of smooth stone in Early Decorated style, the layout including churchyard walls and a superb stone-arched lych with wrought-iron gates. A steep gabled S porch attaches direct to the nave vestibule which emerges clear and unbuttressed at the W. Otherwise, low passage-aisles and tall chancel walls are formally buttressed and have disparately varied fenestration, ranging from foliated rose and spherical triangle to Geometrical tracery and grouped lancets. Big roofs supply the controlling element; kept level from E to W and divided only by the chancel arch cross-wall, they spread down over the aisles with the subtlest shift of pitch. Carried on massive carpentry within, the tile-hung timber W bell-turret has a continuous enfilade of balusters supporting its shingled broach-spire. Inside, arcades are of two bays with a baptistery extension facing the entrance. The nave roof is braced by heavy tie-beams and columnar king-posts, and entirely decorated with texts and patterns by Daniel Bell. It provides an ingenious foil to the much lower stone rib-vault over the chancel. Through an exquisite wrought-iron and brass screen made by Thomas Potter, a profusion of rich furnishings culminates in the reredos triptych painted by Burlison and Grylls.

Later, in 1893, they were called back for the new stained glass, to replace a series by Hardman. [PJ]

West Quantoxhead, Somerset
St Etheldreda

Built 1856 by John Norton, prolific Bristol church and country-house architect. A pink church with a good strong tower and early Decorated Gothic tracery. Separately roofed nave, aisles and chancel as Pugin had recommended. Inside the marble piers of the arcades and well-carved capitals are the best feature. Font of Devon and Cornwall marbles. E window by O'Connor to the Acland family of St Audries. [JO]

West Rainton, County Durham
St Mary

The tall tower with broach-spire makes this church, designed by E. R. Robson in 1864, a landmark in the Wear valley. The height of the nave, which is powerfully articulated on the exterior, is accentuated by the contrast between the lofty clerestory and lean-to aisles. The mosaic reredos is by the omnipresent Salviati. [LW]

Westcott, Buckinghamshire
*St Mary**

An austere grey limestone chapel of ease was built here in 1866–7, its vestigial Geometrical Gothic being the personal invention of G. E. Street. Within its set confines nothing could be so single-minded, nor more sophisticated. The broad nave is left practically unbuttressed and dominated by its enormous tiled roof pulled down low over extremely narrow aisles; but these are confined to the three E bays, and on the S the first resolves into a gabled porch without disturbing the wall-plane. Above this and towards the E, a timber dormer with brick-filled gable is let into the roof as clerestory; it is oddly counter-balanced to the W by a pyramid-capped wooden bell-frame astride the roof-ridge. The short straight-ended chancel has high buttressed walls and a marked drop in roof level; windows are varied in size and shape according to their function, massive early bar-tracery predominating. Pale-pink bricks line the internal walls, making a tensely scaled surface through which are punched the tough Bath stone arcades. Their low

cylindrical columns have plain trumpet-caps with square abaci, running directly into thick unchamfered arches curtailed E and W without responds. The chancel arch is graced with long nook-shafts as well as the distinguishing feature of a hood mould. Otherwise everything comes as logic directs: plain rafter roofs, plain stone pulpit, and straightforward furnishings. [PJ]

Westleigh, Leigh, Greater Manchester
St Peter

The church of 1880–1 is by Paley and Austin, described by Sir Nikolaus Pevsner as 'one of their most thrilling churches in Lancashire'. Traceried bands of red Runcorn sandstone run across the top of the great central tower with its vast pyramidal slate roof. The tower is broadened across the width of the church by gablet-terminated piers between which the tower is twice set out with slated lean-to roofs. The massing of the tower in relation to the rest of the church is beautifully handled. To the N a great spine of brickwork snakes down the roof while the N transept roof sweeps steeply down eastwards over the two-storeyed vestry. At the E end the transom-line of the reticulated window is carried externally across the entire width of the chancel in the blind arcading of the brickwork. [DM]

Wheatley, Oxfordshire
*St Mary the Virgin**

One of the best of G. E. Street's early stone village churches, of boldly effective English First Pointed style with grouped lancets and plate tracery, well-varied buttresses and long low timber roofs. Designed in 1855, the nave of three bays without clerestory, separately gabled N and S aisles, straight-ended chancel and lean-to N vestry, together with the lower parts of the unbuttressed W tower, were built 1856–7. But the idiosyncratic belfry-cum-spire, although included in the original scheme, was delayed a further ten years, only reaching completion from Street's improved design in 1868. This unique stone steeple is a spectacular essay in solid geometry, its image of prismatic clarity achieved through a complex fusion of crossed-gabled and elementary broached forms, the massive octagonal spire having steep projecting lucarnes on the oblique planes. At first the derivation appears French or indeed German, but this is an illusion as the real origins lie firmly in Street's earlier practice in Cornwall – at Biscovey and its own local ancestors. Much else relies on Biscovey here too, as it is hardly more elaborate despite the greater formality of plan. The cool logic of the interior is best characterized by its wide-spacing arcade bays, with curiously corbelled-out chamfering of arch-springs above moulded capitals; and there is appropriate glass in the E lancets by Fouracre and Watson of Plymouth 1875. A truly ungainly S porch was added by an unknown hand in 1887. [PJ]

Whippingham, Isle of Wight
St Mildred

The parish church of Osborne House, although some distance away. It was rebuilt in two stages, the chancel (in Early English style) in 1854–5, and the nave (naively Neo-Norman), transepts and central tower in 1861–2. The designers were Prince Albert and Albert Jenkins Humbert – the latter, subsequently, the architect of Sandringham. The very broad tower, with its bold pinnacles and spired turret rising from a pyramidal base, may have German precedent. The S chapel, behind a screened arcade, contains the royal pew, with the queen's own memorial to Prince Albert (by Humbert and William Theed) and others to members of their family; the N chapel has the tomb of Prince Henry of Battenberg, their son-in-law. Artistically, the best feature by far is the screenwork to the Battenberg chapel, by Alfred Gilbert, 1897. [DL]

Whitby, North Yorkshire
St Hilda

St Hilda's is one of the major works of the great Newcastle architect R. J. Johnson, 1884–5. It is characteristically learned and sensitive, built in a version of the Late Decorated style favoured by Bodley but as forceful as it is refined. The central tower was completed as late as 1938. The interior is richly decorated, with finely carved wooden ceilings and costly fittings: stone pulpit, complete with canopy, excellent rood-screen, reredos, stalls and bishop's throne, all very well detailed. The font, of grey marble, stands in a screened baptistery. There is a considerable collection of glass by Kempe, installed between the mid-1880s and 1906. The calm perfection of this interior, unspoiled by jarring additions, recalls the work of Bodley. [KP]

Whitegate, Cheshire
St Mary

Outwardly this appears to be a totally Late Victorian church by John Douglas of Chester, paid for by Lord Delamere of Vale Royal in 1874–5. It has all his hallmarks; short stumpy tracery, overhanging plastered eaves, a shingled spire and patches of clearly applied but authentic-looking half-timber. The lychgate shows how superb his real timber construction could be. However, the Georgian inner door of the porch, the timber nave arcades and a water-colour inside give the game away. With great skill and sensitivity Douglas cut down the brick walls of 1736, put in new stone tracery, extended the roof outwards in a low sweep and capped off the tower with a spire of Rhineland type. It is a masterly reconstruction which speaks for the architect's skill, frugality and respect for the earlier work. [DB]

Whitfield, Northumberland
Holy Trinity

On the wooded banks of the river West Allen, this is virtually a family chapel to the Blackett-Ords of Whitfield Hall. Designed by A. B. Higham of Newcastle in the Early English style (1859) it has a fine tower and spire over the crossing – stone-vaulted inside – with nave, chancel, transepts and N aisle. The interior is appropriately austere but there is a wealth of fine carving, with mouldings and capitals enriched by naturalistic detail. [TEF]

Whitwell-on-the-Hill, North Yorkshire
St John the Evangelist

Designed by G. E. Street and built 1858–60, this small hilltop church is of grey and brown Whitby stone. The layout is extremely simple, merely a nave and square chancel divided by a wide shafted arch; to these are appended a gabled SW porch and transverse NE vestry with prominent boiler-chimney. But the glory of the church is its campanile-like steeple, hinged onto the SE corner of the nave by a massive cylindrical newel-turret and forming an organ-chamber within. The two tints of stone are built up in layers in its sheer unbuttressed walls, into the thickness of which elaborate belfry-lights are deeply sunk to contain perforated geometrical patterns in chunky plate-tracery. A striated stone broach-spire with big gabled lucarnes is the crowning feature. The subtle polychrome is not carried through to the interior walls which are plastered above a tiled dado, and enclosed by plain, open timber roofs. There is a variation between plate and bar tracery in the windows, that at the E end containing brilliant early glass by Clayton and Bell. Thomas Earp carved the sumptuous stone and inlaid-marble reredos; the pulpit and other carving was done by W. Pearce. Churchyard cross and timber lych-gate are also by Street. [PJ]

Willesden, Greater London
All Souls, Harlesden

This remarkable building on a corner site is by the little-known E. J. Tarver, 1875–6. The impact of this brick octagon with its small iron lantern has increased since the demolition of the more conventional nave added in 1890. The exterior details – canted apse, dwarf gallery and turrets – derive from late Rhineland Romanesque, an unusual source. But it is the wholly original interior that is the surprise: there are no internal supports, and the large space is dominated by the massive roof structure: a complex network of tie-beams, supported by arched braces, meet in a central star; above this rises a web of further bracing to support the lantern. [BC]

Wilton, Wiltshire
SS Mary and Nicholas

A full-scale North Italian Romanesque basilica complete with 108-foot campanile, most improbable in an English town. The church was built from 1841 to 1845 by T. H. Wyatt for the Russian-born Countess of Pembroke and her son Sidney, later Lord Herbert of Lea, secretary-at-war during the Crimean War. Sidney Herbert was an early admirer of Italian medieval art and collected medieval glass and carving, much of which is incorporated within the church. While the smooth stone gives the W front something of the hardness of a steel engraving, the church is of splendid scale and has excellent carved detail. Tall nave with bands of arcading over the arches like a false triforium and vaulted chancel embellished with painted decoration and turn-of-the-

century mosaics. The genuine medieval work includes much of a Cosmati-work shrine of 1256 which Herbert brought from Horace Walpole's collection at Strawberry Hill and some of the best stained glass in England, especially the 12th- and 13th-century French glass in the main apse. Marble effigies of the two founders by J. B. Philip. [JO]

Wimbledon, Greater London
The Sacred Heart (RC)

A long and lofty, minster-like church, with a commanding profile in grey flint with rich stone dressings in a grand Late Decorated style. Built from designs by Frederick Walters between 1886 and 1901, it is one of the largest and most impressive Catholic churches in Greater London. Its smooth, crisply detailed interior, lit by a large clerestory, culminates in a polygonal apse replete with ambulatory and chapels. Elaborate figurative carving and appropriate Hardman, and Lavers and Westlake glass complete the sustained effect of Late Victorian Catholic piety. The altar-rails and Stations of the Cross are by J. F. Bentley (1898; 1900–3). [RMH]

Wimbledon, Greater London
St Paul, Wimbledon Park

Micklethwaite and Somers Clarke, both deeply scholarly pupils of Sir Gilbert Scott, here show a synthesis of Bodley's sensitivity and Scott's innovations at St Agnes, Kennington, yet the church is not a slavish copy. Built in 1888–96 of red brick in the flowing Decorated style, the interior was white from the start; the arcade of arches dying into chamfered piers rises to a wagon roof, and there is a tall dado, like that formerly in St Agnes, round the walls, originally coloured black. The cultivated wooden reredos and triptych in the chapel, opaque stained glass in the flowing tracery, and the rood-screen and pulpit are models of sensitive Late Gothic design by Kempe and Tower. [ANS]

Windsor, Berkshire
All Saints

This gorgeously polychrome early church by Arthur Blomfield (1862–4) rises grandly over Victorian suburbia. In red and blue brick, with stone dressings, it has a tall clerestory above lean-to aisles, bold plate-tracery, and a striking bell-cote over the junction of nave and chancel. The W front has a big wheel-window. The lofty interior has suffered from the taming of the chancel: the E bay has been painted white, and a feeble wooden reredos and screen inserted. But some original fittings survive, as does the rich decoration over the chancel arch. The S aisle is wide, but the N one is a mere passage-aisle. The wooden gallery and organ-case were given by a lady who wished the clergy to have as pleasant a view as the congregation had. In the church hang four drawings by Blomfield, including one for an elaborate reredos attributed to Thomas Hardy, who was in Blomfield's office 1862–7, and certainly annotated some of the drawings for the church. [PH]

Winmarleigh, Lancashire
St Luke

Built in 1876 by Paley and Austin. Two-bay transepts flank the nave and chancel with the three separate roofs all running E–W. A slender broach-spired bell-turret astride the main ridge divides nave from chancel. The chancel walls and boarded ceiling are beautifully painted. [DM]

Witton Park, Blackburn, Lancashire
St Mark

Built in 1836–8. The architect, Edmund Sharpe, was, by 1844, an 'approved architect' of the Cambridge Camden Society. But the Camden Society would not have approved of this earlier church in the Romanesque style. A shallow polygonal apse lies beyond a small sanctuary, itself surmounted by a squat five-stage tower and spire with each stage accentuated externally by corbelling and pilasters. The church was enlarged and restored 1881–7 by Paley and Austin. [DM]

Woburn, Bedfordshire
St Mary

Designed by Henry Clutton for the Duke of Bedford, and built in 1865–8. Outwardly an individualistic version of Romanesque with wide round-headed windows, and a tower which till 1890 carried a spire. Inside it is a masterpiece in Early French Gothic, but in a form very unusual for original medieval churches in that style – it is a hall church, with aisles as high as the nave, all vaulted, and a chancel which continues the nave without a break, though unaccompanied by the aisles. The piers are pairs of slender shafts, linked by double rings half-way up, with foliate capitals from which the vaulting ribs gracefully spring. [DL]

Woburn Sands (Aspley Heath), Bedfordshire
St Michael

By Henry Clutton for the Duke of Bedford, 1868. The W front has two lancets, with a bold thin buttress in between, from which projects a clock. Above rises a circular bell-turret, roundly spiked. The side windows are square-headed, but there is a weird circular window to a N vestry-chapel with a double cross of mullions and transoms. Inside, there are tall slender round columns rising from high bases above the pews, nearly rounded arches, and an E trio of lancets with cusped tracery. [DL]

Wokingham, Berkshire
*St Paul**

St Paul's church, Wokingham, was built in 1863–4 by Henry Woodyer. The cost was borne by John Walter III, the proprietor (and grandson of the founder) of *The Times*. The church has an impressive steeple, 150 foot high, with two tiers of coupled openings in the tower and buttresses with oddly detailed offsets supporting miniature flyers at the top. The inset spire is supported by more, rather slight flying buttresses that rise from the bases of corner pinnacles. The nave has aisles widened in 1873–4, when the nave roof was also remodelled, and long bands of clerestory windows with Decorated tracery of the type used throughout the church. The S side of the chancel has an unusual low clerestory with windows set in two-centred arches. The chancel arch carries a representation of the Holy Spirit flanked by angels. The capitals of the nave arcade are decorated with naturalistic foliage in the way Woodyer excelled at, but the most original decoration of this kind is on the font. The bowl is in the form of eight lobes, carved with flowing, intertwined lilies that have all the delicacy of the Arts and Crafts Movement. The sculptor for all this carved stonework was Thomas Nicholls, a favourite craftsman of Woodyer's. [AQ]

Woodchester, Gloucestershire
Our Lady of the Annunciation (RC)

A Catholic church built 1846–9 by C. F. Hansom for William Leigh, a Catholic convert. The Dominican priory has been demolished but the church remains a monument to the ideals of A. W. N. Pugin, whom Leigh first consulted on his project. Decorated Gothic, with the tower and short spire standing unusually at the E end. Carved and painted fittings and good glass by Hardman, Wailes and Saunders. In the S chapel a fine alabaster effigy of Leigh by Boulton *c*. 1873. He holds a model of the church. [JO]

Woodchester, Gloucestershire
*St Mary**

Consecrated in 1863, this is one of the most attractive of all the churches by S. S. Teulon, restfully composed and constructed in warm Cotswold stone. Teulon was here able to provide a full tower and spire, the only eccentric touch being the placing of the organ-chamber over the vestry which is in turn over the undercroft, all these spaces being combined into a three-storey transept complete with external stairs. The chunky wooden pulpit with simple Gothic decoration over a crystalline stone base is typical of Teulon's Gloucestershire group of churches. There is excellent glass by Preedy and by Lavers and Barraud. [MS]

Woolmer Green, Hertfordshire
St Michael

Plain outside, this is internally a delightful church of 1899–1900 by R. Weir Schultz, who was steeped in the Arts and Crafts tradition. The nave roof is of pointed wagon-form resting on moulded cantilever beams; the screen has delicate tracery; grey-green marble steps lead to the red-tiled chancel with wooden fittings looking almost Art Deco, and bronze sanctuary rails; the walls are of exposed red brick above panelling. [DL]

Worcester, Hereford and Worcester
*St George**

St George's Square is a long strip of grass flanked by handsome brick houses. Its semicircular end is delightfully closed by Aston Webb's church of 1893–5.

The charming W front has a Perpendicular window deeply set within a huge niche between spired turrets. It is of brick with stone dressings, including some chequerboard patterning. The rest of the exterior is very plain. The interior is much bigger than one expects, with aisled nave and large transepts. [PH]

Worsley, Greater Manchester
*St Mark**

This estate church by G. G. Scott stands well on rising ground surrounded by mature trees. From a distance it could be mistaken for a building of the 14th century; perhaps the spire and the regularity of the roofs give it away. Fairly early in Scott's career (1846), it was built at great expense. All the details are English and Geometrical/Decorated Middle Pointed. Internally the church is enriched by the best tiles and woodwork, a mixture of ancient fragments, French, Flemish and English put together with panache. The pulpit and the Earl of Ellesmere's memorial (1857) are notable, the latter with a recumbent figure carved by Matthew Noble. Glass of the Hardman school perhaps designed by Pugin in 1851, bright with much blue. [DB]

Worthing, West Sussex
Christ Church

The original designs for the church by John Elliott of Chichester of 1843 were subject to severe criticism by the Ecclesiological Society, resulting in considerable modifications in the final appearance, including enlargement of the chancel and insertion of a clerestory. Christ Church is large, somewhat austere, with an impressive W tower, a good example of 'Commissioners' Gothic' – the whole constructed in local flint. Inside, the transepts retain galleries. [DRE]

Worthing, West Sussex
St Andrew

The town's first 'high church', begun in 1885, from 13th-century-style designs by A. W. Blomfield. The foundation of St Andrew's met with bitter opposition from local clergy, culminating in an unsuccessful appeal to the House of Lords to prevent its opening. The building is of flint and stone. The well-proportioned interior includes a characteristic Blomfield apsidal baptistery at the W end, transepts, a chancel with elaborate rood-screen, and a fine vaulted Lady Chapel. The Gothic triptych reredos was made at Oberammergau from designs by E. Kempe. Also by Kempe is the chief glory of the church, the stained glass. [DRE]

Worthing, West Sussex
St George

Built in 1868 by George Truefitt to further the strongly Evangelical tradition of Worthing, St George's lacks the tower and spire originally intended, and consists of a large apsed nave with hipped roof at the W end. The apse has five tall windows, and above the W porch an impressive line of six square-headed windows. The interior is very plain. Stylistically the church exhibits a loose version of Middle Pointed, but is a logical and effective composition. [DRE]

Wreay, Cumbria
*St Mary**

A small village church of unique design (1842) having no aisles but an E apse with interior arcade, and an abundance of exotic sculpture better seen than described (recurring motifs are the arrowhead and pine-cone, emblems of death, and life after death). It was built as a memorial to her sister by a highly educated amateur, Sara Losh (1785–1853). She employed village masons and the unusual choice of style is Continental Romanesque, reflecting her extensive travels in Italy, Germany and France. The windows are composed of fragments of ancient glass, and mouldings adorned with highly stylized carvings of animal and vegetable forms. [TEF]

Wykeham, North Yorkshire
*All Saints**

William Butterfield carefully preserved the tower of the late-14th-century St Helen's Chapel, adding a spire and making it into a very grand lych-gate in 1853–4. The new church was set back from the street, with the parsonage to the E. It is a successful expedient, since the old tower was tied stylistically to the new church. Of stone in 13th-century style, the latter is a tough and solid work with typical Butterfield fittings. Of these the font is especially notable: a piece of simple geometry with plain shafts dying into the bowl. [KP]

York
Centenary Methodist Chapel

This is one of the finest surviving works of the leading Wesleyan architect (at least in the Midlands and North) of the first half of the 19th century, J. Simpson (1840). Centenary Chapel has a grand Ionic portico and an equally grand interior, with coffered ceiling, galleries and a splendid organ-case and pulpit (the rostrum backing onto the front wall). It was built to seat 1,500 worshippers. [KP]

York
St Wilfrid (RC)

George Goldie's major surviving High Victorian church in England. Built 1862–4 on a restricted site opposite the W front of the Minster, to which Goldie's Early French Gothic is intended to be a stylistic foil. The nave and N aisle end in apses, the S is a passage-aisle only. There is a conspicuous saddleback tower. Inside, the sandstone piers have massive bases and capitals; nave with coved wooden roof, chancel stone-vaulted. There is glass by Wailes, sculpture by Earp (who also did the W front tympanum), and metalwork by Peard. [RO'D]

Index of Architects

This index lists only those architectural works which are included in this book, so as to avoid confusion. Brief biographical details are given, which are of necessity arbitrarily selective. Dates of birth and death are given wherever known. Where dates of birth are indicated as approximate, this is usually because they are deduced from information giving the person's age at death. Churches that are illustrated are marked in the Index and in the main text by an asterisk(*).

Aldridge, Charles *c.* 1842–95
Partner of C. E. Deacon (q.v.).

   Liverpool: St Dunstan

Anderson, Sir Robert Rowand
1834–1921
Pupil of John Lessels; worked with
Lt. Col. Moody, R. W. Billings, and
G. G. Scott; set up practice in
Edinburgh 1862; briefly partner with
David Bryce 1873; partner with
George Washington Browne 1881–5,
and with H. M. Wardrop 1883–7.

   Dumbarton
* Edinburgh: Catholic Apostolic
* Edinburgh: St Michael and All
     Saints
   Galston
* Glasgow: Govan Old Church
   Greenock
   Kelso: St Andrew

Appleton, Herbert Duncan
c. 1853–1936
Pupil of Henry Jarvis and Son.
Changed his name in 1890 to Searles-
Wood.

   Beckenham

Athron, Joseph

   Leeds: St Bartholomew (with H.
     Walker)

Austin, Hubert James 1841–1915
Pupil of his elder brother Thomas
Austin (of Newcastle upon Tyne);
assistant to G. G. Scott; partner with
E. G. Paley (q.v.) from 1868.
See under Paley and Austin; Paley,
Austin and Paley

Baker, Arthur 1841–96
Pupil and then assistant to G. G. Scott
1864–78; published *Plas Mawr,
Conway* (with his cousin Herbert
Baker) 1888; partner with Harold
Hughes from 1891.

   Llanberis

Ball, J. Henry 1861–1931
Pupil of Alfred Waterhouse; practised
in Southsea until 1896, then moved
to London.

   Portsmouth: St Agatha

Banham, Francis Easto 1862–1924
Practised in Beccles.

   Beccles

Barnsley, Sidney Howard
1865–1926
Younger brother of Ernest Barnsley;
pupil of R. N. Shaw.

* Lower Kingswood

Bentley, John Francis 1839–1902
Pupil of Henry Clutton; set up
practice 1860; became RC 1862.

   Chiddingstone Causeway
   London: Corpus Christi, Brixton
   London: St Mary, Cadogan Street
* London: Westminster Cathedral
* Watford

Beresford-Hope, Alexander James
1820–87
Son of Thomas Hope; politician;
published *The English Cathedral of the
Nineteenth Century* 1861.

   Kilndown

Bidlake, William Henry
1862–1938
Pupil of Bodley and Garner; practised
in Birmingham.

   Birmingham: St Agatha
   Birmingham: St Oswald

Billings, Robert William 1813–74
Pupil of John Britton; antiquary;
practised in London and Edinburgh.

   Crosby-on-Eden

Blanc, Hippolyte Jean 1844–1917
Son of a French Protestant
shoemaker; pupil and assistant to
Robert Mathieson; began own
practice in Edinburgh *c.* 1872.

* Paisley

Blomfield, Sir Arthur William
1829–99
Son of Bishop Blomfield of London;
pupil of P. C. Hardwick; knighted
1889.

* Oxford: St Barnabas
   Portsmouth: St Mary, Portsea
* Privett
   Windsor
   Worthing: St Andrew

Blomfield, Charles James
1862–1932
Pupil of his father Sir Arthur
Blomfield; set up practice 1886;
partner with father and brother
Arthur Conran Blomfield from 1890.

   Chingford
   Portsmouth: St Mary, Portsea

Bodley, George Frederick
1827–1907
Pupil of G. G. Scott; partner with
Thomas Garner (q.v.) 1869–97.

* Brighton: St Michael and All
     Angels
* Cambridge: All Saints
   Cardiff: St German, *see* Roath
* Clumber Park

Cowley
* Dundee: St Salvador
Ecchinswell
* Eccleston
Epping
* France Lynch
* Hoar Cross
Leeds: St Matthew
* Liverpool: St John the Baptist, Tue
Brook
* London: St Mary of Eton, Hackney
* London: St Michael, Camden
Town
* Manchester: St Augustine,
Pendlebury
Roath
* Scarborough
* Selsley
Warrington

Bowman, Henry 1814–83
Practised in Manchester; partner
with J. S. Crowther (q.v.); published
The Churches of the Middle Ages 1845–53
(with Crowther).

Hyde

Brakspear, William Hayward
c. 1818–98
Pupil of Sir Charles Barry; practised
in Manchester.

Bowdon

Brandon, John Raphael 1817–77
Pupil of J. Dédeau of Alençon and J.
Parkinson of London; partner with
his brother Joshua Arthur Brandon
1821–47; published *An Analysis of
Gothic Architecture* 1847, *Parish Churches*
1848, *Open Timber Roofs of the Middle
Ages* 1849 (all with J. A. Brandon).

Datchet
* London: Christ the King, Gordon
Square

Bridgen, Thomas Edward
1832–95
Pupil of N. J. Cottingham; partner in
Manchester with N. G. Pennington
(q.v.) from 1859.

Oxton

Brierley, Walter Henry
1862–1926
Pupil of his father; practised in York.

* Goathland

Brodo, W. K.
Brighton: St Joseph

Brookes, William McIntosh
d. 1849
Pupil of George Maddox.

* Albury

Brooks, James 1825–1901
Pupil of Lewis Stride.

Chislehurst
Dover: SS Peter and Paul
Hastings: St Peter
* London: All Hallows, Gospel Oak
London: Ascension, Battersea
* London: Holy Innocents,
Hammersmith
* London: St Chad, Shoreditch
* London: St Columba, Shoreditch
Marston Meysey
Southend-on-Sea: All Saints

Browning, Edward 1816–82
Son of Bryan Browning, architect;
pupil of George Maddox; took over
father's practice in Stamford.

Fosdyke

Bryce, David 1803–76
Pupil of William Burn; his partner
1841–50; partner with Rowand
Anderson 1873; with his nephew John
1873–6; practised in Edinburgh.

Dalkeith

Buckeridge, Charles *c.* 1832–73
Pupil of G. G. Scott; practised in
Oxford.

* Avon Dassett
Capel-y-ffin

Buckler, Charles Alban
1824–1905
Son of John Chessell Buckler,
architect, who was son of John
Buckler (q.v.).

London: St Dominic, Gospel Oak

Buckler, John 1770–1851
Pupil of C. T. Cracklow; employed
by Magdalen College, Oxford.

Pentrobin

Bucknall, Benjamin *c.* 1833–95
Pupil of Charles Hansom; practised
at Rodborough, Gloucestershire;
translator of Viollet-le-Duc.

Abergavenny

Bucknall, William 1852–1944
Nephew of Benjamin Bucknall;
assistant to G. F. Bodley; partner with
J. N. Comper 1888–1904.

South Norwood

Burges, William 1827–81
Pupil of E. Blore and M. D. Wyatt.

* Brighton: St Michael and All
Angels
Fleet
* Lowfield Heath
Murston
Oxford: Worcester College Chapel
* Skelton
* Studley Royal

Burn, William 1789–1870
Pupil of Sir Robert Smirke.

Dalkeith

Burnet, Sir John James 1857–1938
Son of John Burnet, architect; trained
at École des Beaux Arts, Paris,
1874–7; practised in Glasgow.

* Brechin: Southesk
* Glasgow: Barony Church
* Larbert
Shiskine

Butterfield, William 1814–1900
Pupil of E. L. Blackburne.

* Babbacombe
* Baldersby St James
Bamford
* Beech Hill
Christleton
* Coalpit Heath
Cowick
* Cumbrae
Dropmore
Elerch
Hensall (*see* Cowick)
Hitchin
* Horton-cum-Studley
Lamplugh
* London: All Saints, Margaret
Street
* London: St Augustine, Queen's
Gate
* London: St John, Hammersmith
* London: St Matthias, Stoke
Newington
Manchester: St Cross, Clayton
* Milton
Oxford: Keble College Chapel
Penarth
Perth: St Ninian's Cathedral

Pollington (*see* Cowick)
Rugby: St Andrew
Rugby: School Chapel
* Waresley
West Lavington
* Wykeham

Caröe, William Douglas
1857–1938
Pupil of J. L. Pearson.

Colehill
Exeter: St David
Stansted Mountfitchet

Carpenter, Richard Cromwell
1812–55
Pupil of John Blyth.

Brighton: St Paul
Chichester: St Peter the Great
* London: St Mary Magdalene,
Munster Square
Monkton Wyld

Carpenter, Richard Herbert
1841–93
Son of R. C. Carpenter; pupil of
William Slater (1819–72), the former
pupil of his father who had taken over
his practice; partner with Slater
1863–72; partner with Benjamin
Ingelow from 1878.

Lancing

Chamberlain, John Henry
1831–83
Practised in Birmingham; partner
with W. Martin (q.v.).

Birmingham: St John

Champneys, Basil 1842–1935
Son of the Dean of Lichfield; pupil of
John Prichard.

Hastings: St Mary Star of the Sea
Havering-atte-Bower
Slindon

Chancellor, Frederic 1825–1918
Pupil of A. J. Hiscocks; practised in
Chelmsford; published *Ancient
Sepulchral Monuments of Essex* 1890.

Ford End

Chantrell, Robert Denis
1793–1872
Pupil of Sir John Soane; practised in
Leeds.

* Leeds: St Peter

Chatwin, Julius Alfred 1829–1907
Pupil of Sir Charles Barry; practised
in Birmingham.

Birmingham: SS Peter and Paul

Cheston, Chester (junior)
c. 1833–*c.* 1888
Agent for Lord Amherst's estate in
East London.

* London: St Mark, Dalston

Christian, Ewan 1814–95
Pupil of Matthew Habershon;
architect to the Ecclesiastical
Commissioners.

Hildenborough
Leicester: St Mark

Clarke, George Somers (junior)
1841–1926
Nephew of G. S. Clarke (senior);
pupil of G. G. Scott; partner with J.
T. Micklethwaite (q.v.) 1876–92.

Brighton: St Martin
Stretton
Wimbledon: St Paul

Clutton, Henry 1819–93
Pupil of E. Blore; worked with W.
Burges in 1850s; became RC 1856.

* Ditton
Dunstall
* Hatherop
London: St Francis of Assisi,
Kensington
Moorhouse
Steppingley
Tavistock
Woburn
Woburn Sands

Colling, James Kellaway
1816–1905
Pupil of Matthew Habershon;
assistant to John Brown of Norwich
1836–40; to Scott and Moffatt 1841–2;
published *Gothic Ornament* 1846–50,
Details of Gothic Architecture 1852–6,
Art Foliage 1865, *Medieval Foliage*
1874.

Hooton

Comper, Sir John Ninian
1864–1960
Pupil of G. F. Bodley; partner with
W. Bucknall (q.v.) 1888–1904;
knighted 1950.

Braemar
Little Petherick

Conybeare, Henry d. 1884
Son of William Daniel Conybeare,
Dean of Llandaff and eminent
geologist; engineer of Bombay
Waterworks (1855–60) and various
British railways; published
*Photographic Illustrations of the
Proportions of Medieval Interiors* 1868;
emigrated to Caracas 1878.

* Itchen Stoke

Cory, John Augustus 1819–86
Pupil of J. J. Scoles; partner with
Ignatius Bonomi from 1842;
practised in Durham until *c.* 1860;
then partner with C. J. Ferguson
(q.v.) in Carlisle.

Plumbland

Cotton, John 1844–1934
Assistant to G. Bidlake, A.
Waterhouse, and W. E. Nesfield; set
up practice in Birmingham 1870; sold
it 1889 to W. H. Bidlake (q.v.);
published *Suggestions in Architectural
Design* 1896.

Hockley Heath

Crawford-Hick, A.

* Leeds: St Aidan

Crawley, John A. 1834–81
In India in the 1860s.

Portsmouth: St John's Cathedral

Croft, John 1800–65
Practised in London.

* Lower Shuckburgh

Crossfield, Aaron

Pontypool

Crossland, William Henry
1823–1909
Pupil of G. G. Scott.

Copley
Leeds: St Chad

Crowther, Joseph Stretch 1832–93
Practised in Manchester; partner
with H. Bowman (q.v.).

Alderley Edge
Ashton-under-Lyne
Bury
Hyde
Manchester: St Benedict, Ardwick
Manchester: St Mary, Hulme
Scunthorpe

Cubitt, James   died c. 1909
Son of a Baptist minister; pupil of J.
C. Gilbert of Nottingham; assistant
to E. W. Elmslie 1856–7; to R. J.
Twitchen and W. W. Pocock
1857–60; own practice 1863; later
partner with Henry Fuller; took over
his practice 1874; published *Church
Design for Congregations* 1870.

London: Union Chapel, Islington

Cundy, Thomas II   1790–1867
Son and pupil of Thomas Cundy I;
succeeded him as surveyor to the
Grosvenor Estates.

* London: St Barnabas, Pimlico

Cutts, John Edward Knight
1847–1938
and **Priston**, John   1854–1935
Brothers and partners; pupils of
Ewan Christian.

Tunbridge Wells: St Barnabas

Daukes, Samuel Whitfield
1811–80
Pupil of J. P. Pritchett; practised in
Gloucester and Cheltenham.

Cheltenham: St Peter
Kingsbury
Newport, Isle of Wight
Salford: United Reformed Church

Dawber, Sir Guy   1861–1938
Pupil of Sir Ernest George; knighted
1936.

Matlock: St John

Dawson, Joshua   1812–56
Practised in Preston.

Rainhill

Day, Charles
Pupil of Thomas Allason; practised
in Worcester.

Hereford

Deacon, Charles Ernest
1844–1927
Practised in Liverpool; partner with
C. Aldridge (q.v.).

Liverpool: St Dunstan
Prenton

Derick, John Macduff   d. 1859
Pupil of Sir John Soane; practised in
Oxford, London and Dublin;
emigrated to New York 1858.

Leeds: St Saviour
Marchwood

Dobson, John   1787–1865
Pupil of David Stephenson of
Newcastle; practised there.

Newcastle upon Tyne: Jesmond
Parish Church

Douglas, John   1830–1911
Pupil of E. G. Paley; practised in
Chester; partner with D. P. Fordham
from c. 1884; with C. H. Minshull
from c. 1897.

Altcar
Barmouth
Bryn-y-maen
Chester: St Paul, Boughton
Colwyn Bay
Deganwy
* Halkyn
Hopwas
Maentwrog
Pulford
Shotton
West Kirby
Whitegate

Dunn, Archibald Matthias
c. 1833–1917
Pupil of Charles Hansom; partner
with Edward Hansom 1871–1900;
published *Notes and Sketches of an
Architect* 1886.

Cambridge: Our Lady and the
English Martyrs
Carlisle: Our Lady and St Joseph
Downside

Elliott, John
Builder and architect; practised in
Chichester c. 1832–49.

Worthing: Christ Church

Ellis, Alexander   1836–1917
Pupil of Messrs J. and W. Smith of
Aberdeen; began own practice there
by 1859; partner 1869 with Robert G.
Wilson; retired 1896.

Aberdeen: St Mary

Elwin, Revd Whitwell   1816–1900
Educated at Cambridge; editor of
Quarterly Review 1853–60 and of
Pope's *Works*.

* Booton

Emerson, Sir William   1843–1924
Pupil of W. G. Habershon and A. R.
Pite; knighted 1902.

Brighton: St Mary and St James

Ferguson, Charles John
1840–1904
Pupil of J. A. Cory (q.v.); assistant to
G. G. Scott; then partner of Cory, in
Carlisle.

Plumbland
Tebay

Ferrey, Benjamin   1810–80
Pupil of A. C. Pugin; published
Recollections of A. N. Welby Pugin 1861.

Buckland St Mary
Kingswood
* London: St Stephen, Westminster
Melplash
Merthyr Mawr
Slinfold

Flockton, William   1804–64
and **James**, Thomas   1825–1900
Father and son, and partners,
practising in Sheffield.

Sheffield

Fothergill, Watson   1841–1928
Pupil of A. W. Blomfield and J.
Middleton; practised in
Nottingham.

Nottingham: Baptist Chapel

Fowler, Charles   1792–1867
Pupil of John Powning of Exeter;
assistant to David Laing; own
practice 1818; retired 1852.

Honiton

Fowler, Charles Hodgson
1840–1910
Pupil of G. G. Scott.

West Hartlepool: St Paul

Fowler, James   1839–92
Pupil of J. Potter; practised in Louth.

Lincoln: St Swithin

Fowler, J. Bacon
Practised in Brecon; partner with F.
R. Kempson (q.v.).

    Pentre

Fulford, Robert Medley
1845–1910
Pupil of W. White; practised in
Exeter.

    Washford Pyne

Garner, Thomas   1839–1906
Pupil of G. G. Scott; partner with G.
F. Bodley (q.v.) 1869–97; became
RC 1896.

    Downside
    Ecchinswell
* Hoar Cross
* London: St Michael, Camden
    Town
* Manchester: St Augustine,
    Pendlebury
    Roath

Gee, W. H.
Practised in Liverpool.

    Leighton

Gibson, John   1817–92
Pupil of J. A. Hansom; assistant to
Sir Charles Barry.

    Bersham
    Bodelwyddan
* Todmorden

Giorgioli, Agostino

    Everingham

Goldie, George   1828–87
Pupil and then partner of M. E.
Hadfield and J. G. Weightman; later
worked with his son Edward (d.
1921).

    London: Chapel of Hospital of SS
    John and Elizabeth
    London: St James, Spanish Place
    York

Gollop, W. (or George?)
Presumably the son of George Gollop,
carpenter and architect, of Poole.

    Longham

Goodridge, Henry Edmund
1797–1864
Pupil of John Lowder; practised in
Bath.

    Downside

Gough, Hugh Roumieu
1843–1904
Son of Alexander Dick Gough,
architect and partner with R. L.
Roumieu.

* London: St Cuthbert, Philbeach
    Gardens

Gould, John Ford   *c.* 1840–81
Pupil of W. White; partner with
Richard David Gould (1817–83) in
Barnstaple.

    Down St Mary

Grayson, George E.   *c.* 1833–1912
Began practice in Liverpool 1860;
partner from 1886 with E. A. L.
Ould; from 1896 with son Hastwell
Grayson; retired 1899.

    Liverpool: All Hallows

Gribble, Herbert Augustine
1847–94
From Plymouth; pupil of Alfred
Norman of Devonport; assistant to
J. A. Hansom 1867–*c.* 1877.

    London: Brompton Oratory

Habershon, Edward   d. 1901
Son and pupil of Matthew
Habershon; partner with brother
William Gillbee Habershon until
1863; later partner with Spalding
and E. P. L. Brock (1833–95).

    St Leonards

Hadfield, Matthew Ellison
1812–85
Pupil of Woodhead and Hurst of
Doncaster; assistant to P. F.
Robinson; practised in Sheffield;
partner with J. G. Weightman (q.v.)
1834–58; with G. Goldie (q.v.)
1850–60; with his son Charles
Hadfield from 1864.

    Salford: St John's Cathedral

Hakewill, Edward Charles
1812–72
Son of the architect Henry Hakewill;
pupil of P. Hardwick.

* London: St John of Jerusalem,
    Hackney

Halliday, George Eley   1858–1922
Pupil of E. H. Burnell; assistant to J.
Prichard; practised in Cardiff.

    Nicholaston

Hansom, Charles Francis   1817–88
Pupil of his elder brother J. A.
Hansom; practised in Coventry, and
later in Bristol.

    Bath: St John the Evangelist
    Birmingham: St Thomas and St
    Edmund
    Cheltenham: St Gregory
* Hanley Swan
    Woodchester: Our Lady of the
    Annunciation

Hansom, Edward John   d. 1900
Son of C. F. Hansom; partner with A.
M. Dunn (q.v.) in Newcastle upon
Tyne.

    Cambridge: Our Lady and the
    English Martyrs
    Carlisle: Our Lady and St Joseph
    Downside

Hansom, Joseph Aloysius   1803–82
Pupil of his father, a York joiner;
partner with his brother Charles
(q.v.) 1855–9; with his son Henry
John (b. 1828) 1859–61; with E. W.
Pugin (q.v.) 1861–3; with his son
Joseph Stanislaus (1845–1931) from
1869; inventor of the cab; founder of
the *Builder*.

    Arundel
    Clifford
* Dundee: St Mary
    Leeds: Mount St Mary
* Leicester: Baptist Chapel
* Manchester: Holy Name
    Portsmouth: St John's Cathedral
* Preston: St Walburge
    Ripon

Harris, Henry C.

    Cardiff: Capel Pembroke Terrace

Harrison, James Park   1817–1902
Educated at Oxford and Lincoln's
Inn; practised in London; retired
early.

    Hursley

Harvey, C. W.

    Oxton

Hawkins, Major Rhode   1821–84
Pupil of E. Blore.

    Exeter: St Michael and All Angels

* Blubberhouses
Carnsalloch
Castle Douglas
* Englefield Green
Healey
* Leiston
London: Brompton Hospital
Chapel
* London: St Martin, Gospel Oak
* Prestwood
* Thirkleby
* West Hartlepool: Christ Church

Langdon, John Harris
Builder in London; later practised as
an architect in Newport, Gwent.

Pontypool

Lee, Ernest Claude   1846–90
Pupil of R. W. Edis.

Bentley Common
Brentwood

Leiper, William   1839–1916
Pupil of Boucher and Cousland;
assistant to Campbell Douglas, W.
White, Andrew Heiton and J. L.
Pearson; practised in Glasgow.

* Glasgow: Camphill, Queen's Park
* Glasgow: Dowanhill

Livesay, Augustus Frederick
1807–79
Pupil of James Adams of Portsmouth;
practised in Portsmouth and
Ventnor.

Andover

Lockwood, Henry Francis
1811–78
and **Mawson**, William   1828–89
Practised in Bradford.

Cleckheaton
* Saltaire

Losh, Sara   1785–1853
Daughter of John Losh, of an old
Cumberland family, owner of the
Walker Iron Works, Newcastle upon
Tyne.

* Wreay

Mackintosh, Charles Rennie
1868–1928
Pupil of John Hutchison; assistant to
Honeyman and Keppie; partner as
Honeyman, Keppie and Mackintosh,
1901; practised in Glasgow.

Glasgow: Queen's Cross

Mallinson, James   1819–84
and **Healey**, Thomas   1809–62
Practised in Bradford.

Bradford: All Saints

Manners, George Phillips
c. 1789–1866
Practised in Bath.

Bath: St Michael

Martin, William   d. 1899
Practised in Birmingham; partner
with J. H. Chamberlain (q.v.).

Birmingham: St John

Micklethwaite, John Thomas
1843–1906
In G. G. Scott's office 1862–9; partner
with G. Somers Clarke (junior)
(q.v.) 1876–92; published *Modern
Parish Churches* 1874.

Leeds: St Hilda
London: Ascension, Battersea
Stretton
Wimbledon: St Paul

Middleton, John   d. 1885
Pupil of J. P. Pritchett I of York;
practised at York; moved to
Cheltenham c. 1860; partner with
Goodman; then with his son; then
with Prothero and Phillott.

Cheltenham: All Saints
Clearwell

Mitchell, Arthur George Sydney
1856–1930
Pupil of R. R. Anderson; practised in
Edinburgh.

* Dumfries: Crichton Memorial

Moffatt, William Bonython
1812–87
Pupil of James Edmeston; partner
with G. G. Scott (q.v.) 1835–45.

* London: St Giles

Moore, Temple Lushington
1856–1920
Pupil of G. G. Scott (junior) 1875–8;
succeeded to his practice c. 1890.

Mansfield
Peterborough
* Sledmere

Morris, Joseph   1836–1913
Pupil of J. B. Clacy; partner in
Reading with Spencer Slingsby
Stallwood 1875–86; with his son
Francis Edward Morris till 1905;
became an Agapemonite, and moved
to Abode of Love.

London: Good Shepherd,
Stamford Hill

Mountford, Edward William
1855–1908
Pupil of W. G. Habershon and A. R.
Pite.

Beckenham

Murray, James   1831–63
Pupil of W. Scott of Liverpool;
partner there with T. D. Barry; then
practice in Coventry; then partner
with E. W. Pugin in London; then
back to Coventry.

Sunderland

Nesfield, William Eden   1835–88
Pupil of W. Burn and A. Salvin;
worked with R. N. Shaw 1863–9;
published *Specimens of Mediaeval
Architecture* 1862.

Calverhall
Farnham Royal

Newton, Ernest   1856–1922
Pupil of R. N. Shaw 1873–9;
published *Sketches for Country
Residences* 1882, *A Book of Houses* 1890,
A Book of Country Houses 1903.

Bickley
London: St Swithin, Lewisham

Nicholson, Sir Charles Archibald,
Bart   1867–1949
Pupil of J. D. Sedding; partner with
H. C. Corlette 1895–1914; with
Rushton 1927–49; published *Recent
English Ecclesiastical Architecture* (with
C. Spooner) 1921.

Southend-on-Sea: St Alban

Nicholson, William Adams
1803–53
Pupil of J. B. Papworth; set up
practice at Lincoln 1828.

Haugham

Norton, John   1823–1904
Pupil of B. Ferrey.

  Beulah
  Neath
  West Quantoxhead

Oates, John   d. 1831
Practised in Halifax.

  Buckley

Paley, Edward Graham   1823–95
Pupil of Edmund Sharpe (q.v.) from
1838; partner with him from 1845;
partner with H. J. Austin (q.v.) 1868;
and with his son Henry Anderson
Paley (1859–1946) 1886.

  Blackburn: St Thomas
  Fleetwood
  Lancaster: St Peter's Cathedral
  Preston Patrick
  Singleton

Paley, E. G. and **Austin**, H. J. (qq.v.)

  Atherton
  Betws-y-coed
  Daisy Hill, Westhoughton
* Finsthwaite
  Heversham
  Higher Walton
  Howe Bridge
  Kirkby
  Liverpool: SS Matthew and James
  Manchester: St John, Cheetham
  Manchester: St Margaret,
    Burnage
  Millom
  Salford
  Westleigh
  Winmarleigh

Paley, E. G., **Austin**, H. J. (qq.v.)
and **Paley**, H. A.

* Barbon
  Crawshawbooth
  Dalton-in-Furness
  Field Broughton
* Stockport

Parker, Charles   1799–1881
Pupil of Sir Jeffry Wyatville;
published *Villa Rustica* 1832–41.

  Kingston upon Thames

Parker, Revd John   1798–1860
Son of Thomas Netherton Parker of
Sweeney Hall, Oswestry; Rector of
Llanmerewig 1827–44; of
Llanyblodwel 1844–60.

  Llanyblodwel

Peacock, Joseph   1821–93

* London: St Simon Zelotes, Chelsea

Pearson, John Loughborough
1817–97
Pupil of Ignatius Bonomi; assistant
to A. Salvin and P. Hardwick; own
practice 1843.

* Appleton-le-Moors
  Ayr
  Barnet
  Birmingham: St Alban
* Bournemouth: St Stephen
* Chute Forest
* Croydon: St John the Evangelist
  Croydon: St Michael
* Cullercoats
  Darlington
* Daylesford
* Ellerker
* Freeland
* Hove: All Saints
  Liverpool: St Agnes, Sefton Park
* Llangasty Tal-y-llyn
* London: Catholic Apostolic,
    Maida Avenue
* London: St Augustine, Kilburn
  London: St Peter, Vauxhall
  Perth: St Ninian
  Port Talbot
* Scorborough
* South Dalton
* Sutton Veny
  Thurstaston
* Titsey
* Truro
  Wentworth

Pennington, Nathan Glossop
Partner in Manchester with T. E.
Bridgen (q.v.) from 1859.

  Oxton

Penson, Thomas   1790–1859
Pupil of Thomas Harrison of Chester;
practised in Wrexham and
Oswestry.

  Llanymynech
  Welshpool

Petit, Revd John Louis   1801–68
Educated at Cambridge; ordained
1824; published *Remarks on
Architectural Character* 1846,
Architectural Studies in France 1854, etc.

  Caerdeon

Phillips

  Gosport: Our Lady of the Sacred
    Heart

Pilkington, Fredrick Thomas
1832–98
Pupil of his father, Thomas
Pilkington of Stamford; began
practice in Edinburgh with him 1858;
moved practice to London 1880.

  Cardiff: English Presbyterian
    Chapel
  Dundee: St Mark
* Edinburgh: Barclay
* Irvine
  Kelso: St John
  Penicuik

Piper, Stephen
Practised in Sunderland.

  Hetton-le-Hole

Pirie, John Bridgeford   1852–92
Pupil of Alexander Ellis; worked for
David Bryce and James Matthew;
commenced practice in Aberdeen
1877; took Arthur Clyne
(1852–1923) into partnership 1880.

* Aberdeen: Queen's Cross

Pope, Richard Shackleton
1791–1884
Practised in Bristol.

  Bristol: St Mary on the Quay

Poulton, William Ford
c. 1820–1900
Partner with William Henry
Woodman (*c.* 1822–79) in Reading.

  Batsford

Poundley, John Wilkes   1807–72
Practised at Kerry,
Montgomeryshire; partner with
David Walker (q.v.).

  Abbeycwmhir
  Carno
  Llanbedr Dyffryn Clwyd

Prichard, John   1817–86
Pupil of T. L. Walker; partner with
J. P. Seddon (q.v.) 1852–63.

* Baglan
  Cardiff: Eglwys Dewi Sant
  Cardiff: St Margaret, Roath
  Malpas
  Merthyr Mawr

Prior, Edward Schroeder
1852–1932
Pupil of R. N. Shaw; published *A History of Gothic Art in England* 1900, *The Cathedral Builders in England* 1905, *Eight Chapters on English Medieval Art* 1922.

* Bothenhampton

Prynne, George Halford Fellowes
1853–1927
Pupil of G. E. Street.

* London: All Saints, Rosendale Road
  Staines

Pugin, Augustus Welby Northmore
1812–52
Pupil of his father, A. C. Pugin, published *Contrasts* 1836, *The True Principles of Pointed or Christian Architecture* 1841, etc.

  Alton
  Bicton
* Birmingham: St Chad's Cathedral
* Cheadle
  Derby: St Mary
* Edinburgh: Tolbooth St John
  London: St George's Cathedral, Southwark
  London: St Thomas of Canterbury, Fulham
  Macclesfield
  Marlow
  Newcastle upon Tyne: St Mary's Cathedral
  Nottingham: St Barnabas' Cathedral
  Old Hall Green
* Ramsgate
  Stockton-on-Tees
  Ushaw
  Warwick Bridge

Pugin, Edward Welby   1834–75
Pupil of his father, A. W. N. Pugin, and took over his practice.

  Belmont
  Cleator
  Durham: Our Lady of Mercy and St Godric
  Liverpool: Our Lady of Reconciliation
  Liverpool: St Vincent de Paul
  Manchester: All Saints, Barton-on-Irwell
* Manchester: St Francis of Assisi, Gorton
  Ripon
  Sheerness
  Shrewsbury

Pullan, Richard Popplewell
1825–88
Brother-in-law of W. Burges; archaeologist.

  Pentrobin

Robinson, Frederick Josias
Pupil of H. I. Stevens (q.v.) of Derby, and then his partner.

  Derby: St Luke

Robson, Edward Robert
1835–1917
Assistant to J. Dobson and G. G. Scott (1854–9); architect to the London School Board; published *School Architecture* 1874.

* Durham: St Cuthbert
  West Rainton

Rolfe, Clapton Crabb   1845–1907
Nephew and pupil of William Wilkinson of Oxford; practised in Oxford.

  Hailey

Ross, Alexander   1834–1925
Practised in Inverness from 1853.

* Fort William
  Inverness: St Andrew

Roumieu, Robert Lewis   1814–77
Pupil of Benjamin Wyatt; partner with A. D. Gough 1836–48.

  Tunbridge Wells: St Mark

Rowell, Joseph William
c. 1827–1902
Practised in Newton Abbot; agent to Earl of Devon.

  Collaton St Mary

St Aubyn, James Piers   1815–95
Pupil of T. Fulljames.

  Revelstoke

Salvin, Anthony   1799–1881
Pupil of John Nash.

  Alnwick
  Farlam
  Perlethorpe

Schultz, Robert Weir   1860–1951
Pupil of R. Rowand Anderson; published *The Monastery of St Luke in Stiris* (with S. H. Barnsley) 1901.

  Woolmer Green

Scoles, Revd Ignatius, SJ   1834–96
Eldest son and pupil of J. J. Scoles (q.v.); qualified as architect before entering Society of Jesus in 1860; in British Guiana 1868–73 and 1880–96.

* Preston: St Wilfred

Scoles, Joseph John   1798–1863
Pupil of Joseph Ireland.

* Bath: Prior Park Chapel
  Liverpool: St Francis Xavier
  London: Immaculate Conception, Farm Street

Scott, Edmund E.   d. 1896
Practised in Brighton.

* Brighton: St Bartholomew

Scott, Sir George Gilbert   1811–78
Pupil of James Edmeston; assistant to Henry Roberts; partner with W. B. Moffatt (q.v.) 1835–46; knighted 1872; published *A Plea for the Faithful Restoration of our Ancient Churches* 1850, *Remarks on Secular and Domestic Architecture* 1857, *Gleanings from Westminster Abbey* 1861, etc.

  Ambleside
  Bromborough
  Bwlch-y-cibau
  Cambridge: St John's College Chapel
* Cattistock
* Chantry
  Crewe Green
  Doncaster
* Dundee: St Paul
  Edensor
* Edinburgh: St Mary's Cathedral
* Edvin Loach
* Glasgow: St Mary's Cathedral
* Halifax: All Souls
  Hawkhurst
  Higham
  Langton Green
* Leafield
  Leeds: All Souls
  Leicester: St Andrew
  Liverpool: St Mary, West Derby
* London: All Hallows
* London: St Giles, Camberwell
  London: St Mary Abbots, Kensington
  Nocton
  Odd Rode
  Oxford: Exeter College Chapel
  Ranmore
  Rhyl

Richmond
Ridgmont
Ryde: All Saints
Sandbach Heath
Shackleford
* Sherbourne
Spalding
Stoke-on-Trent
Trefnant
* Welshampton
* Worsley

Scott, George Gilbert (junior)
1839–97
Eldest son and pupil of Sir Gilbert
Scott; became RC 1880; published
*An Essay on the History of English Church
Architecture* 1881; father of Sir Giles
Gilbert Scott.

* Cattistock
Eastmoors
Leamington
Norwich: St John's Cathedral
Sproxton

Scott, John Oldrid 1841–1913
Second son and pupil of Sir Gilbert
Scott; took over his practice.

London: Greek Orthodox
Cathedral, Bayswater
Ryde: All Saints

Sedding, John Dando 1838–91
Pupil of G. E. Street; partner with his
brother Edmund (1836–68) in
Penzance 1865–8; published *Garden-
craft Old and New* 1891, *Art and
Handicraft* 1893.

Bournemouth: St Clement
Ealing: St Peter
London: Holy Redeemer,
Clerkenwell
* London: Holy Trinity, Sloane
Street
Low Marple
Sheffield

Seddon, John Pollard 1827–1906
Pupil of T. L. Donaldson; partner
with J. Prichard (q.v.) 1852–63;
published *Progress in Art and
Architecture* 1852, *Rambles in the Rhine
Provinces* 1868.

* Ayot St Peter
Cardiff: Eglwys Dewi Sant
* Hoarwithy
Llandogo
* Ullenhall

Sellars, James 1843–88
Pupil of H. Barclay; practised in
Glasgow as partner of Campbell
Douglas from 1872.

Glasgow: Kelvingrove
Glasgow: Kelvinside, Hillhead

Sharpe, Edmund 1809–77
Pupil of Thomas Rickman; partner
with E. G. Paley (q.v.) from 1845;
retired 1851; published *Architectural
Parallels* 1848, *Decorated Windows*
1849, *The Seven Periods of Architecture*
1851.

Blackburn: Holy Trinity
Lever Bridge
Manchester: Holy Trinity, Platt
Lane
Scotforth
Witton Park

Sharpe, Edmund and **Paley**, E. G.
(qq.v.)

Preston Patrick

Shaw, Richard Norman 1831–1912
Pupil of W. Burn; chief assistant to
G. E. Street 1859–62; published
Architectural Sketches from the Continent
1858.

* Ilkley
* Leek
London: Holy Trinity,
Hammersmith
London: St Michael, Bedford Park
Peplow
* Richards Castle

Simpson, Edward 1844–1937
Pupil of E. W. Pugin; practised in
Bradford.

Bradford: St Mary

Simpson, James 1792–1864
Practised in Leeds.

York: Centenary Chapel

Slater, William 1819–72
Pupil of R. C. Carpenter (q.v.); took
over his practice; partner with his
son R. H. Carpenter 1863–72.

Edinburgh: St Peter

Smirke, Sidney 1798–1877
Brother and pupil of Sir Robert
Smirke.

Andover

Spence, Thomas Ralph 1848–1918
Painter and decorative designer; in
Newcastle *c.* 1876–86.

Newcastle upon Tyne: St George,
Jesmond

Spooner, Charles Sydney
1862–1938
Pupil and assistant of Sir Arthur
Blomfield; published *Recent English
Ecclesiastical Architecture* (with Sir
Charles Nicholson) 1921.

Little Ilford

Starforth, John 1823–98
Pupil of W. Burn and D. Bryce;
practised in Edinburgh.

Dumfries: Greyfriars
Moffat

Stevens, Henry Isaac
Practised in Derby; partner with F. J.
Robinson (q.v.).

Derby: St Luke

Stevenson, John James 1831–1908
Pupil of D. Bryce; assistant to G. G.
Scott; practised in Glasgow as
partner with Campbell Douglas,
1860–5; recommenced practice in
London, 1872; published *House
Architecture* 1880.

Perth: St Leonard

Stokes, Leonard Aloysius Scott
1858–1925
Pupil of S. J. Nicholl; assistant to G.
E. Street; T. E. Collcutt; and G. F.
Bodley.

Liverpool: St Clare, Sefton Park

Stott, Arthur Alfred
Practised in Heckmondwike.

Heckmondwike

Street, George Edmund 1824–81
Pupil of Owen Carter of Winchester;
assistant to G. G. Scott; published
Brick and Marble Architecture in Italy
1855, *Gothic Architecture in Spain* 1865.

Bettisfield
* Biscovey
Bournemouth: St Peter
* Boyne Hill
* Brightwalton
* Denstone
Dunecht

* East Grinstead
* East Heslerton
  Eastbourne: St Saviour
  Ellon
  Farlington
* Fawley
* Filkins
* Fylingdales
  Helperthorpe
  Holmbury St Mary
* Howsham
* Kingston
* Liverpool: St Margaret
* London: St James the Less,
    Westminster
* London: St John the Divine,
    Kennington
* London: St Mary Magdalene,
    Paddington
* Milton-under-Wychwood
  Oxford: SS Philip and James
* Toddington
  Torquay
  Watchfield
* West Lutton
* Westcott
* Wheatley
  Whitwell-on-the-Hill

Strong, Alfred Pope   1834–93
Pupil of Marchand of Hamburg;
assistant to T. H. Wyatt; began
practice 1864; partner with Samuel
Parr 1867–88.

Eastbourne: All Souls

Tarver, Edward John   1842–91
Pupil of B. Ferrey.

Willesden

Tattersall, Richard   c. 1803–44
Pupil of W. Hayley; practised in
Manchester.

Dukinfield

Taylor, James Medland
1833–1909
Pupil of J. Medland of Gloucester;
partner in Manchester with his son
Henry.

Haughton Green
Manchester: St Mark,
    Levenshulme
Rochdale

Teulon, Samuel Sanders   1812–73
Pupil of George Legg and George
Porter; set up practice 1838.

  Birmingham: St James
* Burrington
  Ealing: St Mary
  Hastings: Holy Trinity
* Hawkley
* Hopton
* Hunstanworth
* Huntley
* Leckhampstead
* London: St Stephen, Hampstead
  Netherfield
  Oare
* Silvertown
* Wells
* Woodchester: St Mary

Thomson, Alexander   1817–75
Assistant to John Baird 1836–49;
practised in Glasgow.

* Glasgow: Caledonia Road
* Glasgow: St Vincent Street

Thomson, James   1800–83
Pupil of J. B. Papworth; assistant to
John Nash; published *Retreats* 1827.

Leigh Delamere

Tite, Sir William   1798–1873
Pupil of David Laing; MP for Bath
1855–73; knighted 1869.

Gerrards Cross

Townsend, Charles Harrison
1851–1928
Pupil of Walter Scott of Liverpool;
assistant to T. Lewis Banks in
London 1883; partner with him
1884–8.

Blackheath

Truefitt, George   1824–1902
Pupil of L. N. Cottingham; then of
Sancton Wood; assistant to Harvey
Eginton of Worcester; published
Architectural Sketches on the Continent
1847; *Designs for Country Churches* 1850.

Worthing: St George

Underwood, Henry Jones
1804–52
Pupil of Sir Robert Smirke; practised
in Oxford.

Llangorwen

Vulliamy, Lewis   1791–1871
Son of Benjamin Vulliamy,
clockmaker; pupil of Sir Robert
Smirke.

Chingford
London: All Saints, Ennismore
    Gardens

Walker, David
Pupil of Messrs J. W. and J. Hay of
Liverpool; partner with J. W.
Poundley (q.v.).

Abbey Cwmhir
Llanbedr Dyffryn Clwyd

Walker, Henry
Practised in Leeds. *See* **Athron**, J.

Walters, Frederick
Arthur   1849–1931
Son of Fredrick Page Walters of
Walbrook, architect; pupil of his
father and of Goldie and Child; set up
practice 1880.

Brighton: St Joseph
Downside
Petworth
Wimbledon: The Sacred Heart

Walton, John Wilson   1824–1910
Pupil of Henry Roberts; assistant to
Sir C. Barry; set up practice in
London 1853; partner in Durham
with E. R. Robson 1859; moved back
to London 1869; changed his name to
Walton-Wilson 1880; retired 1892.

Alston

Wardell, William Wilkinson
1823–99
Trained as an engineer; pupil of A.
W. N. Pugin; became RC 1843;
emigrated to Australia 1858.

Dorchester
Leeds: Mount St Mary
London: Our Lady Star of the Sea,
    Greenwich
London: Our Lady of Victories,
    Clapham

Warren, Edward Prioleau
1856–1937
Pupil of Bodley and Garner; set up
practice 1885.

Bradford: St Clement
Bryanston

Waterhouse, Alfred 1830–1905
Pupil of Richard Lane of Manchester;
practised there until 1865; then
London.

* Blackmoor
  Eaton Hall
  London: Congregational Church,
    Hampstead
  London: Ukrainian Cathedral
  Reddish

Watkins, Alfred Octavius
Pupil of J. H. Langdon; practised in
Newport, Gwent.

  Newport, Gwent

Watson, Thomas Henry
c. 1839–1913
Pupil of his father, John Burges
Watson.

  Loughton

Watson, Thomas Lennox
c. 1850–1920
Pupil of A. Waterhouse; practised in
Glasgow.

* Glasgow: Wellington

Webb, Sir Aston 1849–1930
Pupil of R. R. Banks and C. Barry
(junior); partner with E. Ingress
Bell; knighted 1904.

  London: French Protestant
    Church, Soho Square
* Worcester

Webb, Philip Speakman
1831–1915
Pupil of John Billing; chief assistant
to G. E. Street; set up practice 1856.

  Brampton

Weightman, John Grey 1801–72
Pupil of Woodhead and Hurst of
Doncaster; assistant to Sir Charles
Barry and C. R. Cockerell; set up
practice in Sheffield 1832; partner
with M. E. Hadfield (q.v.) 1834–58.

  Salford: St John's Cathedral

Welch, John 1810 – before 1857
Brother of Edward Welch (partner of

J. A. Hansom); practised in Isle of
Man from 1830; in North Wales from
1838.

  Llandegwning

White, William 1825–1900
Pupil of D. G. Squirhill, builder, of
Leamington; in G. G. Scott's office
1845–7; set up practice at Truro 1847;
moved to London *c.* 1852.

  Great Bourton
  Little Petherick
* London: All Saints, Notting Hill
* London: St Mark, Battersea
* London: St Saviour, Aberdeen
    Park
  Lyndhurst

Wild, James William 1814–93
Son of Charles Wild, artist; pupil of
G. Basevi.

* London: Christ Church,
    Streatham

Wilkins, William 1778–1839
Pupil of his father William Wilkins of
Norwich; Fellow of Caius College,
Cambridge 1803–11; published
Antiquities of Magna Graecia 1807, etc.

* Albury

Willoughby, George Rivis
Son of John Rivis Willoughby,
surveyor to the Corporation of York;
practised in Louth from the 1840s.

  Haugham

Wilson, Henry 1864–1934
Pupil of E. J. Shrewsbury of
Maidenhead; assistant to John Oldrid
Scott; then to John Belcher; then chief
assistant to J. D. Sedding, whose
practice he took over 1891; also a
sculptor and metalworker.

* Brithdir
  Ealing: St Peter

Withers, Robert Jewell 1823–94
Pupil of T. Hellyer of Ryde; brother
of the American architect Frederick
Clarke Withers; set up practice in
Sherborne 1848; moved to London
1851.

  Lampeter
  Little Cawthorpe
  Penrhyncoch

Wood, Edgar 1860–1935
Pupil of James Murgatroyd of
Manchester; practised in Manchester;
after 1900 partner with J. Henry
Sellers.

  Middleton

Woodyer, Henry 1816–96
Pupil of William Butterfield;
practised in Guildford, and later
Grafham, Surrey.

  Bayford
* Clewer
* Dorking
  Eastbourne: All Saints' Hospital
    Chapel
  Grafham
* Greenham
* Hascombe
* Highnam
  Langleybury
  Newtown
* Reading: Christ Church
* Tenbury
  Tutshill
  Twinstead
  Waterford
* Wokingham

Worthington, Sir Percy Scott
1864–1939
Son of Thomas Worthington,
architect, of Manchester, whose
practice he took over; knighted 1935.

* Liverpool: Unitarian Chapel

Worthington, Thomas 1826–1909
Pupil of Bowman and Crowther;
practised in Manchester.

  Eccles

Wyatt, Thomas Henry 1807–80
Son of Matthew Wyatt (first cousin
of James Wyatt); elder brother of Sir
Matthew Digby Wyatt; pupil of P.
Hardwick; partner with David
Brandon 1838–51.

  Fonthill Gifford
  Wilton

Bibliography

A. General Works

Martin S. Briggs, *Puritan Architecture*, London and Redhill, 1946
Kenneth Clark, *The Gothic Revival*, London, 1928 (reprinted)
Basil F. L. Clarke, *Church Builders of the Nineteenth Century*, London, 1938 (reprinted Newton Abbot, 1969)
Roger Dixon and Stefan Muthesius, *Victorian Architecture*, London, 1978
Charles Eastlake, *A History of the Gothic Revival*, London, 1872 (two modern reprints)
H. S. Goodhart-Rendel, *English Architecture since the Regency*, London, 1953
A. Stuart Gray, *Edwardian Architecture: A Biographical Dictionary*, London, 1985
Henry-Russell Hitchcock, *Early Victorian Architecture in Britain*, New Haven, 1954 (reprinted London, 1972)
Henry-Russell Hitchcock, *Architecture: Nineteenth and Twentieth Centuries* (3rd edition Harmondsworth, 1969)
Peter Howell, *Victorian Churches* (RIBA Drawings Series), Feltham, 1968
Anthony Jones, *Welsh Chapels* (National Museum of Wales), Cardiff, 1984
Bryan Little, *Catholic Churches since 1623*, London, 1966
Stefan Muthesius, *The High Victorian Movement in Architecture*, London, 1972
Nikolaus Pevsner and others, *The Buildings of England; The Buildings of Scotland; The Buildings of Wales*, Harmondsworth
M. H. Port, *Six Hundred New Churches: The Church Building Commissioners 1818–56*, London, 1961
Alastair Service (ed.), *Edwardian Architecture and its Origins*, London, 1975
Alastair Service, *Edwardian Architecture*, London, 1977
Christopher Stell, *An Inventory of Nonconformist Chapels and Meeting Houses in Central England*, London, 1986
James F. White, *The Cambridge Movement: The Ecclesiologists and the Gothic Revival*, Cambridge, 1962

B. Particular Areas

Basil F. L. Clarke, *Parish Churches of London*, London, 1966
Mervyn Blatch, *A Guide to London Churches*, London, 1978
Gavin Stamp and Colin Amery, *Victorian Buildings in London*, London, 1980
T. Francis Bumpus, *London Churches Ancient and Modern*, London and New York, N.D.
Roger Homan, *The Victorian Churches of Kent*, Chichester, 1984
Geoffrey K. Brandwood, *The Anglican Churches of Leicester*, Leicester, 1984
Jennifer Sherwood, *A Guide to the Churches of Oxfordshire*, Oxford, 1989
Anne Riches, *Victorian Church Building and Restoration in Suffolk* (a supplement to the 4th edition of H. Munro Cautley's *Suffolk Churches*), Ipswich, 1982
D. Robert Elleray, *The Victorian Churches of Sussex*, Chichester, 1981
H. Hamilton Maughan, *Some Brighton Churches*, London, 1922
Anthony Dale, *The Churches of Brighton*, London, 1988
R. V. Taylor, *Ecclesiae Leodienses* (Churches of Leeds), London, 1875
John Hutchinson and Paul Joyce, *G. E. Street in East Yorkshire*, Hull, 1981

C. Particular Architects

(Books by architects are listed in the Index of Architects)
Winefride de l'Hôpital, *Westminster Cathedral and its Architect*, London, 1919
David Verey, 'George Frederick Bodley', in *Seven Victorian Architects* (ed. Jane Fawcett), London, 1976

Bibliography

J. Mordaunt Crook, *William Burges*, London, 1981
J. Mordaunt Crook (ed.), *The Strange Genius of William Burges*, Cardiff, 1981
Charles Handley-Read, 'William Burges', in *Victorian Architecture* (ed. Peter Ferriday), London, 1963
Paul Thompson, *William Butterfield*, London, 1971
150 Years of Architectural Drawings: Hadfield Cawkwell Davidson, Sheffield 1834–1934 (Mappin Art Gallery), Sheffield, 1984
Edward Hubbard, *John Douglas, Architect* (forthcoming)
Tom Faulkner and Andrew Greg, *John Dobson, Newcastle Architect*, Newcastle, 1987
Recollections of Thomas Graham Jackson, ed. Basil Jackson, Oxford, 1950
Thomas Howarth, *Charles Rennie Mackintosh and the Modern Movement*, London, 1952 (reprinted)
Anthony Quiney, *John Loughborough Pearson*, London and New Haven, 1979
David Lloyd, 'John Loughborough Pearson', in *Seven Victorian Architects* (ed. Jane Fawcett), London, 1976
Benjamin Ferrey, *Recollections of A. W. N. Pugin*, 1861 (new edition by Clive and Jane Wainwright, London, 1978)
Phoebe Stanton, *Pugin*, London, 1971
Michael Trappes-Lomax, *Pugin*, London, 1932
Alexandra Gordon Clark, 'Pugin', in *Victorian Architecture* (ed. Peter Ferriday), London, 1963
Alexandra Wedgwood, *Catalogue of the Drawings Collection of the RIBA: The Pugin Family*, London, 1977
Alexandra Wedgwood, *Catalogues of Architectural Drawings in the Victoria and Albert Museum: A. W. N. Pugin and the Pugin Family*, London, 1985
Jill Allibone, *Anthony Salvin*, Columbia, Missouri, 1987
David Cole, *The Work of Sir Gilbert Scott*, London, 1980
Joanna Heseltine (ed.), *Catalogue of the Drawings Collection of the RIBA: The Scott Family*, London, 1981
Michael Darby (ed.), *Catalogues of Architectural Drawings in the Victoria and Albert Museum: John Pollard Seddon*, London, 1983
Arthur Edmund Street, *Memoir of George Edmund Street*, London, 1888 (reprinted New York, 1972)
Andrew Saint, *Richard Norman Shaw*, London and New Haven, 1976
Matthew Saunders, *The Churches of S. S. Teulon* (Ecclesiological Society), London, 1982
Ronald McFadzean, *The Life and Work of Alexander Thomson*, London, 1979
S. Maltby, S. MacDonald and C. Cunningham, *Alfred Waterhouse*, London, 1983
W. R. Lethaby, *Philip Webb and his Work*, Oxford, 1935 (reprinted London, 1979)
Rhodri Liscombe, *William Wilkins*, Cambridge, 1980
Partnership in Style: Edgar Wood and J. Henry Sellars (Manchester Art Gallery), Manchester, 1975
Anthony J. Pass, *Thomas Worthington*, Manchester, 1988
John Martin Robinson, *The Wyatts*, Oxford, 1979

D. Furniture, Sculpture and Decoration

Victorian Church Art (Victoria and Albert Museum), London, 1971
Peter F. Anson, *Fashions in Church Furnishings 1840–1940*, London, 1960
Martin Harrison, *Victorian Stained Glass*, London, 1980
Marta Galicki, *Victorian and Edwardian Stained Glass* (English Heritage), London, 1987
A. Charles Sewter, *The Stained Glass of William Morris and his Circle*, 1974
Rupert Gunnis, *Dictionary of British Sculptors 1660–1851*, London, N.D.
Benedict Read, *Victorian Sculpture*, London and New Haven, 1982
Susan Beattie, *The New Sculpture*, London and New Haven, 1983
Brian Kemp, *English Church Monuments*, London, 1980
David Meara, *Victorian Memorial Brasses*, London, 1983

ABERDEEN: Queen's Cross Church,
R. Pirie

ADDISCOMBE: St Mary Magdalene, *E. B. Lamb*

ALBURY: The Apostles Chapel (Catholic Apostolic Church), *W. Wilkins and W. McI. Brookes*

ALDWARK: St Stephen, *E. B. Lamb*

APPLETON-LE-MOORS: Christ Church, *J. L. Pearson*

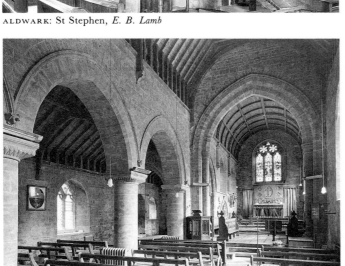

AVON DASSETT: St John the Baptist, *C. Buckeridge*

AYOT ST PETER: St Peter, *J. P. Seddon*

BABBACOMBE: All Saints, *W. Butterfield*. Sanctuary

BAGBY: St Mary, *E. B. Lamb*

BAGLAN: St Catherine, *J. Prichard*

BALDERSBY ST JAMES: St James, *W. Butterfield*. Font

BARBON: St Bartholomew, *E. J. Paley, H. J. Austin and H. A. Paley*

BEECH HILL: St Mary, *W. Butterfield*

BATH: Prior Park College Chapel, *J. J. Scoles*

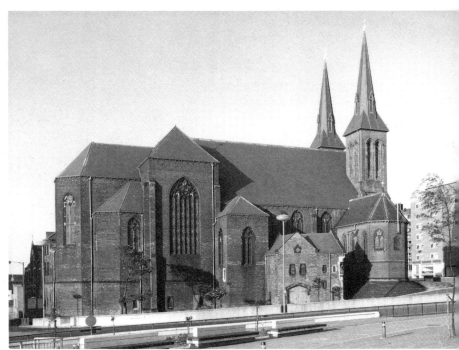

BIRMINGHAM: Cathedral of St Chad, *A. W. N. Pugin*

BISCOVEY: St Mary the Virgin, *G. E. Street*

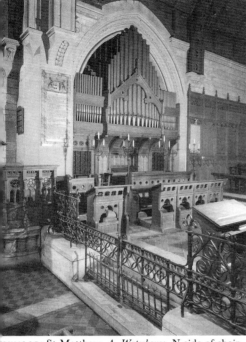

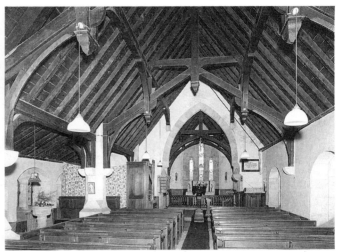

CKMOOR: St Matthew, *A. Waterhouse*. N side of choir

BLUBBERHOUSES: St Andrew, *E. B. Lamb*

TON: St Michael, *W. Elwin*

BOTHENHAMPTON: Holy Trinity, *E. S. Prior*

BOURNEMOUTH: St Stephen, *J. L. Pearson.* Nave to W

BOYNE HILL: All Saints, *G. E. Street*

BRECHIN: Baptist Church, *J., J. M. and W. H. Hay*

BRECHIN: Southesk Church, *J. J. Burnet*

BRIGHTON: St Bartholomew, *E. E. Scott*

BRIGHTON: St Michael and All Angels, *G. F. Bodley*

BRIGHTWALTON: All Saints, *G. E. Street*

BRITHDIR: St Mark, *H. Wilson*

BURRINGHAM: St John the Baptist, *S. S. Teulon*

CAMBRIDGE: All Saints, *G. F. Bodley*

CATTISTOCK: SS Peter and Paul, *G. G. Scott and G. G. Scott junior*. Font

CHANTRY: Holy Trinity, *G. G. Scott*

CHEADLE: St Giles, *A. W. N. Pugin*

CHUTE FOREST: St Mary, *J. L. Pearson*

CLEWER: Chapel, Convent of St John the Baptist, *H. Woodyer*.

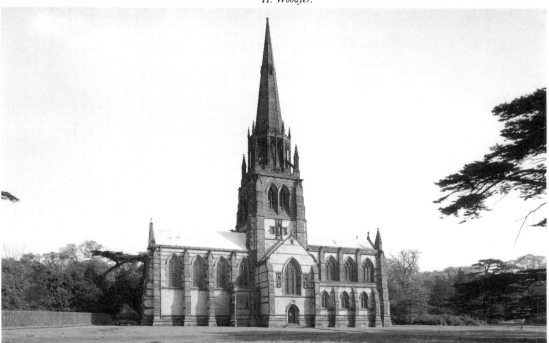

CLUMBER PARK: St Mary the Virgin, *G. F. Bodley*

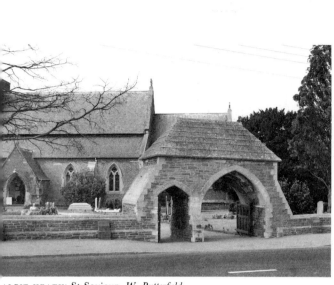

ALPIT HEATH: St Saviour, *W. Butterfield*

CROYDON: St John the Evangelist, *J. L. Pearson*.
Lower part of W gallery

LLERCOATS: St George, *J. L. Pearson*

CUMBRAE: Cathedral of the Holy Spirit, *W. Butterfield*

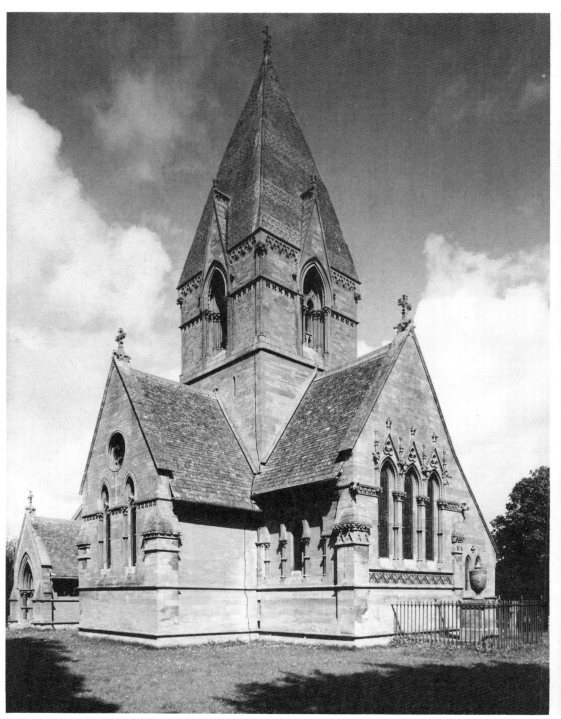

DAYLESFORD: St Peter, *J. L. Pearson*

NSTONE: All Saints, *G. E. Street*. Tower view from W

DITTON: St Michael, *H. Clutton*

DUMFRIES: Crichton Memorial Church, *S. Mitchell*

RKING: St Martin, *H. Woodyer*.

DUNDEE: St Mary, *J. A. Hansom*

DUNDEE: St Paul's Cathedral, *G. G. Scott*

DUNDEE: St Salvador, *G. F. Bodley*

DURHAM: St Cuthbert, *E. R. Robson*

EAST GRINSTEAD: Convent Chapel of St Margaret, *G. E. Street*

EAST HESLERTON: St Andrew, *G. E. Street*

ECCLESTON: St Mary, *G. F. Bodley*

EDINBURGH: Barclay Bruntsfield Church, *F. T. Pilkington*

EDINBURGH: Catholic Apostolic (now Reformed Baptist) Church, *R. R. Anderson.* E wall, mural by Phoebe Traquair

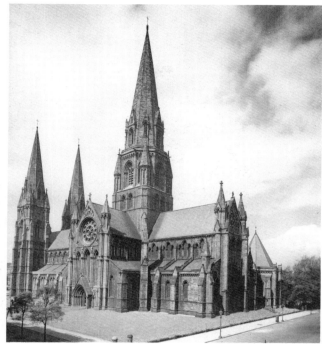

EDINBURGH: Highland Tolbooth St John,
Pugin and Gillespie Graham

EDINBURGH: St Mary's Cathedral, *G. G. Scott*

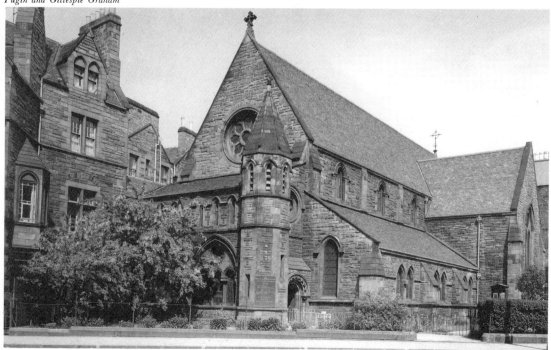

EDINBURGH: St Michael and All Saints, *R. R. Anderson*

EDINBURGH: St Michael and All Saints,
R. R. Anderson

ELLERKER: St Ann's Chapel, *J. L. Pearson*

EDVIN LOACH: St Mary, *G. G. Scott*

ENGLEFIELD GREEN: St Jude, *E. B. Lamb*

FAWLEY: St Mary the Virgin, *G. E. Street*

FILKINS: St Peter, *G. E. Street*

FINSTHWAITE: St Peter, *E. G. Paley and H. J. Austin*

FORT WILLIAM: St Andrew, *A. Ross*

FRANCE LYNCH: St John the Baptist, *G. F. Bodley*

FREELAND: St Mary, *J. L. Pearson*

FYLINGDALES: St Stephen, *G. E. Street*

GLASGOW: Barony Church, *J. J. Burnet*

GLASGOW: Caledonia Road Church, *A. Thomson*

GLASGOW: Camphill, Queen's Park Church, *W. Leiper*

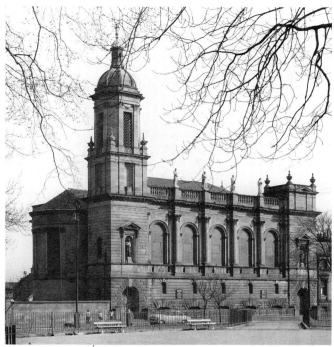

GLASGOW: Evangelical Church, *J. Honeyman*

GLASGOW: Dowanhill Church, *W. Leiper*. Pulpit

GLASGOW: Govan Old Parish Church, *R. R. Anderson*

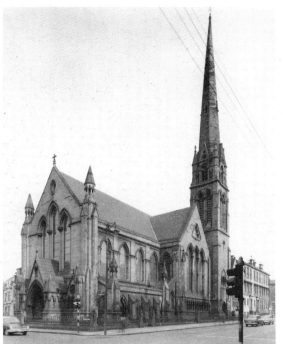

GLASGOW: Lansdowne Church, *J. Honeyman*

GLASGOW: St Vincent Street Church, *A. Thomson*

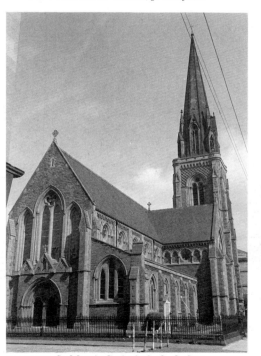

GLASGOW: St Mary's Cathedral, *G. G. Scott*

GLASGOW: Wellington Church, *T. L. Watson*

GOATHLAND: St Mary, *W. H. Brierley*

GREENHAM: St Mary, *H. Woodyer.* Choir

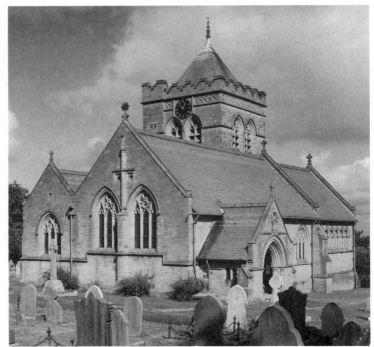

HALIFAX: All Souls, *G. G. Scott*

HALKYN: St Mary, *J. Douglas*

HALLOW: SS Philip and James, *W. J. Hopkins*

HANLEY SWAN: Our Lady and St Alphonsus, *C. F. Hansom*

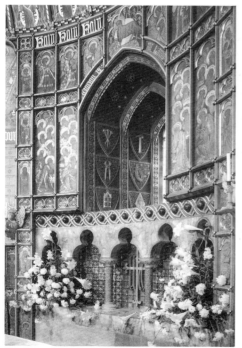

HASCOMBE: St Peter, *H. Woodyer*. Detail of reredos

HATHEROP: St Nicholas, *H. Clutton*. Mortuary chapel

WKLEY: SS Peter and Paul, *S. S. Teulon*

HIGHNAM: Holy Innocents, *H. Woodyer*. Lady Chapel

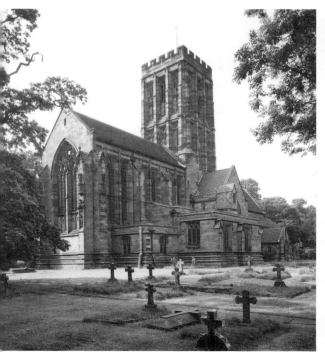

AR CROSS: Holy Angels, *G. F. Bodley and T. Garner*

HOAR CROSS: Holy Angels, *G. F. Bodley and T. Garner*

HOARWITHY: St Catherine, *J. P. Seddon*. Chancel   HOPTON: St Margaret, *S. S. Teulon*

HORTON-CUM-STUDLEY: St Barnabas, *W. Butterfield*.   HOVE: All Saints, *J. L. Pearson*

WSHAM: St John the Evangelist, *E. Street*. Pulpit

HUNSTANWORTH: St James the Less, *S. S. Teulon*

NTLEY: St John the Baptist, *S. S. Teulon*. S side of choir

ILKLEY: St Margaret, *R. N. Shaw*

IRVINE: Trinity Church, *F. T. Pilkington*

ITCHEN STOKE: St Mary, *H. Conybeare*

LARBERT: Stenhousemuir and Carron Church, *J. J. Burnet*

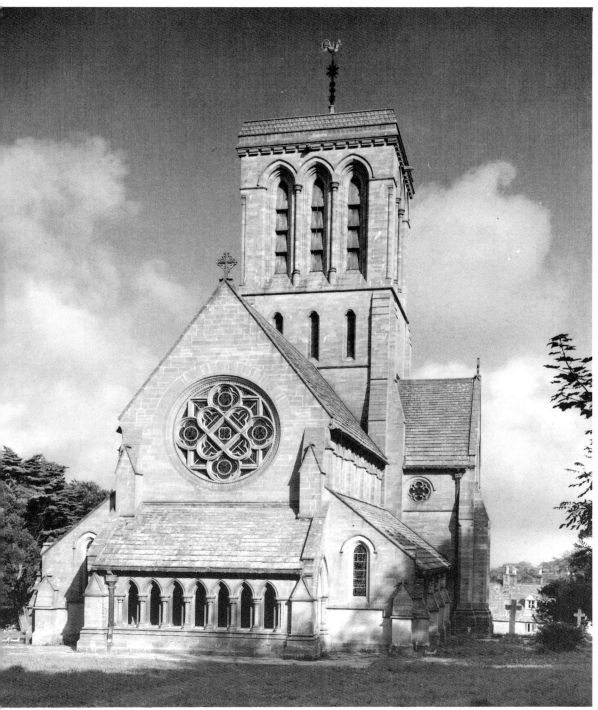

KINGSTON: St James, *G. E. Street*

LEAFIELD: St Michael and All Angels, *G. G. Scott*

LECKHAMPSTEAD: St James, *S. S. Teulon.*

LEEDS: St Aidan, *R. J. Johnson and A. Crawford-Hick*

LEEDS: St Peter, *R. D. Chantrell*. Organ-case and pulpit

к: All Saints, *R. N. Shaw*.

LEICESTER: Former Baptist Chapel, *J. A. Hansom*

TON: St Margaret, *E. B. Lamb*

LIVERPOOL: St John the Baptist, *G. F. Bodley*

LIVERPOOL: St Margaret, *G. E. Street*. Font

LIVERPOOL: Unitarian Chapel, *P. S. Worthington*

LLANGASTY TAL-Y-LLYN: St Gastayn, *J. L. Pearson*

LONDON: All Hallows, *J. Brooks and G. G. Scott*

LONDON: All Saints, Margaret Street, *W. Butterfield.*
Pulpit

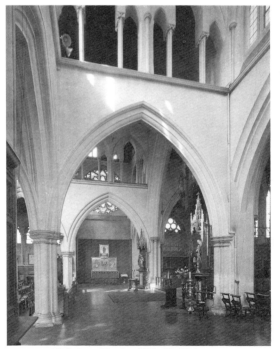

LONDON: All Saints, Notting Hill, *W. White.*

LONDON: All Saints, Brixton, *G. H. F. Prynne*

DON: Catholic Apostolic Church, *J. L. Pearson*

LONDON: Christ Church, *J. W. Wild*

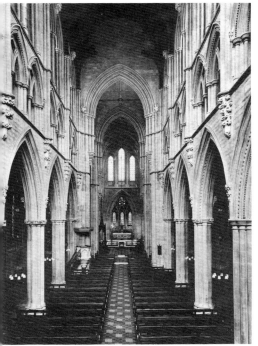

DON: Christ the King, *J. R. Brandon*

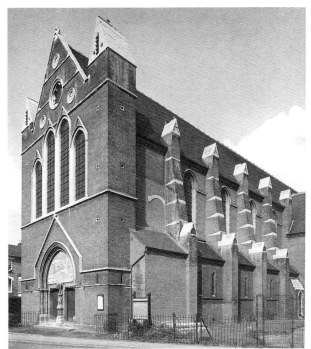

LONDON: Holy Innocents, *J. Brooks*

LONDON: Holy Trinity, *J. D. Sedding*. Pulpit

LONDON: St Augustine, Kilburn, *J. L. Pearson*

LONDON: St Augustine, Queens Gate, *W. Butterfield*

LONDON: St Barnabas, *T. Cundy*

LONDON: St Chad, *J. Brooks*

LONDON: St Giles, *G. G. Scott and W. B. Moffatt*

LONDON: St Columba, *J. Brooks*

LONDON: St Cuthbert, *H. R. Gough*

LONDON: St James the Less, *G. E. Street*

LONDON: St John, *W. Butterfield*

LONDON: St John the Divine, *G. E. Street*

LONDON: St John of Jerusalem, *E. C. Hakewill*

LONDON: St Mark, Battersea, *W. White*.

LONDON: St Mark, Dalston, *C. Cheston Junior*

LONDON: St Martin, *E. B. Lamb*

LONDON: St Mary of Eton, *G. F. Bodley*

LONDON: St Mary Magdalene, Munster Square,
R. C. Carpenter.

LONDON: St Mary Magdalene, Paddington, *G. E. Street*

LONDON: St Michael, *G. F. Bodley and T. Garner*

LONDON: St Matthias, *W. Butterfield*

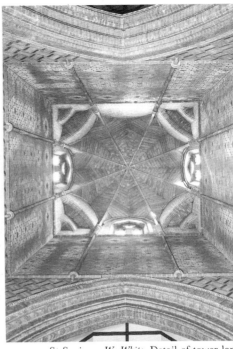

LONDON: St Peter, *J. L. Pearson*

LONDON: St Saviour, *W. White*. Detail of tower lan

LONDON: St Simon Zelotes, *J. Peacock*

LONDON: St Stephen, Westminster, *B. Ferrey*

LONDON: St Stephen, Hampstead, *S. S. Teulon.*

LONDON: Westminster Cathedral, *J. F. Bentley*

LOWER KINGSWOOD: The Wisdom of God, *S. Barnsley*.

LOWER SHUCKBURGH: St John the Baptist, *J. Croft*

LOWFIELD HEATH: St Michael, *W. Burges*

MANCHESTER: Holy Name, *J. A. Hansom*

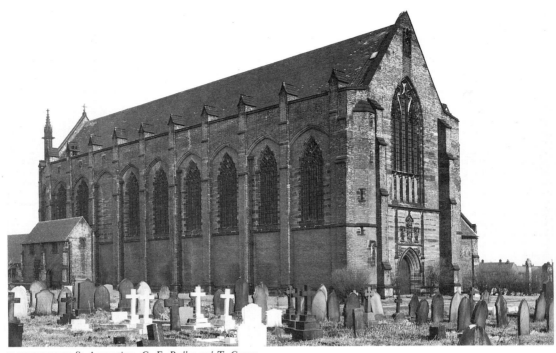

MANCHESTER: St Augustine, *G. F. Bodley and T. Garner*

MANCHESTER: St Augustine, *G. F. Bodley and T. Garner*

MANCHESTER: St Francis of Assisi, *E. W. and P. P. Pugin*

ⲦON: St Mary, *W. Butterfield*

MILTON-UNDER-WYCHWOOD: SS Simon and Jude,
G. E. Street

BURY: Methodist Chapel. View from E in gallery

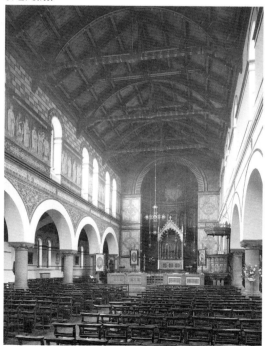

OXFORD: St Barnabas, *A. W. Blomfield*

PAISLEY: Thomas Coats Memorial Church, *H. J. Blanc*   PRESTON: St Walburge, *J. A. Hansom*

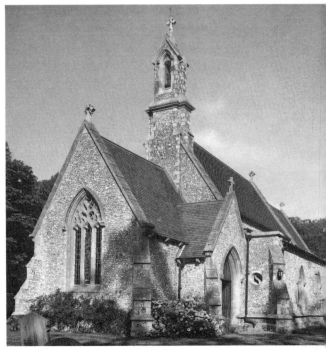

PRESTON: St Wilfred, *I. Scoles and S. J. Nicholl*   PRESTWOOD: Holy Trinity, *E. B. Lamb*

ETT: Holy Trinity, *A. W. Blomfield.*

RAMSGATE: St Augustine, *A. W. N. Pugin.*

RICHARDS CASTLE: All Saints, *R. N. Shaw*

ING: Christ Church, *H. Woodyer*

SALTAIRE: United Reformed Church, *H. F. Lockwood and W. Mawson*

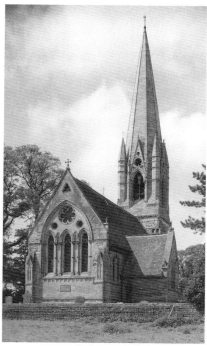

SCARBOROUGH: St Martin on the Hill, *G. F. Bodley*. Pulpit

SCORBOROUGH: St Leonard, *J. L. Pearson*

SHERBOURNE: All Saints, *G. G. Scott*

SELSLEY: All Saints, *G. F. Bodley*.

SILVERTOWN: St Mark, *S. S. Teulon*

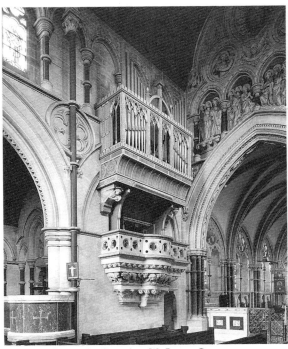

SKELTON: Christ the Consoler, *W. Burges*. Organ-case

SLEDMERE: St Mary, *T. L. Moore*. N aisle

SOUTH DALTON: St Mary, *J. L. Pearson*

SOUTH TIDWORTH: St Mary, *J. Johnson.*

STOCKPORT: St George, *E. J. Paley, H. J. Austin and H. A. Paley*

STUDLEY ROYAL: St Mary, *W. Burges*

SUTTON VENY: St John the Evangelist, *J. L. Pearson*

TANWORTH: Christ Church, *G. Insall*

TENBURY: St Michael and All Angels, *H. Woodyer*

THIRKLEBY: All Saints, *E. B. Lamb*

TITSEY: St James, *J. L. Pearson*. Sanctuary

TODMORDEN: Unitarian Chapel, *J. Gibson*

TODDINGTON: St Andrew, *G. E. Street*

TRURO: Cathedral, *J. L. Pearson*

LENHALL: St Mary, *J. P. Seddon*

ULLENHALL: St Mary, *J. P. Seddon*

ARESLEY: St James the Great, *W. Butterfield*

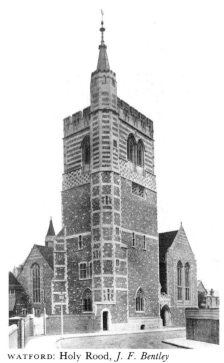

WATFORD: Holy Rood, *J. F. Bentley*

WELLS: St Thomas, *S. S. Teulon.*
Communion rail detail

WELSHAMPTON: St Michael, *G. G. Scott*, Reredos

WEST HARTLEPOOL: Christ Church, *E. B. Lamb*

WEST LUTTON: St Mary the Virgin, *G. E. Street*

ᴛᴄᴏᴛᴛ: St Mary, *G. E. Street*. Clergy stall

ᴡʜᴇᴀᴛʟᴇʏ: St Mary the Virgin, *G. E. Street*

ᴋɪɴɢʜᴀᴍ: St Paul, *H. Woodyer*.

ᴡᴏᴏᴅᴄʜᴇsᴛᴇʀ: St Mary, *S. S. Teulon*

WORCESTER: St George, *A. Webb*

WORSLEY: St Mark, *G. G. Scott*

WREAY: St Mary, *S. Losh.*

WYKEHAM: All Saints, *W. Butterfield.* S porch